Fishwives

a novel

sally bellerose

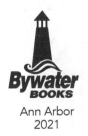

Bywater
BOOKS

Ann Arbor
2021

Bywater Books

Print ISBN: 978-1-61294-189-9

Bywater Books First Edition: February 2021

Cover design: TreeHouse Studio

Bywater Books PO Box 3671
Ann Arbor MI 48106-3671
www.bywaterbooks.com

**Earlier versions, excerpts, and short stories that evolved into the novel
Fishwives have appeared in the following books and periodicals.**

"Fishwives," Saints and Sinners Fiction from the Festival 2011, edited by Amie M. Evans and Paul J. Willis, Queer Mojo, 2011.

"Sunflowers," Bloom, editor Charles Flowers, Arts in Bloom Project, Los Angeles, CA, Fall, 2013.

"Corset," Saints and Sinners Fiction from the Festival 2014, edited by Amie M. Evans and Paul J. Willis, Bold Strokes Books, 2014.

"Mouth to Mouth," Dappled Things, editor Meredith McCann, New Hope, KY, 2014.

"Fishwives," Outer Voices Inner Lives, edited by Mark McNease and Stephen Dolainski, MadeMark Publishing, New York City, 2014.

"Discretion, 1957," Saints and Sinners Fiction from the Festival 2016, edited by Amie M. Evans and Paul J. Willis, Bold Strokes Books, 2016.

"Sunflowers," Walking the Edge, edited by Joan Leggitt, Twisted Road Publications, 2017.

"Corset," Celebrating Writers of the Pioneer Valley, edited by Carol Edelstein and Robert Barber, Gallery of Readers Press, Northampton, MA, 2017.

To My Beloved Brian, Cynthia, Michelle, and Kennedy
in the order they appeared in my life.

Fishwives

Chapter 1

Saturday, February 18, 2017

It's 5:00 a.m. on a winter morning. Ninety-year-old Jackie sits in her boxer shorts counting her blessings. She's taking the advice of her wife, Regina, who came home yesterday from a "Growing Old in the Spirit" meeting at the Senior Center touting "gratitude meditation" to promote sleep, health, and well-being. Jackie hoped recognizing her blessings would buy her a catnap.

Jackie's well-being is the same as it was when she got out of bed. The pain in her hip, as she sits alone on the couch, is sharp.

She says, "Screw this," and stops counting to look down at her thighs. She remembers her skin as olive colored, but her legs match her white boxers in the scant morning light. More expanse of skin than she remembers, too. She was once five feet, ten inches tall and weighed one hundred sixty pounds. Last time she went to the clinic they informed her she was five-eight and told her to get down to two hundred.

Regina, Jackie's main blessing, pads into the living room in her fuzzy pink slippers, pink flannel nightgown, and matching bathrobe. She sets two mugs and a sleeve of saltines on the coffee table and flicks on a light.

"Thanks." Jackie raises the mug and watches Regina fuss with the blinds in the front window. The street of small houses, small yards, and duplex rentals is quiet and shadowy. Regina is as thin as she was when they met sixty years ago, but her eighty-nine-year-old spine has contracted her from five-foot-four to five-three.

"I'll make breakfast," Jackie says. Breakfast consists of dumping Cheerios into two bowls and pouring milk. Lunch and supper have always been Regina's job.

"Let's watch the sun come up first." Regina pins her long braid into a gray halo on top of her head, reaches into the pocket of her robe and applies two perfect sweeps of Plum Elegance lipstick without the benefit of a mirror before she sits next to Jackie. The couch, bought on sale at Railroad Salvage twenty-five years ago, receives Regina with a creak.

"Sun won't be up for a couple hours." Jackie takes a bottle of ibuprofen off the coffee table.

Regina snuggles into Jackie who is twice her size. "Our bio-rhythms are on the same clock," Regina says. They've been up before dawn three days in a row.

"You'd still be asleep if I didn't wake you." Jackie kisses Regina's forehead. "You always smell good." She appreciates the bit of flowery vanilla perfume Regina dabs behind her ear no matter what hour she gets out of bed.

They sit quietly for a few minutes.

"Your hip hurts. Eat those crackers if you're taking pills with coffee." Regina scooches a foot away. "You're in the dumps today." She frowns. "We should get a pain patch for your hip and stay up later so you're not struggling to sleep in the morning. We'll start watching Rachel Maddow in real time instead of recording it for the next day."

Jackie nods and tilts her head against the back of the couch, runs a hand over her buzz cut, and closes her eyes.

Regina has long since stopped wondering how Jackie can be comfortable walking around the cold house in her underwear. Right now, she wonders how to lighten Jackie's mood.

She understands about pain, but the hip has been worse. For the first time in their lives, Jackie isn't bothering to bind her breasts when she gets out of bed. Some days, unless there's a knock at the door, her binder stays off all day. Regina tries to convince herself that this is a good thing. It means Jackie is finally opting for comfort. But Regina can only interpret the expression on Jackie's face this morning as some form of sad and weary. Should Regina just back off and let Jackie be sad and tired? Regina dismisses this idea. Jackie is still Jackie. She's just slowed down. They've been around a long time. They've both slowed down. That's all.

"You okay, honey?" Regina asks.

Jackie opens her eyes. "I was dreaming."

"You were sulking. We're getting you out of the house today." Regina goes back to the window, draws the sheers, and stares out at the glow of the streetlamp in front of their modest ranch house. An eighty-nine-year-old ghost of herself stares back. She wonders, how much longer? "There's not much snow. We haven't been out of the house since . . ." She tries to remember.

"Tuesday," Jackie says. "I dropped you off at the Senior Center." Jackie scratches the back of her head and yawns. "I was daydreaming about The Sea Colony. Old people reminisce. Might look like sulking."

"If you were dreaming about that bar, you were thinking about Bo," Regina says. Jackie's best friend Bo has been dead for a few years. "Did you take the antidepressant? You didn't, did you?" Regina comes back to sit and put her head on Jackie's shoulder. "I'm going to leave that argument for later. There's plenty of gas in the car. The street is plowed."

"I'm tired," Jackie says.

"Of anything in particular?" Regina snuggles in. "We're going out today."

"Tired of everything but you," Jackie says. "Tired of waking up so early."

"I'm tired of you being depressed," Regina says. "Put your feet up on the coffee table." Regina has only allowed feet on the coffee table in the last few years. "We'll take a nap."

"I was counting that bar as one of my blessings." Jackie grunts and hoists her feet. "I was counting you, and Bo, and your sister, too."

"Lynn," Regina sighs her sister's name. "God. I miss her." She drags the afghan over them and anchors a hand between Jackie's heavy thighs. "Me and Lynn, so different and so close."

"You and Lynn," Jackie repeats her name with affection, "had some good arguments. She was a spitfire. So were you." She kisses the top of Regina's head.

"Still am." Regina feigns indignation. "You wouldn't have met either of us if we hadn't stopped at that bar." She's quiet for a while, remembering before she starts talking, mid-memory. "She was reckless and brave, my sister." She rubs Jackie's thigh. "A nap, then breakfast. I'll count your blessings for you," she says, stroking. "Relax. I know how to put my girl to sleep."

October 1955

"Let's get drunk and tell secrets." Lynn grabs her sister's hand and stops on crowded Eighth Avenue in Manhattan. "Like we used to before you clammed up and I got exiled."

"A lady does not get drunk." Regina, just arrived at Port Authority, wags her head, making fun of herself and their mother. "A lady gets tipsy." After several hours on the bus, Regina would love a glass of red wine. She smiles down at the new pumps that almost match her pencil skirt. The pumps make her five feet, six inches tall, which she considers the perfect height for a girl. She likes the way her hair looks, too, staying in place under her new hat for a change.

It's a breezy, sixty-degree autumn afternoon. Regina is determined that her trip to the city, a visit with Lynn, and a good sisterly chat will get them both back on the straight and narrow. A normal life, that's what they both need.

"I thought you quit drinking?" she says.

4

There's a construction boom in the city. Concrete barriers and policemen with whistles funnel people in, out, and around various widths of sidewalk. The sisters are impeding the flow of foot traffic.

"Excuse me!" a girl in high heels, capri pants, and a cashmere sweater set that Regina would die for, complains.

"Don't have a cow, honey," Lynn tells the girl and sits on a barrier to make room for the cashmere sweater set to pass. "Sit," she says to Regina. Regina puts the leather-strapped suitcase she borrowed from their father on top of the squared-off concrete but doesn't sit.

"I told Mom and Dad I quit drinking," Lynn says. "They like to blame my troubles on booze. Easier than blaming them on me." Lynn whacks herself on the forehead. "My baby sister is twenty-six years old today. Happy birthday!" She stands to hug Regina. "You put on a couple of pounds." She holds Regina by both shoulders to get a good look. "Now you're Audrey Hepburn perfect. Let's have a drink. Pick someplace we'll remember when we're old ladies."

"So early?"

"It's almost five. You've come all this way; let's go crazy."

"A drink, but not drunk." Regina loves being told she looks like Audrey Hepburn, and almost forgot how good Lynn's hugs feel, the kind of little-girl feeling of love that comes from remembering your sister pulling leeches off your legs, from knowing come hell or mucky pond water the person you're embracing is on your side. Maybe Lynn doesn't have a "problem" with alcohol. Maybe they can just have a nice time without Regina bringing up her sister's "problem" with men. Maybe Regina should concentrate on her own "problem" with men.

Regina roots around in her purse. Before she can chicken out, she unpins a note secured to the lining. She hands Lynn the paper.

Lynn screws up her face as she reads. "This is my address. I thought we agreed on a drink first?"

"Other side." Regina taps the bottom of the note. "Are

5

we anywhere near?"

Lynn flips over the paper. "The Sea Colony. 52 Eighth Avenue. Near Horatio and West Fourth." She shrugs. "Never heard of it. But I can find it."

"Before she got married, Darla went there." Regina only half believes the place exists. Darla's lies are one reason she and Regina are no longer friends. "She knew the bartender."

"You're finally in Manhattan. If it serves Manhattans, it's what we're looking for. Might be a panic."

"Who needs a panic?" Regina asks, as if she wasn't the one who suggested the place.

"Listen, honey, let's be close like we used to, catch up, have a few laughs. The truth of the matter is I'm lonely as hell. I miss my sister." Lynn picks up the suitcase and walks, using the luggage to wedge through the crowd.

"I'd like that." Regina didn't think much Lynn could say would shock her, but Lynn lonely is a surprise. "Aren't your roommates company?"

"After we order drinks, I'll tell you about my roommates. Let's find this place."

Regina has no trouble keeping up with Lynn's pace until a serious gust of October wind blows up and takes the pillbox hat right off her head. She stops to watch the hat become a blob of turquoise trash as it descends in a nosedive right in the middle of Eighth Avenue where a yellow cab runs over it. The wind dies as quickly as it came. Two dollars and twenty-five cents' worth of hat, representing an hour and a half of piece work in the factory where she works, flattened.

Regina watches Lynn shoulder her way between two old men wearing uniforms that make them look vaguely military. Doormen, Regina guesses.

"Slow down," Regina yells, picking up her pace. For a moment, she can't find Lynn and yells her name louder. But there's Lynn's platinum hair, flashy as a caution light. Regina is mortified to have screamed in public. She should have heeded her mother's instruction: "Be a lady, not a nagging fishwife." Regina remembers her mother's disgust with "fishwives," women who screech their daughters' names from front steps for the whole neighborhood to hear. Regina and Lynn's mother would hate Lynn's hair.

Regina must admit her sister's silvery hair is awfully pretty with the sun on it, bouncing on Lynn's shoulders with every step she takes. If Regina could get her hair to flip like that, she would. But with her wiry hair, a bob held in place with plenty of hairspray is the best she can do.

The sidewalk ends, and the edge of the street becomes the pedestrian way. The foot traffic is so heavy she wonders if it's possible to fall. Or perhaps if she fell there would be a domino effect and she would take down twenty people with her. She feels her head to see how much damage her hairdo has suffered, fluffing it, removing the useless bobby pins that were supposed to keep the hat anchored. Lynn is nowhere in sight. Regina walks faster. The new shoes click against the pavement in a no-nonsense way.

A pinch above Regina's knee is followed by a ping of elastic snapping against her thigh. She stops in a small alcove, the entrance to a souvenir store. She looks down at the garter and dark layer of double nylon where the stocking came unhooked and sags below her hemline. She's worried about losing Lynn, remembers Lynn's address pinned to the lining of her purse.

A young man in a three-button flannel suit stops. "Everything hunky-dory, honey?" The entrance to the store is only a few square feet and the man stands too close for Regina's liking.

And she doesn't like the "honey." She recalls her mother's words about watching out for men in the city and her father's advice to stick close to Lynn. The man lights a cigarette and leans against the window, with its display of postcards, back scratchers, and brassieres with "New Year New York" written boldly across the padded cups.

"You lost?" He offers her a Camel, which she declines. "Where you headed? I know Manhattan like the back of my hand."

Her reflection in the window behind the man unnerves Regina. Her hair is flat on one side and sticking out on the other. She's humiliated by the unhooked stocking. She remembers she gave the slip of paper to Lynn and doesn't have Lynn's address pinned to the lining of her purse anymore. She scowls at the bras in the display case.

The man turns to look. "Tourists," he says with an amused smile.

She tries to sound New York confident. "I'm fine, thank you."

"My offense is what? Offering assistance?"

"What's going on around here?" Lynn is suddenly beside them, setting the suitcase on the sidewalk, teasing Regina, mimicking the words, the heft and tilt of their father's voice when he's in a protective mode.

"Are you accosting my baby sister?" Lynn laughs, planting her hands on her hips, flirting with the man. "She's not used to good-looking men trying to pick her up right on . . ."

Regina cuts her off. "I had a mishap." She points to the hem of her skirt and sagging edge of stocking with as much dignity as she can muster.

"Minor." Lynn waves it off, returning her attention to the man.

"Who have we here?" He gives Lynn the same once-over he has just given Regina, winks, and tips his thin-brimmed hat. "You girls try not to get lost." Regina would love to knock the hat off his head. He squeezes past Lynn, turns on his heels, and walks away.

"He was all right. Why do you have a puss on?" Now Lynn gives Regina the once-over the man just gave them both. "You look like hell."

Regina nods her agreement, taking a comb out of her purse to fuss with her hair.

"He was headed toward Wall Street." The suitcase sags under Lynn's weight as she sits on it. "After hours. But still. I wouldn't mind a rich one for a change."

"I'd rather stay poor than be with a jerk. If Wall Street is that way," Regina points, "half of New York is headed there."

"You just hate men."

Regina looks at her stocking. There's a moment of silence, a skipped beat, while the sisters share the unspoken thought that they don't see each other enough to waste time fighting. "Oh, who cares? More for me," Lynn says offhandedly, like she's talking about asparagus or platinum hair, things she likes herself but can accept Regina not liking.

Regina laughs and grabs Lynn's hand. "You're going to break Dad's suitcase."

"A pencil skirt and heels." Lynn lets Regina pull her up. "Kind of risqué for a Holyoke girl." She takes Regina by the shoulders and turns her body so she can get a look at her from behind. "That is one tight skirt," she nods approvingly. "Looks like you finally grew an ass."

"It's not so tight. For your information, I do not hate men. And, I'm wearing pumps, not heels."

"If you don't hate men, why do you act like such a square whenever a cute guy is around?"

"I don't like rude men." Regina likes nice men fine, but what is she going to do about the fact that she doesn't like them enough? Her chest gets tight with a familiar panic. How will she live her life if she can't train herself to like them more?

"Honey," Lynn says. "Why so glum all of a sudden?" She stares at Regina, interested. "I haven't seen you pull that face in public since we were little. You're a mess too, aren't you?" Lynn sounds hopeful.

"I suppose I am a bit of a mess." Mostly Regina is okay but it's so much work to stay happy with this worry about her future dragging her down. "I'm fine. I just . . . may as well blurt it out. I'm going to end up an old maid."

"You? No. Me and your friend Darla got hitched to the wrong men. Doesn't mean you will. It's almost 1956. A girl doesn't have to get married by twenty-one anymore. Even Marilyn Monroe is single at the moment. I'm single at the moment. Well, not legally. Honey, for God's sake, what's the matter? Mom said you were blue."

"Darla's no longer my friend." Regina flaps her hand in frustration. "Mom told you I was blue?"

"And she told me not to bring up Darla's divorce." Lynn squats on the crowded street, hikes Regina's skirt up a couple of inches, and secures the stocking to the garter. "Come on." She starts walking. "The sooner we get there, the sooner you can tell me all about it."

A few blocks later they stand under the Sea Colony sign.

"Maybe this was a bad idea." Regina puts down the suitcase and stares at an uninteresting door and a sign they could have easily missed.

"We're here. Let's find out."

Once inside, Regina is relieved the place is not too upscale, but not a dump either. Plenty of empty tables in the large, square room at five-thirty. They take one near the bar. A small vase with a single carnation sits at each table. The room is well-lit for a bar, almost as bright as the growing dusk the sisters just came from outside. Two women wearing too much makeup are hunched over a nearby table. They cut their eyes at the sisters and go back to talking quietly. A few people are at the bar, their backs to the tables. Regina mistakes the bartender for a man until the woman calls over, "What'll it be, ladies?" in a voice that doesn't match her button-down collar or James Dean haircut. Except for the bartender, this could be a quiet place around the corner in the sisters' hometown in western Massachusetts.

"Manhattans." Lynn holds up two fingers.

"Neat or on the rocks?" The bartender, tall, with thin muscled arms in the rolled-up sleeves of her white buttoned shirt, a nice smile, and a thick head of very short hair, asks pleasantly. "First time visiting The Sea Colony, ladies?"

"Yes, first time," Regina answers quickly. "One Manhattan. On the rocks. Cabernet for me, please. Do you serve food?"

Lynn gives the bartender a grin. "The two Manhattans are for me."

"We have snacks." The bartender points to a row of bagged chips, peanuts, and pretzels displayed on metal clips on a vertical ladder on the wall behind her.

"No." Regina tries not to openly stare at the barest curve of breast under the bartender's shirt. She adds a flustered, "Thank you." The bartender gives Regina a smile disproportionate to her reply and goes about the business of making their drinks.

"My god, I thought she was a guy," Lynn whispers. "Could that be Darla's friend? So why aren't you and Darla friends anymore?"

"Shush," Regina says. "She'll hear you." The bartender looks in their direction as she draws a beer for the guy at the bar. Regina kicks Lynn under the table, "Talk about your roommates."

"You think she doesn't know she looks like a guy?" Lynn keeps her voice low. "Okay. Roommates. I walk up three flights to share a bunk bed with Candy. She snores. Which is why you'll be sleeping on the couch and I'll be on the floor next to you tonight."

"But your letters?"

"You're the goody two shoes. I tell Mom whatever keeps her off my back and Dad whatever keeps him calm. I'm pretty sure Candy supplements her income." Lynn pumps her hand in a disgusting gesture. "It's not such a bad idea. You try living in the city on a secretary's wages."

Lynn throws her head back and laughs at her sister's reaction. "Don't worry, I don't turn tricks. Stop looking at me like I shot somebody." Lynn puts a hand to her mouth. "Oh my god, I did shoot somebody, didn't I?" She laughs harder. "Loosen up. It's over. It's funny." She holds a hand in front of her, her finger curled around an imaginary gun. "Pistol. Small ladies' weapon."

"I haven't forgotten what kind of gun. Shot *at* somebody." Almost a year later, Regina can't decide whether to laugh or cry over the fact that her sister almost went to jail for shooting at her husband, Jim. "You missed."

"On purpose." Lynn pulls the imaginary trigger. "Would

have fired a shot to the heart if he didn't run." She makes the sign of the cross, suddenly gloomy. "Big Jim, big mistake." She puts her elbow on the table and props her chin on her palm. "I miss him."

"You do not. He beat you up." Anger that Lynn, not her wife-beating husband, had to leave Holyoke rises in Regina. "The injustice of him living in that house you made so pretty." How Lynn tolerates her friends back home gossiping about her private business, Regina will never understand.

"I miss all the friends we had. I miss not having to work a shitty full-time job to share a crappy room. He was a good time until he wasn't. He hates Massachusetts. He'll leave the state sooner than later, and I can move back."

Regina picks up a napkin and dabs at the tear below Lynn's left eye, realizing she's been so busy hiding her own private life, trying not to cause their parents more heartbreak, she forgot about Lynn's heartbreak.

The bartender clears her throat and sets a tray on their table. "Here you are, ladies." All three of them pretend she didn't see the last exchange between the sisters. "Name's Jackie." She looks directly at Regina. Regina can't think of a thing to say. She smiles. Jackie wipes her hands on the checkered cloth tucked into her change apron and takes her time placing the drinks.

Regina is charmed by the way Jackie holds one hand behind her back as she serves them. The proximity of Jackie's low, mannerly voice soothes Regina, but leaves her uncharacteristically tongue-tied. She looks down and sips her wine, grateful that Lynn takes up the slack, small-talking with the mannish bartender.

"Are you going to say hello?" Lynn asks. Regina looks up in time to see Lynn rolling her eyes. "Jackie, this is my sister, Regina. She's not used to big city ways, like saying hello and giving your name when another girl introduces herself."

"Nice to meet you, Regina." Jackie nods. "Welcome to The Sea Colony."

"Nice to meet you too, Jackie," Regina says. "I'm a little

tired from traveling."

"Whenever you get a chance," Lynn says, "another glass of red wine for my sister. It's her birthday."

"No, thank you. I haven't eaten." Regina struggles to make out the outline of the sleeveless T-shirt under Jackie the bartender's oxford shirt. "A second glass will make me sleepier."

"I can bring you a sandwich, if you like? Afraid it will have to be deviled ham, though."

Regina loves the calm attentive way the bartender waits for an answer. She could sit here with the bartender standing calmly to one side all night.

"You want the sandwich?" Lynn says. "You can always have a pickled egg." She points to the huge glass jar of eggs on the counter.

"A sandwich, please," Regina says. "Thank you." She wonders if she can memorize the spicy scent of Jackie's cologne and why people think of spice as a particularly manly smell. The pretty girls at the next table have had their ears cocked since Jackie walked over, listening in an obvious way. The girls' listening in irritates Regina. She says, "A sandwich for my sister, too, please," and both girls laugh out loud. This infuriates Regina but she keeps a neutral expression and appreciates the dignity of the impersonal glance the bartender gives the girls.

"Jackie"—the pretty redhead bats her eyelashes in an exaggerated way. "Are you giving these girls your supper?"

"Mine to give." Jackie looks away from the girl who laughs an unfriendly laugh.

"Oh no, we won't take your supper," Regina insists.

The redhead's companion, a woman with jet black hair to her waist, turns all the way around in her seat to get a good look at the sisters. "Jackie can be very generous when she's in the mood." She juts her chin at Lynn. "Hit on the dye job. She's your best bet." She turns to the redhead. "Let's go to The Drake." The women make a big production out of leaving.

"Do we know you? What is your problem?" Lynn says.

Both women smirk and push in their chairs.

13

"They're not worth the dignity of a response," Regina says. "Ignore them." To make conversation she asks Jackie, "I think you know my friend, Darla?"

"Darla?" Jackie tilts her head.

The redhead snaps her clutch bag shut. "Rack your brain, Jackie. Surely there hasn't been more than one Darla?"

Jackie doesn't blink as the women walk out, swaying their hips. "Sorry about that," Jackie says. "Darla Bodowitz? From Massachusetts?"

"Yes, you have the right girl," Regina says. "From Holyoke, our hometown. Bodowitz was her maiden name."

"I grew up a few towns over. Granby. We worked at a summer camp, right after high school. She came into the city last year, looked me up." Jackie nods. "Darla. Please, say hello." She looks toward two more customers at the bar. "I have a break in ten minutes. Okay if I bring the sandwiches and your drinks over then?"

"Yes. I mean no. Just the drinks, please," Regina says.

"You're hungry. We'll share." Jackie makes a slight bow and stashes the tray under her arm.

"What was that?" Lynn asks as Jackie walks away. "Odd, that's what. Not like you to be rude. I'm getting ideas about this place." She sits back and takes a long sip of her drink. Regina sips her wine blank-faced. "Sometimes when we were teenagers, I used to wonder . . ." Lynn frowns. "Why'd Darla send us to a bar where her friend the bartender is a dyke?"

"Don't use that word," Regina snaps, "and keep your voice down."

"You know those girls who just left are that way, too, right?"

"Yes," Regina says. This is not going the way she hoped. Regina thought she could discreetly mention she had *been* with Darla, explain that *it* was over now, and Regina planned to live a normal life. Then she could lead into how Lynn might pursue a normal life, too, by drinking less, not throwing herself at the wrong men, toning down in general.

A bartender who made her want to peel off her stockings

14

was not part of Regina's plan.

"What do you want me to call them?" Lynn snaps her fingers. "Regina, you with me?"

"Call who?"

"The girls who just flounced out of here. You told me not to call them dykes twenty seconds ago. I'd bet my life the redhead is the bartender's jilted lover." Lynn raises an eyebrow.

"You think so? I was told all kinds of people came here." Regina looks around the bar. "See?" Two well-dressed young men walk in. "It's clean and . . . I thought we could both see that normal people and people who aren't so normal sometimes mix and . . ." Oh, what the hell is she saying? Her eyes settle on her sister. "I went with her." Regina pulls at the hem of her skirt.

"Went where?" Lynn spills her drink. "With who?" She keeps her eyes on Regina and wipes the spot with her napkin.

"Darla."

"You came here with Darla? When? This is the first time you've been to the city." Lynn sips her Manhattan and squints at Regina.

Regina lifts her glass, surprised to find it empty.

"You mean went out with, slept with? Let me get this straight." Lynn cocks an eyebrow and leans halfway across the table. "Your face is beet red. You mean *sex?*" She bounces in her chair.

Regina shakes her head. Why *did* she bring Lynn here?

Lynn takes her sister's head movement as a no. "I would have been stunned," she grins, "but not totally surprised. Did she want to? What about what's his name, the ass she married?" Lynn studies Regina.

"His name is Dan." Regina closes her eyes. "The word is lesbian. Or homophile."

"That's why you have such an on-again, off-again friendship with Darla? Because she's . . . that way? Lesbian? Is that why she got divorced?"

Lynn leans back, still bouncing in her seat, not even trying to contain her excitement over such sensational gossip. "I never liked Darla. But man, she doesn't look it. Now that I think of it, that redhead that just left and her friend didn't fit the bill either." She downs the last of her first Manhattan and starts on the second. "Darla and the bartender? That's how they must pair off. You know, a mannish one and a girlish one." Lynn leans back, satisfied with her reasoning.

"Shut up and listen, Lynn." Regina wonders if it's better to leave well enough alone and stay lonely, keep the truth about herself. She better be smart. She could lose her sister.

The place is beginning to fill up.

Lynn waits, sipping her drink. "I'm listening. You're not talking." She twirls the cocktail glass by its stem. "Hurry up. Our friendly bartender is coming over."

Jackie walks towards them, carrying a full tray. Now there is a second bartender, a young man wearing a half-apron exactly like Jackie's, behind the bar.

"On the house." Jackie sets the wine in front of Regina. "Happy birthday." She unloads chips, peanuts, two sandwiches neatly wrapped in waxed paper, and Twinkies onto the table. "Sorry I can't do better." A mug of beer stays on the tray. She smiles, waits five seconds, says, "Enjoy," places their empty glasses on the tray, and takes a step back, ready to take her leave.

"Awfully nice of you. You're on break, right?" Lynn pushes the chair next to Regina away from the table with her foot. "The idea was that you and Regina share the sandwiches." Lynn pulls the package of cake toward her. "I'm more interested in Twinkies."

Jackie holds up a hand. "You were in the middle of a conversation. I only have ten minutes anyway." She smiles directly at Regina.

"Please, join us." Regina pushes the suitcase under the chair next to Lynn to make room.

Lynn and Jackie carry the conversation again. Regina drinks her wine and attempts to compose a sentence that will make sense to her sister, even as she tries, without success, to ignore the pull of Jackie's warm, low voice. She chews bread and deviled

16

ham as she drifts between the contemplation of Jackie's rolled-up shirt sleeves and worrying that she will never come up with a way to explain to herself why, in the name of heaven, she is so interested in Jackie's arms. She ends up categorizing Jackie as thin, but not skinny, decides her forearms are sinewy. Even when Regina was a teen and locked the bedroom door, she could not conjure up a fantasy partner that so instantly attracted her. What is wrong with her? She brought her sister to *this* bar to get Lynn to cut down on drinking and to get herself to stop liking girls? If she were rich, she'd take herself to a psychiatrist.

Regina is back to appreciating the smell and look of the starched white shirt pushed up against Jackie's forearm when Lynn taps her shoulder. "You can't possibly be drunk on a glass and a half of wine. Jackie asked you a question."

"Sorry, daydreaming."

"Wondering if I can bring you anything else before it gets too busy?" Jackie says. "Believe it or not," she looks at the Bulova on her wrist, "in half an hour every table in front will be taken, and dancing will be in full swing in the back room." She nods at a knotty pine wall with a door in the middle. "Stays quiet all night up here but gets jumpin' in back."

It takes an awkward silence for Regina to stop staring at the back wall and answer, "No, no, thank you. I'm already foggy."

Lynn pulls a pack of Luckies out of her purse. Regina looks up at the layer of smoke hovering just below the ceiling.

"To sisters enjoying the city." Jackie lifts her mug and downs the last of the beer. "Raise a finger if you do need anything."

When Jackie is ten feet from the table, Lynn says, "What the hell? I can't tell if you're afraid of that girl or you want to bump pussies with her."

"Lynn, please." Regina looks around to see if anyone heard. "For god's sake."

Lynn crosses her arms over her chest. "You never thanked her for the drinks and sandwich." She waves her hand over the bags of chips and nuts. "Or any of this stuff."

"I didn't?" Regina glances at the bar where Jackie and the

other bartender tend a rowdy group who just arrived. "All right, I've got to tell you. I think maybe . . ."

"Holy fuck." Lynn tips back in her chair. "You do like girls."

Regina stiffens. Lynn rarely uses the "F" word. "I mean to say, I thought if we could talk I might be able to sort things out." Regina prides herself on honesty, and she is honest, except about this one thing. Her cheeks burn with shame. Embarrassment. And anger. Regina knows she sometimes does foolish things when she's angry. Like tell the truth? She wants to be a girl who tells the truth. But the truth is dangerous.

Lynn stares open-mouthed before she shakes her head and pulls her chair in close. "You never really had a boyfriend. Have you tried boys? It's great. Once you get used to it, you crave it. Maybe with a little alcohol. What about kissing? You like kissing guys?" Regina shakes her head. Lynn takes Regina's hand between hers and rubs like she's trying to prevent frostbite. "But you haven't even tried, right?"

Regina pulls away and wraps her arms around herself. "I just can't."

"Johnny Bell in high school? And that Tim guy?" Lynn frowns. "They barely count. You haven't tried the right one." Lynn holds up two fingers, but the bar is crowded. She doesn't catch Jackie's attention and the other bartender ignores her.

"Please don't drink anymore." Regina wishes they were having this conversation somewhere where she wasn't craving the bartender's beautiful arms. "I'm sorry I brought you to a bar. I was thinking of myself."

Lynn ignores Regina's comment. "Try it after a couple glasses of wine. Some girls don't like it, but that doesn't mean they're funny. I don't like it with some boys myself."

"I didn't like kissing those boys." Regina is adamant. "I liked kissing Darla."

Lynn takes a big drag on her Lucky and lets the smoke curl slowly out her nostrils. "All right." She stabs out the cigarette in a half-eaten Twinkie. "Give me a minute to take it in. Look at you." Lynn opens her palm toward Regina. "You could have any

18

guy you want. Especially in that tight skirt." A low laugh starts at the back of Lynn's throat and builds up steam until tears run down her cheeks. "Come on. It's kind of funny. You're Dad's Queen Regina."

She laughs for a long time before Regina purses her lips and says, "Half the bar is staring at you. You done?"

"Maybe."

Regina juts her chin and whispers, "Darla got to be a pain in the ass. But I liked it." She's surprised by her own insistent tone. "I don't know why I thought this was a reasonable place to talk. What an impossible person I am." She takes a deep breath. "You've got mascara streaked down your face."

"I'd say it worked pretty well as an icebreaker. You got any more tissues? Talk."

Regina hunts around in her purse. "Please stop staring at me."

Lynn grabs the tissue Regina dangles in front of her. "No wonder you got so secretive in high school. This explains the old maid business earlier." Lynn pats under her eyes, leans back and gestures toward the bar with a grin. "You like the bartender. She'd make waves in Holyoke."

Regina should feel some relief, but she feels tense. Lynn has a loud voice. One friend to talk to so she can figure this thing out, she was so sure that was all she needed. Lynn, despite their bickering, would do anything for her, she knows. But a quiet conversation with Lynn? About this? Anywhere?

"Listen, honey, you can talk to me. I tease you but I'm your sister. Hey, I shot my husband and you stood by me. I'm trying to understand."

"You and me both." Regina stares across the table.

Lynn stands. "I need a drink."

"No one needs three Manhattans," Regina's voice trails after Lynn. She watches her sister settle onto a bar stool. Jackie, at the opposite end of the counter, comes right over to her.

Some guy in a sailor suit sits on a stool next to Lynn, and she laughs at something he says.

Lynn flutters her fingers at Regina motioning for her to come over. Regina shakes her head.

A minute later Jackie is at the table delivering another glass of wine. "Compliments of the young man sitting with your sister." She places a glass of water on the table next to the wine. "Thought you might want this, too."

"Thank you." Regina has the urge to stroke Jackie's arm. The fact that she never will makes her want to cry.

"Sorry, did I say something to offend?" Jackie asks. When Regina remains silent, Jackie says, "Enjoy your wine," and turns to go.

Regina's voice comes out hoarse. "I think this is what they call tongue-tied." She touches the back of Jackie's shirt. "I'm sorry. I'm not used to places like this." Jackie must think her a fool. "The back room," she manages to say, "that's where the girls who . . . like each other go?"

Jackie faces Regina. "That's right. If you want to go back there to dance, let me know. Be happy to escort you. Although I can't spend much time in back while I'm working the front." She nods politely and walks away.

Regina thinks of her parents, how unhappy they are that Lynn is here in New York. How unhappy would they be if they saw Regina dancing in that back room?

Two minutes later Lynn and the sailor are at the table. Lynn's eyes are liquid. "This is Tony." Tony places two Manhattans on the table and pulls a chair out for Lynn. They both sit.

"Nice to meet you, Tony." Regina stands, straightens her sweater, and drags her suitcase out from under the table. "I'm sorry, but I'd like to get a cup of coffee."

"They got coffee here," Tony says. He's a big, handsome man with broad shoulders and thick brown hair in a standard military crew cut. "Not to worry." He looks around the bar nodding approval. "I got a twin sister, name of Twilight, comes here all the time. Jackie keeps things quiet. Hardly ever trouble. Me and Jackie," he crosses two fingers, "like this. We were both in the service." He grimaces. "Shouldn'ta mentioned about how

Jackie served at one time. Appreciate if you don't bring it up."

"I'm starting to feel real good." Lynn hangs on Tony's big arm. "Let's stay awhile. Have some fun. Please, Regina. It's your birthday."

"And I'd like a piece of birthday cake." Regina turns to look at the clock hanging between two ornate mirrors in back of the long mahogany bar. It's almost seven.

The music and laughter coming from the back gets louder. A voice in Regina's head, telling her to leave, gets louder, too. Tony and Lynn play a finger game on the tabletop. "You can give Tony your phone number," Regina says. "See him some other time."

"Maybe, if he behaves himself." Lynn winks at Tony and wiggles in her chair. "They're playing an awfully lot of slow ones all of a sudden."

The back room door is open now and music is coming from a jukebox, loud enough to be heard in the front without drowning conversation.

"My kind of dancing." Tony stubs out his cigarette and puts his arm around Lynn. "You want to give it a go? And your sister too, of course." He smiles at Regina. "Nice young lady such as yourself, someone's bound to ask you to dance."

"The juke's playing Nat King Cole," Lynn squeals. Still seated, she pushes her chair back. "Regina, what are you afraid of? Mom danced with Aunt Lidia at my wedding."

"To 'The Bunny Hop,' not 'Unforgettable.'" Regina moves a black plastic ashtray overflowing with butts to the edge of the table, ticking off in her mind a few of the things she's afraid of— that back room, that bartender, disgracing their parents.

"Not all girls back there," Tony says. "Everybody's welcome. You don't have to dance."

Now there are two other bartenders helping Jackie. Regina watches one balance a metal tray on his hip as he delivers drinks through the door propped open with a chair. The music gets louder. People continue to enter through the nondescript front door, size up the place, and take a table or sit at the bar. Some,

21

women mostly, head straight for the back room.

Regina turns back to the bar, disturbed by how drunk her sister is and how ridiculously jealous she is of the women who smile at Jackie as they walk past the bar to the back room. She hits on the idea to invite Jackie to have cake tomorrow. She read about Altman's tearoom in the Big Apple brochure on the bus into the city. She's composing the invitation when she realizes she's been staring in the direction of the bar too long and turns back to her tablemates. She returns her attention in time to see her sister and Tony walk through the cloud of smoke and the open door of the back room. Regina feels, for a moment, like she's in a dream.

"You look lost." Jackie appears at her side, adding to the surreal quality of the moment. "Would you like to join your sister?"

"Yes." Regina places a hand on Jackie's flexed muscle before she hooks her arm through the bent elbow Jackie offers. "I am a little lost."

At the edge of the dimly lit and crowded back room, Regina stays hooked to Jackie. The long rectangular space is large and mostly dance floor.

"It takes a minute for your eyes to adjust," Jackie says.

There's a strong smell of sweat and perfume. A scattering of women sit on wooden folding chairs or lean against the wall, many with drinks in their hands. The song changes to "Sincerely." There are no tables. Regina leans into Jackie, remembers Jackie saying she could escort but not stay long in the back room. She feels the seconds ticking by. Her eyes begin to take in what she already knows. The dancing couples are almost all girls pressed against each other. She feels the pent-up force, created by being held apart too long, building in her own body.

"Do you see Lynn?" Jackie asks.

Regina scans the room. With her platinum hair, Lynn is not hard to find. Through the dim lighting Regina sees Tony's hand resting squarely on Lynn's bottom. Regina looks up at Jackie, who is much taller. "Do you have time for one dance?" In her wildest dreams Regina had not imagined slow dancing with a woman while her sister was pressed against a man on the same dance floor.

Jackie smiles. Before she can answer the lights flicker twice. "I gotta get back to the bar," she says. "Grab your sister, find your table, any table in the front room. Now." And she's gone.

Tony drags a resistant Lynn to Regina, yelling, "Twilight!" over his shoulder.

A woman as tall and broad as Tony, with a shock of the same brown hair, only much longer, answers his call.

Regina grabs Lynn's hand. "What's happening?" she asks Tony.

"Raid," Twilight answers. She has an Adam's apple that matches her brother's and the same low voice.

Lynn frowns. "Of all the rotten luck."

"You two can pass," Tony says to Regina.

"Pass?" Regina says. "For what?"

"Tourists, honey," Twilight's low voice becomes shrill. "The cops don't know you."

"I'm from Brooklyn." Lynn pats her chest.

Tony heads for the back door with Twilight in hand. Someone in the clump of women already gathered at the door yells, "It's bolted shut from the outside."

Through the chaos, Regina manages to get Lynn back to "their table," now occupied by a gray-haired man and woman, and claim two seats as well as her father's satchel under the table. She'd forgotten all about the suitcase. Every seat is being taken by someone who fled the back.

The man seems disgusted. "What's going on?" He folds his arms over his chest.

Jackie flicks a switch behind the bar, the back room lights up, and she calls out, "Best if everyone stays seated." Someone cuts the music, which in the confusion kept playing.

It becomes strangely quiet. The only sound from the back is the scraping of chairs as if everyone is taking a seat around the perimeter of the dance floor at once. The front listens for more signs of what's happening in back. The back seems to be holding its collective breath.

Jackie's voice from the bar is steady. "The doors have been secured by the police. No need to panic, folks. They don't usually bother customers up front." She keeps the reassuring voice as she whips off her tie. "Probably a couple of cruisers outside." She stops speaking when the sound of a door banging open, followed by stomping feet, can clearly be heard in the back room.

A redheaded policeman walks in from the back, looks around, and tips his hat at the crowd. "Sorry to detain you law-abiding citizens. Stay put. Enjoy your beer while we sort out who's who. I'm Officer Riley." He walks over to a table where Tony and his sister Twilight sit.

"They won't bother a serviceman," the gray-haired man insists to the woman Regina takes to be his wife.

Officer Riley speaks into a walkie-talkie on his shoulder. "I got the twins up here, Sergeant. You want 'em both or just Twilight?"

Tony wraps an arm around Twilight who cries quietly on his shoulder. Officer Riley is answered with static that he seems to understand because he says, "Okay boys, both of you, back you go." The cop walks the twins to the back room.

"Bartender, is this a raid?" The man sitting across from Regina asks Jackie loud enough for most of the people in the room to hear. "I demand to know what's going on here."

The woman answers, "Of course it's a raid. I tried to tell you, Thomas." Her hair is in a neat little knot at the back of her head, not a strand out of place. Regina is reminded of their grandmother. Except their grandmother wouldn't be caught dead at a bar and couldn't afford the dress the woman is wearing. "It's the vice squad," the woman announces to the room. "They are looking for homosexuals, females mostly, by the looks of who walked into the back." She turns to the man, "Are you a homosexual, Thomas?" The man gives her a disgusted look. "Then they are not looking for you," the woman says.

Some of the other patrons have begun speaking quietly.

The woman looks Lynn up and down. She turns in her seat to give Regina the same scrutiny. "That man's twin was his brother, not his sister," she says.

"Get out," Lynn squeals and pulls the empty cocktail glass she left on the table toward her.

Regina grabs Lynn's hand on top of the table, decides it's a bad idea, and releases it. "Let's keep our voices down."

"My voice is down," Lynn says loudly.

"We live in Manhattan. My husband," the woman gestures, "did not believe places like this exist in our little borough."

Her husband glares at her. "Congratulations, you were right."

The only thing heard from the back room has been shuffling and instructions of "stand up" or "sit down." Now the disembodied voice from the back room booms, "Okay, ladies and gentlemen." Everyone in the front turns to the sound, staring at the open door, seeing only the back of the officer barking the order, "You two against the wall, that's right, you two in bobby socks, too drunk or stupid to pull yourselves away from each other. Did you think you were going to an all-girl hop? Riley," the voice snaps, "stop gawking at the blonde, do your job, collect ID, gather up the girls who dress like boys. Line them up next to the kissing cousins. Anyone gives you lip, any sissies, any undetermined—against the wall."

Regina has heard of homosexuals getting beat up. She never dreamed it might be the police who beat them, thought it only happened to guys, "fairies," their dad would say. She sits up, shoulders back. Sisters out for a birthday drink, no reason for police to give them a second look.

Someone in the back room is crying. The big voice booms, "Officer Heinz, put a stop to that blubbering. Stick a sock in her mouth if you have to."

"That could be Tony's brother." Lynn glares at the back wall. "Or sister." She shakes her head. Concentrates. "I'll ask Jackie."

"Stay right here," Regina says.

Lynn trips getting out of her chair then walks a straight line

25

to the bar. Regina grabs her suitcase and follows. Two women jump off bar stools and take the sisters' seats at the table. Lynn and Regina sit on the vacated stools.

Jackie comes right over, dragging a dishrag across the clean bar in front of them. Lynn wastes no time asking her, "Girls dancing? Is that . . . unlegal?"

"Illegal. Girls together, boys together—crime against nature." Jackie stares at the back wall. "Sounds like they're getting rougher than usual." She bends to untie her wingtips and slip into penny loafers she keeps under the bar. "Excuse me." She turns so she's not facing them and takes a comb out of her back pocket. When she faces them her slicked-back hair has been pulled forward and she has a fringe of Brylcreemed bangs. "I hate to ask," she lowers her eyes, scratches the back of her head, and asks with a tense smile, "Can I borrow your scarf, Lynn?"

"What?" Lynn lifts herself off the stool and sits back down.

"I need three pieces of women's clothing." Jackie's brow creases as the noise coming from the back escalates. "I usually keep a couple of scarves and a bracelet here. I don't know where they went."

"Why?" Regina unties the scarf from around her sister's neck.

"So they can't charge me with pretending to be a man."

"No numb girl." Lynn giggles, stops, abruptly serious. "Dumb girl. Not in America." Other customers are whispering. Lynn speaks loudly, "No girl's gonna think you." She frowns. "Well, I did."

"Shush, Lynn." Regina takes a chiffon scarf from her purse. "Unbutton your top two buttons. Let me." She kneels on the stool and unbuttons Jackie's collar.

"Try to sober up," Jackie tells Lynn as Regina arranges the scarves. "You may land in jail if you don't."

Regina is handing Jackie her charm bracelet when the cop with the big voice makes an entrance into the front room. "You lost sheep, come to the wrong watering hole, don't worry," the cop says. He stands in the doorway between the rooms. "We are the NYPD Vice Squad." Everyone on a bar stool swivels to watch the cop approach the bar. He's a tall white man with a thick neck. He surveys the hushed room with his back to the long mahogany counter. "My name is Smithe, with an *e*. Sergeant Smithe at your service. Keep your noses clean and you'll walk out of here with a good story to tell the family back home."

There's a thud followed by the sound of glass breaking in the back room. Two bodies struggle in the doorway, bounce against the door frame, and stagger a few feet into the front room. One is a cop who keeps telling the person he's struggling with to "calm down."

"Enough," Officer Smithe bellows, raises his nightstick, and brings it down.

"Shit." The person struggling with the cop falls to their knees.

"Officer Johnson," Smithe's laugh is mean, "see that thing hanging off your belt? You got bested by a short fat girl with your nightstick just dangling there."

Officer Johnson unhooks the nightstick, which slips out of his hands and skitters, stopping when it slams into Regina's suitcase.

Smithe shakes his head. He turns his attention to the person on the floor whom he just hit. "Well, who have we here? Bonnie Louise Meeks. In men's pants and suspenders."

Anyone who can turn or stretch their neck to watch the show does. Regina is close and sees that the person still on all fours is Black. And female? Jackie hurries from behind the bar and picks up the nightstick. She exchanges a nod with Officer Johnson as she hands it to him.

"Take it easy, Sergeant," Jackie says and looks down. "You okay, Bo?"

Bo makes it from all fours to a squat, straightens her suspenders, and rubs her thigh.

The sergeant looks around the room and feigns a pleasant attitude. "Do I look like a man who takes orders from a bartender?" He drops the fake tone to growl at Jackie, "You want to join your pal on the floor there?"

"Just trying to be of service." Jackie extends a hand to help Bo upright.

"She don't want no one to get hurt, Sarge." Johnson reattaches the nightstick to his belt loop.

Smithe slaps his stick against his palm. "Keep your mouth shut if you want to keep your job, Johnson. Get back behind the bar, Jackie." He uses the tip of his nightstick to snap one of Bo's suspenders. Bo glares at him and tugs up her pinstriped pants. "Those pants are kind of raggedy. You laid off again Bonnie?" the sergeant taunts.

As wide as the officer but a foot shorter, Bo looks him in the eye when she hisses, "My name is Bo."

"I'll call you whatever I like." The whole room hears Smithe snarl, "spic." He slaps the nightstick against his palm again.

Lynn leans forward on her stool. "Did the cop call her a 'spic'?"

Regina clutches Lynn's shoulder. "Don't say another word."

Smithe drags Bo by the arm the few feet over to Lynn. "You two know each other?"

"Hello, Miss." Bo grins at Lynn. "This fool . . ." She nods at Smithe. Smithe squeezes Bo's arm tighter. Bo winces and continues, ". . . can't get his racial slurs right."

Lynn holds out her hand like she expects Bo to kiss it.

"Shut up, Bo." Jackie wedges herself between Lynn and Bo. "I got bail." She takes a twenty out of her change apron. "Don't be stupid." She sticks the bill in Bo's pocket.

"You want to talk about stupid?" Bo glares at Smithe, who still has her by the arm. "Man don't know Puerto Rican from Jamaican."

"How drunk are you?" Without warning, Smithe brings his nightstick down hard on the wooden bar, then with a ninja's grace swings it between Bo's legs. Bo yips and crouches. Smithe finally releases Bo from his grip. "That ought to sober you up."

Regina jumps off her stool. Jackie helps Bo take the seat.

"If your pal was a real man, that might hurt," Smithe glares at Jackie. "Didn't I tell you to get behind the bar?" He makes an arc with his arm to take in the whole room. "You gave these folks a good show, Bonnie Lou." He gestures to Johnson, standing like a sentinel five feet away. "Get her out of my sight." Smithe's voice becomes almost pleasant as he announces charges. "Drunk and disorderly, resisting arrest, impersonating, assaulting an officer."

Regina stands with her hand on Lynn's shoulder, hoping to keep her quiet and seated.

Lynn looks at Smithe, still within feet of them. "Big Jim would give this guy what-for."

Smithe sticks his face close to Lynn's. "You got something to say?"

"Drunken tourist," Jackie says. "I'll take care of her."

"Mind your business," Smithe hisses like a pressure cooker about to blow.

"I'm so sorry, officer." Regina smiles for all she's worth. "My sister just lost her husband." She touches her throat. "A tragedy. We're from a small town. Not used to alcohol."

"Boom." Lynn shoots Smithe with her finger.

"A night in a cell will take her mind off her troubles," Smithe says.

"My sister wouldn't let me get drunk." Lynn grins idiotically.

Regina pats Lynn's arm. "We have to let Officer Smithe do his job." She smiles sweetly at him. "Her husband, may he rest in peace, he gave her a hard time. She's not herself." Regina tries to think of something flattering to say. "She hasn't gotten over him, you see. He was very handsome. We were just saying how much you look like him."

"Handsomer," Lynn says.

Smithe seems to think this means *he* is the handsomer. Something like a smile crosses his face.

From the back room a woman's voice screeches, "Son of a bitch!" followed by what sounds like a chair smashing into a wall. Static comes through Smithe's walkie-talkie again. He

29

concentrates on the controls.

In Smithe's moment of distraction Jackie tells Lynn, "Sober up and shut up. Jail is a bad place for a drunk." She touches Regina's elbow. "If they take you in, cry and ask for Johnson."

"Don't feel so good." Lynn teeters off the stool and vomits, hitting the tip of Sergeant Smithe's shoe.

"Jesus." Smithe shivers with disgust and raises his baton.

Jackie points to Regina's suitcase. "Sisters, right off the bus. I'll be responsible. Bound to mess up your paddy wagon." Jackie locks eyes with Smithe.

Smithe's stick hovers above Jackie's shoulder. "Tourist my ass." The baton slices sideways into Jackie's arm. He leans in and whispers in Jackie's ear, "You thought your little girlfriends could puke on my shoe because I lost a few bucks to you in a poker game?" He shakes his foot and yells, "Towels!"

Jackie holds her bruised arm. Another bartender runs over and hands Jackie mop towels.

As she wipes Smithe's shoe, Smithe studies Regina's ass as she bends to hold Lynn's hair back. "This one's cool as a cucumber. A pro?"

"I told you," Jackie stands and rubs her arm, "a tourist."

"Jackie got a boo-boo?" Smithe yanks the walkie-talkie off his shoulder "Riley, I got two more out here for you."

Jackie steps close to Smithe. The officer's frown turns menacing as Jackie speaks. "When you come to the bar after hours, does whoever you're collecting money for know you stay to play cards?"

"Lower your voice before this baton finds your head," Smithe snarls.

Jackie lowers her voice. Before she's done talking, Smithe pulls his head back and claps Jackie's bruised arm so hard Jackie lurches. He says, "You're right, I don't want a sloppy drunk in my wagon. Clean up and close up. We're even. I owe you nothing."

"Bo," Jackie says.

"Bonnie Lou won't get a free ride in my paddy wagon

tonight. But that is it." He appraises Regina and Lynn with a sneer. "Your lucky day, ladies. Or whatever you are. This one is wasting a big chit on you."

He turns to the crowd. "Good night, ladies and gentlemen. This establishment will be closed for the evening in a few minutes and you'll be free to go. By the way, Jackie"—he walks away laughing—"you look nice in those scarves."

Chapter 2

Saturday, February 18, 2017

Jackie and Regina are slouched, asleep on the couch. Regina has her head on Jackie's shoulder. A car horn honks and partially rouses Jackie who mutters, "Bo's in trouble."

The horn honks again.

Regina stretches. "Bo is still dead and completely out of harm's way, honey." She pulls a tissue from the pocket of her bathrobe and dabs at a bit of spittle. "That's Lotti getting picked up for work at the bakery." Lotti is their friend, next-door neighbor, and supplier of day-old baked goods.

"Bad dream." Jackie rubs her face. "But I got to see Bo."

"Bo asked you to look after Yvonne. You should call her." Regina grabs the phone off the end table and tries to hand it to Jackie.

"Before breakfast?" Jackie shakes her head, refusing.

Regina makes the call. Yvonne answers with, "This better be good. It's not seven o'clock and I was having a good time in a dream for a change."

"Morning, Yvonne. Jackie was having a bad dream. She said it was too early, but you know me," Regina says brightly.

"Headstrong. We couldn't sleep. Well, woke up and napped on the couch. You want company?"

"Not at the crack of tweet o'clock, I don't. You mean your woman couldn't sleep? Still got the blues? Not being able to sleep is a classic sign of depression. She still having bad dreams?"

"Yes, yes, and yes," Regina says. "Dreamed Bo was in trouble. I was dreaming about Bo myself. Just before we fell asleep I was talking about the raid at that bar in Manhattan where we first met."

"Let me drag myself up into a sitting position." Yvonne huffs with effort. "I love that story. The Sub Colony," Yvonne says. Regina corrects her, but Yvonne talks over Regina's correction. "Bo had lots of stories about that place. Let's get Jackie telling those old stories. Put her on the phone."

Regina holds the phone out. "For you." Jackie shakes her head again. Regina puts the phone on the coffee table, walks across the room, and stands with her hands on her hips.

From her end Yvonne yells, "You woke me up; now pick up the phone. Stop making me yell, Jackie."

Jackie picks up the receiver of the old-fashioned rotary phone, puts it to her mouth and ear, and says nothing.

"There's my favorite heavy breather," Yvonne says. "You miss your buddy?"

"Yes," Jackie says.

"Me too. How I miss waking up next to my Bo in the morning."

"I'm sorry. I didn't mean to bring up Bo."

"You didn't. I did. I like bringing up Bo. Matter of fact, you need to come over here and tell me stories. Much as you claim to hate to talk, you talk up a storm when you're in the mood. But I was trying to make a point about all of us needing medication from time to time. You remember a few months after she died, I'd wake up, realize Bo would never be there next to me again, and I got so depressed I could barely get out of bed? You and Regina had to force me to take the damned meds. And me a doctor. Not that that matters when it comes to depression, when it comes to coping. You remember that?"

"Yes."

"Me and Regina love you enough to gang up on you and kick your ass in our sweet womanly way. Take your antidepressants. Please?" Yvonne says please sweetly. She doesn't wait for a response. "That's my friendly and professional advice. You need to go see your doctor again, too. In case something besides being ninety and depressed is going on. All right, I'm done harassing you. For this morning. Now, as the wife of your best friend, I'm going to tell you what Bo surely would if she hadn't had the bad manners to die on us. First, I'm walking to the den. Lemme sit down." She groans with the effort. "You ready?"

"Does it matter?"

"Not one bit." She laughs. "This is what you get for rousing me out of a sound sleep. Dreaming about one of those good parties we used to have, too."

"I didn't want to call," Jackie says.

"Bo would tell you that white girls take the blues too damn hard."

Jackie nods. "Told me that many times. Tell Regina. I'm not worried about being blue. You and Regina are the ones worried about me being depressed."

Yvonne ignores Jackie's observation. "Bo would tell you to get off the couch and go do something that makes you happy. Wait a minute, what day is this? Saturday already? You can't come visit me today. I got a bunch of old lady doctors coming for lunch. And no food in the house. Eh, doesn't matter. We try to outdo each other with food. They'll bring plenty of food. Come tomorrow. Noontime. We'll have fancy leftovers. Reheated. Don't call first. Just come. Let me speak to Regina. I have an idea for you for today."

"The dump," Yvonne tells Regina. "Bo and Jackie's happy place."

"Yes," Regina says. "Good idea. Poetic. The dump to lift her out of the dumps."

"Yes, poetry, first thing I think of when I take out the trash,"

34

Yvonne says. "When you come for lunch tomorrow, remind me to tell the story about the first time Daddy met Bo. We'll make Jackie tell about the bus ride to Holyoke, scaring your poor father."

"And pissing off my mother," Regina says. "I'm going to make her tell that story over breakfast."

"You do that. We're getting so old. We've gotta tell these young lust stories while we're still kicking." Yvonne laughs and hangs up.

November 1955

Jackie wakes up slumped in the horsehair chair that belonged to her grandmother. She runs her tongue over her teeth. The remnants of Johnnie Walker make her groan. She tries to sort out last night: half a week's pay gone to seven-card stud, zipping Beulah's dress, collapsing on the chair as the big bottle-blonde let herself out, gone to tell her husband some elaborate lie, no doubt. Unless the ring on Beulah's left hand was the lie, or even her name, maybe? How did a high-strung woman with a Long Island accent come by the name of Beulah?

She rubs the back of her head. Whatever dream she was having is gone, but she's sure Regina was in it. Regina again. Jackie's done a halfway decent job of blocking the girl from daytime thoughts. She's less successful with dreams. A one-night stand weeks ago. Regina was so receptive to Jackie's every touch, every move, still asking Jackie to help her "keep things a little cool." They never did get completely naked. Regina keeping things at a slow burn all night. Because, "My sister's in the next room." Because, "Oh, Jackie, we've only just met."

Jackie smiles. Knows she's still at a slow burn. They weren't even under the covers, but had a good time sliding around on top of the blanket while Regina's sister slept it off sprawled on Jackie's couch under an afghan. Jackie was surprised then by how attracted she was to Regina. Is surprised now by how much

35

effort it takes to keep Regina off her mind three weeks later.

Jackie stretches her long legs, stands, and pulls the shade up. The slant of the sun tells her it's almost noon. Damn. She needs to do something different. Something that doesn't end up with her falling asleep in a chair and feeling like shit in the morning. She's okay while she's at work, mostly okay. It's been quiet enough at the bar, but waiting for the next raid is taking its toll. And after-hours has become a time to get through with the help of Johnnie Walker and a seat at a poker table. She had been ecstatic when she moved to the city and found so many like herself, the same elation she felt when she first enlisted. She fell out of love with the army in short order, too.

She should get out of the city before the city dishonorably discharges her. Leave her job at The Sea Colony? Yeah, she could make a living doing something besides bartending six nights a week. Never beat the money, twenty dollars in tips on a good night. Unbelievable that between rent, alcohol, and gambling, she hasn't saved a dime. Leave Manhattan? Leave her best friend Bo? Bo's been threatening to leave the city herself. Her friend and sometime lover, Lou Ellen, is already gone. The thought of moving makes Jackie feel even more tired. She's twenty-seven, pushing thirty: no wonder she feels old. Maybe she'd feel better in the morning if she cared more that Beulah's probably going home to her husband.

In the kitchen, Jackie bends over the sink and lets cold water wash over her short hair. She straightens up, swishes water around in her mouth, and spits. She dries her head on a kitchen towel that has *Jacqueline* hand-embroidered on both sides, a gift from her mother. She stares at a number stuck to the wall where Regina's sister, Lynn, left it. Lynn, still half-drunk that morning three weeks ago, had said, 'This is our number in Holyoke. Stay in touch. We owe you a big favor,' as she used a bent safety pin to impale the matchbook cover on the wallpaper next to the phone.

Jackie unpins the number that's been dangling there, leans against the sink, and rubs her thumb back and forth across the matchbook cover. "HAMpden 7-842." She says the number out loud before lifting the receiver off the cradle and sticking her finger in the first digit. The return of the spinning dial reminds her of roulette. Not her game—still, she smiles. Pick a number, take a chance. She likes a long shot because the payoff is such a kick when it hits.

She knew Regina was only visiting her sister for the week. She could have called the number Lynn stabbed the wall with sooner. Apologized to Regina. How was Jackie to know Regina was going to show up in her dreams, night after night? The girl lived in another state. At best Jackie thought she might look her up when she visited her own parents in Massachusetts. Lou Ellen showing up at Jackie's was a fluke. Jackie hadn't seen her in weeks. Still, Jackie should have anticipated Lou Ellen might come by. But how to explain to a nice girl who lives with her folks in a small town: why Lou Ellen had a key to Jackie's apartment, how sometimes girls take comfort from each other, how sometimes a girl just needs a safe place to stay. Explain that every place is not Holyoke, Massachusetts. Maybe she *could* explain it to a girl like Regina, who moved her hips in a slow steady wave, careful of Jackie's bruised arm, suddenly gripping Jackie's uninjured arm and moaning, all before her stockings were off. Then snuggling, admitting she'd had some trouble accepting that she likes girls.

Now, as then, Jackie is unsure if she should be impressed or put off by Regina's candor. Oh, but the girl could moan. Jackie shakes her head. Regina took getting walked in on by a third woman hard. Jesus, did she ever take it hard.

Jackie listens to the phone ringing on the other end, coils the phone cord around her finger, and waits for someone to pick up. As Jackie uncoils the cord, the pull toward Regina and the anxiety about seeing her increase in equal measure. Anxiety fuels resentment that Jackie didn't know she had. Angry, sure: Regina had cause to be angry, but she was so self-righteous that morning. Being mad at Jackie made sense, but snubbing Lou Ellen while Lou Ellen did her best to smooth things over? It was Jackie, not Lou Ellen, who maybe owed Regina an explanation. If Jackie and Regina ever did get together, the girl would drive Jackie nuts.

Jackie sticks her finger in the "0" and waits for the operator to connect her with the number.

"Yes, I accept the call," Lynn answers. "Regina's out. But come to Holyoke. Today," she says without hesitation, as if it's been days, not weeks since they've spoken, assuring Jackie an impromptu visit will be fine with their parents who are "good as gold."

Jackie hangs up, realizing Lynn said nothing about her visit being fine with Regina.

Two bus transfers later, Jackie is dropped off in Holyoke. She grew up on a farm a couple of towns over. She knows the neighborhood, if not the street, where Regina and her family live, which may be one reason she and the sisters hit it off so quickly when they visited Manhattan and wandered into the bar.

"Hello," a gray-haired man in his fifties answers when Jackie knocks. The house is a small ranch, a tract house built after the war on a small lot. On the ten-block walk from the bus stop, Jackie saw at least thirty houses built from the same blueprint, differing only in color, maybe a porch, a breezeway. This one has a paved driveway.

The unassuming working-class neighborhood gives Jackie courage. "Hello, Mr. LaFleche. I'm Jackie. Lynn and Regina's friend?" She stands awkwardly as he takes her in. She twists one of the tiny gold hoops that her mother bribed her to punch through her earlobes when she was sixteen in exchange for permission to get a driver's license. The earrings, an heirloom from her great grandmother, made Jackie a boyish girl with pierced ears years before ear-piercing came back in style. She feels sorry for Mr. LaFleche, who smiles at her, but is clearly confused. Jackie, with her close-cut hair and button-down collars, gets second looks in Manhattan, never mind Holyoke. She never meant to be someone who caused so much notice. If she wasn't nervous, she might be amused to have thrown another otherwise stable-looking man off balance. Mr. LaFleche's mouth opens as if he's about to say something, but he doesn't speak.

"From New York," Jackie offers. She has Regina's chiffon scarf in the pocket of her coat. She could have covered her hair with it, but Lynn said her parents probably wouldn't be home, and Jackie is slow to wrap a baby blue scarf around her head. "I'm a little early. Jackie. From New York City."

"Yes. Yes. Come in. Come in." Righting himself, Mr. LaFleche opens the door as wide as it will go. The tidy living room is barely large enough to hold a couch, two chairs, and a coffee table. He gestures to the couch. As if to make up for his lack a moment ago, he speaks rapidly with enthusiasm now. "Please, have a seat. Yes. She told us. Just a few minutes ago. That you were coming." He claps his hands together in a gesture of goodwill. "So, you took the bus? How was the trip? Are you hungry? What can I get you to drink?"

"Yes, sir. Slept most of the way. A glass of water, please." Jackie holds her hands behind her back. November is turning colder. As she walked from the bus stop, Jackie was glad she had put on her toggle coat.

"Lynn, your company is here," he calls up the stairs. "Can I get you something to drink? Oh yes, water. We have Coca-Cola. Cake, too. It's our anniversary. My wife's and mine."

"Happy anniversary." Jackie stands in the middle of the small living room. There are coats draped over one of two chairs. The several feet to the couch seem a long way to walk.

"Why thank you." A pretty woman enters the room. She gives Mr. LaFleche a smile that is clearly a question, maybe more than one question. "Why is the door open, dear?"

"This is Jackie." Mr. LaFleche closes the door. "Regina and Lynn's friend." He waits a beat between each statement. "From New York City." He gestures to his smiling wife. "This is Mrs. LaFleche. Eugenie. My wife."

"Hello, Mrs. LaFleche." Jackie bows from the waist, realizing

39

too late this might not be a gesture that will put either Mrs. or Mr. LaFleche at ease.

"Nice to meet you, Jackie. Do sit down." Mrs. LaFleche gestures and pulls on her long gloves. "Take her coat, Armand." She is dressed to the nines in a clingy narrow sheath. She looks like Lynn, but is small-boned like Regina. She has Regina's poise and smile. Jackie wonders if she has Regina's temper.

Before Jackie reaches the couch, Lynn bounds down the stairs. She gives Jackie a quick hug, her hair damp against Jackie's cheek. "This is the lady who saved my backside in Brooklyn; well, Manhattan really. Sorry, I was in the shower. Sit." Jackie sits on the couch and Lynn sits next to her. "Go." Lynn waves her parents away. "You'll be late. They're seeing *East of Eden*. They made it into a movie. Have you seen it?" She fluffs her hair, which is now auburn.

"I haven't." Jackie wonders how much of that night Lynn has told her parents.

"Bet she read the book," Lynn informs her parents. "She had a million books in her apartment."

Mr. and Mrs. LaFleche stand near the front door exchanging a look.

"You girls have a good time. The number of the Victory is on the fridge." Mrs. LaFleche slips her arms into the mohair coat her husband holds open. She holds the sides together with one hand. She has a clutch purse in the other hand. Jackie has seen this type of coat in the city. She's surprised to see a winter coat without buttons in sensible western Massachusetts.

Mr. LaFleche grabs his hat off the back of the chair and kisses Lynn on the cheek. In heels, Mrs. LaFleche is taller than her husband. "Do eat that cake," she says. "And there's popcorn and *The Perry Como Show*."

Jackie smiles her thanks. She wonders if she'll still be here by the time Mr. and Mrs. LaFleche get out of the movies. She was born and raised in this area. This is the first time she's had to consider whether cabs drive out here. She could call her parents. They would happily come and get her, but they're farmers who go to bed at nine and she has no idea how this night is going to go. She's not even sure if Regina is home.

"Why'd you take so long to call?" As soon as the door closes behind her parents Lynn points to the ceiling and the sound of the shower. "She doesn't know you're here." She speaks in a loud whisper. "I'll lure her down. She may kill you. She's definitely gonna kill me. She's been such a drag. If I had known you two had gotten, you know, close, I would have marched her back to your place the next day."

Lynn considers her last assertion. "Or maybe not, I don't know. I was so hungover that morning. I had just found out Regina was," she grimaces, "like you. But she didn't tell me you two had a thing that night until I moved back home last week. Another story." Lynn waves her hand, changing the subject. "My poor parents, stuck with two spinsters. At the time, I thought Regina was stomping around your place because she was mad at me. But she was mad at you for not telling her you had a girlfriend. So, who was that girl in your apartment that morning anyway?" Lynn lifts an eyebrow.

"Not my girlfriend," Jackie says.

"Good. If you want to make my sister happy you might start by telling her that." Lynn holds out a hand, asking for a name, "Ellen?"

"Lou Ellen," Jackie says.

"Lou Ellen is not your girlfriend anymore."

"Never was," Jackie says.

"Oh. Even better." Lynn looks at the ceiling. "She's hurt you haven't called. But now you have. And she's mad about Lou Ellen who is not your girlfriend. I'll remind her we would have landed in a paddy wagon without your help." She runs into the kitchen and comes back with a tall piece of cake and a glass of milk in a jelly jar. "German chocolate. Regina baked it."

She sits on the chair across from Jackie with her feet on the coffee table. "So." She holds up her hand. "None of my business, but if you care to tell me, why didn't you just say Lou Ellen wasn't your girlfriend? I had two roommates, and neither one of them was my girlfriend, not that way, not any way; they were awful."

Jackie sighs. "Didn't say she wasn't a lover."

"A lover?" Lynn sits up, enjoying the jolt of the word. "But not a girlfriend?"

"A friend." Jackie fidgets in her seat. "A good friend." She feels protective. Lou Ellen takes enough abuse. "Some mornings she needs a place to stay. She has, she had, a night job." Jackie can't believe she's telling Lynn this, but it feels good to try, at least, to tell the plain truth.

Lynn leans forward on her chair. "So, she's a friend with a night job who sometimes stays at your place and sometimes you have . . . " Lynn bites her bottom lip. "Relations?"

"You're right, none of your business." Jackie arches her neck against the back of the couch and closes her eyes.

"Sure," Lynn says. "I'm not exactly squeaky clean myself. Here's some advice that is also none of my business. Tell Regina the part about how Lou Ellen works the night shift, maybe an all-night drug store." Lynn snaps her fingers. "The Automat. Regina loved the Automat and it's open all night. Lou Ellen sometimes needs a place to stay and she's never been your girlfriend. Drop the rest of it." Lynn is talking at a clip that leaves her breathless. "Regina's awfully prissy, real straightlaced for a girl who . . . likes girls, but she's also a big mush, a romantic really. Thinks she's a poet. She'll want to believe you, but she's scared to death of you. Well not, you know, *you*." Lynn laughs. "Here's the thing: my sister would like nothing more than to settle down with a husband she could boss around, but she just doesn't like boys. Or kids for that matter. She doesn't care about Lou Ellen. I mean not if you quit her. She just needs an excuse to run away from you." Lynn sits back. "Uh oh, you look scared."

"We spent a few hours together." Jackie is scared. Lynn seems to have their lives all wrapped up with maybe a cat and a lawn to cut on the weekend. Jackie doesn't know any girls who have pulled off living happily ever after. She's not sure how that would look or if she'd want it if she could have it. She's been in and out of love too many times to believe in forever. Love Regina? She barely knows her. Simone and Gretta live together in Queens, have for years, but they both date guys. Maybe the guys are homosexuals, too; Jackie often wonders. What a crazy thing she's done, coming here. "I'd like to speak to Regina."

"Of course." Lynn pops out of her chair, still talking as she moves toward the stairs. "I'm not saying you should go steady after, let's face it, one night." Lynn grins broadly at the fact of Regina having had a one-night stand, with a girl yet. "I'm just saying, don't give her an excuse to stay mad about something that really is none of her business. It's not like you were cheating on anybody. But," Lynn puts her hand up, "none of my business."

Lynn disappears up the stairs. Jackie rubs her face, wondering if The Sea Colony found another bartender for tonight and how long it will take Bo and the guys to realize she won't be playing poker after hours. She doesn't know how hungry she is until she takes a bite of cake. The sound of the shower stops. After the soft padding of feet and the closing of a door, not a sound comes from upstairs. Jackie looks at the front door, thinking it's still not too late to take off.

The cake is chocolate, three layers with pecan and coconut frosting on top and between each layer, fussy and delicious. Just the kind of cake Regina would make. Jackie cannot understand why she thinks she knows what kind of cake this girl would make. Maybe she would have forgotten her by now if Regina had yelled that morning. But after Lou Ellen opened the bedroom door and walked in on them, Regina had sat up in bed, straightened her clothes, and become a wall of furious dignity. Lou Ellen had smiled, saying, "You dog, Jackie," and left the bedroom almost as soon as she'd barged in, closing the door softly behind her. It happened so fast, Lou Ellen walking in and out, Regina's fury.

Lynn had snored on while Lou Ellen made coffee and breakfast, which Regina had refused. Regina had refused even to answer Lou Ellen when she turned from the stove to say, "Good morning." Lou Ellen had handed Lynn a bag

43

of still-warm biscuits, and Regina gave Jackie a look of pure disdain.

That moment when Lynn was putting on her coat and slipping into her shoes, that's when Jackie could have tried to massage Regina's wounded dignity. And the next moment when Regina had had no choice but to stand there fuming as she waited for Lynn to pee and splash water on her face, Jackie could have spoken then. But she hadn't liked Regina in that moment, hadn't liked her haughty arms crossed against her chest. Jackie liked least of all the tight self-righteous set of Regina's lips then, how the expression made Jackie feel like she had to justify the way she lived. Yet here Jackie is, eating cake on the girl's couch, hoping she can come up with some words to smooth things out.

Jackie takes another bite of cake. Where did Regina learn to moan like that? Besides the fact that Regina makes great bed music, what does Jackie know about her? She takes another bite. She knows Regina bakes a good cake. She knows Regina can handle drunks and crooked cops. Jackie shakes her head. She's got it bad. And that ain't good. That night—by then it was morning—Jackie had put Frank Sinatra's latest, *A Swingin' Affair!*, on the hi-fi in her bedroom. Regina had whispered, "I love this," when Sinatra sang "I Got it Bad." Said she loved Billie Holiday's version even more.

Jackie downs the milk, wishing it were beer. She might be able to see herself clear to mow a lawn for a girl who loves Billie Holiday and who hums the words to her music low in her throat while she's making love. Sexy, how straitlaced she seems at first glance, how she holds herself apart until she doesn't. Smart, too. She did handle herself like a pro with those cops. She and Lou Ellen, smart and willful, probably would have gotten along like gangbusters if Regina wasn't on her high horse. A strong-willed pretty hick, Regina reminds Jackie of Jackie's mother. A door opens on the second floor. Jackie looks toward the stairs. She snaps to attention at the sound of Regina's voice, which she hears clearly.

"Why are you bringing this up anyway?" Regina says. "Are you trying to upset me?"

"Because she's here," Lynn answers.

"Here?"

"On the couch."

"You're full of it." Regina laughs and stops laughing abruptly. "Lynn?"

"Put your robe on. We're being rude."

"I don't believe this," Regina says in a tone that acknowledges she does. "Who do you think you are, making this decision?"

"You weren't home when she called. If I'd told you, you might have said no."

The sisters are standing in the hallway outside the closed door to their bedroom, Regina wearing a lacy nightgown. Always keep the door closed; this is Lynn's rule for keeping their mother from complaining about the mess on her side of the room. Regina opens the door, sits on her paisley bedspread, and presses the matching pillow to her chest. Lynn's bed is unmade, the sheets greasy from a bowl of popcorn turned on its side.

"Get a move on." Lynn steps inside the room, grabs Regina's robe off the hook, and throws it at her. "You know you want to see her."

Downstairs, Jackie leans forward on the couch straining to hear the exchange above, but all she hears is the sisters' bedroom door closing.

Regina sits on her bed with the robe on her lap, barely registering Lynn's buzzing in her ears. She recalls Jackie's bedroom was neat but horribly decorated, really not decorated at all, barracks spare, but washed by a lovely stream of yellow light that came through the window as dawn broke, washed beautiful, she thought at the time, by the rightness of Jackie's hands on her. She remembers feeling strong, finally, in her longing, strong enough to be a girl who let another girl, this one, this

45

Jackie, kiss her long and deep, without having to shroud her mind, staying alert and alive the whole time, and still being able to listen to know if Lynn was all right in the next room. In those moments with Jackie she had been a girl who might have lived a happy enough life knowing the rightness of another girl breathing heavy on top of her.

Then Lou Ellen walked in, and Regina dived for the army blanket tangled at the foot of the bed. In that moment, every place Jackie had touched felt dirty. Her half-nakedness felt horrible in front of Lou Ellen. Everything after Lou Ellen walked in was wrong: Jackie trying to stroke her hair and saying "okay" as if Regina's agitation was the problem; the percolator sitting on a trivet dead center of the table; Lou Ellen pouring coffee like this was just another morning in the big city. It all felt ugly. "Eggs and biscuits?" Lou Ellen had asked, like coming here to find Jackie in another girl's arms was as common as bread for breakfast.

"Enough dillydallying." Lynn wraps the robe around Regina's shoulders. "Don't look so shell-shocked. You know you want to see her."

Regina whips to attention. "You had no right." She has a brush in her hand. If Jackie thinks Regina is just another girl to bed when she feels like it, Regina would rather not think of Jackie at all. She throws the brush against the far wall of the bedroom.

Jackie hears a thump, then a louder noise like something hitting the wall. Lynn comes tearing down the stairs and plunks herself on the couch with her arms crossed and her face set in a determined grin. Regina comes next, slower, but not slowly. Even in the pink nightgown and robe, as she descends the stairs, Regina looks like she's ready to take out the third battalion.

"Three weeks." Regina lowers herself into a chair across from the couch as if it's a throne. "Why are you here now?"

"I told you, I invited her." Lynn slides over until she's right next to Jackie. "Fix your robe. God's gifts are showing."

"Tough shit." Regina yanks the two sides together.

Lynn opens her mouth in mock horror. "Queen Regina said, *shit*."

"I should have phoned sooner." Jackie would bet three days' tips Regina is aware of how good she looks in that getup. She can't help being impressed by a girl who dresses like that in her own house when she's not expecting company. She wipes her hand across her face, knowing that even a nervous smile would not be well received.

Regina frowns. "The two of you, making fun of me, Lynn right to my face, Jackie clearly amused and doing a bad job of hiding it." She rises a little in the chair. "How dare you invite her here without consulting with me first."

"Consulting?" Lynn arches an eyebrow. "Your Highness is the only one who thinks I need permission." Lynn pats her hair. "Do you like it, Jackie?" Her reddish-brown hair is short and pulled away from her face in crimped waves like a movie star from the thirties. She turns to show off the back. "Short in the back, but no duck's ass for me. Oops, no offense. A DA looks good on some girls."

"Very becoming," Jackie says.

A horn honks. Regina walks to the door and peeks out the slit of window near the top.

"That's for me," Lynn says. Jackie stands to help her pull on her coat.

"You're leaving your invited guest?" Regina says.

"Soften up." Lynn steps close and takes both her sister's hands. "Or toughen up. I'm not sure which." She shakes her head. "Maybe it's not right, girls together. I don't know. Who does it hurt? You've always been brave. Maybe Jackie's not the one for you." She gives Jackie a smile and a shrug by way of apology. "But don't be alone. Don't do that to yourself, Ginny."

Regina only glances at Jackie, who has grabbed her coat and stands quietly with her eyes lowered. Regina wonders if what Lynn says is true. Is she brave? Lynn has no idea how hard it is to be a girl who likes girls. You can't even hold hands at the movies.

The car horn honks a second time. Lynn opens the door and waves. Someone laughs and yells, "Shake a leg, Lynn."

Jackie steps back from the door not because of the cold, but so the girls in the car won't see her.

"Gimme a minute," Lynn yells back and shuts the door.

"Don't worry. They're not coming in. We're going out, because you," Lynn says pointedly to Regina, "convinced me I shouldn't stay home, cowering. You," she pauses for dramatic effect, "marched me over to Auntie Gerri's so the old biddy could 'Tsk, tsk, tsk,'" she wags her head to demonstrate, "about my 'circumstances.' You convinced me that the family could just get over the fact that I'm a fool who married a wife-beater and pulled a gun on him. At least you won't make the newspaper. Wasn't it you who said, 'No one can make you feel inferior without your permission'?"

"No, it was not me, it was Eleanor Roosevelt. I repeated it. What does that have to do with this situation?"

Lynn opens the door, holding a finger up to let her friends know she's almost ready. "I thought it was so clever of you, and all this time it was Eleanor Roosevelt?" Lynn adds in a stage whisper, "She came all this way. Swallow your pride and flaunt that superior view of yourself you got from Mom."

"Swallow my pride *and* flaunt my superior view? Honestly, Lynn."

"You know what I mean." Lynn buttons her coat. "Talk to her."

"Surely, standing in an open doorway in this peignoir set counts as swallowing my pride."

The girls in the car are laughing, blowing cigarette smoke out of the open car windows. One of them yells something about Regina being "*Oh là là.*"

"Oh, grow up." Regina shuts the door with her slippered foot.

The sisters stare at each other silently. Jackie doesn't know if this is a good or bad sign but breaks the silence. "For the record," she says, "I invited myself. You have your reasons to be upset. Getting walked in on that morning. I'm sorry. You deserved an explanation. The way they treat us, like we're criminals, it's not right." She shakes her head. "But that doesn't give me call to treat you badly. We should go out of our way to be nice to each other." Jackie knows she's no good with words. "Try to," she scratches her head, "be understanding."

The sisters stare at Jackie as if her words came out of nowhere. As if she had not been standing two feet away, privy to every word of their conversation.

Lynn cocks her head at Regina. "I have to admit, if another girl walked in on me, I'd probably go crazy. But sometimes things aren't anyone's fault." She looks thoughtfully at Jackie. "You look rough and tumble, but you're awfully nice." Her thoughtful look dissolves. "Well, have a good time, kiddos." She kisses Regina, then Jackie on the cheek, opens the door for the last time, and runs to the car calling to her friends. Regina closes the door behind her.

Jackie puts on her coat, sliding her hands into the pockets. "The cake was delicious. Thank you. I'll be staying with my folks for a few days." She puts a hand on the doorknob. "Lynn has the number if you should change your mind and want to see me." It's only 7:30. She should have asked to use the phone to call her father for a ride before she made this little speech.

"Please stay," Regina says flatly, feeling anything but flat. "I'll get dressed so we can talk."

Jackie sits on the couch for the fifteen minutes it takes Regina to get dressed. She wishes Regina would hurry so whatever is going to happen will. More talk? Jackie has already said more than enough for one night. Her attraction to this girl is so strong that, if Regina wants her, she's got her, for now anyways or for as long as the temporary insanity of it lasts. It always feels this way at the beginning, the driving too fast in a convertible down a mountain thrill. Crashing, that's the hard part.

Upstairs Regina tries to tame her feelings and her hair. She prefers them both neat. She fusses, wishing she could take a hair iron to her feelings. Regina couldn't help but be moved and confused by the way Jackie had exposed herself, and Regina, too, with her talk about "the way they treat us." That "us" muddies Regina's thoughts, makes her feel ashamed of her own shame. Why dis Jackie have to lump Regina in with the messy "we"? Regina had quit The Ladies Auxiliary because the president kept going on about how "we" represent the church. Regina represents herself, and she didn't need a lecture on decorum by some battle-axe in an ugly dress. And damn Lynn, bringing up Eleanor Roosevelt, as if Regina giving in to her attraction deserves a merit badge.

Jackie's "doesn't give me call" are old-fashioned words Regina's father would use. Oh, everything gets so tangled up. Why is this girl able to make Regina feel things just by lowering her eyes that Darla couldn't make her feel when she pressed her whole body against Regina's? When Regina asked her to stay, Jackie stuffed her hands in her coat pockets, looked Regina in the eye, and nodded. Now why in the world, Regina wonders, should she be so moved by that?

Regina gives up on her frizzy hair and pushes it out of her face with one of Lynn's plastic headbands. "God." She moans her regret over her indiscretions with Darla. *Indiscretions.* She laughs bitterly over the ladylike word she uses to describe what she and Darla did. Once in this very bathroom. She covers her face with her hands. What kind of person is she?

In the mirror, the red plastic headband clashes with her lipstick and looks ridiculous with her yellow dress. She blots her lips and takes a deep breath.

Jackie smiles when Regina walks down the stairs, high heels followed by shapely calves in silk stockings, crinoline under billowing skirt, cinched waist, darted breasts, hair pulled away from her face the way it was that morning just before things went bad. She stops smiling when Regina's eyes meet hers, unsure of what Regina's look means. She smiles again when Regina sits next to her on the couch.

"By *us?*" Regina smooths her skirt. "By *we* you meant homosexuals, girls who are?"

Jackie allows herself a cautious smile, trying to remember her own words.

"Right before Lynn left, you said something about the way they treat us. You said *us.*"

"That's right," Jackie says. "Maybe not you and me together, but sure, girls like us, guys like us."

"And by 'they' you mean?"

"Almost everyone. Sometimes you'll find a Lynn, a freethinker who treats you right."

"Lynn? A freethinker?" Regina turns sideways to face Jackie. "I suppose so." Regina tucks her feet under her on the couch so both knees almost touch the side of Jackie's leg. She puts her hands flat on the couch cushion, trying to balance. "We barely know each other."

Regina's brain races faster than her heart. She was so close to convincing herself that she could stop thinking of Jackie, maybe stop being one of those girls. And yet the words Jackie just spoke—"Maybe not you and me together"—have her nearly panicked.

She takes a deep breath. "I haven't slept through the night since we met. I'm not even sure what I'm ashamed of. Well, of course I know," she says as if Jackie had challenged her statement.

Jackie's brow creases.

"I'm ashamed of the wanting. You. Still." Regina is adamant. "I've been so angry. Not just at you. It meant something to me, that it didn't mean to you."

Jackie gives her an uncertain smile. "I've been thinking of you, too."

"I didn't ask for this. I didn't mean to be like this," Regina says in a hoarse whisper. "Did you?"

Jackie shakes her head, relieved that the scold has drained out of Regina's voice.

"I was okay, glad even, until that girl. When she walked in, I didn't know you had someone. Else." Regina takes a deep breath. "The days are all right. I go to work, see my girlfriends. But the nights. I'm awake, ashamed, and frightened."

"Her name is Lou Ellen," Jackie says. "She is someone special. But not my girlfriend. Not my special girlfriend." Loneliness and fear, Jackie understands perfectly. She's no stranger to shame or anger either. "I dream of you."

Regina nods stiffly when Jackie says, "Lou Ellen," frowns when she says, "Not my special girlfriend," and smiles when she says, "I dream of you."

Then Regina talks for a long time, saying things Jackie has heard before: "Don't want to hurt my parents . . . I thought as I got older . . . the girls at work . . . my parents wonder why I haven't been to confession . . ." Why does Jackie always fall for talkers?

Clearly Regina wants Jackie to explain what's what. Jackie is not so much tuning Regina out as listening with one ear while she tries to translate what the girl is saying. Regina wants to be assured that it's all going to be all right. Well, it's probably not going to be all right. Things are what they are. The two facts Jackie's sure are true about being a dyke are that some girls like to have sex with other girls, and lots of people, most people, find that disgusting. Regina wants to know how to make it easier. Jackie's damned if she has an answer.

Regina's voice lifts to a heartbreaking note. "It's all so impossible."

They stare at each other so tragically that Jackie grins. She thinks how lucky she was to get this bullshit over when she was very young. How lucky *and* cursed to be a tall, thin, muscular girl that most people think of as a freak of nature at first glance.

Regina starts talking even faster in urgent, unfinished sentences.

Jackie holds Regina's hand. She can see the immediate future in Regina's brown eyes: Regina crying on her shoulder, Jackie kissing Regina's neck, putting an arm around her waist, pulling her in. The sex: frenzied, unstoppable, glorious for weeks or months, draining and sad over time. Jackie moving back in with her parents, slinking around, working at the paper mill, helping on the farm, her father taking her aside to make sure she's all right, her mother putting a defiant arm through Jackie's whenever they're in public. Jackie and Regina meeting in nearby towns pretending to be sisters, trying to keep it from Regina's folks. Regina hating the lying. Jackie hating it too, not so much for moral reasons. People force you to lie, then call you dishonest when you do. Lying makes Jackie tired. And lonely. One of the reasons she hates talking to most people is that it's hard to have a conversation without lying. She massages Regina's hand and wonders if the look on her face matches Regina's, a mix of lust and suffering. She remembers Lynn saying her sister writes poetry. She hopes Regina's poetry isn't awful.

Regina mentions something about confession again. There's a crucifix on the stair wall with the bleeding heart of Jesus. Catholic. LaFleche—even the name screams sex and salvation.

"It's all right," Jackie hears herself cooing. What she means is it's inevitable. Worth the heartbreak to come. Jackie must believe that because she knows what's to come but doesn't want to stop. Knows sooner or later, Regina will be more drawn to being normal, to keeping her good name than to keeping Jackie. Yes, it's all right. Jackie left Granby to get away from pretty, prissy girls, soft one minute, hard the next, pushing and pulling her like taffy, but here Jackie is, hoping this girl will somehow be able to live with the fact, at least for a while, of who they both are, without punishing herself, without punishing Jackie, without Jackie throwing up her hands and finding comfort somewhere else before Regina is ready to call it quits.

Regina cries on Jackie's shoulder, asking why God made them this way if He didn't want them to be this way. Jackie doesn't answer, a little drunk on too much talk, the smell of

Regina's perfume, and the fact that she's only had a piece of cake to eat all day.

Regina pulls away and repeats another question she's obviously already asked, "Do your parents know?" She stands abruptly. "Have you heard a word I've said in the last five minutes?" She puts her hands on her hips. Tears run down her cheeks.

Jackie stands, too. "My parents have known since I was twelve." This crying and blaming is the part Jackie hates. "Talking. I'm no good at it." She pauses for a long moment, searching for words, making her point with silence.

Regina swipes at her cheek with the back of her hand. Jackie reaches in her back pocket and hands Regina a neatly folded handkerchief. Regina looks at Jackie like there's something on the other side of her eyes that she's straining to see.

"Go easy," Jackie says gently. "Give yourself a break."

"You make me feel"—Regina takes one of Jackie's hands, kisses the palm, and looks up into her eyes—"so much."

Jackie should call her parents, go home, give the girl a few days to think, give her a chance to back out before they really get involved. But Regina is clinging to her with parted lips and whispers into Jackie's ear, "Do you believe we can have happy lives? Girls like us?" She pulls her head back and smiles. Jackie is moved by the smile. It's the determined smile of a girl who has made up her mind. Regina runs her fingers along the nape of Jackie's neck, making the short hairs stand at attention.

Jackie puts her hands on the sides of Regina's waist, pulls her close, and feels the press of Regina's hips against hers. "Yes," she says, not lying exactly, not knowing anyone whose life is all that happy. At this moment, she feels as happy as she ever does, but she has this one thing to say before she can feel right. "You left my apartment without saying a word to Lou Ellen. She's a nice girl." Lou Ellen would laugh if she knew Jackie was defending her on the grounds that she's a nice girl. It's not Lou Ellen that Jackie is defending. Lou Ellen has gone back to Kentucky. Jackie will never see her again. Jackie is defending her right to see things her own way. She wants Regina to know she'll only bend so far. "She didn't do anything to you."

Regina is taken aback, unsure if she wants to apologize or protest. Jackie still holds her close and seems content to have made the statement without asking for a response. Regina puts her head on Jackie's shoulder. "I'm sorry if I hurt Lou Ellen's feelings," she says and waits.

Jackie puts an end to the uneasy moment by putting her lips on the soft skin of Regina's neck. They both remember that first kiss in Jackie's bedroom, the slow slide of Regina's sweater, one arm of the sweater and then the other moving off Regina's arms as they kissed, neither one of them conscious of helping it along until eventually the sweater, blouse and skirt became a tangle on the floor. The awkwardness of trying to untangle their feet had made them smile. They took a break from kissing to laugh and kick the clothes aside. The clunk of Jackie's belt buckle hitting the hardwood had startled the laughter out of them and made Regina put a finger to Jackie's lips to shush her so she could listen to see if they had wakened Lynn. Jackie's boxers, socks, and the thick elastic that bound her chest then, and binds it now, had remained in place all night. Regina's slip had stayed on even after her bra came off. A sleepless night, two tired, excited girls making love around a rayon slip, which got hitched up or down as necessary.

Now, when their lips finally part they wonder if they can hold back, even to laugh, this time. "Shouldn't you be pushing me down on the couch?" Regina teases, but is serious about wanting Jackie on top of her. Her dress buttons in the front. Jackie unbuttons the first button, takes Regina's face between her hands, and kisses her again. Regina fumbles with a second and third button, grabs Jackie's hand and places the palm flat against her cleavage. She is shocked by her own boldness but has kept her longing at bay for weeks.

Jackie turns her hand over and runs the back of it across the soft mounds of flesh. With a fingertip, she traces Regina's warm skin down the curve of one breast. "Shouldn't you be taking me upstairs?"

Even before they enter the bedroom Jackie can smell the mingling of the sisters' perfumes. She's more aroused than uneasy about having sex in the room Regina shares with Lynn. Truth be told, having sex with Regina here, with the possibility of her parents or sister coming home at any moment, does nothing to lessen her desire. It's what she knows: the danger of getting caught, the charge of it. Still, she doesn't really want to get caught. She's sure Regina doesn't want to get caught.

Regina closes the door. She walks to a small chair standing in a corner, and with skill that makes Jackie think she has done this before crams the back of the chair under the doorknob.

"Welcome," Regina points to the bed with her eyes, unbuttoning her dress to the waist.

Jackie watches Regina loosen the belt that up to this moment was invisible because it's made of the same material as the rest of the dress. The dress falls, followed by the petticoat, making a puddle of fabric on the floor. She pushes it aside with the toe of her high heel. Jackie bides her time with a serious smile on her lips and a growing but patient need that makes every breath press harder against the binder she removes only when sleeping alone.

Regina puts one foot on the wooden slat that frames the bed and reaches to unhook the garters. The angle is awkward. Her heel gets caught under the slat. Jackie steadies her so she doesn't fall.

"Thanks." Regina hangs on to Jackie's arm and slips out of her shoes. "This worked better in my fantasies." Regina laughs, embarrassed.

"Working fine from where I'm sitting." Jackie allows the rawness she feels to be heard. She really likes this girl. "Please," she invites Regina to continue.

Regina steps back. She bends, unsnapping the garters and peeling the stockings off slowly, looking up at Jackie through mascaraed lashes. Jackie's eyes move from Regina's eyes to Regina's legs to her thin waist and small still-covered breasts. The unpracticed and slightly clumsy way Regina moves as she undresses excites Jackie. "You are my fantasy," Jackie says.

56

Regina tugs off her garter belt, determined to be more graceful as she steps out of her pink panties. She has a moment of feeling utterly ridiculous, and exposed, and just plain dirty when the panties hit the floor. But she is unwavering in her desire to finish what she started, and Jackie is leaning back on the bed, smiling and sloe-eyed, openly appreciating. Regina's whole body responds to the excruciating attention. The urgency is almost painful. She could almost climax with just the thought of Jackie's touch. She turns her back to Jackie and reaches around to unclasp her bra, turning back to face Jackie with the bra dangling in one hand. She shivers. Jackie stands. They kiss and sit on the bed still kissing.

"You're cold." Jackie pulls back the quilt.

"Not yet." Regina unbuttons Jackie's white shirt. Jackie takes the shirt off. "The T-shirt, too," Regina says. Jackie stands to take off her wingtips, her black socks, her pants, and boxers, before pulling the sleeveless shirt over her head. She stands a second longer than necessary to take in the flush of Regina's skin on her slight, sturdy body. "And this." Regina puts a finger on the eight-inch band of elastic double wrapped around Jackie's breasts. Jackie shakes her head. Regina puts her arms around Jackie and runs her lips over Jackie's, initially pulling back when Jackie tries to kiss her fully, before giving in to a deep kiss, Jackie understanding too late that Regina is groping for the fasteners that hold the strip of elastic together in back. Regina expects snaps or hooks but finds two metal clips with teeth that bite into the material holding the sides together. She tugs at the first clasp. It comes right off. She holds it in her palm as she pulls at the second. The teeth of this clip bite her finger as it lets go. Regina says, "Ouch." They both pull away. Jackie tries to catch the length of material before her breasts are exposed, but the binder slips between them and falls to the floor.

"Son of a bitch," Jackie hisses.

Regina picks up the strip of elastic. She does not understand what is happening. Until she looks up to see the look on Jackie's face. Then, Regina is mortified to understand that she has humiliated Jackie. Regina looks away and hands the strip to Jackie. "I didn't know."

Jackie holds the binder. It dangles from her hand. She says nothing.

Regina closes her eyes and waits until she can't stand to wait. "I've ruined everything," she says, her eyes still closed. "I didn't want to be naked alone." She's still holding the clasps. She puts them on the night table without looking up. "I didn't mean to embarrass you."

"Be quiet," Jackie says gently.

Jackie takes an excruciatingly long minute to collect her dignity, fold the elastic, and place it neatly on the table on top of the clasps. Regina remains quiet.

"You're shivering," Jackie pulls Regina to her. "Damn, you're a handful."

"Now I know," Regina says, finally looking Jackie in the eye.

And then they are in each other's arms falling on the bed, kissing, their skin touching the full length of their bodies.

Jackie's breasts are small, but bigger than Regina thought they would be. She's dying to know if Jackie has ever held them against another girl, excited to think this is the first time, maybe the only time. She knows enough, now, not to ask, not to reach for the lovely weight and soft flesh of them so different from the rest of Jackie's muscular body. "I'm bossy," Regina says between kisses. "Everyone says so. But I'm not mean. I'm. Nice. I try to be . . ."

"Shush, sweetheart," Jackie says.

Jackie has eaten two ham sandwiches, and Regina and Jackie are sitting on the couch in the living room holding hands when the lights of the LaFleche's car turn into the driveway and shine through the front window. The doorknob turns. Jackie lets go of Regina's hand.

"How was *East of Eden*?" Regina asks as her father helps her mother out of her coat.

"Tragic, of course, the lies, the war." Mrs. LaFleche hangs the coat in the closet. "The young couple separated."

"Very good movie," Mr. LaFleche says. "You girls should see it." He holds his hat in his hands and offers to drive Jackie home.

She accepts his offer and stands to go.

Regina remains on the couch, takes Jackie's hand and nods for her to sit back down. "Can we all sit a minute, Dad?"

Mr. LaFleche watches his daughter's hand reach for Jackie's. His expression is confused.

Jackie thinks he may be wondering where his daughter picked up this strange old-world custom.

"For you, Princess"—he can't take his eyes off their entwined hands—"sure."

Jackie wants to help him out, remind him about *Little Women* or one of those other girlish books he probably refused to read in high school, a story where sisters walk through a garden arm in arm.

Another car light flashes in the window.

"Ah, here's Lynn." Mr. LaFleche smiles, his attention drawn away.

Lynn rushes in. "Look." She holds up a radio.

"A transistor. Does it get good reception?" Mr. LaFleche asks. "What'd you pay for it?"

"Just borrowing it," Lynn says. "If you fiddle with it, it comes in pretty good."

"Regina?" Mrs. LaFleche, about to take a seat on the armchair, stares at her younger daughter's hand wrapped around Jackie's.

Jackie, waiting to pull her hand away discreetly, pulls it away now.

Lynn turns her head toward Regina and Jackie so only they can see the bug-eyed look she gives them. She turns back to her father, says, "It was coming in great outside," and hands him the radio. He plays with the dial but gets only static.

"For heaven's sake, girls can hold hands in their own living rooms." Regina sits up straighter.

"Little girls, perhaps," Mrs. LaFleche says. "You're not a child anymore, Regina."

"No, I'm not." Regina closes her eyes and sits very still for a good thirty seconds.

"Oh, god," Lynn groans, "she used to do this when we were little."

Regina opens her eyes. "Lynn's right. I don't mean to be childish. Jackie, forgive me, I should do this when you're not here. But I'm afraid my courage will leave me. I want you all to know. I'm a certain kind of girl." She inhales slowly. "Who likes other girls."

Mr. LaFleche stops trying to find a station. "Oh?" he says.

"What?" Mrs. LaFleche finally sits in the chair. "What do you mean, Regina?" She turns to Lynn but says, "What does she mean, Armand?"

"She means she's a lesbian." Lynn puts a hand to her mouth and sits on the arm of her mother's chair. "That means a girl who's a homosexual. Homophile. I asked around. Jesus, you should have eased them into it. And you thought I had balls, Mom."

"Lynn!" Mrs. LaFleche glares at her before she throws up her hands at Regina. "Is that what you mean?" Mother and daughter have a twenty-second staring contest. Then Mrs. LaFleche shakes her head in disbelief. "We knew you were different, but this?"

Regina stands. "This has nothing to do with Jackie. I mean..." she blushes. "It's separate from Jackie." She shakes her head. "It would have happened without Jackie. She helped me to be brave. Not Jackie exactly, but how I feel. Lynn helped, too."

"Stop talking." Lynn shoots Jackie a look. "You didn't know she was going to drop this bomb, did you?"

Jackie shakes her head. She glances up, knowing Regina's bed covers are a bump in the middle of her mattress. Did they close the bedroom door?

Mr. LaFleche turns the hat in his hand. "I don't know who

is more in shock, your mother or me."

"Me." Mrs. LaFleche says. "I am more in shock." The bewildered look on her face turns to anger. "For god's sake, stop standing there like someone's going to put a gold medal around your neck. Come with me, Regina." She stands and walks to the landing. Regina does not follow. "Never mind then. We'll talk right here in the living room. Armand, give Lynn your keys. Lynn, drive her home." She scowls at Lynn. "Inviting that girl here. I'll deal with you later." She faces Jackie. "Young lady or whatever you are, you won't be seeing our daughter again."

"Maybe not here." Regina folds her arms over her chest.

Jackie is more frightened than she was on the night she got pulled out of The Sea Colony and thrown in jail. Despite her best effort to keep a poker face, the sides of her mouth curl up a bit.

Chapter 3

Jackie and Regina step carefully down their front steps. Then, arm in arm, they teeter-totter through the inch of unshoveled snow on their sidewalk, heading for their car on the curb, and eventually the dump. They stop halfway down the walk to discuss the dead Christmas tree in their front yard. They've missed the city's curbside pickup by over a month.

"We should have asked the kids to help us get rid of that tree when they were still home for Christmas break," Regina says.

"The kids are adults living their own lives like they're supposed to." Jackie stops to wince and give the tree a dirty look. Over a year has passed since her surgery, and her right hip still hurts.

Even without stopping to disparage the dead tree on their front lawn it would take Regina and Jackie a few minutes to maneuver their way down the walk.

When they reach the car, Regina flaps her hand, "We should at least try to get TJ to drag the thing to the curb." Of the four neighborhood kids Jackie and Regina are close to, only

TJ still lives on the street. But even TJ is rarely around. Sobriety, weight lifting, and assistant sales associate at Costco are TJ's steady jobs now.

"You're mad that I played the lottery," Jackie says. She promised years ago to forgo gambling, excepting the occasional lottery ticket. "That's why you're harping about the tree."

"You lost five dollars and you told me about it. That was the deal. You're mad at yourself about the lottery. Depressed."

"Would you really make me go back to Gamblers Anonymous if I bought another ticket next week?"

"You know I would. One lottery ticket a month. Part of the deal. Anyone who knows anything about gambling problems would say that's foolish enough."

Jackie grunts, knowing Regina is right.

They stand on opposite sides of the car, hanging on to the door handles, thinking their separate thoughts, catching their breath. Even holding a car door handle in the cold morning air seems like an escape from their routine.

Regina wonders if they could shove the tree in the trunk. Probably not without getting dead pine needles all over the puffy down parkas she got almost new at The Survival Center, because the fashion of encasing yourself in four bushels of airy feathers went out of style when the new synthetic fibers came along. Regina tries not to care about being out of fashion but can't seem to stop. She thinks about being poor. She's been thinking about being poor as the third rail in their relationship, causing as many sparks as any of Jackie's women ever did.

What were they thinking—living beyond their means and working shitty jobs without putting a single penny toward retirement? They were thinking IRAs and 401(k)s were middle-class scams. A simple CD was too bourgeois for them. And where would they have gotten the money to contribute? The unlikely fact of old age, why be bothered? Any shot they had at a comfortable old age was lost as they job-hopped, never finding a job that paid them a living wage, hired, and promoted a girl without humiliating her. Taking night courses in Poly Sci and

Comp Lit made Jackie a well-informed forklift operator and Regina a failed poet. No one in either family had ever dreamed of a college degree, never mind sending a girl. And Regina had blown her scholarship to nursing school.

Jackie is thinking about poverty too, how it's a fishwife who gets louder when ignored and meaner in old age. If it weren't for poverty shrieking, "Where's the milk money?" she could skim off a few bucks for a lottery ticket without feeling like shit. For them, a few missing dollars means no pork chops that week. Ironic, because buying a ticket at the grocery store is the only way Jackie gambles now. This was her first "slip up" in months. At least poker exercised her mind, kept up her math skills at calculating odds. She opens the door on the driver's side.

When they're both inside, Regina says, "How are we ever going to get that tree to the dump?"

"Lousy home and car repair person, disabled trash hauler, that's me," Jackie says.

"Honey, it wasn't a comment about you. Grilled cheese, frozen pizza, prewashed salad in a bag with a can of tuna dumped on top." Regina refers to the fact that she has become a lazy cook. "We have our good points. They just haven't shown up yet today."

"I never promised to give up the lottery completely." Jackie would sound angry to someone who doesn't know her. Regina recognizes her tone as regret.

"No, you didn't. You promised one ticket no more than once a month." Regina pats her hand. "So let it go. At least you're talking. I don't think you said ten words yesterday."

The dead pine needles and snow stuck to their boots make the inside of the car smell clean. Jackie folds her hand around the screwdriver handle she jury-rigged in place of the shift knob that fell off. She sucks in a lung full of air and sits quietly for a second, feeling to be sure the makeshift handle is securely in place.

Regina says, "We could ask Papi."

"To help with the tree?" Jackie frowns. "We're not people

64

who bother the neighbors to dispose of our dead holidays. Not yet."

"I suppose we should save our favors for falls and heart attacks. But it's the dead Christmas trees that drive you crazy," Regina says.

They sit in the pleasantly cold air of the car, resting their eyes, content to be out of the house and not irritated with each other, although someone listening to their conversation might think they were irritated.

Before she got old, Regina supposed her thinking would slow down as she aged. Sometimes Regina's mind spins like a tire stuck in a muddy field. Now her thoughts move like a young dog circling back on its tail. She looks at Jackie through the little cloud-breaths of February air that form in the front seat of their once gold, now faded to tan, 1992 Buick. How did they get so old? The calendar, the mirror, their joints scream, "Old!" Regina looks at Jackie all day, every day, and elderly is still a shock. Ninety is too old to fathom. She nods to herself. Elderly, that's an achievement of sorts.

"This car is older than the kids," Regina says. "TJ wouldn't mind helping us."

"He helps us plenty."

"When he comes over to pull out the cans on trash day, he always asks what else we need." Regina watches Jackie's breath. She likes being able to see it.

"We're not bothering TJ with the tree," Jackie says.

"Remember what cute little kids they were?"

"Cute little shits. Especially TJ." Jackie moves to put the key in the ignition.

Regina puts her hand on Jackie's. "Let's just sit here a minute."

"The windows are gonna fog up."

"I want to look at the neighborhood, watch you breathe," Regina says, "and think of that time TJ got us kicked out of the pool."

"Heard that story so often I feel like I was there." Jackie

presses her head against the seat. "I wonder how those kids tell that story?"

July 2005

Regina and Lotti are poolside, at the Olympic-size municipal pool, perched on the end of matching plastic lounge chairs. Lotti makes an awning over her eyes with her hand of perfectly lacquered nails so she can watch her eight-year-old grandson Ramon and his friends splash around in the shallow end. She glances at Regina.

"A man cheats on me and I find out"—Lotti slaps her hands across each other like she's just disposed of trash—"it's the last time he cheats on me. You made it perfectly clear from the get-go you wouldn't put up with any nonsense?"

She's returning to a conversation that was cut short last night and had to wait until the kids were in the pool to be revived this morning. "Jackie, of all people, a cheater?" Lotti shakes her head. "*You* got cheated on. Incredible."

"Decades ago." Regina slips off her flip-flops. They have arrived early to get the good seats in the shade near the two-foot end. "Perfectly clear? Nothing was perfectly clear those first few years. Proper young ladies were not homosexuals in those days. Darla, my first, cheated on me with a man she eventually married. But then, I never loved her." Regina sighs. "I was propped up by lust when I first fell for Jackie, brave enough when it came to telling my parents, but the rest of the world?" She adjusts the chair farther back. "I don't know why I was so shocked by people's reactions. I was still me, but no one believed a sweet young thing and a lesbian could possibly coexist in the same person."

"A sweet young thing? You?"

"Well, maybe not." Regina roots around in a tote bag. "Who can remember?" They both laugh. "I kept hoping I'd come to my senses and straighten out. By the time I met Jackie I was twenty-six and my entire experience of sex was with Crazy Darla."

"Wasn't there a thing with your mother's cousin?" Lotti

holds up a hand. "Okay, sorry. I've got bullshit in my past too, as you know."

"I swear I was buck naked under the covers with Darla and didn't think of what we were doing as sex." Regina groans. "Not at fifteen."

"First I heard of fifteen. Where was Lynn? Off with the first fool she married?" Lotti takes her eyes off the kids in the pool to pull her head back and peer at Regina. "You sure you're not from the Island? You know I have a cousin in Puerto Rico who was married at fifteen."

Regina grins and puts on sunglasses. "The longer I was with Darla, the worse I felt after being with her. Jackie was a revelation. Someone worth taking on the world to be with. But . . ." Regina pulls back her hair, which she stopped coloring a year ago and which is finally gray down to her shoulders with only a bit of auburn at the very end. And frizzier than ever.

"But?" Lotti says. "She cheated. You kicked her to the curb and took her back?"

"More complicated. The world was harsher than I'd imagined those first few years, I kept wishing I wasn't what I was. She felt that, of course. It wasn't only Jackie who wasn't all in. Most of the girls we knew in those days were pretty loosely coupled."

Lotti slaps Regina's thigh. "A damn shame you took five years to tell me. When was this? Late fifties?"

"Late fifties. Early sixties."

"Christ, how many times did she cheat?" Lotti laughs at Regina's frown. "You are old, girl. I wasn't born until 1945. 'Loosely coupled' sounds like something you'd sue a mechanic over." Lotti shades her eyes with both hands this time. She sees Pock, the nervy neighborhood girl with the strawberry mark on her forehead who came to the pool with them. Pock is talking to a little girl wearing goggles. The boys are roughhousing a few feet away. "Hey," Lotti yells to the boys. "No dunking."

For some reason, when Lotti annoys Regina the irritation doesn't stick. She and Jackie have lots of friends from the days

67

when lesbians, lucky enough to find each other and if they lived within an hour's drive, became friends whether they had anything else in common or not. Some of them became good friends, too. But few became friends that Regina finds as easy to get along with as Lotti. Yvonne, maybe. Regina has the opinion, which she realizes is shameful and probably internalized homophobia, that lesbians are more annoying than most people. With the notable exception of her sister Lynn. Lynn is more annoying than the average lesbian.

"How come you look so young?" Regina says. She thinks it's partly Lotti's long, thick hair dyed a deep maroon color that she twists in a complicated braid for the pool.

"I'm ten years younger than you and I'm pleasingly plump. Fat faces don't show wrinkles." Lotti scrutinizes Regina who is sitting up slathering sunscreen on her thighs. "You look good. Look at those legs."

Regina squints. She considers the fact that Jackie's face is fatter than hers and less wrinkled. Yvonne and Bo, too. But then Regina is thinner and more wrinkled than all her friends.

Lotti stands and tugs at the legs of her Slenderizer swimsuit. She's sixty-five, but in that suit she looks like an in-shape fifty-year-old.

Regina likes the fact that Lotti is ten years younger. It takes a certain amount of energy and discipline to keep up with her.

"TJ, that's far enough," Lotti yells. "I told you only up to your chest until you pass the tadpole test." She turns to Regina. "God, I hate those baggy trunks the boys wear. They spend half the time pulling them up so their junk doesn't fall out."

Forty feet away, eight-year-old TJ splashes Pock. "Why's your gramma gotta yell about me not passing the tadpole test so the whole pool hears?" he asks Ramon as if it's Ramon's fault.

"Ramon," Lotti yells. "Stick close to Pockie."

Ramon nods yes to his grandmother. "Why's Abuela yelling at all?" Ramon says to TJ. "And why I gotta stick close to Pock?

68

She's your cousin."

Pock holds on to the edge of the pool near the boys. She stands up straight, hands on her hips. "I am not TJ's cousin. TJ's Uncle Luiz is Mommy's boyfriend. Mommy's husband is my daddy. His name is Tommy."

"Little Miss Know It All is right." TJ shakes his head vigorously. "No cousin of mine. She ain't even Puerto Rican."

"You're not even half Puerto Rican." Pock sticks her tongue out at TJ. She splashes them both and turns away to avoid their retaliation head-on. The boys pummel her with water. Pock puts her head in her arms on the edge of the pool and waits for the boys to lose interest in splashing so she can ask the little girl with the goggles if she can borrow them. Pock won't be eight until August, but she's smarter than either of the boys. She knows that if your mother is half Puerto Rican and your father is Italian like TJ's you're only part anything. She knows her mother is half Irish and half German, and Tommy is half Kentucky and half Georgia so Pock knows she's only part anything, too.

The boys stop splashing. Pock turns around, smiles at the little girl with the goggles, and, while she's at it, waves at Regina and Lotti. She wants to keep being invited to the pool.

Regina smiles and waves back. She hands a tube of lotion to Lotti. "Put this on my back? I'll keep an eye on the kids." Regina is still surprised to find herself around so many kids so late in life. It's taken her a long time to understand Jackie's longing to have children.

"Push forward." Lotti sits behind Regina in the lounge chair. "I wonder how Jackie and Oscar are doing?" Oscar is Ramon's brother, Lotti's other grandson. She feels her earlobes to make sure she hasn't lost a hoop. "I wish that boy wasn't so afraid of water. Thank God Papi took Ramon to the Y to learn to swim when he was a baby." Lotti spreads the warm lotion on Regina's back.

Papi is Lotti's son and Ramon and Oscar's father. Regina

finds it strange that Lotti calls her own son Papi. But then, everyone, including Regina, calls Lotti's son Papi. Lotti lifts the straps of Regina's suit to smooth the cream on her shoulders. Regina only half listens to Lotti's chatter about what a good father Papi is to Ramon and Oscar, how Papi's mother-in-law didn't like the idea of her daughter marrying a Hispanic guy at first, but now the mother-in-law thinks Papi is the best thing since white bread. Regina is barely listening close enough to laugh when Lotti says "white bread" instead of sliced bread. She's heard the story twenty times and understands that it's the kind of story that needs to be retold so the teller can continue to make peace with it. Regina wants to concentrate on the feeling of Lotti's hand spreading lotion on her back.

In the water, Pock is trying to get the little girl to hand over the goggles. Pock's hair is pulled back into a bathing cap so the strawberry mark on her forehead is on full display.

"What are you staring at?" TJ challenges the wide-eyed little girl with goggles who still has the Buddha belly of a five-year-old.

Pock likes TJ standing up for her, but wants the goggles more than TJ's loyalty. "Fair trade," she bends toward the girl so the girl can get a better view of the angry red mark that extends beyond Pock's hairline inside the cap and under her hair. "You can touch it if you let me use the goggles."

The girl shakes her head, steps backward, and hands over the goggles. She stares at Pock. TJ knocks the goggles out of Pock's hands, pushes her in the water and says, "Freak show." They are only chest deep and Pock rights herself without really falling.

The girl plucks her goggles out of the water and hurries out of the pool.

"You guys scared her," Ramon says. "She's just a little kid."

"If you push me, I'll tell." TJ wags his head and mimics Ramon. Ramon pushes him.

"I didn't scare her," Pock says. "TJ scared her."

"Done." Lotti rubs what suntan lotion is left on her hands onto her own shoulders.

Regina's eyes pop open. She hasn't been watching the kids. It takes her a second to adjust to the water's glare. When she focuses, she can only locate Pock who is out of the pool. Her heart pounds, but before she has a chance to panic Ramon and TJ come springing out of the water and hold on to the side of the pool. A teenaged girl in a bathing suit with *Lifeguard* written across the front stands within twenty feet of them. Regina reminds herself that this is 2005, and children don't drown in public pools these days. She shakes off an unwanted memory and sits up.

"You sure you're not a lesbian? You apply suntan lotion like you're gay," Regina says.

"If I was, I'd be gay for you." Lotti grins. "If you were a little younger. You think butch women cheat more?" She tosses the tube of lotion in Regina's bag.

"I think cheaters cheat more."

"That's no kind of answer." Lotti lies back in the lounge chair. "People seem to think men, straight men, cheat more than women. Straight women."

Regina cocks her head. "Do I think butches cheat more than femmes? Old-school labels. Me and Jackie, pretty clear, but people don't identify as butch or femme so much anymore."

"Play the game," Lotti says. "This isn't going to be published in *Psychology Today*. I've met your friends, manly girls or girlie girls, mostly."

"Mostly," Regina nods her agreement. "Not all. Old ladies, old school. There's still a problem with your question. For argument's sake, let's say every human being thinks of themselves as either male or female and is attracted to their *opposite*." Regina fingers air quotes around opposites. "Who are all these males cheating with? Females, right? So, unless some females are super-cheaters, and fucking lots of different males, the males and females must be cheating in equal numbers. Am I right?"

Lotti frowns, unconvinced by Regina's logic. "I hope the woman my ex cheated with cheated on him with ten different people," she says. "The whole time I was crying on your shoulder about Leo messing around, you never mentioned Jackie."

"It was so long ago. We were isolated in the early days. Jackie had a dogged will to hang on to her independence. She still hates other people telling her who she should be."

"But you're so, no offense, bossy. I just can't see you putting up with that shit. You two are so committed to each other now."

"Demanding Jackie's fidelity, out loud, I thought I might lose her." She glances at the pool and sees the lifeguard with the ponytail talking to the boys, but she walks away, so Regina continues. "There were no rules for us. After I sobered up from the first wave of sex, I got confused about what was possible. I wanted Jackie to come to the conclusion she wanted only me all on her own. I wanted that romantic ideal."

"I've always wanted that too." Lotti nods, mulling this over. "Can only gays say *queer?* Like the older boys use the 'n' word, which I still say should be out of bounds, period. In my day *queer* was a nasty word. Well," Lotti answers her own question, "if you don't say it with the wrong 'tude, if you don't spit it out." She wags a finger at the tolerant look on Regina's face. "You two aren't the only lesbians in the world. My niece lives with a bull of a girl. They have a sign on their bathroom door that says 'Queers.' By the way, I know for a fact my niece keeps that woman on a short leash for good reason."

"Making the mortgage and car payment is what I worry about these days."

"You see Pock?" Lotti frowns.

"I'm right here." Pock's chin rests on the back of the lounge chair.

"How long have you been there?"

"I wasn't spying. I walked right by you. You just didn't see me. It's called hiding in plain view. My cousin taught me. You just be

72

quiet and wait until the grown-ups aren't paying attention."

"Sorry, honey, of course you weren't spying." Regina smiles.

Lotti scooches sideways so Pock can squeeze in beside her on the lounge chair behind Regina. "I don't say the 'n' word," Pock says. "Bad words are for punks and fags."

"But you know *punk* and *fag* are not nice words either," Regina says.

"My mom's boyfriend Luiz says punk all the time," Pock says.

"I say it sometimes myself," Lotti says. "But Regina is right. It's not a nice word."

"Like retard?" Pock says.

"That's right, honey." Lotti puts her arm around Pock. "We call Oscar 'delayed' or better still, just plain Oscar."

Lotti changes the subject to the penny-ante poker game at her house last week. "How much did Jackie lose to my gangsta brother?"

"Let's talk about this later." Regina tickles Pock's foot, which is lying next to her. "Why are there three of us on this chair?"

"Because my boys are lousy cuddlers." Lotti hugs Pock and Pock giggles. "Can playing for pennies really be called gambling?" Lotti asked.

"Can a seventy-year-old man who plays the horses once a week really be called a gangster?"

"No," Lotti agrees. "That was sarcasm. How much did she lose?" she repeats.

"Ten bucks maybe. Not the point. She promised not to gamble." Regina twists to give her friend a look.

"Ten bucks. Let the woman live a little." Lotti laughs. "I might cheat on a tight-ass like you myself," she mouths the words over Pock's head.

"I'm happy with my spouse. Maybe you should stop bringing up other people's history in front of the children."

"True. Sorry." Lotti touches Regina's hand. "Really." She starts talking about how nice it was of Jackie to stay home with

Oscar. How Jackie could teach TJ to swim and Papi could teach Oscar.

Pock snuggles in and stays quiet. She knows the ladies are talking about Jackie because she's not here. More than what the ladies are talking about, Pock loves that they're talking in front of her. She wonders if Ramon really isn't a good cuddler and what gambling is. The best thing is being cradled in Lotti's arm with Regina's hand on her foot. The only thing to make it more perfect would be if the ladies were talking about Tommy. Her father has been in jail ever since Pock can remember. Pock visits him sometimes. She's not sure what goes on in the big brick buildings after the families leave the visitors' room. Until Pock heard her mother's boyfriend talking about a fight in the prison cafeteria, she thought Tommy only ate stuff from vending machines. Pock likes to think of Tommy in the cafeteria. Not the fighting part, the pizza and hamburgers and tuna noodle casseroles part. The thought of Tommy in the cafeteria makes her think he has friends to eat with. Pock has a cat and a mother and TJ and Ramon and Ramon's brother Oscar, who likes to play with her.

Three sweaty bodies on a plastic chair are too many for Regina. She stands and stares at the water. She thinks of herself as the kind of old woman who refuses to be shamed by her aging body. Still, she's intimidated by the thought of all the eyes that will be on her if she takes the plunge and struggles with the doggie paddle. Eh, she thinks, no one is going to pay attention to an old lady for long. Besides, she's thin. People love thin.

Lotti and Pock slide into the pool after Regina. Almost immediately a whistle blows, shrill and loud. For a second the only noise is the sound of the filter's pump. The lifeguard perched on her high white chair points at four boys, including TJ and Ramon. "You four, out of the pool," she yells.

Ramon gestures to himself. TJ grins.

The other two boys, older, jump out of the pool laughing. TJ has just intercepted a Frisbee tossed between them and hidden it in the back waist of his baggies. The Frisbee digs into the hump of his butt and makes him stand unnaturally straight.

Regina, Lotti, and Pock huddle and listen, across the pool from the boys. The lifeguard, ponytail bouncing, climbs down her chair and walks over to the boys. She stands with her hands on her hips. "Patrick and Joey," she says with disgust, "out for the day."

"Really?" Lotti breaks the silence of the poolside onlookers. "For a Frisbee?"

The lifeguard, managing to summon a lot of authority for a sixteen-year-old wearing a navy-blue Speedo, turns to TJ. "Frisbee," she extends her hand.

"I see no Frisbee," one of the older boys taunts.

The other boy holds up both hands, "What Frisbee?"

TJ holds up his empty hands, too, smiling like he's about to take a bow.

"Get kicked out with these idiots or hand it over." The lifeguard rolls her eyes. "Or can't you feel a piece of plastic the size of a dinner plate in the seat of your pants?"

TJ hands over the Frisbee with a grin.

The lifeguard points her chin at TJ and Ramon. "Twenty minutes on the bench."

The older boys walk to their towels. "Your sister's kind of a dick for a girl." The boy, Patrick, blows the lifeguard a kiss as they walk out through the door to the men's locker room.

"She just threw her own brother out of the pool?" Lotti wonders out loud.

"Toys flying around a pool are dangerous," Regina says. "Lifeguards need a clear view." She looks down at her painted toes through the shimmery water. The memory of a girl being pulled from dirty gray water all those years ago comes back to her— Regina's father and a few other men diving into the deep part of the pool and feeling around the bottom with their hands, a lady screaming, a lifeguard, who was a grown man, crying over the girl. What was the lady screaming? Regina tries to put the horrible incident out of her mind as she watches Ramon and TJ follow the lifeguard to a bench near her tall white chair at the deep end of the pool.

"Lookit." Pock points. The minor spectacle of the girl life-guard herding the boys to a bench and pointing her finger at them before she climbs up into her throne-like chair excites her. "She's gonna make them sit in time-out. She can do that."

"For a Frisbee?" Lotti repeats. "I'm the first one to admit our boys can be little shits." She shakes her head. "Well, plenty of times they didn't get benched when they should have."

Regina nods. *Rosie, my baby, save my Rosie,* that's what the lady at the pool had screamed.

"Want to float, Aunties?" Pock hangs on to the side of the pool letting her legs drape out behind her. Pock knows she isn't blood to them, but she doesn't have any real aunties and her real grandmother died. Lotti and Regina smile at her. Lots of kids in the neighborhood call women they aren't related to "Auntie."

They all hang on to the edge of the pool and float. Pock kicks her feet and hums.

Regina thinks about fighting for territory on the edge of a municipal pool when she was a girl. What year would that have been? All four sides of that big pool were hung with kids. "Like garland on a Christmas tree," her father had said. "That pool is so filthy and crowded no one can keep track of their children; that's why that little girl drowned," her father had said. Her grandfather had said, "That's what happens when you mix whites and coloreds." Was it 1939?

Pock sings the Dora the Explorer theme song in her high, thin voice.

Regina kicks her feet without splashing. She was once an excellent swimmer. She hoists herself out and sits on the edge of the pool. Her mother had yelled at her grandfather, "She was white, you old fool." Her grandfather had spit on Mama's clean floor. "Muddy the water," he said, "everybody drowns." That was brave of her mother, in those days, to yell at her own father. She remembers yelling at her mother when she made homophobic remarks. She's glad both she and her mother soft-ened before her mother died. Her mother had even specified in her will that the house Regina and Lynn had grown up in be sold, the profits split between her daughters, leaving enough money for a substantial down payment on a small ranch house next to Lotti's.

Pock sits next to Regina. Regina kisses the side of her head. "You're a good girl, Pock."

Pock could die happy right now. Right now, Pock doesn't mind that the boys only play with her because Lotti makes them. Sometimes girls get things that boys don't get.

The boys sit on the bench. TJ rocks sideways, purposely banging shoulders with Ramon, trying to get him to laugh. "I got a better arm than those punks," TJ says.

He's a natural athlete. Ramon, tall, smart, more or less well-behaved, has the sturdy build of an average eight-year-old boy. TJ is short and muscular with a quick mind and body, quick to move, quick to become agitated. TJ needs Ramon to mess around with him right now, to take his mind off worrying about his father. Sometimes all Ramon has to do is bump shoulders with TJ and say, "Calm down" and TJ calms down, *snap* like that!

TJ starts singing the wrong words to "Justify My Thug" and knocks knees with Ramon. Ramon could at least play around a little if they have to be in time-out together. But Ramon just sits there like a big baby.

"Cut it out," Ramon says. "I'm sick of you getting us in trouble. That's a stupid song."

"My father says Papi's turning you into a punk." TJ's never called Ramon a punk before even though it's his favorite insult. TJ's father loves Jay-Z. His father has been staying with TJ and his mom for the last few days. If TJ didn't have to sit still on this stupid bench, if he could move, he'd be okay. What if Lotti or Regina tells his father he got benched?

"You're a fag." Ramon thinks about saying TJ's father only comes around when his real wife and kids are giving him trouble.

77

Even when Ramon is mad with TJ, Ramon doesn't want to hurt him bad, just bad enough to make him shut up.

"You looked at that lifeguard's feet when she was talking." TJ kneels on the bench and gets right up in Ramon's face. "My father says punks don't look people in the eye."

"Your father broke your shoulder." Even the little kids in the neighborhood know it.

"Dislocated." TJ stands up. "My shoulder's fine. It was an accident." After it happened, he stayed with Jackie and Regina while his mother went to stay with his aunt to calm down.

"Papi says there's too many accidents when your father is around." Ramon stands too.

"Papi's a fag and a punk. Say it was an accident."

"Say Papi's not a punk." Ramon looks TJ in the eye. "Say he's not a fag."

TJ pretends he's going to sit but clips Ramon in the back of the knee. As Ramon stumbles on the wet concrete he grabs for TJ and they both lose their footing.

TJ says, "Shit." His strength as he grabs Ramon adds to the momentum of their fall.

"Why you have to be like this?" Ramon hisses in TJ's ear. "Get off me." They wrestle, banging against the bench, rolling closer to the pool. The whistle blows.

"Say it was an accident." TJ doesn't understand why he doesn't have Ramon pinned by now. If they were on the grass or in Ramon's room, TJ would be sitting on Ramon and both boys would be laughing or crying. Either way, it would be over. But they're at the pool and TJ is terrified of deep water and they are both on their sides panting.

Regina notices the empty bench where Ramon and TJ should be. "Where are the boys?"

'It's our responsibility,' Regina's father had said, 'to keep the children safe.' 'That little girl drowned on our watch,' her father had said.

The whistle blows again.

"Ramon." Regina hoists herself out of the pool. "TJ."

Lotti and Pock stare toward the sound of the whistle and pull themselves out, too. Everyone stops to look toward the sound of the whistle.

"Fighting. See 'em," Pock points, following Lotti and Regina as they rush to the boys who are still wrestling on the opposite side of the pool.

"Say it was an accident," TJ says loud enough in Ramon's ear to compete with the whistle that blows and blows.

"Okay, an accident," Ramon screams. He feels the raised edge of the pool press against his back. He hears the lifeguard yelling and Lotti calling his name, her voice getting closer. "Calm down, TJ. You gotta calm down."

TJ might have calmed down enough to at least roll in the right direction, but the lifeguard grabs at his shoulder, the one that still hurts sometimes. Seems to TJ like everyone is always pulling at him. He pushes hard into Ramon. They wrestle at the edge of the pool for a split second before they slide into the water entwined, and, because TJ is too panicked to let go of the bear hug he has on Ramon, they drop to the bottom. As they sink, TJ thinks maybe this is dying. He thinks, *I'm sorry, Ramon,* and hangs on tighter. The water stings TJ's wide-open eyes. TJ clings and sees Ramon staring back. He sees bubbles come out of Ramon's mouth.

"Calm down, TJ," Ramon's bubbles say.

"Good Ramon," TJ's bubbles say. "No insult. For real," TJ's bubbles say. He watches their bubbles mix and rise, feels the skin of his chest close against Ramon's chest, their legs and arms entwined, hips pressing, bodies sinking.

Lotti, Regina, and Pock reach the edge where the boys have fallen in and stand on the lip of the pool looking down.

To Pock, the boys look like the twin babies she saw suspended in a huge bottle at the traveling circus last year. Her mother said the babies were fake. Pock could see those baby boy twins up close and they were real dead babies, joined and clinging

79

chest to chest just like TJ and Ramon are now, only those boys had naked bottoms and Pock's mother said it was a spectacle and hurried Pock out of the tent. Everyone is out of the pool now except Ramon and TJ. Everyone is looking at Ramon and TJ. Pock thinks this might be a spectacle. She's glad Ramon and TJ are wearing bathing suits.

Regina sees what Pock sees and thinks at least this pool is clean and the lifeguard is right here. Poor children don't drown in municipal pools in 2005. Not today. Not in this pool. She turns to see the lifeguard grab a float off a hook on the fence surrounding the pool.

Lotti jumps in.

Regina grips Pock's shoulder. "Stay here," she says and jumps in after Lotti.

"Jesus Christ." The lifeguard throws the float in the water where the boys should surface, blows her whistle, and yells, "Get out of the pool, ladies."

TJ sees two quarters on the bottom of the pool and feels his toes hit the concrete as Ramon's bubbles tell him, "Push." He sees the sunlight breaking through the water. "Push," TJ's bubbles answer as the light splits the quarters into a hundred coins of light. Both boys push their feet against the solid turquois cement. TJ has no more bubbles to fill with words and he swallows *Good Ramon* as they both push for all they're worth straight up, back to the surface, only partially untangling when they hit the air.

Ramon pants, treading water frantically with one arm and leg, holding onto TJ with the other arm, trying to unhook his other leg from TJ's so he can kick. "Let go," Ramon shrieks.

TJ sputters and coughs, flailing in the water. He spits out, "The quarters, man, did you see the quarters?"

Lotti and Regina resurface in time to hear the lifeguard yell, "Get out of the pool, ladies." They see her throw the life buoy shaped like a small surfboard and jump in just as the boys break the water sputtering for air.

"You're gonna drown us!" Ramon grabs the float with

his free hand.

Pock picks a second float off a hook on the fence and throws it at TJ. TJ grabs the float without letting go of Ramon.

The lifeguard grabs the ropes on the floats, throws a loop over each shoulder and drags the boys to the aluminum stairs at the side of the pool.

A second lifeguard is on the scene, an older man in trunks and a polo top. He kneels at the edge of the pool glancing at Lotti and Regina as they pull themselves out. He tells the young lifeguard to let the boys hang on the floats and catch their breath before they try to climb up the ladder. He instructs the women and Pock to sit on the bench and not interfere. He stands to tell everyone else to stay out of the pool until further notice.

When the young lifeguard and the man in the polo shirt are satisfied that the boys can maneuver the ladder, the boys are taken to the Lifeguard Station. The man in the polo shirt decides they are physically fine. He informs Lotti and Regina that the boys can't return to the pool for a month, and it's a good idea for Lotti and Regina to stay home for a few weeks, too.

Before anyone gets in the car, Lotti talks to Regina. Then Pock and Regina get in the car while Lotti talks to Ramon and TJ by the big tree in the parking lot for a long time before the three of them get in the car.

Driving home no one says a word.

Lotti cuts the engine in Regina's driveway and nods at her. Regina turns all the way around and reaches into the backseat to touch TJ's shoulder. "Listen," Regina says. "We're not going to tell your father. He goes too far. Never a good enough excuse to put a hand on a child. But help us, okay? Can you try to behave so we can just leave your father out of it?"

TJ winces. His face becomes hard with the effort of not crying.

Ramon sits in the middle of the backseat between TJ and Pock.

Pock leans over Ramon to stare at TJ who looks like he doesn't know it's okay, doesn't know he's not going to get in trouble. Pock almost says she's sorry out loud, almost forgets that she has nothing to say sorry for. She feels sorry for TJ. She's not sure why. Probably TJ's a punk. Tommy would say TJ's a punk. Tommy only knows what her mother tells him about TJ. He doesn't know that sometimes, when nobody is listening, TJ talks nice to Pock. Tommy doesn't know TJ won't let anyone, besides himself, make fun of her strawberry mark. He doesn't know TJ says the other kids are jealous because Pock is smart. Pock holds Ramon's hand. Ramon looks at her when she takes his hand, but just for a second.

Then Ramon pushes his other hand near TJ's so the sides of their hands touch.

Regina and Lotti are both turned around looking right at TJ, waiting for him to say he's going to behave. "You can behave, can't you, TJ?" Regina asks again.

TJ feels the side of Ramon's hand and calms down just a little bit, enough to be able to look at the back of Lotti's seat without crying, maybe enough to answer Regina's question. TJ looks at Ramon to let Ramon know he better not say something punk and make TJ cry.

Ramon holds his hand steady next to TJ's.

TJ nods. He can behave. He wants to tell Ramon about the quarters so bad. But that might make him a punk.

"Well good. I bet Jackie would like you to stay with us for dinner and a sleepover tonight. I'll ask your mom if that's okay."

Oscar runs out the front door waving a Lego spaceship yelling, "Me and Jackie made it." He pokes his head in the car's open back window. "TJ sad?" Twelve-year-old Oscar speaks directly to TJ. He has Down syndrome. "You naughty, TJ?" Oscar often says what he means straight at the person he wants to hear it.

"Come on, Oscar." Jackie is behind him. "Let's carry in the cooler, give the kids a minute to gather their stuff."

Lotti steps out of the car. "Don't leave any wet towels in my backseat."

The women and Oscar stand on the sidewalk by the front steps.

"What happened?" Jackie glances back at the kids huddled in the backseat. "TJ?" She looks over her shoulder at a small ranch a few houses up the street. "His father's car is in the driveway."

"Get him settled. I'll tell you all about it. First, I have to get permission for him stay with us tonight."

Lotti sets her big beach bag down to kiss Oscar on top of the head. "How was my guy?"

"Oscar is always good. Aren't you, buddy?" Jackie says.

"No," Oscar says.

In the car Pock stretches around Ramon to talk to TJ. "They're not going to tell!"

Ramon slides his hand over TJ's. TJ looks out the window but hooks his baby finger in Ramon's.

"Come on, kids," Lotti yells. "Grab your stuff and get out here. I got work tonight."

"Okay, man," Ramon says, normal, like they've been goofing around all the way home. "You're gonna stay with Jackie and Regina tonight."

Not for the first time, Pock thinks about saving her money to have an operation to get rid of her strawberry mark so she can marry Ramon when she grows up. Sometimes she feels sorry for TJ, sometimes she likes him so much, sometimes she doesn't like him at all. But Ramon, Pock always loves.

Chapter 4

Saturday, February 18, 2017

Regina and Jackie disagree about whether they ever made it back to the pool that summer. They're settled into separate thoughts when Jackie startles and says, "Jesus," in response to TJ rapping on her window.

TJ squats next to the car, his face right up against the glass, his grin full force. He makes a *roll down the window* motion with his fist. "Why are you ladies sitting in the car with your eyes closed? Me and Ramon thought you got wasted and never made it into the house last night." He stands up to laugh at Ramon over the top of the hood. "Told you they were okay."

Regina rolls her window down to speak to Ramon. "We're off on Jackie's favorite adventure."

"The dump," TJ says. "Let's go with 'em. I'll drive."

"You forget about Pock?" Ramon says.

"Pock and Eugene." TJ jumps in the backseat behind Jackie. "Gotta uninvite myself on your adventure, ladies. I got the day off work. Me and Pock gotta meet Eugene. Ramon got him-self a Eugene." TJ grins at Jackie in the rearview mirror. "We're meeting him at Sip." TJ holds up a pinkie and pantomimes holding a cup. "Like sip tea."

"It's a coffee shop." Ramon, in the backseat now, too, gives TJ his newly acquired *I can't be bothered* smirk. "His name is Gene. And you don't *gotta* meet him."

"Oh, I *gotta* meet him. Let him see you got family. Pock says he's got blond hair."

Lotti's already told Regina that Ramon's young man is a blond.

"Pock's never seen him." Ramon sticks his head into the front seat. "You're still using that screwdriver? You see this, TJ? Why you letting the ladies drive around like this?"

"Me? What do I know about cars? You being a college boy didn't turn me into a grease monkey. No offense, Jackie, but an old lady with a bad hip driving an old car with a stick shift?" TJ shakes his head and crosses his bulky arms over his chest.

"Leave poor Jackie out of it," Regina says lightly. "This is like old times, you boys in the backseat, poking at each other. Be happy you're still friends after all you've been through."

"Oh, for heaven's sake," Regina responds to the look Jackie gives her. "These boys know what they've been through."

"It's true." TJ claps Ramon on the thigh. "You the man who went through all that with me. You always been the man, Ramon, always be the man."

"Just a college boy." Ramon looks out the window.

"Papi should look at the car," TJ says. "What else you need, ladies? Something the handsome young TJ and good citizen Ramon can do for you while he's home for the weekend?"

Ten minutes later Ramon and TJ have the tree strapped to the roof of The Bucket. TJ slaps the hood and says, "For real, you ladies have to take care of this car. Papi fixes it up—another ten years it'll be vintage. And in twenty years you leave it to me in your will."

Ramon says, "Leave me the screwdriver handle."

Jackie puts the key in the ignition. The boys stand clear of the car. The women sit forward, listening, exaggerating the curves of their spines. The car starts, and The Bucket slides into

85

first gear. Jackie and Regina exchange satisfied nods.

"Let's bounce." Regina waves, her hand out the window like a beauty queen.

The boys grin and laugh harder as the women drive off because Regina is acting out something they haven't said for years.

Regina's head bounces and it starts shaking before she and Jackie are off the street. Jackie slows down to five miles an hour and grabs Regina's chin to steady her bobble head. "Thanks. I'm fine," Regina says. "Good to see the boys."

Jackie lets go of Regina's chin and pulls at the stubble on her own face. This always gets Regina feeling kindly toward her wife, who calls the little plot of hair on her chin her soul patch.

"I miss them. Pock and Oscar, too." Jackie accelerates, still going slowly.

"Too bad they have to grow up." Regina sighs.

"Oscar in Horace's doghouse." Jackie laughs.

Regina smiles. "Lotti's going to put the poor dog down."

"What?" Jackie skids. There are no cars in the opposite lane and she's driving slowly, so no harm done. She pulls The Bucket into a neatly plowed driveway without turning off the engine. "Horace? When?"

"Black ice." Regina frowns. "Soon. Maybe driving today is a bad idea?" She puts a hand on Jackie's thigh. "Sorry, shouldn't have told you while you were behind the wheel. How long has it been since we've seen that dog? He can't walk anymore. Sleeps day and night."

Jackie starts backing out. "He gave up his house for those kids."

"Stop. Let's just sit in this driveway for a few minutes," Regina says. "You heard the boys say Pock's home, too. I'll bake cookies."

"That dog was old when the kids were teenagers," Jackie says. "I wonder if they know."

"Wait," Regina cocks her head. "Aren't they still teenagers? My god, we went to Oscar's twenty-first birthday, didn't we? The other three are right behind him, aren't they?"

May 2012

Fourteen-year-old Pock is practicing her stealth moves. She steps quietly into Lotti's backyard where fifteen-year-old Oscar is flat on his back in the doghouse. Not his whole body, just his head, shoulders, and the hand that's holding the joint, his right hand. Pock can only see Oscar's body from his mid-chest to his feet. She squints at the part of him she can see. Hands on her hips, she's determined to make an informed decision. Informed decisions and masturbation are Pock's newest obsessions. Just lately, since she got over the fact that Ramon may not marry her but discovered an excellent use for the second pillow on her bed, Pock has decided that the convent is not her only option. With a little help from Regina, Pock has concluded that becoming a judge might suit her as well as becoming Mrs. Ramon Soto.

"What are you doing?" Regina stands behind Jackie who is looking out the open window into the backyard they share with Lotti.

"Spying on Pock who's spying on Oscar. He's in the doghouse."

"Ahh. You want tea?" Regina clicks on the heat under the kettle. "What makes you think she's spying? It's her job to watch him after school." She doesn't ask why Jackie is spying on the kids because they've both been doing this since they retired, if you can call quitting a minimum wage, part-time job in your eighties retiring.

Spying on the kids is somewhat redundant since the kids spend so much time at Jackie and Regina's. But they were kids once and know that kids behave differently when no adults are around. The way the sun hits the kitchen window in the afternoon makes it easy to see out, but impossible to see in. These lovely spring afternoons are the best days for being nosy.

"She kind of snuck up on him. To catch him smoking

marijuana, I suspect. Do we have chamomile?" Jackie steps to the right to let Regina see what's going on outside their window.

Regina stares out, considering the doghouse and the first time she saw TJ sitting inside it where Oscar's head and chest are now. TJ, growing into a short, strapping teenager now, was a sniveling four-year-old then. She feels a renewed affection for Lotti, such a good neighbor, who banned Horace from his own house and turned the tiny building over to the kids. She had cleaned the doghouse inside and out when she saw how sitting inside it calmed TJ. TJ, a lovable little shit prone to little tantrums then, and who is a less lovable big shit prone to big tantrums now.

"Why isn't Pock making Oscar come out?" Regina asks. "Where would he get marijuana? Surely the boys don't give it to him, and Lotti hides hers. And why smoke it in the doghouse?" She holds up two boxes. "Ginger or Lipton?"

Jackie points at the ginger. "How would I know where he gets it? Could be he's just taking a nap. TJ uses the doghouse like a big bong. Economical. Oscar's probably seen him."

"Now you're teasing me." Regina would be surprised if Jackie knows something that goes on in Lotti's backyard that Regina doesn't know. Regina and Lotti have coffee every evening and Lotti is not one to keep anything to herself. "I've never seen TJ smoking pot in there."

Jackie shrugs. Jackie and Ramon are two of the few people TJ has real conversations with these days. Jackie knows what she knows.

They watch, leaning on the sink, sipping tea. Nothing much happens. Pock unfolds a chair, places it near Oscar's feet, sits on it. Except for Oscar's head in the doghouse, everything in the yard seems to be in order, balls and Frisbee in the plastic tub, lawn chairs folded, everything stacked on the slab of concrete under the awning. Horace is nowhere to be seen.

As they watch her sit, Regina talks about Pock. Regina knows quite a bit about Pock, a girl who thinks big. Regina tells Jackie a story that features Regina shepherding Pock through her nun phase. Jackie has heard the story, in fact lived through it, but sips her tea and listens. A while ago Pock heard the term *Mother Superior* and decided she'd become a sister and work her way up the ranks. Regina, aware that Pock was an unlikely candidate for a nunnery, bought Pock a book about Ms. Lou Ellen Lewis aka Judge Magistrate Lewis and informed her that most nuns take vows of obedience, poverty, and chastity. Pock became interested in the law. She joined debate club. Soon after, Pock found out that the birthmark on her forehead is not a pock at all but a port wine stain that can be removed with laser surgery. "She wants to get rid of the bangs because Judge Judy and that other TV judge, Judge What's Her Name, don't have bangs. Unprofessional," Regina says. "Pock should make people call her by her given name. I'm going to start calling her Patricia."

"Her name's Patricia?" This is the first thing in the story Jackie hasn't already heard.

Oscar beats out a rhythm with both feet on the bald patch of earth in front of the doghouse door. He taps a counterrhythm with a hand on his bent knee. Pock thinks this is a fancy maneuver for a guy who has trouble getting more soup in his mouth than on his shirt. She's pretty sure what he's doing now is creativity, not self-stimulation. Since being in charge of Oscar, Pock has become aware that there are all kinds of self-stimulation and, even if it's not the sexual kind, self-stimulation bothers some people. Lotti wants Pock to interrupt Oscar when he taps the table or kicks his heel on the floor too long, so she taught Pock interruption techniques. Most of Oscar's self-stimulation can go on for quite a while before it becomes too long for Pock who has boy cousins: tappers, leg-jigglers, heel-thumpers, every one of them. Sometimes Pock puts Band-Aids on Oscar's thumbs so he can't pick at the skin around his nails, not because the habit itself annoys her, but because Oscar does it until his thumbs bleed.

"Look," Jackie says after a few minutes of watching Pock watch Oscar tap his feet. A curl of smoke hangs above Oscar's feet. A breeze breaks up the little cloud and carries it off toward the high fence that hides the yard from the street.

"Smoke?" Regina strains to see a thin trail wafting out of the doghouse. Her eyesight has never been as good as Jackie's and she needs a new prescription. "We better go over there."

"Let's see what Pock does first," Jackie says.

Pock just sits. She doesn't particularly care about Oscar smoking pot. Her cousins all smoke pot. She thinks Oscar's grandmother, Lotti, whom Oscar calls *Abuela* smokes pot. Pock's not even supposed to be on Oscar duty yet. Her bus was ten minutes early. Usually Oscar's on his own for at least ten minutes after his squatty bus lets him off. She doesn't like the thought of him lighting a joint though. Oscar and matches seem like a bad combination.

She frowns. Lotti would consider it part of Pock's job to take the joint away from Oscar. The back of the lawn chair comes up off the ground as Pock bends and speaks softly into the few inches of doghouse door not obstructed by Oscar's belly. She touches his knee. "Stub out that joint. But not on the rug." The doghouse floor has a carpet of AstroTurf.

"Pockie!" Oscar is always glad when she arrives. He starts to drag himself out. Then, realizing he could be in trouble, he shimmies back in and hands out the joint. "Am I bad?"

"Let me think about it." Thinking is Pock's favorite thing. She takes the stubbed-out joint, still relatively long, which means he didn't smoke much. She considers keeping it, but her concern about her mother's boyfriend catching her with it over-takes her thrift. She digs a little hole with a stick and buries the marijuana.

"What's happening?" Regina says. She and Jackie lean on the sink, shoulder to shoulder. Scrutinizing other people's lives takes up more of their old age than either one of them thought it would.

"Not sure. Think she took the joint away from him and put it in her shoe." Jackie squints. A passing cloud obscures her view.

"Good girl."

"Okay for Pockie to have marijuana, but not Oscar?" Jackie asks to accommodate Regina's love of a good argument.

Regina flaps a hand. She enjoys their ongoing conversation about Oscar's safety versus his liberty but has no interest right now. She wants to watch what action there is to watch, not argue over which kids, barely teenagers, get to smoke marijuana without getting turned in.

"Dignity is about getting to make choices," Jackie deadpans and mimics Regina. "Choice involves risk."

"Really?" Regina swallows the last of her tea. "The guy's head is in a doghouse."

"So?" Jackie puts both of their cups in the sink. "Why should Oscar be different?"

"Because he is. He takes meds. He needs more watching than most," Regina says.

"We both take meds," Jackie answers, thinking, not for the first time, that their arguments are getting more predictable and interchangeable as they age.

"And you've always needed more watching than most," Regina counters. "I'm glad Pock took the joint away before Oscar got wasted, and so are you."

Jackie grabs a banana off the hook Regina hangs the bunch on, cuts it, and offers Regina half by way of agreement, vaguely remembering it was she herself who first made the argument about dignity and choice.

Pock is still busy thinking. She stretches her legs to bridge Oscar's. She's earned over three hundred dollars for being in charge of him. Lotti doesn't like to say *babysitting* because Oscar is not a baby. Oscar's grandmother calls this arrangement Pock "being in charge." Pock loves the sound of it. She is the *being* in charge. She loves having a job at fourteen, loves the wad of fives and the ten-dollar Christmas bonus in the tea tin. She loves Oscar because he loves her and because she doesn't have to make excuses not to hang around with her cousins or, worse, babysit the younger ones for free. And Ramon comes to check on his brother almost every day. Lotti works funny hours, but if she's working day shift, always gets home from work earlier than Ramon and Oscar's parents. But Pock still doesn't know why they don't give Ramon the five dollars to watch his own brother at their own house. She thinks it's because Ramon's best friend TJ is sometimes nice, but sometimes crazy, and the two boys are always together.

Pock arches her back and stretches her neck. She only smoked dope once. Some kids don't care if they can't make a sentence without falling on the ground laughing. Dope, a good name for it. She wishes there were girls her age in the neighborhood, although the girls at school are as dopey as the boys. Pock needs to concentrate. Pretend this is debate club. What is the central question regarding Oscar and marijuana?

"Where do these kids get the money to buy marijuana anyway?" Jackie wonders.

"They can't all be stealing marijuana from their grandmothers," Regina says. "If we don't go talk to those kids now, I'll have to let Lotti know Oscar may have found her stash when we have coffee tonight."

"Coffee," Jackie grumbles. She'll never understand how Regina and Lotti can drink two cups of coffee after supper and still sleep like babies while Jackie has to drink the damn herb tea after her first cup in the morning or be up half the night.

Oscar starts humming "Rack City." Between verses, in his happy voice, he asks, "Can I stay in here for eight more minutes?" Eight minutes is his favorite length of time.

"You totally forgot you might be in trouble, didn't you? Okay. Eight minutes." Pock checks her flip phone, which she wishes was an iPhone but not really because she'd have to pay for it herself.

Oscar starts on a Spanish song that Pock doesn't understand. She shakes her head. Oscar is totally bilingual, while she's studying like crazy and maybe still won't get an *A* in Spanish. Lotti's slow-moving dog Horace galumphs around from the side of the house and puts his head on Pock's knee. She stares into his big dog eyes until the solution to the Oscar and marijuana question comes to her. She will tell Lotti that Oscar may be smoking pot, occasionally, before Pock is in charge. She will stress *before*. She will say, "I may have smelled marijuana on him." Maybe Lotti doesn't care. She's one of those pretty grandmothers with a cute old man boyfriend. She should care about the matches, though. Pock kisses Horace's giant head before she pushes it off her knee. "Okay, eight minutes, time's up, Oscar."

Regina makes a plate of crackers with peanut butter and marshmallow. They eat, sip tea, and watch more of nothing much in the yard, without comment, until Oscar comes out of the doghouse.

"Pock looks pleased with herself," Jackie says.

"You can't possibly tell that from here." Regina wipes a crumb off the front of Jackie's shirt.

Pock stands on her tiptoes to check out Oscar's eyes. His eyes look normal.

Horace waddles over to the corner of the yard to do his business before he wanders over to the opposite corner to plop down and sleep in the sun. "Lotti picks it up with a plastic bag," Oscar giggles. Which is normal. Any boy in the neighborhood, except Ramon, might giggle about Horace doing his business, especially if the boy just came out of the doghouse.

Oscar keeps giggling, which he sometimes does, is not normal, and drives Pock crazy. She claps her hands at waist level, which is the cue Lotti taught her to get him to stop giggling without having to scold him.

He claps his hands back at her. She finds this confusing and funny because he's never done it before. He giggles harder. She doesn't want to go down the slippery slope into an afternoon of Oscar giggling, but can't help herself and giggles back. He claps again and she stops giggling. Oscar stops, too. Oscar is learning. Even after the joint, he figured out he could clap back. He learns something new every day. This makes her a little sad.

"Don't get too smart on me," she says. "And no matches."

"No matches," he repeats. "Snacks."

"Snacks," Pock agrees. Lotti has the best snacks, rice custard and cookie balls, day-old stuff she brings home from JimmyZ's Puerto Rican Bakery where she works.

Just as they decide to head inside, Ramon sticks his head out the back door. He's out of breath and his face is red. He looks at Pock. "Where's Lotti?" Before Pock can answer he turns to Oscar, "Abuela?"

"JimmyZ's. It's only 3:30," Pock says.

Jackie puts both hands on the edge of the sink and leans over it with her ear to the window screen. Sometimes, if the wind is right and the kids are speaking loud enough, she can catch what they're saying.

"That's just Ramon coming by to see Oscar," Regina says.

Jackie puts up a hand to shush Regina. They both say, "Shit" after Ramon says, "Fuck," loudly and disappears inside the house followed by Pock and Oscar. Any of the neighborhood boys might be heard yelling, or laughing, or singing "Fuck." Neither Jackie nor Regina would be surprised to hear Pock use the word if Pock thought an adult wasn't listening, but they both think of Ramon as a boy who swears only with good reason. Something is not right over there.

Inside Lotti's living room, the kids stand around TJ who is slouched on a chair and manages to look cocky even though his knuckles are bleeding and his right arm throbs. Ramon dabs at TJ's hand with a wet facecloth. TJ flinches and pulls his hand away. "What, you're my nurse now?"

Pock pulls out her flip phone.

"Who you think you're calling?" TJ snarls. "No ambulance, drama queen."

"Macho jerk. At least a doctor." Pock looks at Ramon for confirmation.

"We need a car," Ramon says. He and Pock look toward Jackie and Regina's house.

"No doctors." TJ pulls himself up a little straighter. "Get Jackie. Regina's a worse old lady than you, Ramon."

"Are you afraid of shots?" Oscar asks.

Pock puts her hands on Oscar's shoulders. "Can you do something for us? The cabinet under the bathroom sink. Get the box Lotti keeps the Band-Aids in. With big red letters on it."

"The first aid kit," Oscar says solemnly and runs out of the room.

"Maybe something's broken," Pock says to Ramon.

TJ closes his eyes. "I'm fine."

95

"Who beat him up?" Pock says. TJ opens his eyes. Pock watches the boys bounce glances back and forth. "Oh," she says, "my mother told me his father's back. You walked here?" Pock says. "He can walk okay, right?"

"Why do you keep asking Ramon questions about me? I'm sitting right here. I walk fine. You and your mother want to talk about fathers? Talk about your father in Walpole."

There's a knock at the front door. TJ snaps to attention.

"Think that's him?" Pock stares at the door. "Go out the back, TJ."

TJ turns around in the chair to stare at the front door, too. "What do you care?"

"Why you have to be hundred percent asshole? She's trying to help." Ramon moves toward the door. "I'll get rid of him."

"Let me," Pock says. "He'll know TJ's here if you get it."

Ramon frowns, but takes a step back.

"Don't answer," TJ says.

Pock ignores him and walks to the door, "My father's never been in Walpole. He's in Shirley, minimum security," she says as she looks through the widow beside the door to see if she can tell if it's TJ's father on the step. The door opens before she gets a chance to find out.

Regina uses the key she's had for years and walks in saying, "Hello."

Jackie, close behind says, "Everything all right in here?"

Regina gives Jackie an irritated look. "It certainly is not." She kneels next to TJ. Oscar comes into the room and holds the first aid kit out to Regina who says, "Thank you. You're right on top of things. Ramon, can you get me some soapy towels in a big bowl?" She twists her neck to address Pock who is standing behind her. "Can you take Oscar into the kitchen and make us some lemonade?" Lotti always has lemons.

"Come on, Oscar," Pock huffs, tired of jerks like TJ getting all the attention. Still, she can see why he has problems. Her father may be in Shirley, but he loves Pock like crazy.

Jackie sits on the couch directly across from TJ. Looks to

her, like it's his right side again. She wipes her hand across her face remembering the last time, the only time, she called the cops on TJ's father. When the police showed up, his mother, father, and TJ swore it was an accident. Then, TJ wasn't meant to see Jackie and Regina until TJ's father went back to his other family. Jackie wonders if calling the cops would make things better or worse for TJ this time.

"I'm all right." TJ pulls the hand Regina is examining away.

Ramon places the bowl of wet hand towels on the floor next to Regina. "You gotta see a doctor," he tells TJ. "You afraid of your father or afraid of getting him in trouble?"

"Why are you talking?" TJ starts to stand.

"TJ," Jackie says sternly, and TJ stays seated. "Sit, Ramon."

"Just trying to figure out why he doesn't want to act like a normal person for once." Ramon sits heavily on the couch next to Jackie. "You get beat up, you get stitches or some shit. Go to a doctor. Find out if something's broken."

"Normal person? How long you been telling me I'm a wind-up crazy boy?" TJ circles a finger next to his head. "Beat up? He looks worse than me."

Regina raises her eyebrows at Jackie and hands her a wet cloth.

Jackie gets off the couch, puts a hand under TJ's chin, and pats a cut on TJ's cheek. Regina hands Jackie a tube of antibiotic and Jackie swipes some of the ointment on TJ's wound.

"Thinks he's a thug." Ramon is talking about TJ's father as much as TJ. "Why you taunt him? Guy wales on his own kid. How do you think your mom feels seeing you two? How many times you think I'm going to get in the middle of your mess?" He remembers TJ all sleepy, but serious, lying next to him in the pup tent in Ramon's yard last summer right before they started high school saying, "You know everything about me and still." TJ shaking his head, tears falling, saying, "I love you, man. Not this queer stuff. That ain't shit. That's just, you know, till we find girls. I love you cuz you always got my back. I love you right here." Then TJ putting his palm flat on Ramon's chest over his heart. "Because you're strong, man. You're fucking ironman, right here." Why is Ramon thinking of this now?

Jackie is still dabbing at TJ's face. He pulls away. "What do you know about fighting with your father, Ramon?" He smirks at Jackie. "His Papi still tucks him in at night."

Jackie takes the Band-Aid Regina offers. "Enough out of both of you. Get off your knees, honey." She nods at the couch and Regina sits.

The boys glare at each other.

"No messes for pretty Ramon," TJ hisses.

"Punk." Ramon slides over so Regina can sit next to Jackie on the couch.

"Boys," Regina says firmly, "shut up, sit quietly, while Jackie and I go into Lotti's bedroom to call Yvonne."

"Old lady doctor," TJ snorts.

With a glance, Jackie asks Regina to let her handle TJ. "Listen to me," Jackie says.

TJ closes his eyes.

"Don't punk out," Ramon says. "It's Jackie. You gotta look at her." TJ opens his eyes.

"We're on your side." Jackie keeps looking at TJ as she stands. Standing takes more effort than she thought it would. "Let the people who care about you, care about you."

In the bedroom Regina reaches Yvonne and Bo on the second ring.

"Yvonne says they'll meet us at the ER," she tells Jackie when she gets off the phone.

"Let me tell TJ," Jackie says. "Give him a minute to get used to the idea of the hospital."

"He's all yours," Regina agrees.

The women sit on the couch next to Ramon across from TJ again.

Oscar and Pock come in from the kitchen, Pock carrying a tray of lemonade, which she sets on the coffee table between the sofa and the chair TJ sits in. "Real lemons." Oscar hands a glass to Regina.

She takes a sip. "Very good."

"After we drink this," Jackie looks at TJ, "we're going to the hospital."

"Your arm needs to be seen," Regina says in answer to the glare TJ gives Jackie, "by a doctor."

"Ramon will come with us," Jackie says.

"Yvonne's a doctor," TJ squirms in his chair. "She can come here."

"She'll meet us," Regina says. "Yvonne hasn't practiced in years."

"Relax," Ramon says.

"Why can't I go to a normal doctor?" TJ's words come out fast and loud. "At an office."

"You need an appointment," Pock says.

"The ER?" TJ looks from person to person, accusingly. "You're making me go to the ER?"

"We'll be with you," Ramon says. "Calm down, man." They all stare at TJ.

"In the meantime, I'm the entertainment? Sip lemonade. Gawk at TJ. No wonder I'm fucked up. The fucking ER!"

"What a waste of space." All Ramon really wants is for everyone to leave so he can shake TJ then rock him. When there are other people around Ramon has to say something to burn TJ just to get him to stop talking shit.

"People shouldn't stare at you." Oscar picks up a glass and offers it to TJ. "Lemonade will make you feel better."

TJ closes his eyes again, but Oscar keeps on talking, something about drinking when it's hot out. Ramon's always telling TJ what to do, what not to do. Now the retard Soto brother is telling him what to do. Never throw the first punch, Ramon says. Would Ramon throw the first punch if his father showed up after being gone for months, then sat up shirtless in his mother's bed complaining that the coffee was cold? Ramon and Oscar with pretty Mommy and perfect Papi and Lotti to take care of Oscar when he's too much for pretty Mommy and perfect Papi.

"Here you go." Oscar leans in to give TJ the glass.

"Just leave his glass on the table, Oscar." Pock starts to sit in the only empty chair in the room, decides to let Oscar have it, and sits on the arm at the end of the couch near Ramon.

Pock's advice comes too late.

It's not that TJ wants to hurt Oscar. TJ is trying not to hurt Oscar. He puts up a hand. He means only to clear the air in front of Oscar, to warn him to stay away, to let him know this is a bad time to push a glass of fucking lemonade on him. TJ gets the bad feeling he got before he hit his father or before his father hit him. Who hit who first? Like it matters. Like it fucking matters. Oscar and TJ's hands collide or maybe TJ knocks the glass away. He sees the lemonade fly out of the glass, something you see on TV, some special effect. The yellow, separating from the glass, a fountain of liquid. *Let go of the glass, let go of the glass,* TJ is screaming, he thinks he's screaming to himself, but maybe he's yelling out loud to Oscar, he's not too sure.

"Jesus," TJ says. "Jesus. I'm sorry, Oscar. I'm sorry, man." He shakes his head and looks at the floor. Without looking he knows how this is going to turn out. He won't be cut a break. It won't be some little accident where a glass gets broken and the carpet gets wet. There's gonna be blood. There's gonna be blood, and Oscar's gonna have a messed-up hand, and it's gonna be nobody but TJ's fault. TJ's heart pounds. The blood rushes to his head.

"Now what?" Regina says. "We're way too old for this." Jackie and Regina both take a deep breath before they stand.

Pock springs to her feet. "It's Oay, Oskie." She studies the broken glass in his hand and the trickle of red. Oscar and everyone else in the room stares at the cracked glass with the red spider lines. "You did good, hang on till I say let go," Pock says almost immediately. She takes Oscar's hand above his wrist and moves his arm in a careful arc until it's over the empty spot on the couch where Ramon had just been sitting. "Okay, let go."

"It's gonna make Abuela's couch all wet," Oscar cries.

"The glass is empty," Ramon says. "It's okay; listen to Pock."

"Lotti loves you more than the couch," Jackie says.

"Of course she does." Regina unwinds a roll of bandaging from the first aid kit. "Open your hand, honey. Let go of the glass, Oscar."

"You'll get to wear a bandage, buddy," Ramon says. "You can probably wear it to school."

Oscar lets go of the glass. It falls to the couch. "You can't squeeze too tight when you wash glasses." He looks at his brother, his eyes wide. "Lotti lets me wash everything now. Even the good plates."

"Because you're careful." Pock squints at Oscar's hand to see if any shards are stuck in the web between his thumb and first finger, the only place he seems to be cut. Ramon dabs at the blood with a square of gauze.

"Put pressure on it," Jackie says.

"Right." Regina cuts more bandaging and hands it to Pock who smears the hand with antibiotic before she wraps it. "Just stop the bleeding for now," Regina says. "You're going to be fine, Oscar." She thinks this is true. "We'll wait for Lotti. She should be on her way home. Oscar needs to be seen, too. Ramon, call your parents."

"This is Lotti's late night. She goes out with her boyfriend after work," Pock says.

Ramon is already calling. "No answer," he says. "Sometimes the phone cuts out near Mom's work." The Soto household shares two cell phones. The boys' parents work near each other and ride back and forth together on their long commutes.

Regina and Jackie go back into the bedroom and sit on Lotti's mint green bedspread while they call JimmyZ's and then Lotti's cell phone, with no luck. Regina searches through her purse for her little address book. "We need to find someone under eighty to take them." She calls two other families on the street. Mr. Martin is home and willing but carless and sounds like he's been drinking. Louisa is home alone with a croupy newborn and a two-year-old. "I'm not asking Silver to leave Lynn alone or to drag her out of the house. She's too sick," Regina says.

"We can squeeze six in The Bucket. Or Pock and Ramon

can stay home," Jackie says.

"We need Pock for Oscar, Ramon for TJ," Regina says. "Sliver's the only good man Lynn's ever had. let's not abuse him."

"Does it hurt, man?" TJ asks Oscar as they gather in the kitchen, about to leave.

"Yes, does it hurt?" Regina repeats, realizing no one has asked Oscar this question.

Oscar shakes his head. He looks at his brother. "Why'd TJ do that, Ramon?"

"The boy's messed up." Ramon puts his arm around Oscar. "Looks like it stopped bleeding, buddy. He didn't mean it."

"I am messed up." TJ squeezes his bicep on the injured arm. His whole body shakes. "I'd never hurt you on purpose, Oscar. Come on, Ramon, I wouldn't hurt him on purpose."

"I just said you didn't mean it." Ramon keeps an arm slung over his brother's shoulder.

"I never meant to hurt you," TJ says again as Oscar slides into the front seat between Jackie and Regina.

Ramon climbs in the backseat, in the middle, between Pock and TJ as usual. "'Never meant to hurt you, the last thing your father said before he broke your arm, TJ," Ramon says.

Jackie drives slowly so as not to jostle Oscar or TJ in the tightly packed car. Everyone is quiet until TJ leans his head back on the seat, looks up at the ceiling and whispers, "Fucker thinks he's gonna walk by me in his boxers, hand me a dirty plate, and I'm gonna run to the sink and wash it like his little bitch." Still looking at the car's roof, he asks, "Am I crazy?"

Jackie takes TJ's question seriously. She tells him she doubts he's crazy, guesses he's just angry, but bets he'd have to stop smoking marijuana and drinking, be off all drugs completely and away from his father for a while, to find out for sure. She tells TJ and everyone in the car that for a time, when she was

102

a girl, she thought she was crazy. "After my brother took my niece Selma away because he didn't want her around me." She tells them about the months she spent out of school, working on the farm, speaking to no one but the cows, not saying a word to another human being for weeks, not even her father. How a boy from a failing farm down the road started coming around at dusk to help milk the cows for a free gallon. How the boy talked and talked, never shut up, until every now and then Jackie would throw out a word or two just to get him to close his piehole.

"Piehole?" Oscar has never heard the term. He doesn't understand what it has to do with shutting up and laughs nervously.

Ramon laughs, too, so his brother won't be laughing alone. Then Pock laughs. TJ laughs, a sad laugh, then coughs and looks back up at the car's roof, cradling his arm and rocking, thinking about how no one remembered to feed the dog, how poor Horace was probably waking up hungry in the backyard right now and that was TJ's fault, too.

The rest of the way to the hospital all Regina can think of is Ramon saying "before." TJ's father said, "I never meant to hurt you" *before* he broke TJ's arm.

Chapter 5

Saturday, February 18, 2017

Jackie has always been content driving. Regina has always been content being the passenger. They relax into the ride to the dump. Regina enjoys the cocky look Jackie settles into behind the wheel.

"It was just five dollars. I'm sorry." Regina is back on the lottery ticket, feeling guilty about threatening Jackie with Gamblers Anonymous if she bought another one next week, tired of being stuck in the worry rut of losing the house. She appraises Jackie and decides She has kept her physical appeal: meaty, cropped gray hair, steel blue eyes with droopy lids, dignified. Jackie can't do the swagger anymore, but the facial expression is about the same as it was half a century ago. "Butches fare well, looks-wise, in old age. You're still handsome."

Jackie says nothing but gives Regina a sideways glance.

Regina decides Jackie's wry humor is visible in her profile. Jackie's way of saying so much by saying so little cracked Regina open from the start. Infuriated her, too. Regina looks down and notices that the quilting of her parka is frayed. No wonder she lives in the past. If she weeds out the arguments, money woes, the gambling, Jackie refusing monogamy in the early days, Regina's own bossiness, justified and unjustified jealousy, it's all Regina and Jackie, screwing around, having a good time. Poor and young, Regina can translate in her mind, romanticize. Poor and old? No charm in frayed polyester when you're poor and old.

Jackie catches Regina looking at her in the mirror. "You're all right," she grins.

Damn if Regina's thighs don't catch a ghost of the ache this statement used to bring on. The first time Jackie said, "You're all right," was the late 1950s. It means "Thank you" or "Nice tits" or "I love you."

Regina pats Jackie's leg, well below public viewing range. Regina feels Jackie squirm.

Inside a moving car is a public place to Jackie. Instead of saying she hates public shows of affection that aren't strictly in front of friends, Jackie says, "I hate Xmas," which Regina knows is not true. Jackie likes the decorated tree and the company that shows up at Christmas. And she likes sacrilege. Loves Mary because her mother loved Mary but hates the Blessed Virgin part. And just as her mother did when Jackie was a child, a few years ago Jackie started kneeling before bed, her lips moving silently. Maybe she prays to win the lottery. Regina never asks. Their days are long, the house is small, and Regina feels a little privacy is not too much to ask of someone who loves you.

Jackie pulls her head back sharply and adjusts her seat, a reaction to her hip hurting.

"Tell you what," Regina says. "If the social security checks are in the mailbox when we get back, I'll buy a fat chicken with a dollar off coupon and roast it with those tiny red potatoes. See if the boys and Pock want to come over for supper. Maybe Lotti and Yvonne." Their company meal. "And Oscar if he's around." When did they last make a meal for company?

Jackie drives slowly down the dirt road to the dump. They head toward a shack with smoke curling out the chimney. Regina hugs her handbag. Getting rid of stuff makes her optimistic.

Maybe they can float in this world a little longer if they have less stuff. She squints. The Bucket's belly scrapes the ground as the plowed road becomes a channel of frozen tire ruts. They park next to a sign near the shack that reads "Honk if You Need Help."

Jackie doesn't honk. She gets out of the car and limps toward the shack. Jackie's parka is blue; Regina's is maroon. A hairy guy, also in a parka, green and grease-stained with what might be real matted fur on the hood, comes around the tar-papered building.

He glances at the tree. "Got a sticker, buddy?"

Jackie looks at him sideways until he recognizes her and says, "Jackie? Sorry. Been a while."

"Thom." She nods hello. Maybe his name is Dick or Harry, but it said *Thom* on a hat he used to wear. He was young when he wore that hat, younger than now anyway.

Regina gets out of the car, because even though Jackie is the gambler, she won't play the poor-old-lady card. Their sticker has run out. It costs twenty-five bucks for a new one.

"Regina." He scratches his woolly beard and leans on the "Smoking Prohibited" sign.

Regina blushes because it's come to this, a thrill that the dump guy remembers her name. "We're short on cash." She can't decide if she should appeal to his possible love for his mother or just look needy.

He looks around. Not another soul in sight. "Five bucks. I'll help you dump it."

"We'll manage." Jackie could pass for seventy when she takes her wide-legged stance and looks you in the eye. "Thanks just the same." She pulls four singles out of her wallet.

Regina digs in her handbag for change.

"Keep it." Thom holds up a hand. Regina smells a whiff of whiskey on his breath, which may explain why he's letting them in.

"Can you believe this?" Jackie says as Thom opens the gate. She's been trying to figure an angle to roam around unescorted in The Bucket through this dump for years.

"He thinks we'll unload the tree and come right back like good little old ladies," Regina says. Jackie snorts. Regina didn't realize how worried she was about Jackie's state of mind until the relief of that snort. She watches Jackie drive as they bounce over the uneven road. "I went too far? Making you go to Gamblers Anonymous for so long?"

"Doubt it." Jackie shrugs. "Jesus, what made you think of that?"

"Things pop into my head." Regina shrugs. "What's that look on your face? I can usually tell if you're about to laugh or cry."

"Your mother's corset." Jackie takes a slow one-hand-on-the-wheel turn.

Regina follows Jackie's train of thought from GA to the corset without having to ask how Jackie got there. She starts to correct Jackie, to ask her to use two hands on the wheel, and remind her the corset was Regina's grandmother's, not her mother's.

But Regina decides to just sit and enjoy the ride and the bitter sweetness of remembering.

April 2006

Cupping one of her own breasts, waking from a dream about bread rising in a warm oven, Regina pulls up the comforter and turns over to spoon Jackie. She finds the depression in the mattress where Jackie should be and looks toward the bathroom. Silence from that direction, but the creak of a cabinet door and the smell of pancakes rises from the kitchen. She hauls herself up to sitting, surprised, as she is every morning, to find her body an old body getting older. Her thoughts meandering like water over stone, she smooths the flannel of her nightgown and runs her fingers over the mound of thinning hair that Jackie calls "no-man's land." Not the impressive bush it was, but still

107

a considerable hank of hair. Regina has heard from Lynn and Lotti, her main sources for keeping up—well, for not falling as far behind—that it is the fashion for young people to shave their pubic hair. Who are these young people who don't appreciate a full bush? She laughs out loud, vain of her pussy, at her age.

She smells maple syrup, warming no doubt in the same tiny enamel pot with the long handle and short spout that they have warmed their syrup in for years. "My wife." She giggles like a schoolgirl. They've been legally married in the state of Massachusetts for one year today. Now they have two anniversaries, October when they first met, which served them for over forty years, and this new April date. Regina would give up the October date, but Jackie won't hear of it.

Like most citizens of their state, Regina and Jackie were shocked when Massachusetts became the first to sanction same-sex marriage. They belonged to GLAD and Mass Equality, groups that lobbied for marriage equity. They marched down Main Street alongside Bo, Yvonne, Lynn, Lotti, even Papi and the mayor of their small city, to celebrate.

On May 16, 2004, the day before registrars in town halls all over the state braced themselves for an onslaught of couples taking out marriage licenses, Jackie had gotten down on her left knee, as the right knee was way beyond taking her full weight at that point. Regina winces, thinking of Jackie's poor knee. Smiles remembering the rest of it. "Will you marry me?" Jackie had asked in the stockroom of Sally's Card Shop where Regina was taking her fifteen-minute break.

Regina had touched Jackie's cheek and answered, "Hell, no," because she knew, notwithstanding Jackie's belief that same-sex marriage was a step forward for civil rights, that Jackie's view of the military and matrimony as suspect institutions had not changed. "That's what gay rights has come down to, marriage and the military, the right for the state to be legally involved in our relationship and the right for queers to get shipped off to Iraq and Afghanistan." Jackie had repeated this view even as she cheered the Massachusetts Supreme Court for declaring it unconstitutional to allow only opposite-sex couples to marry and applauded the military for becoming less sexist and homophobic.

It took Jackie almost a year to convince Regina that what Jackie wanted was to be inextricably tied to Regina so there could be no doubt that their house belonged to them both, there could be no question who should be let in the hospital room. Their friends Martha and Jill shared a life for forty years. Still, Martha lost the house she and Jill shared because she couldn't pay capital gains taxes. Money she would not have had to pay when Jill died if they'd been able to legally marry. Yes, Jackie wanted to say, "I do" so it would be clear to whoever it needed to be clear to that they belonged to each other. It was a shame that it took a piece of paper issued by the state. If that's what it took, so be it. Jackie wanted the piece of paper. When Regina finally said "yes," Jackie was happy. Bo was ecstatic. Bo had bought a tuxedo when she married Yvonne. As best man for Regina and Jackie's barbeque ceremony, Bo would get to wear the tux again.

"So?" Regina says. It's a question she often asks the day. It appears she gets two anniversary breakfasts this year, maybe every year. She'll make an anniversary cake and pick up Jackie's favorite wine. Sitting up in bed and looking toward the drawn shade, she wonders about the daffodils right outside the window, if they'll open today.

She stretches, considering their previous fifty Aprils together, well, mostly together, wondering if this is the spring the sap finally stops running. What a fool she is. What a species she belongs to. Humans need the whole earth and sky to understand themselves. She does like the idea of comparing herself to a sappy tree. But sex is sex. The birds and the bees aren't a metaphor; they have sex. She decides to give up on the foolish poem she's working on. No need to compare the hummingbird with its tiny beak in a petunia with the fumbling of human beings.

Poets are fools. She said that to Jackie recently. What was Jackie's reply? What's wrong with foolishness? Something like that. She rolls her shoulders, stretches her legs, and extends her arms over her head, her practice every morning before getting out of bed, the way the yoga teacher at the Senior Center taught her.

A shudder of unfocused worry confuses her. What now? Yes, she remembers the pact, the silly pressure she and Jackie imposed on each other. A mistake they made over forty years ago when they came up with their first anniversary date. A time when neither of them believed old age, slowing down, drying up, would come. And dying? None of it would ever happen, not to them. Sex on your anniversary. Now there is a cliché.

She stops brushing her long gray hair, frizzier than ever, to grab a handful and press it against her cheek. She may never get used to the way her hair looks, but she loves the feel of it, and rubs it back and forth against her skin. For the life of her, she can't remember what arguments some fools have against same-sex couples. Oh yes, it's the sex. Fuck them. Pleasure should exist for its own sake. Regina smiles at her own thoughts. She's becoming someone who tries to understand, but after trying can be content succeeding *or* failing.

She leans to witness her smile in the bureau mirror. Smile therapy. The kind of treatment offered to people who get free "therapy" by going to talks at the local library. Not a bad tactic. She exaggerates the smile. She's been lucky enough, in sex anyway. Never, like some of her friends, has Regina been afraid of that sticky mess of herself. Afraid of sap? Not Regina. Jackie has certainly never been afraid of sex. Afraid of getting caught, maybe, in the early years, when the horror and thrill of that possibility got tangled, when getting caught meant a beating or a berating.

This is not where she wanted her smile therapy to bring her, not on their first anniversary of being legally wed. She has often wondered if Jackie's cheating was mixed up with the sexy thrill of the illicit. Regina's one indiscretion certainly was.

She breathes in the yeasty sugary smell coming from the kitchen, puts the brush on her lap, kneads some warmth into her arms, and worries for Jackie. She has always responded to

Jackie on their anniversary. Her reaction was sometimes exaggerated but never false. They made the pact to always hold each other, that was all, to hold each other on their anniversary. But Regina knows her Jackie. She knows, even at seventy-eight, Jackie will consider herself a failure if she can't inspire Regina to hit the high notes. Hit the high notes and let the sap run, as close to dirty talk as Jackie gets. Randy as they come, but don't ask Jackie to speak her lust. Not that Regina was much for dirty talk herself before she realized how much Jackie enjoyed hearing "Fuck me hard, honey." Regina would have preferred to just stick with the action. But wouldn't you know it, the one place Regina wanted to hold her tongue, Jackie wanted her to talk more. All that porn star yammering. No harm.

Regina did reap the rewards of a few strategically moaned phrases. They were foolish and brave in equal measure, she supposes. They were trying. Trying young women, and now they're trying old women. Herself and her beautiful Jackie. Human beings, the whole lot are tiresome. But worth it. She smiles wide at herself in the mirror. Life is mostly worth the trouble. At least it feels that way this morning.

Time to move. Regina remembers she's working today and plunks the brush on the night table. She and Jackie are both working today, at their age, Jackie from ten until two taking money at the car wash, and Regina sitting behind the counter at the card shop. The fact they're both still quick enough in their minds and sturdy enough in their bodies to stand and make change from twenty-dollar bills is a happy thought, but if there is one piece of advice Regina would like to bestow on the youth of today, it would be make and save money when they're young so they don't have to work part-time in a card shop when they're in their seventies. Also, they should stop taking razors to their pubic hair. It will be gone soon enough.

Jackie is radiant, standing over the kitchen table, smiling that smile that still manages to come across as both shy and brash. Jackie pours the warm, sweet syrup on the buttered pancakes. Her glance admits she's pleased with herself and entreats

Regina to be pleased, too. How could Regina not be pleased with her big-hearted girl? Regina is hungry. Jackie is a good cook. They both have to be at work in an hour. Jackie bows her head for a moment, long enough for Regina to register that this gesture is a little prayer, even though Jackie would probably not agree that a bow to love is a kind of prayer. The crown of Jackie's bent head and the pink scalp beneath her cropped hair makes Regina pick up her napkin to wipe away a sappy tear.

That evening, Regina picks the daffodils. She arranges the fisted buds in a jelly jar on the table, hoping the warm kitchen will encourage them to open. Jackie has gone out to pick up Chinese food, splurging for their anniversary. Regina sets a book of matches down next to the candle in the middle of the table. She wears Jackie's favorite dress, a light blue shirtwaist that has become too tight. She tugs at the bodice, trying to get rid of the gulf between the buttons. Regina has always been and expects always to be a small woman. But in the last few years, her shape has changed. Her breasts and belly are larger, her arms and legs thinner, her clothes loose in some places, tight in others. She remembers her waist-cinching days, thin as she was.

Thin as she is, she thinks this dress could use a little help from a girdle or, better yet, a corset. She is wearing her prettiest slip, her only slip, pink and faded, worn every time she wears a dress, which doesn't happen as often as it used to. Jackie likes to slip off the straps one at a time, kissing Regina's neck and shoulders as she goes. When was the last time this happened? Six months ago, on their October anniversary? She wishes she had a slip or even a bra that wasn't several years old. The days when Regina had money to spend on lingerie have passed.

She walks into the den to shut off the TV that Jackie has left on and bends to reach for the remote wedged between chair cushions. It's a small room filled with a television, a La-Z-Boy recliner, and a couch that converts to a twin bed. When the recliner is stretched to its full length it almost touches the "Big

Ass," as Jackie calls the oversized TV, which is the newest thing in the house, purchased six years ago. Bookcases line one wall. A tower of dusty eight-track and VHS tapes stands in the corner. It's been years since they had an eight-track or a VHS player. As far as Regina knows, no one in the Western world has had an eight-track tape player in decades.

She studies the pile of outmoded technology. Jane Fonda workout tapes, *Desert Hearts*, *The Color Purple*. She picks up a tape with the handwritten title *Fire in the Air* on the cardboard sleeve. It's a tantric sex tape, a pseudo sex tape really, nice lesbians and a couple of straight-ish women channeling their chi. It was made by that women's group she joined the last time she and Jackie split up. What was that group called? The . . . Something Collective? The Lesbian Collective? Surely something more inclusive. What year would that have been? She was at least forty when she found Jackie and Bo at Dawn's Den. Dawn herself sitting in Jackie's lap. A woman with an afro that swayed as they moved was slow dancing with Bo.

Regina turns over the tape in its cardboard sheath. The date, *1970*, and the name of the group, *Daughters of Sappho*, is inked on the box right under the glued-on photo of herself and three other women in beads and flowing dresses. She groans, hopes they at least argued about the name. In the picture the four women sit close together on a huge granite boulder. 1970? Regina shakes her head. She could fathom this artifact trying to convince her they sat on that rock fifteen years ago, but more than three decades? Time lies. Numbers lie. She sniffs the cardboard. Swears she smells patchouli oil.

She sits in Jackie's recliner and lingers on the faded image. Jackie had claimed that what Regina saw at Dawn's Den was innocent flirting. Whatever it was, Regina went looking for some of her own. Which she found in Alisa, the woman in the photo with an arm around Regina's shoulders.

Alisa, holding all four women in tight for the shot and looking boldly at the camera, stares now at Regina with the arrogance of a beautiful, smart woman who wants you to appreciate her power. Alisa, the largest woman, the biggest personality in the collective. Alisa of the long legs and smart, full mouth, who Regina hasn't seen since that crazy Halloween party in the late '80s. Alisa dead for at least a decade now.

Could that tape player still be in the cellar or did it get tossed when Jackie was in her *Apocalypse Now* cellar-cleaning phase? Could it be hooked up to the Big Ass? Probably not. She'd love to see herself, Rose, Wildflower, all those women moving through space and time. Maybe a glimpse of young Jackie? She closes her eyes and remembers that Jackie and Bo showed up for the first meeting, Regina feigning irritation but glad Jackie came even though she and Regina had split. Jackie caught on tape. Regina recalls the captured moment because no amount of cajoling would make Jackie consent to anything more. One quick shot of Jackie looking for all the world like a man. Jackie's breasts flattened under her white button-down shirt, her torso as ever triple covered, no matter the weather, bound under a sleeveless T-shirt. The T-shirt under a starched long-sleeved white shirt. So shy, so brave, and bold. So much shit she had to take just for being herself in those days. And brave handsome Bo, not the only person of color in the photos, but the only person who sometimes referred to themselves with male pronouns. Earnest Bo with those big, beautiful eyes. Tough as nails, Bo. It was Bo who suggested, "The personal is political" for the group mantra.

Regina laughs out loud and reclines all the way back in the La-Z-Boy. Personal for sure. Breathing and looking into the eyes of women who were not your woman. Sitting on each other's laps while facing each other, touching, calling up your *kundalini*, imagining your *yoni* a breathing flower or a panting animal. Your rose or your mongoose inhaling and exhaling with you as you called up erotic energy. Touching, fully clothed. Then, at the end of the night, going back to your take-home partner. If you had one. Bo questioning their use of another culture's tradition but staying in the group for another month. Regina cringes, knowing Bo's question had deserved more consideration.

Jackie had read both Kinsey Reports and called the collective the Kegel Group, because of the way the whole gaggle of them got a rhythm going, tightening and releasing vaginal muscles in sync. The point of the practice was energy transfer, and? What? Regina holds the tape at arm's length, cocking her head, screwing into the memory of Alisa leading endless discussions about higher energy and joyous intimacy. More chaotic talking than coordinated breathing, more breathing than touching, endless questions about how to ethically channel your life force, how to ask for and give or deny permission to touch each other's shoulders, arms, faces. The Daughters of Sappho attempted to interpret thousand-year-old traditions every other Wednesday evening. Before the end of the first and only meeting she attended, Jackie saved the group hours of discussion by defining how to *contain* sacred energy. "No coming," she had said, putting on her ball cap. "Clothes on, no touching private parts," she had said as she walked out the door.

Regina feels a swell of love for those flawed, ridiculous, brave women. She also feels hungry. She hasn't eaten since lunch, saving herself for Chinese food and German chocolate cake. The cake Regina baked herself, doubly delicious because rich chocolate cake with gooey frosting is forbidden on the low-salt, no-refined-sugar diet the nutritionist at the clinic prescribed for them both. She even sneaked in a bottle of Jackie's favorite wine to go with dessert. Jackie must have smelled the cake baking when she came in from work. Sweet, that Jackie chose not to mention it, saving Regina the pleasure of her little surprises.

Jackie is taking a long time. It's all Regina can do not to go in the kitchen and cut herself a piece of cake. She needs a distraction. She tries to sit cross-legged in full lotus position on the couch. Her hips and knees don't fall open the way they once did. She arranges pillows beneath her. Rocking her hips, she settles into her sit bones so she can feel the lump of padding press against her. What did Alisa call the area Regina is rocking against? A gynecologist would say *perineum*. A libido-killer that

Regina lets float out of her head before it corrupts her chi. She squeezes and wiggles, delighted that she can still contract the muscles on first try. Alisa's word, what was it? The pillow presses between her legs just so. She exhales, relaxes, sucks in her muscles and her breath, in and up, into her belly, up between her ribs into her solar plexus, lungs, breasts, throat, mouth. She closes her eyes and exhales, "Sacred vault," in a confident tone she recognizes as Alisa's as soon as the words leave her lips. *Sacred vault*, good lord. She laughs, but her hips keep rocking.

"Boun . . . da . . . ries," she draws in slowly, syllable by syllable, sounding silly, clenching harder, trying to relax in the tension as she was taught, trying to focus on the energy as it moves in and up. The first time she heard Alisa say, "One must define her own boundaries," she thought it an odd use of the word, more suited to real estate and land surveys. That was Alisa, surveying the lay of land, expanding her territory. Despite her rhetoric about each woman finding her own autonomy, Alisa always attempted to include everyone else's borders within her own.

Regina exhales and surveys her body as the letting go drips down. Yes, she remembers this feeling of warm wax dripping down her torso, over her nipples, tingling the skin of her belly, sliding between her legs, pooling in her root chakra; what was the other name for that chakra? Holy grove? Yes, but Regina wants the Sanskrit word.

As if she could remember a Sanskrit word uttered forty years ago. How irritating, searching for words to complete a fantasy. Just as well. She doesn't mean to bring herself to climax. No need to worry. The red light on The Big Ass flashes, indicating that a Red Sox game is starting to record, reminding Regina how late Jackie is. She squints at the tiny bright numbers of the TV's clock that flashes her fear and worry. And her anger mixed with shame, which makes her angrier. Regina has done nothing wrong. Masturbating, big deal. Jackie is all right; late, is all. She rejects thoughts of Jackie crushed in the front seat of The Bucket. How many times has Regina told Jackie to drive slower and brake sooner? Jackie's fine, not grabbing at her chest at The

Chinese Place, and an ambulance with its red dome swirling is not on its way to suck her into its hatchback. Just this morning Regina convinced Jackie to use less cream in her coffee.

Regina sits on her pillows and tries to rechannel her chi, but her anxiety mounts as she watches the clock on the Big Ass change from 5:21 to 5:22, 5:22 to 5:23, 5:23 to 5:24. She listens for the crunch of tires on gravel. By 5:29 Regina wills herself into irritation instead of worry, convinces herself that Jackie has just lost track of time, that their food is getting cold at the Chinese place while Jackie shoots the shit with Old Man Chaffee or flirts with Bad Maddy.

By 5:41 she has flipped the tension of worry and irritation on its back and is busy rocking on her pillows. She gives up on summoning Sanskrit words. To hell with language. To hell with boun . . . da . . . ries. Regina gives in and lets Alisa enter as she did all those years ago. All Regina has to do is close her eyes and there is Alisa, sucking in Regina's exhaled breath, sitting on Regina's lap, wrapping her legs around Regina's waist, cunt to cunt, a word an American woman is not likely to forget until the very end; Alisa holding Regina firmly in the circle of her strong right arm, pressing her right hand against Regina's back, pulling their breasts closer, at the same time snaking the fingers of her left hand between them; Alisa's fingers reaching and stroking, mimicking the lapping movement of her tongue that would begin minutes later, more exploding than awakening Regina's *muladhara*.

Muladhara, the Sanskrit word for the root chakra. Regina laughs out loud, loses tension, clenches, fighting to hold on to the fire down below. "God," she whimpers, chasing "Fire Down Below" from her mind, refusing to lose her climax to rock 'n roll lyrics from 1976. She wills back the memory of Alisa's mouth, the encouraging shape and pressure of it, the things that came out of that mouth, the things that mouth took in. The girl was talented. Insistent. Animal instincts, her own needs outweighed every other consideration. Not an easily likable person. But when did that stop a body from responding? Give a girl a

117

boundary, she'll want to know what's beyond it.

Regina comes in Alisa's mouth. When it's over, she finds herself spread open with one foot on the floor next to the couch and the other hooked over the couch's back. She slides off the pillows, pulls her panties up, her hem down, and straightens the bodice of her dress. She spent herself on their anniversary. Damn chi. Where the hell is Jackie?

Regina throws a pillow at the Big Ass. It blinks 6:28. She goes to the junk drawer in the kitchen to check for the free cell phone ElderCare gave them. The phone is there in the drawer. Jackie didn't remember to take it, and Regina won't be able to use one of their ten allotted monthly calls to find her. Regina sits at the kitchen table and stews for a minute before she decides to soothe herself with a generous glass of the wine she bought to go with dessert. The cabernet works better than she expected. She smiles at her reflection in the toaster. By the time she's done with her second glass Regina is no longer hungry and decides to give Jackie another half hour before she lets either worry or anger ruin their anniversary. She has given Jackie a lifetime of half hours. What's one more? Jackie, after all, did not say exactly when she would return.

In the bedroom, Regina opens the hope chest her grandmother gave her mother as a wedding present, inhales cedar, and sorts through lace tablecloths, wedding dresses, and tatted linens. She deposits the contents of the chest on the bed and finds what she's looking for. The corset is hand-stitched ivory brocade, beautifully faded, exquisitely lined in ages of yellow, like an elephant tusk she once saw at The Natural History Museum. She runs her fingers over a yellow streak on the bodice. "Bosoms," she says. Or is it bosom? She likes the plural, which seems more of her grandmother's era. She runs her fingers along the stays and is reminded that they are whalebone, the actual thing from the live creature that swam in the ocean.

She holds the corset at arm's length. It would be a twenty-year lapse since she fastened the hook and eye closure in the front—since she felt the boning press and the ruffle trim on the sweetheart bustline tickle her *décolletage*. She wonders if she can get into it, thinks it might be pleasant to feel the bottom of Jackie's foot on her butt as Jackie tugs at the laces. When she slips into the corset, she understands that her body is so changed that tugging at the laces won't be necessary, maybe won't be possible. And good thing. One of the laces is frayed and probably could not survive a good yank. Regina is sleepy. She feels a bit flushed and lies on top of the comforter. Perhaps she should have had a piece of bread with the wine. She looks at the alarm clock; the neon numbers flip to Six forty-two. They usually eat around 5:30. 6:42 is late, but not unforgivable. Jackie is all right. Regina rests her head on her pillow. If Jackie is not back in five minutes, Regina will call The Chinese Place. If Jackie is not at The Chinese Place, she'll call Bo.

In her dream, Regina puts her dress on over the corset, a little surprise for Jackie after dinner.

Chapter 6

Saturday, February 18, 2017

Jackie and Regina drive to a fork in the road and turn right, as Thom instructed, taking in acre after acre of his backyard. Everywhere they look they see heaps of trash. Regina needs new glasses, and a thin layer of white snow covers the dump, making things even harder to recognize.

"Tires." Jackie drives slowly and identifies the heaps for Regina, "Appliances. Appliance doors. Compressed cars."

The pile of compressed cars is taller than their house. Shiny blue-black crows, smudges against the snow, flit from heap to heap. Regina opens her window to hear the crows caw and the seagulls squawk. She doesn't have to ask why Jackie pulls over and stops alongside the remains of an industrial-sized freezer whose huge door has been ripped off. From this vantage point the waste is endless, dune after dune of white-blanketed stuff as far as the eye can see. Used-up stuff, huddled in the cold, tucked in for the winter.

"Sorry I've been so much trouble over the years," Jackie says.

"For god's sake, enjoy the view." Regina pats Jackie's hand. "Trouble and joy. Both of us."

"You were off daydreaming for a few minutes there. What were you thinking about?" Jackie asks. She's been staring out The Bucket's big dashboard window herself.

"The corset, gambling, that time you were late for our anniversary," Regina says. I never really understood. About addiction. You're the only thing I've ever been addicted to."

"I still miss five-card stud," Jackie says. "And I still love you more than gambling."

"Tell me about that night," Regina says. "What really happened?"

"Why would I bring that back? It's over."

"Because it's over. And I want to know. You love this view. Let's just sit and talk some more. I want to understand."

April 2006

"Hey, Mac." Jackie has called the Hawaiian guy who owns The Chinese Place Mac for as long as she's known him. Bo calls him Mac, too. She has heard others call him Ho and Sam.

"Hello, Jackie," he says. "Where's your better half?"

"Home, waitin' on her anniversary dinner."

"Congrats." Mac scratches his chin. "How many years?"

"One," Jackie says.

"One?"

"One legally married. Fifty unsanctioned by the state. Regina might figure it more like forty-seven. I got a couple years lopped off for bad behavior."

"This same-sex business is fair and square far as I can tell," Mac says. "Haul the ball and chain like the rest of us."

Jackie orders spring rolls and fried rice with shrimp and chicken. While the kid with the hitch in his gait makes up the order, Mac tells Jackie about the poker game going on in the back room.

"Open game?" Jackie's head turns to the door leading the way to the game. She has forgone poker longer than she cares to remember.

"Not really. But Old Man Chaffee went upstairs to check on his wife. Might want a fourth till he comes back." Mac pushes the bowl of free pork crisps toward Jackie. They both eat a few and watch the door. "Since they all know you."

"Henry, James Junior, and Bad Madeline?"

"Same old gang." Mac snorts, as close to a laugh as he gets. "Tuesday lineup shrunk down to the die-hards." He frowns. "Thought you swore off, though. Now that I think of it."

Jackie fingers the twenties in her pocket. "How much is the food?"

Mac rings up the order. "Eighteen twenty-five."

Just the thought of taking a seat at that table makes Jackie feel more alive than she's felt in a long while. Bad Maddie will cackle like the crazy old bird she is if Jackie walks into that surprisingly big back room. Jackie can already feel the edge of the table press against her belly as she pulls up a seat. She can see the shine, a new deck every time, feel the crisp cards between her fingers, feel the ridges on the circumference of the chips taking tiny love-bites as she rakes them in. Even her ass hitting the too-small seat of the metal chair would feel good. Right, wrong, good, bad, indifferent, the risk in each throw of the card is a thrill that belongs to Jackie alone.

"Eighteen twenty-five," Mac repeats.

She hands him a twenty. Three twenties and change from a fourth, that's all she's got. None of them will stake her, not since she lost the tax refund. None of them wants Regina in here making another scene. Sixty dollars should have been enough to get Regina the CD player on sale at Walmart, but they were sold out. The rain check in her back pocket would make a shitty anniversary gift. No wonder she has the blues. She can't even afford a CD player from Walmart that's not on sale. Regina has never understood the blues. Not a hint of depression in Regina. Under stress, mania is more Regina's style.

All Jackie needs to win is thirty more dollars, plus tax, so maybe forty, to get the next model up, which, what a surprise,

122

is still available. But even if she loses, since Old Man Chaffee lives above the place and the stakes are low, she probably won't have time to lose it all. What's ten minutes? She has to wait for the food anyway. And she might win.

Mac hands her the dollar seventy-five change.

Jackie fights with herself for twenty seconds before she hands Mac another twenty. "Still five bucks to get in?" She's seventy- eight, old enough to decide to play a hand of poker. She needs a pick-me-up, and Regina deserves a partner who doesn't have the blues on their anniversary.

"Same as ever." Mac gives her back three fives. "Bad Maddy will be happy to see you." He turns to the kid. "Put the order under the lights when it's ready."

The back room is better than Jackie remembers. Madeline flings her arms around Jackie, steps back, holding her at arm's length, passing red-tipped fingers across the top of Jackie's close-cropped gray hair, pretending, as she always has, that they're both interested in more than the theatrics of the moment.

Jackie hides her shock at how much older Madeline looks and tries to remember how long it's been since they've seen each other. Maddy has let her hair go gray. Jackie is no connoisseur of makeup, but Maddy's trademark cherry red lips don't seem glamorous tonight.

Maddy leans in to whisper, "Glad you're off the leash this evening."

Jackie doesn't flinch outwardly. It's the kind of thing Maddy might say to any of the guys at the table. Still, Maddy has hit a nerve. Jackie does feel the leash. Maddy's remark reminds Jackie of the limitations of her hips, knees, and bank account as much as the restraints Regina puts on her. She rubs her neck and wonders, as she always has, whether Madeline has ever had any real attraction to her. Unlikely. Just part of the sport. It's okay, Jackie's a sport too, and appreciates the effort. To make things more interesting there are three whiskey sour glasses in front of Maddy's spot at the table. When Maddy loses, it's usually to whiskey sours. Jackie wonders if she and Maddy need to feel like they're

123

in the game as much as they need to win.

Henry and James Junior are close-mouthed. Jackie is as comforted by the familiarity of their silence as she is by Maddy's chatter. Both men offer Jackie a nod and a tight-lipped smile. James Junior has, by far, the biggest pile of chips in front of him, mostly blue. Jackie counts the chips and does the math—three hundred dollars' worth. Not the most Jackie has seen on the fake leather tabletop, but enough to make her put on her poker face and decide not to mention that she's only got fifty-six dollars and change on her.

"I'm only in till Chaffee comes back," she says, as if she's considering how many chips to start off with. She asks for twenty-five blue chips, fifty dollars' worth.

"Chaffee comes through the door, we finish the hand and you're out," Henry says.

Four at a table has always been the rule. Jackie remembers when there were five tables of four playing and people holding numbers waiting their turn for a seat. The space, the room itself, seems desolate with just one table, set up near the back window. The shades are drawn as always. Tonight the only overhead bulb turned on is above their table.

Sad.

Until the cards are dealt. Then the room expands. Jackie notices every nuance, every shadow passing over the other players' faces. James Junior's face colors as he labors to get a lung full of air. Bad Maddy's powdered face stiffens to block an expression. The green tarnish under Henry's wedding ring shows as he moves the cards a fraction of an inch farther away from his chest and squints to read them. Something skitters in the wall. The ding of a customer ringing the bell sounds far off. Jackie feels her own heart speed up and slow down, dancing with the cards.

Apparently Old Man Chaffee's wife needs more than ten minutes' worth of help. Jackie wins fifty-five dollars, loses twenty, wins twenty-five. In between hands they relax for a minute at a time, eat a handful of chips, down a few gulps. Jackie drinks the warm free water. Maddy tells Jackie she looks good with a few extra pounds on her. Jackie doesn't return the compliment. The red of Maddy's lips looks more appealing as Jackie pulls in her winnings.

After twenty minutes, Jackie's up by one hundred eighty dollars. Then the worst and best thing that could happen does. Old Man Chaffee is back and watching as she wins her biggest round yet, one hundred five dollars on her "last" hand. Two hundred eighty-five bucks. Might be enough to calm Regina down about gambling. Or maybe Jackie will keep the thing to herself.

Jackie is glad for the rules of the game. The rules will save her, get her home on time, in enough time anyway. She rises to leave. But Old Man Chaffee says, "Sit your ass down. I ain't gonna steal your chance to give some of that back." Jackie's heart races. She looks around the table. Her heart steadies and squeezes out her better judgment. She could kiss the old man's dry lips. She sits and allows the sad and sorry of staying when she should be leaving give way to her coursing blood.

Jackie doesn't kiss Old Man Chaffee and she doesn't give a penny back. Jackie keeps winning. She wins like the heart attack that hasn't happened, knowing sooner or later this could kill her, but not right now; right now there is the pure rush of it, her arms wide, raking it in, stopping to allow herself a half smile at the other cardiac cases witnessing her win. Even James Junior, who has lost most of his winnings, gives her a grudging nod. It's Bad Maddy who finally says, "Okay, Chaffee, tell Jackie she can go home now while I still got cab money in my bra."

Jackie pulls up to the curb in front of the house and wipes the self-satisfied smirk off her face. It's hard to be contrite about winning $500 so soon after the fact. Regina would have expected her to be gone an hour. Jackie might have stretched it to two, claiming she had a hard time finding an anniversary present, which she did, but almost three hours late for their anniversary dinner is beyond forgive and forget. Jackie pats the CD player, a purple shiny thing. Even without the evidence of dried-out Chinese food, Regina probably figured out that Jackie is late because she's been gambling. Only thing to do is walk in and tell the bold-faced truth.

The kitchen door is not bolted—good. "Baby?" Jackie opens it slowly, expecting Regina to be standing there with fire in her eyes. If Jackie is lucky, a minute or two will pass while the fact that Jackie is home safe and sound settles in. If only Jackie had called Regina with some bullshit about a flat. "Baby?" She places the grease-stained bag of food on the counter. She almost got a new order, but decided to use the ten minutes to run into Walmart for the CD player instead. She walks into the living room. Maybe she can still use the flat tire excuse? No. Regina would march out to the car and see that the tire hasn't been messed with. "Regina?" she whispers the question. Where is she? Heart attack? Stroke? Not Regina. Has she left without leaving a note? Wouldn't be the first time.

Jackie walks down the hall to the bedroom, opens the door, and stops dead in her tracks. Regina is sprawled flat on her back on their bed, a position Regina never assumes in sleep. Jackie stares at the soles of Regina's bare feet. She takes a step into the room. Besides Regina's chin and nostrils, Jackie can't see much of her face. Her long gray hair is a cloud around her shoulders. She's wearing something old and impossibly tight, some kind of lingerie that only covers her torso and makes her breasts seem large. It seems important that Jackie retrieve the word for the garment Regina is wearing.

Jackie holds her breath to see if she can hear Regina breathing. She cannot. Her intellect tells her that this is Regina, her partner of fifty years, asleep on the bed, wearing some old-fashioned sexy undergarment. A lump in Jackie's throat expands to her chest. "Please, some sign of life," she whispers.

Regina does not oblige. This could be a scene in a bad movie; it looks staged, which is some comfort, but elaborate, even for Regina. If she is trying to give Jackie a scare, it's working. Jackie stops herself from running out of the room. The thought that this may not be her Regina on the bed runs through Jackie's mind followed by the thought that Jackie's gambling may have finally killed Regina, as Regina has more than once claimed it would.

Just how much she left on that card table comes roaring home as Jackie stares at the delicate tuft of gray hair peeking out of the panties that are themselves peeking out of the bottom of the complicated, constructed thing Regina is wearing. Jackie rubs her head, which is starting to pound. Maybe she's losing her mind. Come home too late, gambled one time too many, and lost everything. She concentrates on the rigid cups covering Regina's breasts. The swell of belly below might be moving in and out. Jackie is hopeful that this is the case.

"Regina," she exhales the name and moves to the side of the bed, where she stares down at Regina's face. She kneels and strokes Regina's cheek with the back of her hand.

Regina's mouth is slack until her dream of eating chocolate cake with chopsticks merges with the reality of Jackie's hand on her cheek. In the second it takes a tear of relief to slide down her temple, Regina is furious. Her body jerks, one quick tremor.

Jackie feels Regina's fury before Regina's eyes open. She removes her hand from Regina's cheek. "I thought you were dead." Jackie stands. Her knees ache from kneeling.

"Because you're a fool." Regina sits up too fast. She's a bit dizzy, but otherwise the effects of the wine have worn off along with her inclination to calmly accept whatever explanation Jackie has for ruining their anniversary. She looks at the pitch black outside their bedroom window. "Maybe I'm the fool." How humiliating to be found in this getup.

She holds out a hand. "Give me my robe." Then, with a break in her voice, relief squeaks out. "Did you think of me at all, how worried I'd be?"

"I'm sorry, baby, so sorry you worried." Jackie is truly sorry even though she's not sure how much worrying Regina did in her sleep. She makes a vow that this is the absolute last time she will gamble. The lottery is exempt. She doesn't vow to entirely give up the lottery. "Corset. I couldn't remember the name. It was your mother's." This forgetfulness feels like something outside of Jackie, something alive and willful worming its way in. Her mother became forgetful before she lost all memory and then all speech. "I first saw you in that corset in our little apartment, a walk-up on the fourth floor."

Regina scowls, for how dare Jackie call up past sex acts, as if she had the right to mention making love at this moment? Simultaneously, Regina is also thinking what Jackie is thinking—sex on the kitchen floor, cracked linoleum, witch hazel on the scratches on Regina's back and Jackie's knees. "Grandmother's corset," Regina spits out, as if the mistake about which dead relative was the original owner of the corset is another transgression to be thrown in the black hole of Jackie's sins. She is suddenly full-blown mortified to have Jackie see her in this archaic piece of underwear. "Hand me my fucking robe," she yells.

Jackie grabs the robe off the hook on the back of the door.

"Is that a tear? Please." Regina wraps herself in the robe. "How much did you lose?"

Jackie shakes her head and wipes the tear of relief off her cheek. If she doesn't watch herself, she'll smile. Regina is not only alive; she's wearing a corset. And behind Jackie's shame, before and after the fact of coming home late on their anniversary and worrying Regina, Jackie won. She won big. She won going-out-to-dinner- and-a-movie-and-a-drink-after-with-plenty-left-over BIG.

Regina ties the robe's belt in a double knot. "How much did you lose?" She slams a fist on the bureau. She rants about the lost money. She rants about "this ridiculous situation." How they could have gone to night school, "not just one fucking course at a time." How they both should have chosen a career. "Hairdresser, manager at Walmart, butcher, baker, candlestick maker." She contradicts herself, saying they never had a chance to "be out and make a living, to have opinions and be women at the same time." She starts in on an outburst about Jackie's "irritating uncomplaining ways" that ends with "my big mouth lost me a shot at being a nurse."

She paces and rants, "Hopes and dreams? I just wanted to be in charge, of something, somewhere." She rants about sexism, homophobia, the shitty school system, her mother training her to be a suitable wife. She waves her arms and yells about young lesbians who have no idea what it was like growing up in that time. She glances out the window and rants about how the grass needs cutting.

Trying to answer is futile. Jackie listens to Regina stomp around the room, careful not to let what pleasure she takes in the energy of Regina's momentum crack her poker face. A force of nature to be respected, Regina nipped Jackie's "You're beautiful when you're angry," response in the bud years ago. Well, not the response, but any outward sign.

Finally, when there's a lull in Regina's railing Jackie says, "Over five hundred," adding "Won," quietly, because Regina is in full force again. She needs to get it out and Jackie needs to tamp down the after-a-win mania that, despite Regina's anger, has barely subsided. How quickly the world turns sometimes. Despite how badly she has messed up, if Jackie plays her cards right, if she lets Regina see how sorry she is, despite the worry, despite every time she has ever fucked up; if Jackie can show her honest feelings, like Regina is always trying to get her to do, because Jackie is sincerely in love with Regina after all these years, as much or more now than she has ever been, because she is genuinely sorry and ready to do better, ready to quit altogether; if Jackie can hold out, hold back her increasingly good mood, let Regina have her well-deserved say, let her vent, do what she needs to do; if Jackie can hang in and not blow it by trying to make everything all right too soon, there will be a celebration, eventually, sooner than later, she hopes; they will have their own little party. Jackie's mind spins, making her heart race. She takes a breath to calm herself. It will be after, Jackie understands, after Regina calms down and realizes this is not a relapse into losing the mortgage money and negotiating a budget with the electric company. That happened more than a year ago. It's not what's happening now. Except for being late, tonight turned out okay.

After a while, Regina will smile at Jackie again.

For the moment, Regina has murder in her eyes. "Where the hell did you get $500?" She really belts it out. "$500, you piece of—"

"Won," Jackie says quickly, not sure if Regina heard over her own yelling, but Regina stops short of calling her shit so maybe she did hear. The windows are open. Well, they've heard as bad or worse come through the windows from Lotti's house. Besides, Regina will probably give Lotti a blow by blow over coffee.

Regina looks like she might explode, which she does. "On our fucking anniversary." She throws up her arms. Her head shakes, her face contorts. She looks Jackie in the eye, speaking in a normal volume, slowly, like the words hurt. "After the time and money we spent on that counselor, money we didn't have, time." She lowers her voice and gives Jackie a look that breaks Jackie's heart. "We're running out of time."

Regina looks at the wall for a long moment before turning back, "Do you get that, Jackie?"

"Yes," Jackie forces herself to admit before she sits on the bed.

Jackie bends forward, head bowed, hands clasped between her knees. Regina stands over her, saying nothing. Irritation starts to erode a bit of Jackie's remorse. She would like to know the total amount she has wasted on gambling compared to the total amount Regina has spent on the things that make her happy: clothes, entertainment, fancy food, an embroidered duvet cover from the craft fair. Also, there is the fact of winning. "Won," Jackie says firmly. "Won," she repeats, for what, the fourth time?

"You stayed away from this thing for over a year. Why now? I will not borrow from Lynn and Silver again. I will not borrow from Bo and Yvonne. They're not rich, just comfortable, and they've earned every penny. It's not right to ask people to sacrifice. If you think I'm going to take on more hours so we can eat *and* have electricity . . . " Regina cocks her head. "Won?"

"Can we just be happy about it?" Jackie nods. "I thought you were dead for a minute. I'm so happy you're alive. Sit down, honey." Jackie pats the mattress.

Regina does not sit. "Won is no better than losing when it comes to satiating you once you feel those cards in your hand," she says. "And sooner or later we both lose."

Jackie doesn't disagree. Still, in her heart she doesn't believe that gambling fifty bucks is proof of relapse. She was never totally convinced she has an addiction in the first place. Can't she be allowed to hang on to the rush of the win for one evening? She lets her tears fall on the gray, once blue, carpet. It's what she's got, tears and five hundred bucks.

Regina stands and stares down on Jackie. Above and below the belt, the sides of Regina's robe separate.

Jackie's tears are mostly real. She hopes they work. Hopes the undignified sighing makes Regina see how much she loves her. Hopes at some point she can tell Regina how happy she is that Regina put on that corset for their anniversary. Because Jackie is grateful for all their years together. Jackie is also tired and hungry, and all she can think about is how to get Regina to forgive her as quickly as possible. The smell of chocolate cake bolsters her resolve to get them both to the table. She reaches for her handkerchief, feels the money, and pulls the roll of bills out of the back pocket of her chinos, a big bundle, mostly fives and tens, more money than twice the combined weekly income from both their part-time jobs. She offers the wad of money open-handed to Regina. She has blown a chance to show Regina how good she looks in that corset, the chance to feel Regina's soft flesh and listen to the pounding of her still ardent heart. Tonight will not be a night when sated, pleased with herself and Jackie, Regina will sit up in bed and carry on about TV commercials selling youth by making old people ashamed of their skin, hair, minds, and teeth. Jackie won't get the wrinkles on her face and neck kissed tonight. Jackie shakes her head, accentuates the sorry in her expression.

Regina snatches the money and points a finger at Jackie's

chest. "Stay seated on that bed. Do not move an inch."

Jackie listens as Regina goes from room to room, slamming doors and drawers, flushing the toilet, banging windows shut. She allows herself a knowing smile. Regina is hiding the money, taping it to the bottom of the silverware drawer, or putting it in a plastic bag and sticking it in the urn with her mother's ashes. She is gone, making clattering noises, for a long time. It gets quiet. It stays quiet. Jackie would be wondering if Regina left, but Regina wouldn't leave wearing a robe and corset.

Jackie retraces the steps she took to get to the bedroom, down the ten-foot hall, into the kitchen.

Regina listens to Jackie's approach. She has a plan, her only plan. She has lived through Jackie losing the mortgage money and the tax refund. She might be able to live through Jackie falling off the wagon again, but she'll be damned if she's going to. Even if she could get Jackie to a therapist, that $500 is not buying a month's worth of twenty-dollar lunches for a counselor. Gamblers Anonymous, tough love, that's Regina's plan.

She closes her eyes to conjure up the face of gambling. Regina has her own definition of poker face. It is not neutral or impassive; it is the smarmy, smiling face of Richard Milhouse Nixon, arms and shoulders raised in his split-fingered victory salute as he debarked from a jet coming back from who remembers where. Regina doesn't care that this image is ridiculous, doesn't care that she has never, not even once, met a gambling buddy of Jackie's who had any resemblance whatsoever to this picture. Not a disgraced smug-faced politician among them. She can't even pin this image on the people who make money off gambling. As far as Regina knows, Jackie has never been to a casino or a horse race, never had her money snatched up by some greedy millionaire leeching cash from lower class losers. No, her Jackie has always been lured into overheated back rooms of local restaurants or cheap hotels. Her consorts have always been the poor dealing to the poor, seated at a folding table. No matter; the image of Nixon doesn't have to make sense, as long as it fuels Regina's fury, as long as her fury feeds her resolve. She's not going into her eighties worrying that her wife has blown their grocery money.

Jackie finds Regina sitting at the kitchen table, her robe wrapped tightly around her, eyes closed, sitting up straight, relaxed in her chair. She looks serene, more like a Zen master than an angry aging lesbian. Jackie sits opposite her without speaking.

"Here's what's going to happen." Regina opens her eyes, sits back in her chair, and folds her arms over her chest. "That money is dead to you. We will not go out to eat, go to the movies, buy me a new dress, order cable. You will not get one iota of pleasure connected to that money." She holds up the sales slip she has removed from the Walmart bag. "Nor will you ever see me get one smidgen of pleasure from that money. The CD player is going back." She stares at Jackie, ready for an argument that she doesn't get. "You think I'm biting off my nose to spite my face. You think I spend as much money on Christmas ornaments, throw rugs, and fancy face creams as you spend at the card table? That argument held water years ago, but wake up, Jackie, I haven't spent a dime on anything we don't really need in a long time."

Regina enunciates the next sentence as if English is not a language Jackie is overly familiar with. "We're poor and you can't gamble." She takes a sip of tea. "You think I'm punitive, manipulative? Tough."

Jackie shakes her head. She's not thinking punitive or manipulative. She's thinking smart move to kill the buzz, smart move to bring up her own sacrifices. She's thinking maybe we really can't afford to take a chance on even fifty dollars anymore. She's thinking old age is a bitch she can't bet on. She's thinking she may never see Regina in that corset again.

Chapter 7

Saturday, February 18, 2017

Regina and Jackie both get out the passenger side to avoid having to step on the slick road, which has not been sanded. They stand in the snow. The morning sun bounces off every piece of dented chrome and broken glass that manages to stick out of the snow; even the corrugated cardboard shines. Except for the cawing of the crows, squawking seagulls, and the occasional flapping of paper, plastic, and wings, the place is eerily quiet.

"The Starship Enterprise crash-landed on a deserted planet," Regina says.

Jackie takes over Regina's thought in voice-over mode. "A new world with new forms of danger and beauty."

Regina smiles and strokes the sides of her parka with her puffy-gloved hands, feeling fondness for the dump and Jackie and the old coat. The temperature hovers below freezing. A clear winter's day. Her feet are warm and her ankles doing fine in her quilted boots. There really is otherworldliness here. She half expects the robots, shackled laborers, or ogres who maintain this place to appear from behind one of the trash heaps.

THIS PLACE IS A DUMP
IF YOU WANT TO PLAY
FIND A PLAYGROUND

Regina reads the message, painted in block letters on a piece of plywood, propped next to the freezer.

"Look." Air curls out of Jackie's nostrils. She points.

Regina follows Jackie's gaze between the piles of rotting boards and wooden skids to a gigantic circle with a slight swell in the center. "What is that?"

"Frozen garbage. They dig a big hole, fill it with trash, and bury it. Must be too cold to work now. Probably stay uncovered till spring."

Regina takes her glasses out of her purse even though they will give her only a few seconds of improved eyesight before the heat of her breath hits the cold and crystallizes on the lenses. "A lake," she says, "a frozen lake of garbage filled with the unsorted stuff of kitchen cans and dumpsters." There's a road to the lake, but it's covered with snow. "How come there's no snow on the lake?"

"Melted. Makes its own heat similar to a compost pile." Jackie studies the horizon like she might be asked to manage the operation sometime soon. "Thirteenth biggest dump in the Northeast."

"How do you know these things?" Regina is always amazed at the vast difference in the facts they've accumulated in such connected lives. Jackie has no response. Regina can see by Jackie's focused squint that she plans to walk the thousand feet to get a better look.

"Old with a fake hip. Snow is dangerous," Regina says.

Jackie nods as if considering the information that snow is hazardous to old women with bad hips. It's clear to Regina wthat Jackie is going, and if Jackie is going, Regina is going. Regina circles the lake with her eyes. Through her foggy glasses the giant swell reminds her of an animal on its back, belly up.

"The underbelly of the material afterworld, alive and exposed, vulnerable," she says.

Jackie rolls her eyes and smiles.

Regina leans her head on Jackie's shoulder and coos, "If you break your neck, I'll bitch about taking care of you till the day you die."

Jackie kisses Regina and bends to pick up a metal rod that looks somehow related to the freezer. She sticks the bar in the snow. It's the perfect height for a cane, even takes a right angle at one end so she has a grip of sorts.

She offers Regina her arm. They plod. The few inches of snow are stabilizing, firm enough to help steady their ankles, but not so deep they can't walk, fluffy enough that it might soften a fall. One step at a time they reach a huge mustard-colored piece of equipment, a rusty bulldozer, poised near the edge of the frozen pit of rubbish.

Regina is ready to sit or lie down. Jackie's cheeks are pink with cold and exertion, but otherwise she looks better than she has in weeks. Several crows flap up nervously and land again in the same spot not five feet from them.

Jackie pats the rubber tracks banding the tires of the bull-dozer. "Hello, dinosaur." The inert machine does look like a sleeping giant. "Wake up," she says. The big shovel of its mouth rests on the ground and is loaded down with frozen dirt. "In years to come, people won't know this dump existed. It will be a retirement home for kids who are in nursery school now."

When they first met, Jackie claimed a whole section of Boston was built on top of a dump. They were drinking tequila at the time and Regina didn't believe her, but Jackie was right. Jackie looks up four tons of backhoe and stares longingly at the driver's seat, high above them inside the open cab.

"Oh no, absolutely not," Regina says.

"The world is full of danger. Old age. Winter. Politicians." Jackie rubs her hip. "Old and used-up are the whole point here." She knows it's unreasonable, two elderly women standing in snow in thirty degrees, one with a hip replacement, arguing

136

about climbing onto a bulldozer, but they only made it for sixty years together because they're both unreasonable.

Regina doesn't mind unreasonable if it makes Jackie happy. This is the closest to happy Jackie has been in weeks. But Regina considers it her job to keep Jackie from killing herself and leaving Regina to carry on with only one Social Security check. "Another Tonka toy you can't play with. If I could hoist you up there I would, my love."

"Shame to waste an opportunity." Jackie steps back and considers the step up to the cab which is at least three feet from the ground.

"The last time your foot was raised that high was in water aerobics sometime in the late nineties," Regina says.

Jackie sits on the step. Then, remembering who she is, out of habit and manners, she stands back up with a wince, offering Regina her seat.

"Just scoot over," Regina says. "We can both fit."

Jackie struggles to sit back down, which surprises Regina. Down is easy. It's up that's the problem. "You all right?" Regina squeezes in next to Jackie on the surprisingly generous and almost comfortable step.

"I'm all right." Jackie scans the horizon with a satisfied look. "You know I love a pretty mess." She gives Regina the same pleased look. "Tell me a long story."

"Aren't you sick of my voice?"

"I love your voice. The Halloween Party. You tell that one different every time."

October 1988

Jackie stands in front of the bureau mirror scowling at the bra she's wearing over her binder. She reaches in the cups, pulls out tennis balls, and throws them on the bed.

"I have to agree, not the look I was after." Regina snaps her fingers. "I've got just the thing." She rushes out of the bedroom

137

and returns holding two skeins of navy blue yarn. She stuffs each cup of Jackie's bra with a ball of yarn, which Jackie allows without giving up her frown. Regina stands back. "Let's see it with the dress on."

"Looks like real tits." Jackie stands sideways taking in the effect with a less pronounced frown. "I'm scary in drag. I wouldn't flirt with me."

"You'd flirt with anyone in a dress." Regina sits on the bed. "Sure you want to do this?"

"Yes." Jackie wants to do this. Damn if she knows why. Forty and fifty didn't faze her, but sixty—sixty seems like a corner she should turn with an attitude that includes revisiting clothing she was forced to wear in childhood. This one time. Maybe she wants to see what all the fuss over dressing like a girl was about. Be in Regina's skin for an evening. People assign so much meaning to clothes and hair and all the rest. Damn if she'll give up her binder, even for one night, though.

Regina gathers what they need from the closet, the bathroom, and her lingerie drawer. Between the Salvation Army and Goodwill, Lynn and Regina spent days looking for the right dress. Finally, their mother remembered something she couldn't bear to throw away.

At eighty-four, with her husband dead for three years, Mrs. LaFleche asked no questions about why Jackie suddenly wanted to borrow a dress. She decided long ago that she didn't have to like "Regina's situation" to accept it. Regina's mother lives alone now and is happy enough to have Jackie and Regina visit once a week and take her grocery shopping.

"You'll be glad to know your costume cost us nothing." Regina is trying to make up for the fact that she spent a small fortune on this party.

Despite Regina's insistence that bringing home the bacon is both their responsibilities, Jackie hears what she always hears when their tight budget is brought up in any way. She hears that she has failed to make and save enough for them to buy a house.

"It's going to be fun." Regina hands the blue dress patterned with tiny violets to Jackie. "This is actually kind of pretty."

The fabric has a luxurious silky feel Jackie didn't expect. She holds the dress away from her body as if she's got a rat by the tail. It's the kind of material she likes to rub up against when it's on Regina's body. She looks down at her hairy legs. "I'm not wearing a garter belt."

The party, unknown to their guests, is in part a celebration of their thirtieth anniversary. It has been thirty-three years this fall since they first met at that bar in Manhattan. Regina insists they cut off a few in recognition of their shaky beginnings.

"Nobody wears garter belts anymore." Regina laughs. She wears an apron over her dress, so it won't get dirty while she does up Jackie. She pulls tan support hose out of the apron's pocket. "*Voila.* Panty hose. You can wear them under your boxers."

Jackie pulls the dress over her head as she's seen Regina do thousands of times. Her head gets stuck.

"You have to unzip it." Regina tugs at the zipper as Jackie tries to poke her head through the small neck hole, fighting blindly with the dress, trying to find an armhole.

"Motherfucker!" Jackie says.

"Be still," Regina steps back so she doesn't get whacked by one of Jackie's flailing arms. Jackie holds her breath while Regina sunzips. "Now raise your arms." Regina pulls the dress off over Jackie's head. "I thought we agreed you wouldn't use that word."

"Motherfucker? I agreed to save it for extreme circumstances."

Once Regina has gotten all of Jackie's body parts through the correct holes, the dress is on, and the battle of the panty hose has been won, Regina turns Jackie around so she can see herself in the mirror. "Lynn was so right: high neck, skirt below the knee. Perfect."

Jackie's not convinced. "Republican from the neck down. Aging butch, small *d* democrat from the neck up. The hair's wrong." Jackie's vanity is her dark hair, which doesn't have a strand of gray.

"I have plans. Barbara is only three years older, but she has more wrinkles. Turning your crowning glory white is the easy part."

"Didn't I used to be thin?" Jackie doesn't expect and doesn't get an answer. "How many people did you invite to this party?"

"I told Bo and Yvonne they could invite whoever they wanted." Regina shrugs. "What could I do? Bo's bringing the beer."

"We'll get shut down by nine o'clock when Mr. 'whores, whores, whores' on the third floor calls the cops."

Jackie and Regina live in a fourth-floor walk-up in a tenement block in the center of Holyoke not far from the homes where they grew up and only a half mile from the factory where Jackie has worked for the last few years. When they first moved to this block, Regina was in her Prince phase and had played "Soft and Wet" over and over until the guy below them banged on his ceiling with a broom and shouted in his Italian accent, "Who-ores, who-ores, who-ores."

Regina dismisses Jackie's concern with a flap of her hand. "Our party will have plenty of competition. Kids will be running all over the building tonight. I invited Mr. and Mrs. Whores. Never mind that look. He won't come. She might show up. Anyway, that incident was years ago. Mrs. . . ." Regina stops to think. "What *is* their last name? Vahillio? I've called her 'Ro' for years."

"Says Vecchio on the mailbox. You call her Ro?"

"You've heard me say hello to her. Her name is Rosemary. We have our little talks on the stairs. I've seen you and Mr. Vecchio grunt at each other from time to time."

"I tend to grunt at people who conflate lesbian and whore. Not that I have a problem with either." Jackie feels a festive spirit coming on despite the hundred bucks Regina spent on this party. "Any other surprise guests I should know about? You invite Sappho?"

"No. You can't stand her. Her name is Alisa. She's been Alisa who volunteers with me at The West Street Shelter, not Alisa from Daughters of Sappho, for years now."

A knock at the door is followed by Bo's baritone. "Make yourselves decent. Where you want the cooler?"

"Put it in the kitchen, please," Regina hollers back. "Is

140

Yvonne with you?"

"With the best jerk chicken this side of Kingston." Yvonne is out of breath from climbing the stairs. "Where else would I be?"

"Put that in the kitchen, too, please," Regina says. "Wait till you see what we've done with Jackie."

"Wait till you see what we've done with Yvonne." Bo, pushing a cooler on wheels that squeak, is even more out of breath than Yvonne.

Jackie picks up an aerosol bottle of spray-on hair coloring Regina has placed on the bureau. She reads from the can, "Moon Glow."

"Cheaper than a wig. Happy Anniversary. Happy Halloween." Regina hands Jackie a towel. "Cover your face."

Bo walks in from the kitchen. "Jesus, god, yes, cover your face. Never thought I'd see this." She sits on the bed, her hands flat on her wide thighs and explodes with laughter. She's a tank of a woman, low to the ground, wide, slow, strong, likely to go directly for what she's aiming at. Bo would usually wear a vest, slacks, and spit-shined loafers sans socks to a party. In deference to Halloween she's wearing her Bob Marley T-shirt and carrying a huge cigar with *Jamaican Gold* written with a gold glitter pen down its length.

Yvonne, five foot nine in sandals and a toga with her braided hair piled high on her head, picks up the copy of *Time* magazine with Barbara Bush and Kitty Dukakis on the cover. She looks from the picture to Jackie and gives Regina a thumbs-up before she puts the magazine back on the bureau and runs her fingers through Jackie's slicked-back hair, pulling it straight up. "It's actually pretty long in front," she says, considering the possibilities. "You know I'm always interested in transformation, anything to do with gender." She lets go of Jackie's hair and pulls her head back. "I can see it. Yes. This is going to be good, Regina."

"Even better because more and more often Jackie is taken for being a man." Bo laughs.

141

"This is true. And less and less often you are taken for being a woman, my handsome husband." Yvonne nods her approval at them both.

Regina picks up the hem of Yvonne's tunic, remembering visiting Yvonne in DC when she was in med school, Yvonne coming back for a few days, accompanying Regina to a night class, Bo and Yvonne's experiment with non-monogamy, the predictably bad results, the rules around what Yvonne called *nonexclusivity* that made the Geneva Convention seem simplistic.

"Sappho." Regina looks at the twist of hair piled on top of Yvonne's head. Leave it to Yvonne to figure out how to leave her buff sixty-year-old arms bare.

Yvonne and Regina still have conversations about the ethics of playing at seduction that amuse Bo and irritate Jackie. Bo has never had a girlfriend that Jackie has found more attractive and flirted with less than Yvonne. It's not that Jackie and Yvonne don't tease each other in various ways. But Bo's and Yvonne's relationship was tentative years after Regina and Jackie became a stable couple. Even play flirting seemed like a bad idea in the early years. Now Jackie and Yvonne are not in the habit.

Regina often strains to control her envy of Yvonne, who is not only beautiful but a doctor. Now Regina smiles, proud to have a friend who transforms a white sheet into something lovely with only drapes, tucks, and a few pins.

Bo runs her hand down one of her extended dreadlocks. "You got nothing to say about my pretty hair?" she asks Jackie, who is busy staring at Yvonne as Sappho. Bo's own dreads are gray and barely reach her shoulders. She has added rainbow-colored extensions.

"You've insulted our hosts with your rude laughing." Yvonne sits next to Bo, resting a hand on Bo's thigh. "They're not speaking to you."

"You may have stolen this one's voice. Stop staring." Regina slaps Jackie's arm. "That is a great costume, Yvonne."

"Creative," Jackie agrees. She turns to Bo. "A T-shirt, hair extensions, and a cheap cigar? Now that is a lazy costume," she says with envy. "You going to sing 'I Shot the Sheriff'?"

"In a roomful of white people?" Bo laughs and considers. "After a few beers, I might sing 'One Love.'"

"Joy and Lee," Yvonne checks her makeup in the bureau mirror, "will be interested to know you think of them as white."

"May I yank my friends' chains in peace? I must get myself a beer so I can toast the womanly charms of you three." Bo stands. "While my beautiful wife was getting into her costume, I tried to explain the drama that happened in The Daughters of Sappho while she was off becoming the world's best doctor."

"Daughters of Sappho, now there was a bag of trouble," Jackie says.

Regina puts her hands on both hips and gives Bo a face full of attitude. "Do we want to discuss that era? Maybe go a few years back while we're at it?" Regina winks at Yvonne.

Yvonne grins. "As I understand it, a *kundalini* consciousness-raising group in the late sixties, early seventies that these two walked away from, called 'The Daughters of Sappho?' I can only imagine what they were walking toward. I am all ears."

"No, no, no. Sorry I brought it up." Bo raises both hands in a gesture of surrender. "My lady knows enough. We played it by ear in those days."

"Emancipate yourself from mental slavery," Yvonne sings Marley, almost in tune.

"And you, Jackie," Regina says. "You want to talk about those early days? No? Good."

Regina and Yvonne work on Jackie's hair and her costume. When they're done tugging, painting, and fouling the room with aerosol products, Yvonne stands back. "Yes, Jackie, your woman is a genius. Look in the mirror." She puts down the blow-dryer.

"Good helmet hair in the front," Regina says." "Can't do anything about the shaved back."

Jackie sees her mascara-covered eyelashes, pancake makeup, and painted mouth. She touches the pearls Regina has hung around her neck. "Be a good time to rob a bank."

"Mrs. Bush has a bit of Ma Barker in her," Yvonne says.

"I always thought of Barbara Bush as a butch in drag." Regina pins a name tag that reads Mrs. George Herbert Walker Bush to Jackie's bodice.

"You're prettier than Nancy Reagan." Yvonne pins the name tag on Regina. "But the hair's right. You're the same size."

"Not much of a stretch," Regina says. She and Mrs. Reagan are both thin-faced and slender-hipped, with small breasts and frosted gray-brown hair. "People always comment on how much we look alike." It irritates her every time.

Bo appears with a Kodak Instamatic and four Heinekens. "Let's get this party started."

In the living room Regina sits on Jackie's lap. "We should have dressed you as Ronald," she says, putting a hand on Jackie's knee, and inching it upward. "You could have called me 'Mommy' all night."

Jackie grabs Regina around the waist and kisses her. Regina kisses her back before pushing away. "You'll ruin our makeup."

"This is why we need a camcorder," Bo says. "Proof of what the old butch can do in a dress."

Mr. and Mrs. Vecchio, dressed in old bed sheets as twin Holy Ghosts, are the first guests to arrive. By his third Pumpkin Ale, Mr. Whores has abandoned his holey sheet and sits in the kitchen in his impeccably ironed dress shirt and Dickies work pants answering the intercom with a mild "Boo," and buzzing up people when Regina gives him the nod to do so. The block is awash in costumed kids, ghouls, and princesses from neighboring tenement buildings, knocking on every door, taking advantage of so many households to loot. Mrs. Vecchio volunteers to hand out mini candy bars.

Regina's friend Jaime shows up with a red star on her forehead and a red cape over her shoulders. Regina has no idea who Jaime is pretending to be, but Carl, a man in a catsuit, calls, "Mortification" from the couch as he covers the eyes of his boyfriend, Lou. "Don't look, Sweetie. Another Wonder Woman."

"Oh, let him look." Jaime points to her jeans and Doc

Martens. "We'll be a makeover. I'll be the 'before' Wonder Woman. Lou can be the 'after.'"

Lou is fully decked out, including bustier, hot pants, and tights under his high red boots. He clicks his wide indestructible bracelets in greeting. "Twins," he says happily.

Jaime hugs Regina. "I hope it's all right I brought a date." She gestures to the tall, athletic-looking woman standing next to her.

"Welcome," Regina says. Jaime's date is wearing a store-bought Kitty Dukakis mask and what looks like a ribbon borrowed from a Girl Scout uniform slanted across her chest with a NOW button, a Rainbow Coalition button, a Jewish star, and an AA pamphlet pinned to it.

Regina points to the Nancy Reagan name tag on her own dress. "Well, this could be awkward. My girlfriend is Barbara Bush. You're outnumbered." Regina tilts her head. "Alisa?"

Kitty Dukakis removes her mask. "Regina?"

"Of course, you two know each other from the shelter." Jaime spots Jackie and squeals, "Oh Jesus, Jackie's in a dress? Catch up for a minute. I'll be right back."

By eleven most of Jackie's, Regina's, Bo's and Yvonne's friends, all Jackie's coworkers from the mill, and Regina's workmates from Big Y Supermarket have gone home.

Bo and Yvonne, Jackie and Regina, and Lynn who just moved back from Vegas with her husband, Fred, sit with the leftover chips, dips, and candy corn in the living room. To Jackie and Regina's amazement, the Vecchios are huddled on one end of the couch holding hands.

Jackie and Bo sit on the other end of the couch talking about the winter Olympics. They spent three weeks in front of the TV together watching the games last February. Bo takes every opportunity to bring up the Jamaican bobsled team who, she contends, will medal in '92. "I should have come as Devon Harris," she says. "Put my Jamaican flag to good use." She considers this. "Not sure I could hack tights or whatever they wear instead of proper pants."

145

"I'd trade my soul for proper pants right now," Jackie says. "I'm starting to feel like that cross-dressing psycho in Hitchcock."

"The nurse or Bates? He had more than one cross-dressing psycho, didn't he? The man's obsessed." Bo looks around the living room, feeling beer-induced nostalgia. "Remember the day we moved you and Regina? How empty this place was?"

"I remember." Jackie knows by the smirk on her face that Bo is remembering finding Jackie and Regina half naked on the kitchen floor. Bo had been driving the truck with the furniture in it and had arrived earlier than expected.

"On cracked linoleum." Bo raises her glass. "Now that is the way to christen a new home."

"Financial planner." Jackie huffs and grabs a fistful of her dress, trying to get at the panty hose beneath that is pinching her crotch.

"So now we're going to talk about Alisa, fast cars, and big jobs? And we were having such a pleasant conversation. You want to talk or fight with your underwear?"

"Chivas," Jackie says.

"Now you're being sensible." Bo goes to the kitchen and comes back with a bottle. She pours them each a shot. They sit back and sip the whiskey. "You're still jealous because Alisa opened your woman's root chakra in the old days," Bo says, lowering her voice when Jackie gives her a look. "Long time ago. Let go of that shit. You will forgive me for reminding you that it took that whole mess to help you understand that open relationships seem less desirable when it's your girlfriend and not you involved in the opening. Oh please, go ahead, put your hands over your eyes. We've been friends since before you knew Regina. You nap. I'll keep talking like one of those subliminal tapes supposed to help you learn a new language. Why do you act like Regina is the only jealous one?"

"You know we're in the middle of a party?" Jackie asks, her hand still covering her eyes.

"Half-drunk party talk. The best kind. You ever ask yourself why you keep so many talkers so close?" Bo stops speaking to sip the Chivas. "You're still not sure what happened between Regina and Alisa? You want to break open that conversation? Open your mouth. Ask. Old business." Bo shakes her head. "Be prepared for an answer you don't want." She stops talking in case Jackie has something to say. "And maybe some questions you don't want asked."

Jackie raises her glass. "To sleeping dogs."

Lynn's husband Fred, dressed as Madonna, pulls off his cone-shaped breasts and asks loudly, "What are you two whispering about over there?" He places the cones on the coffee table next to the clip-on earrings, pearls, bra, and balled yarn Jackie has already discarded. He looks pointedly at Jackie's knees which are stretching the hem line of Barbara Bush's dress as far apart as the fabric allows. "To sitting like a lady." Fred lifts his glass and smiles good-naturedly enough, but there is something sneering in the way he says it.

"Fred," Lynn warns. Chairs have been brought in from the kitchen. She's sitting on one of them dressed as The Bride of Dracula in a torn wedding gown. "You're drunk. Behave." She has marks on her neck, drawn with eyeliner and lipstick, meant to represent bites. She tucked her fangs in her purse hours ago.

Jackie is pleasantly drunk herself. She watches Fred who shakes his head and laughs derisively. Jackie thinks that sober Fred likes to play at being a gentleman, but drunk he's just a guy with a big mouth.

"What is it you laugh at?" Mr. Vecchio, who has been quietly observing for most of the party, asks Fred.

"Women." Fred nods knowingly at the only other man in the room. He throws his hands in the air. "Usually I like 'em even more when I'm drunk."

"We like you less." Lynn's eyes are ringed in kohl, which makes her look crazed.

Fred downs another shot. "The guy in the Wonder Woman getup had nicer legs than you, Lynn." It takes him a minute to understand that Lynn is frowning at him. "What?" He looks around the room. "Tough crowd. It's Halloween. I was a female impersonator myself tonight." He looks at Jackie. "These girls can't take a joke." He hooks his thumb over his shoulder as if females, not the wall, are behind him.

"Women," Jackie corrects. She pushes her hair straight back from her forehead. When she takes her hand away there's a film of white on her fingers. She and Fred stare at each other. Unlike her behavior toward most of Lynn's men, Jackie has never attempted to like Fred for Lynn's sake. Fred and Lynn have been married two months. Jackie gives them until Christmas. If she can hurry the process along, so be it.

Regina gets off her chair to sit on the arm of the couch near Jackie. She puts a hand on Jackie's shoulder and whispers, "Let him make an ass of himself. He doesn't need any help from you." She passes Jackie an orange and black napkin to wipe her hand.

"Wait a minute. Where's the one with the nice figure? Not Cleopatra here. The other shapely gal." Fred winks at Yvonne, seated in an armchair matching the one he sits in. No one answers. Fred keeps talking, "I know she's like the rest of you, but I like a big-boned girl." He snaps his fingers and stands. "Alisa." Standing is more than he can manage. He sits back down.

"You know the man is about to say, 'What a waste she's gay,'" Bo says.

"We're going home." Lynn holds out a palm. "Hand over the car keys."

"We got Bush's wife and what's his name's wife. Come on, ladies. Let's hear why we should vote for your husbands." He looks Bo up and down. "Are you anybody?"

"I'm Shirley Chisholm." Bo shakes her dreads and points to Bob Marley's face on her shirt.

"I wondered who you were. Go ahead, Shirley. Why should we vote for your husband?"

"You don't know who Shirley Chisholm is?" Lynn hands Fred his jacket. "Of course you don't."

"Jessie Jackson's wife?" Fred gives Lynn a fake pout. "Married two months and already giving me the stink eye." He hunkers into the armchair and slaps his knee. "Who's the one that caused all the trouble? Malcom X? Bet his wife doesn't lead him around by the nose."

Yvonne folds her arms over her chest. "Malcom was assassinated in '65."

"You don't say?" Fred points his chin at Bo. "Where's he . . . she from?"

"Holyoke, Massachusetts," Yvonne answers stone-faced. "Where are you from?"

"You know what I mean. Could be a lotta things. Korean even." Fred folds the coat Lynn threw at him on his lap. "I fought in Korea."

"I am so sorry." Lynn glares at him. "You cannot imagine how sorry I am."

"Pretty soon—" Bo holds up a clenched fist and abruptly lets her fingers fly open "—somebody may explode. You might want to get your Fred gone before that happens, Lynn."

"Come on." Jackie takes his arm and tries to hoist Fred up out of the chair.

"I can't ask where her people are from?" Fred resists, looking around, appealing for reason.

"Thanks, Jackie." Lynn shrugs on her coat. "I'd sneak out alone. But then you'd be stuck with him."

"The ladies want to tell us what's what in this election," Fred insists.

"The ladies are not interested." Mr. Vecchio stands. "You and I will speak of this downstairs." He looks at his wife. "Come, Rosemary. Please."

Mrs. Vecchio, sober as a judge, needs a moment to comprehend that her husband is trying to help get Fred out the door. She gathers their holey sheets. "Thank you for inviting us. We had a wonderful time."

"Yes, thank you." Alcohol helps the neighborly feeling that rushes through Mr. Vecchio make it to his mouth. "I want to

149

say . . . I wasn't the good neighbor when you moved in . . ." He looks at the floor, saying, "Yes," agreeing with himself. He steps toward Regina and takes her hand. "An apology." He bows slightly toward Jackie. "We do not get invited so often. My wife has not had a night out." He lets go of Regina's hand. "Too long." He turns to Fred. "A cup of coffee with the wives, Fred?"

Mrs. Vecchio leans in to whisper to Lynn, "Come, dear."

Lynn links arms with Rosemary. "I think I'm in love with both you and your husband, Mrs. Vecchio."

"Then you must call me Ro."

Fred looks around the room, uncertain. "The party's breaking up?"

"Time to go," Mr. Vecchio says. "These ladies invite us to their home, we eat their food, drink their beer. We try not to offend. You understand?"

"Sure." Fred looks for Lynn, already out the door arm in arm with Ro. He throws an arm over Mr. Vecchio's shoulder. "Sure."

Regina is bent over the sink elbow deep in dishwater. Her face is framed in a halo of escaped hair. The hairspray she used on herself and Jackie is failing them both. She turns to smile at Jackie, who is stripped down to boxers and a sleeveless T-shirt and carrying a tray loaded with glasses and beer bottles.

"Marlon Brando," Regina says.

"Yah? Is it the spray-painted hair?" Jackie's hair is a slick of white running straight back from her forehead. "You want to think of me as Brando—" she pecks the back of Regina's head "—be my guest."

"It's the wife-beater T-shirt and the arms." Regina touches a finger to Jackie's bare bicep, leaving soap bubbles. "And the full lips. And those lashes don't hurt." She turns back to her dishes.

Jackie puts the tray on the counter. "Thirty years." Jackie circles Regina's waist from behind. "Come to bed. I'll clean all of this up tomorrow."

"Thanks for helping with Fred, dressing up, all of it," Regina says. "You only agreed to the party because I wanted it."

They both understand that Jackie's not making a fuss about Alisa showing up is one of the things that Regina is thankful for.

Regina kisses Jackie's cheek without taking her hands out of the water. "Roaches."

"The food is put away. Let the roaches drown in beer," Jackie says.

Regina sighs, and the back of her head falls against Jackie's chest. She turns to embrace Jackie. Dishwater drips down her elbows, hitting Jackie's ass and the floor.

Jackie pulls her in abruptly for a kiss, aware that the booze, rubbing up against silk all night, and Alisa's cameo appearance are somehow inspiring her to be a little rougher than normal. She pulls Regina closer. Stripped down to her slip, Regina pushes her silk-stockinged leg against Jackie's crotch.

Jackie would love to hoist Regina up on the counter and yank down her panty hose. She's not sure if it's the booze making her think she can still manage it.

Regina puts both hands on Jackie's chest to push her away. "Help me rinse the dishes and wipe down the counters and I'm all yours."

Jackie dumps the dregs from the beer bottles down the drain and starts on the dishes.

Regina, quick with a dishrag, sweeps crumbs into the sink. She likes parading around in her new slip and nylons. She has not felt this sexy in a while. Earlier Alisa had whispered in her ear, "You're hotter than ever." Regina picks up a half-empty bag of candy corn. "Will we eat this? Or will it just attract vermin?"

"Garbage," Jackie says.

When they are finally under the covers, Jackie takes Regina's face in her hands. She traces the wrinkles deepening around her lover's eyes and whispers, "Desire in the kinks of our skin." It's an unlikely thing for her to say and Jackie is embarrassed.

Regina presses closer.

Jackie washed the makeup off her face halfway through the party, but underestimated the staying power of mascara, some of which clings to her lashes and exaggerates their length. How Regina loves Jackie's long lashes, the vulnerability and unlikeliness of them. She kisses first one eye and then the other. Regina has never told Jackie how much those lashes move her. It would make Jackie uncomfortable. It's enough that Regina gets to love them. She rolls onto her back laughing and pulls Jackie on top. They move against each other, their rhythm a long-practiced dance. They are both lost to the motion when Jackie lets out a shivering groan that could be mistaken for pain. Regina, inspired, does not stop moving until her own familiar series of "Yes, yes, yes," rushes out.

"You okay, baby?" Jackie collapses on top of Regina, worries her weight is too much, and rolls to her side. She strokes the side of Regina's face and traces a finger around the hard seed of Regina's nipple. Regina enjoys the attention while she catches her breath.

The bed linen is streaked with Regina's makeup and Jackie's hair goop. "Your pillowcase is wearing our costumes," Jackie says.

Regina twists to look at the pillowcase. "Showers," she says.

Later, showered, lying on clean sheets reading *The Bonfire of the Vanities*, Jackie puts the book down to watch Regina towel dry her hair.

"Can you believe Lynn married that idiot?" Regina slips in next to Jackie.

"Booze and Vegas. She should never have taken a job in a casino."

"She shouldn't drink if there's an eligible man in the building." Regina shivers. "Fred."

"Some jerks hide who they are at first." Jackie picks up the book.

"Fred thinks everything he does is wonderful. Why would he hide any of it?"

"So Lynn would have sex with him." Jackie flips the pages trying to find her place.

"Did we do that?"

"Hide who we were when we first met?" Jackie closes the book. "Sure, I had no idea you would charm the Vecchios into liking us. Charmed me into fidelity."

"Fidelity? You do remember I was there?" Regina raises herself up on an elbow and narrows her eyes at Jackie. She lowers herself back onto Jackie's shoulder, trying to regain the easy, after-sex glow. "As far as putting a spell on the neighbors, I've been massaging the Vecchios with flattery and chitchat for years." Regina rests a hand on Jackie's slight swell of belly.

Jackie changes the subject. "I wore those pumps for an hour and my feet are killing me." She flexes her feet and stretches her toes. "How do you do it?"

"Asks the woman who wears a binder all day." Regina sits up. "I didn't invite Alisa."

Jackie sits up, too. "Did she know the party was at our place?"

"No idea." The irritation rises in Regina's voice. The lengths of their legs touch from hip to ankle. Regina's leg stiffens a little. Jackie moves her leg slightly away.

Neither of them want to be angry after such good sex. But the same long-standing resentments—that Regina should have been enough from day one and that Jackie was asked to settle down before she was ready—poke through the sex, the anniversary, the successful party, and the alcohol.

They sit up against the headboard silently until Regina says, "I didn't get the promotion at the store. Why do I always mouth off to my superiors?"

"Because they're so often not superior." Jackie touches Regina's arm. "I'm sorry. You deserved that promotion."

"It was only about fifty cents an hour. I'm still mad about having my Saint Ann's Scholarship taken away because some homophobe complained I had a 'girlfriend.'" Regina makes air quotes around girlfriend.

"1966?" Jackie asks.

"'65." Regina feels disgust for her gutsy, stupid younger self for sitting opposite the church lady members of the scholarship committee and answering "lovers" when asked "the nature" of her relationship with Jackie.

"Prideful anger," Regina says, remembering. "Still closeted to some of my friends and family, I came out to those assholes."

"What a firecracker you were. Are." Jackie tries to smile but thoughts of Alisa buzz in the background like static from an off-air TV station. "Sorry I've been so bad at bringing home the bacon," she says to stop herself from mentioning Alisa, and because apologies over money come easily to her.

"I've made less over the years than you have." Regina doesn't mention spending. She could mention the sums Jackie has lost from time to time gambling. Gambling hasn't been a problem lately, not that Regina is aware of. She prefers the high road for now. If they steer away from Regina's taste for designer shoes and Jackie's taste for seven-card stud, lamenting their financial situation is a safe way to stay clear of the more immediately dangerous subject at hand.

Regina wants to say something about Jackie not having to play the breadwinning husband. But that would be hostile, too close to Regina's old accusations of Jackie "acting like a man" when Jackie cheated. For all Jackie and Alisa's dislike of each other, Regina can't help but notice that in the old days they shared a common language of "open relationship."

"Be nice to have two cars in running order at the same time," Jackie says. The only conversation she had with Alisa all night consisted of the woman bragging about her cars, a brand-new Audi sedan and an older model Ford F Series pickup truck. Jackie admitted she'd kill for the truck and gave her condolences that the Audi hadn't helped Alisa find a girlfriend.

"We were happy fifteen minutes ago. Now there's a pall hanging over us." Regina hears the criticism in her voice and tries to pull back. "Let's not give her the power to take us backward."

"A pall?" Jackie's not sure why, but the word bugs her. "How did I get accused of giving Alisa anything? It sucks being poor," she says, knowing Regina hates being called poor.

"We're not poor." Regina juts out her chin. "Are you happy I said that on cue? Compared to who?" She's daring Jackie to say Alisa's name again.

"Some of our friends."

Regina fluffs up the pillow and slides down to lie on her back. She looks up at the ceiling. Jackie holds her book open in front of her without reading.

After a minute, Regina says, "We're not as poor as most of the world."

Jackie doesn't answer. They have both deliberated on how fortunate they are compared to many. There's no real disagreement. They both believe that the system is rigged, that lack of opportunity and outright discrimination keep poor people poor, keep people earning low incomes stuck in low-income jobs. Still, they blame themselves for not pushing harder, for having too little ambition.

Regina looks at Jackie leaning back against the headboard with a hand over her eyes. She wishes she could just stop being angry at Jackie once and for all. She likes how Jackie behaves in the world most of the time. She conjures up images of Jackie sneaking the eviction-worthy terrier that belongs to the old couple upstairs out for a walk after the old man broke his foot, and Jackie waiting at the bus stop with the Henderson's first-grader when he was getting bullied. Jackie who thinks of these acts not as charity or even kindness, but as things that need to get done.

Jackie's eyes pop open. "Somebody's jiggling the door handle." She jumps out of bed and pulls on a sweatshirt and jeans.

"I hear it." Regina grabs her robe as Jackie grabs the baseball bat they keep in the corner. Last year drunk teenagers from the next block broke into the Vecchios' apartment on Halloween.

"Stay by the phone." In her haste, Jackie has forgotten that their phone receiver is not tethered to the base.

Regina picks up the mobile receiver and follows Jackie out

155

of the bedroom.

"Who's there?" Jackie hollers at the door, her bat in the air over her right shoulder.

The door swings open. "It's me," Lynn says.

"Don't shoot," Regina yells, meaning don't swing the bat.

"Motherfucker." Jackie lowers the bat and leans on it to catch her breath. "Tell me Fred's not behind you."

"Motherfucker." Regina collapses onto the couch.

"I'm such a loser." Lynn, still in her Bride of Dracula costume, puts down her suitcase and hugs a paper bag with a pillow sticking out the top. "Fred's passed out. I left him a good-bye note. You gave me a key. Remember?" She holds it up. "I'm sorry." Lynn falls onto the couch next to Regina. "Three-time loser. I'm done drinking. Forever." She throws her hands over her face. "I just want to hide."

"Two-time loser. You didn't marry the last one." Regina gathers her weeping sister in her arms and cries with her. "Don't cry. No, do cry. Cry all you want."

Jackie squeezes Lynn's shoulder. "Stay here. It'll keep me off the couch."

"Thanks," Lynn coughs out.

Regina's eyes slide toward the bedroom, asking Jackie to make herself scarce so she can talk to Lynn in private.

"I'll get the sheets," Jackie says.

"It's over," Regina says and rocks Lynn who smells of perspiration and beer. "New leaf." Regina wonders how much effort it's going to take to fend off Fred.

"Sixty years old and still falling for motherfuckers." Lynn dabs her kohl-streaked cheeks. The hem of her torn wedding gown is filthy.

"You look a fright." Regina tries to grin.

Jackie falls asleep for almost an hour. When she wakes, the sheets for Lynn are next to her on the bed. She pads back to the living room and stands in the doorway, unseen by the sisters, who are still on the couch, drinking something out of mugs. Lynn's face is washed, and she's wearing pajama bottoms and a baggy *Vegas is for Lovers* T-shirt. She looks pale and more defiant than sad. It's almost three o'clock. The sisters speak in low voices. It takes a minute to understand what they're saying. Patience has never been a problem for Jackie. She sees only the back of the couch and Regina's and Lynn's profiles.

Regina says, "I thought age would be more mellow, more forgive and forget. I keep waiting to be comfortably bored."

"Shit." Lynn holds her mug between both hands. "This is the beginning of old-ladyhood, isn't it?" She sits up straight and says earnestly, "We have to dump the bullshit. I dump the Freds. You dump the crap from your past. You and Jackie are never breaking up, so be happy."

"Seriously?" Regina pulls her head back. "You're giving relationship advice and it's 'be happy'?"

"Seriously. My love life is fucked. Always has been. We've established that. My goal is to find my Jackie before I die. The love of your life screwed around. At least she never lied about it. I was there; I remember. You left her, and she screwed around a little more because you said it was over. Now, some bitch shows up that you, not Jackie, had some kind of a thing with that you won't even tell me about!" Lynn's arms fly up. "You got payback. Move on. Oh, don't be mad." Lynn starts crying. "Who else is going to tell you what's what if not your fucked-up sister?"

Regina hands Lynn the tissue box. "You give halfway decent advice for someone who makes such bad decisions. The thing is when you're together this long you hold it all. Everything that's happened, then, now, what may or may not happen in the future, it's all in the mix. You know?"

"No, I don't know. Fuck Fred. Fuck Alisa," Lynn says vehemently. "You've got each other. What's she got?"

"The Audi." Jackie steps into the room.

The sisters turn in unison. "You were eavesdropping," Regina says.

"Waiting for an opening," Jackie says.

"Besides the Audi." Lynn blows her nose for the twentieth time. "I might fuck her for the Audi. I thought Fred was going to hump the hood."

"Fuck Alisa," Jackie says. "Fuck Fred."

"Fuck Fred, fuck Alisa," Regina agrees.

"That's the spirit. Go to bed, you two." Lynn takes the sheets out of Jackie's arms, flaps one open, and starts making up the couch.

As Jackie and Regina climb into bed again Lynn yells, "The Impala's in Fred's name. I wonder if technically I stole it. We were only married two months."

"Shut up, Lynn," Regina yells at their closed door. "You'll wake the Vecchios." She turns on her side and sighs. "Are you sorry," she says, reaching behind to touch Jackie's arm in invitation for Jackie to spoon her, "that I charmed you into fidelity."

Jackie throws a leg over Regina's hip and kisses her shoulder. "I had no idea two women could survive fidelity, never mind love, especially if one of them was me. Not in the world that existed then. I'm still surprised it's possible."

Chapter 8

Saturday, February 18, 2017

"I wish I brought a thermos of coffee. It's getting cold sitting here." Regina's been talking for a long time. "It didn't occur to you not to invite Lynn to stay with us, did it?"

Jackie's been staring out, one hand tucked beneath her thigh and the step of the big machine. She realizes her hand has fallen asleep. She turns her head to ask, "Which time?" before she pulls the hand out from under her.

"You asked me to tell the Halloween party story and you didn't listen." Regina slaps Jackie's forearm.

"Just wanted to hear your voice." Jackie rolls her wrist and puts an arm around Regina.

"Are you cold? Let's go." Regina shrugs off Jackie's arm.

"I heard most of what you said. We did have some good parties." She grins, remembering. "It's nice with the sun on us." She lifts an inch to take the pressure off her butt for a second. "Sitting here reminds me of Gamblers Anonymous."

"Gamblers Anonymous?" Regina frowns. "The bulldozer or the dump reminds you?"

"Just the step. Hard on the ass."

159

"All the more reason to go," Regina says.

"Wait till my backside wakes up. I need my butt in working order to walk."

Regina flaps her gloved hand at Jackie's feet. "Wiggle your toes and circle your ankles."

"I love sitting here." Jackie circles one ankle then the other even though she doesn't think it's going to help her ass. "But I thought I was done with hard metal chairs."

"Your butt's never going to wake up as long as you're sitting on it," Regina says. "Lift up again. Lean forward, put your weight on your thighs. Not too far. Okay, put your legs straight out and squeeze your butt muscles. Get the blood flowing." Regina demonstrates.

"Okay, no more excuses," Regina says when Jackie's exercise routine is over.

"I made sure never to sit on a damn folding chair at our parties," Jackie says.

"Come on, get up. You're stalling."

"I'm not getting up because I don't want to leave yet. I'm happy here."

"Okay, honey. I just worry; it's cold, your bad hip. Grin away. You know I can't resist that grin. We can sit awhile longer if you tell me about Gamblers Anonymous. Then we have to get you home. Warm us up."

September 2008

Jackie doesn't mind that the coffee is cold and the donuts are stale, but she's tired of hard metal hitting her ass every time she sits on a folding chair and waits for the circle in the basement of the Unitarian Society to fill in. She likes the 4:30 Friday meeting because it's always the same couple dozen people who show up for this Gamblers Anonymous group, and she can stop in right after her noon to four shift at the car wash. Also, at eighty, she's not the oldest person here. Eighty-one-year-old twin brothers mention their age every week. Charlie, a kid with metal embellishing his body in unlikely places, takes a seat next to her and stares at her hair. Jackie's regular guy was not at the barber shop this morning, and his stand-in thought that by buzz cut she meant a thirty-second of an inch shy of bald when what she meant was a sixteenth of an inch shy of bald. She stares back, hoping Charlie will speak while he's looking directly at her. Jackie wants to get a look at Charlie's tongue. Larry and Grant, the old twins, swear Charlie has a split tongue. Charlie's a talker. Every week he sits next to Jackie, making comments, looking straight ahead while other people speak from the podium.

Sometimes Charlie speaks from the podium himself. Jackie liked what he said last week about why he comes to meetings. He said his parole officer *suggests* that he come, but he also shows up for the stories. Charlie said he thinks of the twelve steps as a way into stories that are better to listen to than to live.

The meeting hasn't begun, and Jackie is already bored with tonight's topic: "Come to believe that a Power greater than ourselves can restore us to a normal way of thinking and living." She's heard enough GA discussions to know that *normal* and *Greater Power* are flexible ideas, jumping-off conversational points. Still, there's not a word in Step 2 that doesn't grate on her.

She smiles, thinking about how many times she's been stared at without any body modification besides a haircut, pierced ears, and chest binder. The kid thinks she's smiling at him. He smiles back, sticks out his tongue, and holds it out for a good ten seconds. At first it seems to have a deep groove down the middle, then the two sides arch up like a double headed snake.

"Control," Jackie says.

He high-fives her. She lifts a hand to meet his, thinking this is an old-fashioned gesture for a boy with a forked tongue. When he first showed up, Jackie thought Charlie might be female. But he's a boy. Not a boy. Eighteen or twenty. A young man wearing a skirt made of black canvas, the hem covered with

161

fake diamonds that sweep the floor when he walks. Chin stubble. Low voice. Born male, anyway. Probably. Regina insists if Jackie had been born a few generations later she'd be an F-M trans man. Maybe. Jackie doubts it. It's other people who have always been bothered by Jackie's mannishness, her sexuality, her gender, who she's drawn to. It's other people who are bothered that her body doesn't seem to fit who they think she is. She doesn't keep up with what people have to say about the workings and desires of other people's bodies or minds. It's always been other people who wanted to put a name to who she is in the world. Jackie does like that Regina stays informed about this stuff and passes on what information she will. Yvonne calls herself queer, calls Bo her husband. Jackie nods. She wouldn't mind being called husband. But doesn't mind that Regina says "spouse." Queer is not a dirty word anymore; she misses dirty words, but fair enough.

She glances at Charlie. She likes this kid. Maybe TJ will grow up to be like this kid. Jackie is leaning forward with her elbows on her thighs. This last thought, that *her* TJ will grow up to be like Charlie, makes her sit upright in her chair. TJ spending several nights a week at twelve-step programs? This kid Charlie is homeless for all she knows. She grunts at the floor.

Charlie hisses to get her attention. "You having a good time in there? Arguing with yourself?" He taps his own head and grins.

"Recovery," Jackie says, "ruins your poker face."

The circle fills in. Charlie goes to get coffee before the meeting starts.

A big fan of Step 4, Jackie makes a fearless and searching moral inventory regarding Charlie. Nope she doesn't give a shit one way or the other whether he's a boy, girl, man, woman, some combination, something completely different. A Bud and a bowl of kale soup at the Portuguese place with Charlie might be interesting. Be good to hear what's on the kid's mind, remember when she was the young weirdo. Skip the beer. Charlie has shared that he goes to Narcotics Anonymous, too. She doesn't have any judgment about the addictions. No, she hates addictions.

This week's leader, Ted, a guy with shoe-polish hair, walks to the front of the room and taps the mic, the cue for last-minute seat adjustments, throat clearing, and nose blowing.

Charlie hands Jackie a paper cup full of coffee, hikes his skirt, sits, and says, "Suck on this," offering a Lifesaver from the flat of his hand.

Jackie doesn't like his "Suck on this" comment but plucks the Lifesaver from his palm.

"No disrespect." Charlie stares front and center and whispers, "You got a scary face when you don't like something, lady."

They get a patient look from the leader who announces that this is an open meeting and recites the bit about confidentiality. When no one offers to be the first to share, Ted tells the group that one year ago yesterday he lost his vehicle, a 2003 Prius, to a twenty-three-year-old who drove off without even asking for the title. Jackie has heard this story, how it took Ted the better part of a month to find the kid and get the kid to register the Prius in his own name. She thinks about how lucky it is that she never managed to get into a game that allowed cars, houses, or diamond rings to substitute for money. She's lost every cent of ready cash, but never their transportation, never the roof over their heads. Maybe the roof over her own head since Regina has thrown her out several times in the past. Once for gambling.

"This guy was in the military," Charlie whispers. "Who else calls a Prius a vehicle?"

Doreen, one of the few other women in the group, tonight or any night, is speaking when Charlie kicks Jackie's foot. Clearly, Doreen expects Jackie to respond to a remark she's made. Jackie smiles and nods at the pretty woman. Jackie's been daydreaming. Talking isn't required. Witnessing is all that's required. Probably her head was bobbing, and it looked like Jackie was asleep. Maybe she was asleep, caught shirking her witnessing duties. Doreen looks offended.

Jackie says, "Sorry. Hard to witness sometimes."

163

Doreen gives Jackie a kindly look and continues her story, which, Jackie can now testify, is about Doreen's battle with Power Ball.

During the break, Charlie and Jackie stand apart from the larger group milling around on the sidewalk outside the Unitarian Church. Charlie asks if Jackie has a cigarette.

"Still don't smoke. Same as last week and the week before that."

"I'm trying to look more mature." Charlie picks at the black nail polish on his thumbs. "Smoking gives you wrinkles."

Two guys who look like they spend a lot of time in the gym walk toward them. The smaller guy stands close to Charlie. "Hello, Chuckie. Nice skirt."

Charlie sneers. "I gave Rudi ten bucks yesterday."

"And Rudi gave it to me today," the big one says. "You owed ten yesterday, twenty today, forty tomorrow. You see a pattern here?"

"He needs a lesson in compound interest." The small one strains his neck to look at the back of Charlie's skirt. "Don't have the ass for it."

"They came all the way from Gleason Street for a stinking twenty?" Charlie seems to be talking to himself, more discouraged than fearful. "Psychopaths."

"You owe me ten." The big one sounds disappointed. "This boy does not listen. Twenty minus ten equals ten." He tips his Red Sox cap to Jackie, says, "Have a nice meeting, ma'am," and lays a muscled arm across Charlie's shoulder. "Let's take a walk."

Jackie pulls her wallet out of her back pocket and hands the big guy a ten.

The guy bows and takes the bill. "Nice doing business with you."

Jackie and Charlie watch them walk away. Charlie doesn't start shaking until they're out of sight. "Thanks," he says. "I've got money in my backpack inside. I'll pay you back."

"You need to skip the rest of the meeting? Go somewhere to calm down?"

Charlie looks at the sidewalk. "Those people in there. I'm being an asshole when I bitch about them. Anyway, I gotta go back in and eat or I won't be able to sleep tonight."

"Stale pastry is your dinner?"

"My coffee is always half milk."

They stand in silence until the light on the side of the building flicks on and off signaling the second half of the meeting. "My wife's having a surprise party for me after the meeting," Jackie says. "Old people, dykes your grandmother's age mostly. Potluck. Brother-in-law's bringing venison meatballs; they're awful. Wife makes great coconut cake with lemon frosting."

"Potluck means I gotta bring something?"

"You're the conversation starter."

"I like old ladies." Charlie looks much younger when he's trying not to cry on the sidewalk than he does when he's talking out of the side of his mouth in the church basement.

"These women will love you. Might have opinions about whether your skirt matches your chin stubble." Jackie has a bit of chin stubble herself. She scratches it.

"Well, good evening." Regina is placing baby carrots on a vegetable platter when Jackie and Charlie walk through the kitchen door. "Introductions, please?" She raises an eyebrow.

"This is Charlie." Jackie kisses Regina on the cheek. "I invited him to my surprise party."

"I'm a waif from Gamblers Anonymous." Realizing he's blown confidentiality, Charlie says, "Shit, sorry."

Regina feigns a startled look. "I thought you'd taken the yacht to the harbor, Jackie."

Jackie opens the refrigerator door and gives Regina a private look that asks her not to be angry.

Regina gives Jackie, then Charlie, a strained smile. "You must be the surprise in Jackie's surprise party." She turns to Jackie. "Get dressed, please. Our guests will be arriving shortly."

"Charlie's hungry." Jackie closes the refrigerator door.

165

"He can help cut vegetables and sample the appetizers while he tells me his life story."

Jackie comes out from the shower in dress pants, vest, and tie to find Charlie and Regina in the bedroom. Charlie holds a pair of Regina's jeans by the waist in front of him, measuring for length. The pants stop halfway down his shin.

While Charlie takes a shower in the bathroom off the bedroom, Jackie thanks Regina for not giving her hell for bringing Charlie home.

"We haven't had a minute alone," Regina says. "What do you know about this kid?" Jackie shrugs. The washer and dryer are in a little alcove in the bedroom, hooked up in the only place in the house where they fit. Regina holds up Charlie's dirty backpack. "I think this will survive a spin. His clothes and sixty-three dollars in filthy bills are already cycling through."

"But for the grace of god and my Regina." Jackie grins.

"Sometimes I forget what a bullshitter you are." Regina rolls her eyes. "That boy is not sleeping here. Did he tell you his grandmother died, and the state took the house she raised him in for back taxes? That a true story?"

"Maybe. He has pastry for dinner at a twelve-step program most nights."

"Claims to be four months sober. Short-term shelter. Long-term, subsidized room somewhere. Hard to get a job without an address. Yvonne or Bo might be able to help."

"Drafted his short- and long-term future while I was in the shower?" Jackie smiles.

Regina tosses the backpack on top of the sudsy clothes. "We're not taking this kid in."

"My plan is to give him some stew and drive him to the underpass where he's been sleeping." Jackie breathes in Regina's freshly washed hair. "You smell like coconut."

"He knows how to put together a veggie platter." Regina turns to face Jackie. "We've already got one boy sleeping here some weekends. Don't give me those eyes. Enough is enough. That kid could be a serial killer. We couldn't take in a stray

166

cat and survive." Regina allows Jackie to circle her waist. "If it wasn't your birthday, old woman."

"You'd still feed him. You're a fucking angel."

"No one in their right mind thinks I'm an angel. The Chinese Place is always looking for help. Maybe Mac will hire him." Regina smirks. "You're going to have to give him a pair of your boxers." She straightens Jackie's tie.

"They'd be three sizes too big. He can go commando."

"Easy for you to say." Regina gives the tie an aggressive tug. "He's not wearing your jeans. Jesus, my wife is eighty."

"Seventy-nine until six-thirty. Mama waited until the cows were milked."

Regina is pressed against the washing machine and Jackie pressed against her when Charlie comes out of the shower wearing a towel and Regina's jeans that fit like pedal pushers.

Regina whispers in Jackie's ear, "You bet your ass you're driving him to the shelter before it closes," before she pulls away.

The backup alarm on a van sounds. Regina says, "That'll be Lynn. See if she needs help, honey. Let's find you a clean shirt, Charlie."

Charlie chooses one of Jackie's white dress shirts that's huge on him. He rolls the sleeves neatly to the elbows, keeps the top buttons open to expose his hairy chest, and hangs a bolo that's hung on the door handle unworn for years around his neck.

Lynn has a key to the house. Her husband, Silver, pushes Lynn in her wheelchair up the ramp into the house. He's finished pivoting her from wheelchair to La-Z-Boy when Regina and Charlie arrive in the living room.

Silver shakes Jackie's hand. "Welcome to eighty. You are officially an elder."

"Thanks for moving your chair into the living room," Lynn says. "Now I can give orders in comfort." She pulls Jackie into a hug that leaves them both winded. "I forget my own strength." Lynn laughs. "Legs barely work, but my upper body . . ." She pats her arms which are covered in silk. "Okay, lovely young man." Lynn points her chin at Charlie and straightens her skirt to cover her leg braces. "Where did you come from?"

Charlie tells the story of the ten bucks and the thugs, talking fast, careful not to mention GA again. He wants these people to like him, wants their sympathy. He's dying for a smoke, doesn't have a cigarette, and bets Regina doesn't allow smoking in the house. "You do stupid stuff when you're hungry," he says.

"Hungry." Lynn nods knowingly. "I met Silver at a food pantry." She beams at her husband. "He was a volunteer. Still is. It was summer. Regina wheeled me to the back of the line, and we waited for free bags of corn, kale, and tomatoes."

"And I wheeled you out," Silver says on cue.

"Stroke." Lynn speaks directly to Charlie. "Thought my life was over. But Regina, Jackie, and Silver pushed and pulled me back. Silver owned a construction company. He built the ramp to Regina and Jackie's side door."

Yvonne and Bo arrive with their little dog Pee Wee standing on his hind legs, turning in circles as he yaps. They scrutinize the bolo Charlie's wearing and banter about whether it was a present to Jackie from Bo in 1990 when Yvonne was still in New York breaking Bo's heart, or a present from both of them in 1991 after Yvonne had returned to Bo and Massachusetts for good.

Charlie sits on the floor rather than sit in another metal folding chair and tells a story about giving up Big Macs for jars of peanut butter. Jackie wonders if the story is a con, thinking more power to him if giving Yvonne a chance to expound on nutrition, and Lynn a chance to relive her honeymoon with Silver, gets him a shot at getting the two couples to rally around him.

A half hour later there are more guests than seats. Charlie makes a second veggie platter. Yvonne and Regina huddle in the hall to discuss whether they should let Bo try to arrange a surprise Skype call for Jackie with her niece Selma who lives in Georgia. "The test run was a disaster," Yvonne says. Yvonne is wearing a mostly red, twenty-year-old dashiki that originally belonged to Bo who wore it with pants. Yvonne wears the multicolored top over a long black skirt. "Whoever was helping on Selma's end is worse than Bo at this computer nonsense. It took two hours to finally get a good view up Selma's nostrils."

"Old-fashioned phone call." Regina nods her agreement.

"Now, about the young man." Yvonne arranges an escaped piece of wiry gray hair behind her ear. "The shelter closes at ten." She spent much of her career as an MD working with homeless people. "I'll call ahead. They know me. Will he go?"

Regina has no idea if he'll go.

They find Charlie alone in the kitchen looking in a cabinet. He turns when they walk in. "You ran out of chips. My gramma used to make popcorn for company. It's cheap and easy. If you have some, I can make it. Grams called it a celebration in a bowl. You look like her, Regina." He closes the cabinet door. "Just trying to make myself useful."

Yvonne pulls out a chair at the kitchen table. "Sit with us, Charlie?" Yvonne waits. Charlie doesn't sit. "You know the Howell Street Shelter?" she says. "How do you feel about staying there tonight?"

For the first time since he arrived, Charlie has nothing to say.

Regina roots around in the cupboard. She places an old-fashioned looking popcorn popper in the middle of the table. The popper is a silver bowl with four small silver balls for feet and a round silver cover that turns the pot into a silver globe when placed on top. She takes a seat at the table.

"Man, I love this thing." Charlie, still standing, avoids eye contact with either of the women and bends to get a closer look at the popper. "Looks like a tiny spaceship. Either of you ladies could take command of the Starship Enterprise." He laughs and scratches his head. His left foot taps as he speaks. "I saw a *Twilight Zone* episode; a thing like this landed on a lady's kitchen table and a bunch of tiny spacemen poured out. The lady doesn't notice because she's turned away from the camera doing the dishes, looking out the window onto this big prairie, and you only see her back. It's the olden days. The little spacemen swarm around in her kitchen, hiding behind the sugar bowl and shit.

169

One of them knocks over a spoon or something and she turns around. She has a warty green face and antennae. One of the spacemen raises a tiny American flag. Turns out the spacemen are aliens from earth."

He smiles and the women smile back. "Do you have popcorn?" He runs a hand over the popcorn popper. "Can I use it? It's like something I saw on a field trip to the Springfield Museum when I was in high school. At a modern design exhibit. It's from like, the fifties, right?"

"Forties. It was my mother's," Regina says. "What about the shelter tonight?"

He puts a finger on the electric cord, which is thick and covered in gray and black stripes. "I can manage. Am I talking too much? I thought it was okay to talk. I used to talk to Grams. Bossy old lady, real good to me. Big talker. After she died, I learned to keep my mouth shut in front of most people. I thought you wanted me to talk."

"Are you high, Charlie?" Yvonne sits back in her chair and settles her folded hands on her belly like she's prepared to settle in for the long haul if necessary.

"It's fine to talk," Regina leans in. "And it's fine for Yvonne to ask the question."

"My mother used to accuse me of being high when I was like, ten years old. The first time I didn't even know what she was accusing me of."

"We're not accusing. We're asking," Yvonne says. "You have a sponsor?"

Charlie nods, half-turned to the counter so he's at an angle to them, not facing them, not quite turned away. "Some days I don't talk to anyone all day until a meeting. I didn't sleep last night. I'm not stupid. Surprised Jackie even let me know where she lives. I know you don't want me here too long . . . a young guy, an addict, two old women. It's warm enough outside, under the bridge, protected, sort of; you hide behind the girders."

Regina and Yvonne exchange a glance. Charlie stares at the popper and keeps talking. "Last night a guy I didn't know showed up under the bridge. My jeans and hoodie were on top of my pack, easy pickings. He must have stolen them just before dawn, so maybe I did sleep for, like, five minutes. Thanks for these." He looks down at the jeans he's wearing, not feeling bad about being high or lying to the nice ladies about it but feeling bad about taking the Oxy from his gram's cabinet that first time. Why do all old ladies keep drugs from the last century in the back of their cabinets? Charlie is barely high, just high enough so he can relax; maybe he could figure out a few things if he could lean against the girder under the bridge, watch the moon come up in Jackie's clean shirt with his belly full of baby carrots and cheese and guacamole. He should get out of here while he and Jackie are still friends. "Sometimes," he says, patting the jeans that cover his thigh, "it's just not the right occasion for a skirt, you know?" His laugh sounds easy.

The women laugh with him.

The sound of the kids shrieking "surprise!" comes from the front room.

"I have guests to tend to," Regina stands. "Are you high, Charlie?"

"No, I'm just," he turns the pot around, "socially awkward." Until tonight, he'd been sober four months. It feels good and bad at the same time to be just a little high, to know he has six, and only six, more Percocet from 1997 in his back pocket. He left two in the bottle in the back of Jackie and Regina's kitchen shelf where he found them. Two left in the bottle, that's good. That shows restraint.

"Someone will drive you to the shelter before ten." Regina pulls a bag of popcorn, a bottle of oil, and a measuring cup from the cabinet over the stove. She motions at the oil and popcorn. "Half cup of each. No on or off switch. Just plug it in. When there are four seconds between pops unplug it. Watch it like a hawk. Don't burn down my house." She nods at Yvonne.

"Go," Yvonne says. "Greet your guests."

The kids are settling in on the rug in the middle of the living room with a Game Boy when eleven-year-old TJ sniffs the air.

He yells, "Popcorn!" jumps up, weaves around the adults, and runs into the kitchen. Ramon and Pock follow. Thirteen-year-old Oscar is too interested in watching Pee Wee walk on her hind legs to trot off with the rest of the kids.

Charlie is standing in front of the counter answering or avoiding Yvonne's questions when the three kids burst in. They stop in their tracks to stare at him. Yvonne introduces them.

Their awkward "hellos" hang in the air until the popcorn starts to pop, which animates Pock who says, "Charlie's got Jackie's shirt on." She drags a chair from the corner and pushes in next to Yvonne. Ramon takes a seat across the table from them.

"Why you here?" TJ takes a step closer to Charlie. He can't decide if this guy is cool or not cool so he laughs. Since he turned eleven, TJ laughs at anyone who confuses him. "Jackie know you're using that?" Sometimes Jackie lets TJ and Ramon make popcorn. TJ also can't tell if this guy is a kid or an adult, but he knows Charlie is intruding on his territory.

"Manners," Yvonne says.

"Yes, ma'am." TJ has learned that "Yes, ma'am" followed by shutting up is one of the few answers Yvonne will accept from "rude" children.

Pock says, "Is that a tie or a necklace? How come your pants are short? Are you a model?" She competes with the popcorn, which is at full pop, and lifts in her chair to get a better look. "How many earrings does he have?" she asks TJ who still stands a foot away from Charlie.

Yvonne puts up a hand. "And now you are forgetting your manners, young lady."

"Sorry, ma'am," Pock says. "Sorry, Charlie."

"It's okay." Charlie, happy to be rescued from the conversation about future housing and employment, holds up the bolo, "Half tie, half necklace." He points a thumb at the two rods in his right eyebrow. "Way too many piercings. Makes it hard to get modeling gigs." He winks at TJ like TJ's in on the joke. The popcorn slows, Charlie pretends he's not sure what to do, and

TJ pulls the plug. Charlie says, "Thanks, man. You know where there's another bowl?"

Oscar comes in rubbing his eyes. He has his shirt collar grasped in his hand and pulled up covering his chin. He bites the nail of the thumb of the same hand that holds the collar.

"Hey, buddy," Charlie says. "You want some popcorn?" He puts the bowl on the table, pulls out a chair, presses gently on Oscar's shoulders to get him to sit down, and sits next to him, handing Oscar a kitchen towel. "Wipe your hand before you stick it in that bowl, my friend."

Ramon watches the way his brother Oscar grins back at Charlie. Ramon smiles at them both. TJ watches them all. TJ catches Ramon's eye, and wordlessly the boys agree that this guy Charlie is okay.

Yvonne is watching, too. She decides the kids will be okay for a few minutes alone and announces that she's joining the rest of the party and that Charlie and the kids should make another batch of popcorn, bring it into the living room, and, "All of you, be sure to unplug the spaceship."

After Yvonne leaves, Pock says, "Even TJ likes you, Charlie. And TJ doesn't like anyone except Ramon. And sometimes me."

"Shut up, Pockie." TJ laughs. "I never like you."

By the time the popcorn is ready Charlie is tired, tired of being watched, tired of talking, tired of entertaining. He's lost the knack of socializing, especially with kids. Maybe he shouldn't have taken that second Percocet. Especially since he didn't sleep last night. Suddenly the kids are laughing and Charlie's not sure why. One of them says something. Ramon and Pock look at him like he's supposed to answer.

TJ grins. "Told ya he's not gonna tell us why he's here."

Charlie sits on the floor with his back against the wall in a corner of the living room. The kids sit around him.

Ramon passes TJ the Game Boy. "You like that song, 'Control Myself?"

"Who doesn't like Cool J?" Charlie says.

TJ looks up from the game. "What's your favorite song?"

"'I Write Sins Not Tragedies,'" Charlie says.

"That's Cool J?" Ramon asks.

Charlie shakes his head. He needs to nod off, even for a few minutes. "Panic! at the Disco. Want to hear it?" He pretends to pull the iPod stashed in his back pocket out of Oscar's ear.

"Ouch." Oscar joins in the joke and rubs his ear.

Pock scoots closer to Charlie. She likes his sleepy eyes.

Charlie hands Ramon the iPod. Ramon turns it over.

"Sucker, you don't even know how to turn it on," TJ says.

"Go ahead, Little Man." Ramon hands it to TJ. "Find us Cool J."

"Sometimes Ramon calls TJ 'Little Man,'" Pock informs Charlie. "Usually when they're fighting, but they're only play fighting now."

The girl's eyes follow Charlie's every move. But Pock's watching doesn't bother Charlie. He thinks the girl is just curious. A kid crush that will move along. Now TJ, he's a craver. Charlie knows all about being a kid that needs too much. The way TJ watches, the way he craves attention bothers Charlie. Charlie's too tired to give TJ whatever it is he needs.

"Right there." Charlie shows TJ the magic button.

"I know." TJ pushes where he's shown. He frowns.

"You gotta put the earbuds in," Ramon says.

"No shit." TJ sticks the buds in his ears.

Charlie pulls one of the buds out. "Be careful with my fucking iPod." He grins at TJ and gets up off the floor.

The kids watch him walk toward the hall, Pock with her mouth open, not because Charlie said *fucking* but because he said it to a kid in a room full of adults.

The adults only hear the Nina Simone CD that Jackie got as a present.

Jackie and Regina stand in the small archway of the short hall watching their guests.

The party is in full swing. Lynn, who has an iPod at home,

174

helps TJ find Cool J. Lotti is interested in buying an iPod. She convinces TJ to be a gentleman and let her have a turn. Yvonne is amused by all the ways Cool J can't control himself, but skeptical that this is the best music for Pock and the boys. Bo decides that even though Nina Simone is Jackie's favorite, an hour of Nina is enough. Silver ejects the Simone CD. In the living room every chair is taken. Bo and Silver bring in the lawn chairs. Silver sits in Lynn's wheelchair. Lynn regales Papi with stories about her crazy first and second husbands. Pee Wee gets passed around.

"Remember when parties started at 9:30 and we danced all night?" Regina asks Jackie.

"I only danced to the slow ones. I remember when parties started at midnight."

"New York, before my time." Regina snuggles against her. "Sit on the bed with me a minute? I have a present for you."

In the bedroom, Jackie begins to move coats piled on their bed.

Regina waves a hand and sits on top of the pile. "Fuck it."

"When did you start saying fuck so much?"

"1969, same as everyone else." Hip to hip with Jackie, Regina reaches for a small black box on the nightstand. "I was a nice girl before I met you."

Jackie kisses Regina full on the mouth. Regina is not as turned on as her full-bodied response implies. She's on a mission. This is the first time she's wanted to get naked with Jackie for a long while and she wants there to be no mistaking that she's ready, or expects to be, later on tonight. She figures at their age you can't start foreplay too early. She pulls away with a sigh, reaches for the little box, and hands it to Jackie. Jackie turns the box over in her palm and places it on her lap to run her thumb over Regina's bottom lip. She plays with a button on Regina's new dress, a well-made yellow print with a full skirt, a Donna Reed number that fits Regina to a tee.

"Remember when we first met, you could make me come just playing with my nipples?" Regina laughs.

Jackie's smile is serious.

"You think you're going to fuck me in the middle of the party?" Regina says, not really thinking of it as a possibility, just enjoying the question.

"On top of our guests' coats? That would be wrong." Jackie grins.

"Open it, sweetheart," Regina says.

Jackie loves unbuttoning. This dress must have twenty buttons running down the front. This is not a Walmart dress. She's sure that some of the $500 she won two years ago at the last poker game she'll ever play paid for the dress. She unfastens two buttons exposing small pillows of cleavage. So much for Regina's declaration that Jackie will never get one iota of pleasure from the money she won gambling.

Regina giggles. "Not me, the box." Someone is knocking on the bathroom door in the hall. The bathroom also has a door to their bedroom. Regina glances over to be sure that door is closed.

Jackie takes the top of the box off and stares at the ring inside. "This is my Dad's wedding ring." She stares at Regina.

"I had it cleaned and sized to fit you." To her dismay, Regina can't read the contortion of expressions that wash over Jackie's face. Regina holds her breath, afraid she's made a big mistake. Jackie's face softens. Regina exhales. "I thought you'd like it. I should have asked. Oh, I'm a fool. It wasn't mine to alter."

Jackie pushes the ring over her knuckle. Once over the knuckle the ring fits well. She puts her hands on her lap and turns the gold band in circles round and round her finger.

Regina sits quietly and watches until she can't hold back. "You okay, honey?"

"Regina," Jackie says. It's the only word she has. "Regina."

They rock side to side, trying to have a quiet moment as the knocking gets louder.

"That's TJ calling Charlie's name," Jackie says.

"We're all right?" Regina says. "You and me?"

"Thank you." Jackie wipes a tear with her baby finger. "We're

176

all right. The ring is good. Thank you."

"Well, then." Regina hoists herself up. "We better check out that racket."

In the hall seconds later TJ tells them, "Something's wrong with Charlie. He's been in there fifteen minutes."

Jackie reaches above the door frame. "Charlie, answer or I'm unlocking the door and coming in." She bangs once and sticks the key in the lock.

"TJ," Regina says. "Go whisper to Yvonne and Bo that we need them. Whisper," she repeats.

Charlie is slumped on the floor between tub and sink. Jackie and Regina move to give Yvonne and Bo access. Yvonne hikes up her skirt, kneels, and tries to put a hand on his chest.

"Charlie, can you hear me?" Yvonne says. Charlie has fallen forward, doubling up on himself. She holds his chin and pulls up an eyelid. "Call 911, Regina. Get your guests to move their cars so the ambulance can get through." She turns to Jackie. "Help me prop this boy up against the tub." She turns to Bo. "Get my bag from the car." Pee Wee can be heard whining in the living room. "And get someone to take our dog away."

Bo, already halfway to the floor, uses the sink to pull herself back up.

Jackie sits on the side of the tub, working her way to Charlie, thinking maybe she can somehow grab him under his arms and help him sit upright that way. TJ bolts through the door from the bedroom side. "You did good, TJ. Go back to the living room," Jackie says.

But TJ is quick and strong and somehow able to maneuver himself so he's sitting on the floor against the tub holding Charlie from behind before Jackie can even lower herself anywhere near Charlie. TJ props Charlie up, Charlie's back against TJ's chest, TJ's legs splayed around Charlie's hips. Jackie nods and gets up to stand by the door out of the way.

"He needs Narcan, ma'am," TJ says to Yvonne.

Bo, back from the car, opens Yvonne's big blue bag on the sink. Beads of sweat form on Bo's brow. She unbuttons her vest and loosens her tie.

"Do you know what he took?" Yvonne has already pushed up the sleeves of Charlie's mercifully large shirt and found no tracks. "TJ? Jackie?" She unbuttons the shirt and pulls down a shoulder.

TJ shakes his head. "My cousin was like this. Narcan saved him."

Yvonne nods. Bo, who was once an EMT, holds out an airway tube. Yvonne shakes her head saying, "He's breathing on his own, but barely."

"He takes pills," Jackie says. "That's what I've heard him say in meetings."

"Jesus." Papi squeezes into the bathroom, making the sign of the cross, falling to his knees, replacing TJ who does not argue, but leaves when Papi says, "Good boy. Go."

By the time the ambulance pulls up to the ramp, Yvonne has administered the Narcan and taken both Charlie's and Bo's blood pressure. Jackie is standing in the living room next to TJ, thinking how sad it is that an eleven-year-old knows about Narcan. The ambulance lights flash. Charlie is lifted onto a stretcher in the hall. The kids, Lotti, and Papi are all still there. Yvonne and Bo talk to the EMTs. Lynn and Silver are in the kitchen cleaning up, respectfully out of the way. Otherwise, the guests have all left.

Papi tries to calm Oscar, who clings to him and keeps asking if Charlie drowned in the tub like the Marconis' cat. Oscar's and Ramon's mother, whose name is Mary, is a reserved, introverted woman. Mary declined the invitation to the party but came running when she saw the ambulance. She's been here only long enough to understand a young man is in big trouble because of drugs. Mary puts a hand on each of her sons' shoulders.

Lotti says, "These kids shouldn't be watching this, Papi."

Mary gives her mother-in-law a serious look and kisses the top of each of her boys' heads. "They should watch and so should we."

Papi gives his wife a nod of agreement.

It breaks Regina's heart to agree with Mary and Papi.

"Is he going to die?" Ramon asks softly. He was ordered by his father to stay in the living room to watch Oscar and Pock when Papi went to help. No one answers Ramon's question. Ramon takes TJ's hand. The boys haven't held hands in public for years. Ramon would hold hands with Pock too, but Pock's hands are wrapped around Regina's waist in a full body hug.

"He's not gonna die." TJ starts out angry. He looks down at his hand in Ramon's. His voice cracks. "Why you wanna say that?"

Jackie stands close so TJ can lean into her and hide his hot tears in her big side.

Chapter 9

Saturday, February 18, 2017

Regina rummages in her purse for Jackie's pills, trying not to think about all the bad drugs that are on the street now. She takes a breath, glad her loved ones are sober. She watches Jackie who is leaning forward with her elbows on her thighs.

"Your expression keeps changing," Regina says.

Jackie grins. "Remembering the trailer in Florida. How I almost lost you."

"Almost losing me makes you smile?" Regina hands Jackie two pills. "Take these before we walk back. Thinking about fucking Pearl is what put that grin on your face."

"I was thinking about how lucky we are. How lucky I am," Jackie says. "I thought I wasn't supposed to take these without water." She frowns at the pills. "After Florida I figured out how much you meant to me. That's when we really got to know each other."

"Work up some spit." Regina pulls a cough drop out of the pocket of her parka and hands it to Jackie. "1962. Make it or break it year."

"Sixty-three, the year Kennedy was shot." Jackie pops the

180

cough drop in her mouth followed by the pills.

"Right. The year from hell." Regina steadies herself on Jackie's thigh, about to rise.

Jackie swallows hard. "Ibuprofen doesn't work so quickly." She puts a hand on Regina's arm. "You said you wanted us to get out of the house." She exaggerates her grin. "Blues gone. It's good to remember."

"Good to remember Florida?" Regina grimaces. "I remember being outraged at the time, and for years, decades, after."

Jackie sighs. Old regret.

"I remember the outrage now, but I don't feel it." Regina puts her head on Jackie's shoulder. Jackie wiggles to get in a better position to put an arm around Regina's shoulder. "That anger is so time-softened," Regina says, "it feels like it happened to someone else." She tilts her head to look at Jackie. "Or were we completely different people then?" She shakes her head, "Why would you want to remember something so painful?"

"Because it's ours."

"Now if I said something that corny, you'd roll your eyes. Remember whatever you like. I'll be right here watching the birds."

But they look out at the swell of snow-covered trash and they both remember.

September 1963

Before she arrived in Drinkwater, Florida, the TBO Relocation Company sent Jackie paperwork asking for height, weight, and a history of any criminal record or serious medical problems. Jackie was fit as a fiddle and knew the information about her brief time spent in a jail cell in New York for the crime of having short hair and wearing men's pants was almost seven years old and had not followed her to Massachusetts. TBO's correspondence made it clear they were looking for strong men. *Skilled or unskilled labor needed to help relocate a cemetery. Excellent $$$$ paid to help with*

excavation, the general announcement read. Jackie foreshort-
ened her legal name of Jacqueline to Jacque on the application.
There was a box to check if you had a wife but no box to check
if you had a husband. There were no boxes to check male or
female. There was a notation explaining that single men were
preferred, and wives and children were not allowed to live with
the men in the small trailer the company provided. The job was
for one year only. It paid four times what Jackie was making at
the brake shop.

It was the money, the promise that every "man" got "his"
own living quarters, and a chance to learn the excavation trade
that had finally sold Jackie on the job. The plan was for Jackie to
come back to Regina in Massachusetts in a year with a bundle
of cash and experience in excavation. Regina in the meantime
would live at her parents' house, saving even more money, maybe
going to night school.

Two men quit on the May morning Jackie arrived. She didn't
know yet that most days at least one man quit. She didn't know
that the reason they quit was because the job was so damn dirty
and hard. She thought her luck was changing for the better. She
wasn't surprised that the foreman was brawny and soft-spoken.
She was surprised that he and many of the men who worked
under him were Black. When the foreman shook his head and
said, "Sorry Miss, no females," Jackie handed him the paperwork
with "approved" stamped across it, told him he had nothing to
lose, and promised to leave quietly if he decided she couldn't do
the job. He shook his head again and said, "Some of the men
wouldn't take to you being here." She said she had never worked
a job where some of the men didn't take to her being there. She
was as terrified that he would hire her as she was that he would
not. He held his hat in his hands the same way her father did
when he was speaking to a lady. Jackie was also holding her hat.
The foreman looked her in the eye. They nodded in unison and
put their hats back on their heads. He took her to the supply

trailer and had her pick out two pairs of steel-tipped boots and overalls in her size. The overalls were easy. Lots of men were five foot ten and thin. They had to search through all the boxes for two pairs of boots in Jackie's size. The foreman told her most of the men worked so hard they didn't have energy left to cause a commotion, and if she kept her head down, she just might stay out of trouble. He handed her a pickax and a shovel, pointed in the direction of the Quonset hut where she'd be eating, and assigned her her own tiny trailer and a crew boss.

Four months later, most of the men speak to Jackie only if talk is necessary and work related. She had imagined using her brain as well as her brawn in learning to use the dozers, power shovels, and backhoes. But even the least motivated, most unreliable men are considered more suitable than Jackie to run a big machine. Her coworkers find it strange enough that she's allowed to swing a pickax. Mostly she helps exhume graves. So far, the caskets have been intact. She eats lunch with a stray one-eared cat. She keeps her head down. Does her job. Jackie has two friends in Drinkwater, the cat with no name and a girl named Pearl.

Regina has never traveled farther than New York City. In September she's on a Greyhound bus traveling the back roads from Holyoke, Massachusetts, to Drinkwater, Florida. On her lap is the newspaper with the article where she and Jackie first learned of the place called Drinkwater, the January 14, 1963 edition of the *Morning Union* with a headline below the fold, *Opportunity for Common Laborers*, followed by *Florida makes way for tourism. TBO Relocation Company seeks help displacing and relocating one of the South's largest cemeteries.*

Regina has been on the bus for close to twenty hours. She smooths her skirt, picks up the newspaper, and taps the window with the rolled paper while she stares out.

When Jackie left for Florida, she promised she would call Regina every night from the nearest phone booth. And until two nights ago, she had kept that promise and called every night like clockwork at 8 p.m., spending more time in conversation with Regina on the pay phone than she had in the two rooms they shared at Mrs. Malloy's Efficiency Apartments back in Massachusetts. Then the night before last the phone call was late, and when she finally did call Regina heard something in Jackie's voice that made Regina decide to surprise Jackie with a visit.

Regina stares out the bus window and twists the newspaper tighter. She sees nothing but corn and something she can't identify, cotton maybe, for miles. The decision to be apart for a year with Jackie alone in a trailer and Regina alone in her childhood bedroom was such a risk. But they couldn't go on the way they had been, telling the landlord they were sisters, the neighbors giving them dirty looks. Breaking up. Coming back together. Moving three times in six years. She frowns at the field of vegetation flashing by. How are they supposed to figure out how to make a life together when people make it so hard for them to just live together? And so many things they don't agree on. Like if it's okay to flirt, or kiss, or fuck another girl, for example. She slaps the newspaper, twisted now into a short crop, against her palm. When Jackie left for Florida, they both knew a year apart would either make or break them.

Regina wakes up to a baby cooing in the seat in front of her. For a moment she feels optimistic. Maybe it will all work out. Neither Regina nor Jackie argued the fact that if they didn't get an apartment with a real kitchen and private bathroom, they'd lose their minds. She wonders how much money they've really saved by her moving back in with her parents. They've been spending a dollar a night on phone calls that, to both their pleasures, sometimes end with Regina describing her longing in pornographic detail. In phone booths. How seedy. Regina feels the uneven road bouncing beneath her. She steals a glance at her seatmate, a young man with his nose in a paperback. She blushes to have become the kind of girl who can say such things on the phone and feel such things through thinly padded bus seats with a strange man's thigh beside hers. Why is she kidding herself? She's always been a fan of raunchy. Discreet raunchy. The sex with Jackie has always been good. But their phone sex has been great.

Until two nights ago, when Jackie was late, and Regina sensed that strain in her voice.

"Tired," Jackie said. "People are waiting to use the phone," Jackie said.

Regina asked straight out, "Is there someone down there?"

"I love you, baby," Jackie said. That dodge of an answer made Regina buy the bus ticket.

The man sitting next to Regina has not said a word since the trip began.

He says, "Miss?" and brushes a few pieces of torn newspaper off his pant leg.

It takes her a second to comprehend she's been shredding the paper. "Sorry." She brushes newspaper off her own lap, runs a finger over the limp flip in her heavily hair-sprayed, shoulder-length hair, gives him her best Regina smile, and hands him a brownie from her overnight bag.

In Drinkwater Jackie and Pearl slow dance to Nina Simone's "My Baby Just Cares for Me." Pearl brought Simone's *Little Girl Blue* album all the way from England. But she has no record player. Someone left a small player in Jackie's trailer. But she has no records. Pearl is Black and British by way of Trinidad. She keeps the books for the TBO Relocation Company, which she refers to as "The Bloody Outfit." She carried Nina Simone's voice with her across the ocean six months before she carried the music across the trailer park. Although they will never say so to each other Jackie and Pearl both blame the singer's strong, sexy

185

voice for their affair as much as they blame their own separate loneliness and depression.

Nina sings, "Love Me or Leave Me." Jackie and Pearl sway in each other's arms in the few square feet of open floor between the bed that converts to a table and the small bathroom with a shower that spits a weak stream of water if the faucet is turned just right. Pearl wraps her arms around Jackie's neck. She's wearing Jackie's T-shirt, which is long on her. Jackie slides her hands under the hem and rests them on the shelf of Pearl's ass. This maneuver does nothing to erase Jackie's feeling that Regina is somehow watching all the way from Massachusetts.

Pearl tilts her head and narrows her eyes at Jackie. "Penny for your thoughts."

"You stopped relaxing your hair." Jackie breathes in the flowery smell of it.

"What does a white girl with two inches of hair know about relaxing?" Pearl laughs.

"Curlier, shorter." Jackie pushes a twist of hair away from Pearl's face. "Pretty. Smells good."

"I am an exotic bird," Pearl says.

One corner of Jackie's mouth turns up, the half smile she smiles when she's being cautious with Pearl, which is much of the time.

Pearl wraps a coil of hair around her finger. "You get a kiss for paying attention."

At 5:45 the bus carrying Regina pulls up in back of a brick building with an empty parking lot. Regina, four men, and a teenage girl carrying a sleeping infant step off the bus. The station is deserted, but the bathrooms are open for use.

There are six stalls in the ladies' room. Every stall door has a metal lockbox that allows access to the toilet only after it eats a dime. The girl with the baby stares at a lockbox, crazy-eyed. "Can you make change for a quarter?" she asks Regina.

"I'll hold the door for you when I'm done," Regina says.

The girl points to the sign that takes up the entire back wall. *Each patron must pay 10 cents for one-time use of each stall. Any infraction of this rule constitutes theft. Make change with matron on duty.* There is no matron on duty.

"I only have one dime," Regina lies.

The girl's bottom lip quivers. She can't be sixteen. She pulls the baby close. "I don't wanna give no one no reason to make trouble for me and Lorelie." Her eyes never stop moving around the room. The fluorescent lighting gives her pale skin a blue cast.

Regina wonders how the girl made it through the summer with that skin. She hands the girl a dime. "I'll hold the baby." The baby is sleeping, which is the only reason Regina offers.

The girl squints at Regina and moves her lips without making a sound. Praying or discussing with herself whether she should hand over her baby, Regina couldn't say.

Finally, the girl holds the baby straight out in front of her. "Jesus gonna bless you."

Regina rocks little Lorelie in her arms. Even after a day on the bus, Lorelie smells good. Holding her is not so bad. Regina hopes the baby doesn't wake up and start bawling. She buries her nose in the crocheted blanket, taking in talc and baby breath, wondering how Jackie came by so much maternal instinct while Regina came by none. She looks down at the sleeping child and wonders if Lorelie's father is any help. Thinks about how much Jackie loves kids, how Jackie might willingly conform to whatever conventions she had to if it meant she could raise a child. She wonders if she overreacted, jumping on the first bus out of Holyoke. Jackie is working six ten-hour days every week so they can afford a decent place together. Regina cradles the little girl, feeling shamed by her jealousy for the baby they'll never have and the thought that Jackie would commit herself to a child but has never really committed to Regina.

Regina sighs. Something in her—jealousy and pride she supposes—makes her want to find out in person if her worries are justified. And the desire to see Jackie squirm if Regina's worst instincts are correct.

Regina's arms are tired of being in the same position. She doesn't want to move for fear of waking Lorelie. "You all right in there?"

The girl comes out. Regina maneuvers her backside to catch the door before it slams shut.

The girl's eyes dart back and forth between the stalls and the entrance to the ladies' room. She takes the baby and runs out like the place is on fire.

The door slams and the metal box clanks as Regina steps all the way in and hikes up her skirt. Alone in the stall she thinks that maybe not having a husband is making her crazy. She's sure Jackie would have offered to hold that baby on the bus so the poor girl could get some sleep. Jackie could raise a kid just fine without a husband.

Pearl throws her head back and laughs. "My goodness. You might think I liked that by all the noise I made." She's lying on her back on the thin mattress. Jackie sits on the side of the bed pulling on clean work boots. She takes pride in always having a clean pair of work boots, takes a rag to the muck as soon as she gets in from work, in case she doesn't have time to clean them before she needs to go out again. She doesn't want to drag the burial ground of people's dead relatives everywhere she goes. People have no idea what live and lifeless things their loved ones mingle with when they're six feet under.

"What's the matter, love?" Pearl rubs Jackie's back.

Jackie straps her watch on her wrist. "Almost eight."

"Oh, you were late to ring up Regina last couple nights, weren't you?" Pearl sits up and hugs her knees. "Sorry."

Jackie is back in ten minutes.

Pearl is sitting up on the bed, wearing Jackie's T-shirt again. "Did you know some nutter murdered Medgar Evers?" She doesn't look up from the *Life* magazine she's reading. "How did I miss this? How old is this magazine? You know it was some white bastard and he'll go free. Why don't either of us have a radio?" She taps the black and white photo of Evers's widow and son in mourning clothes on the cover of *Life*. "Did you know about this?" she demands.

Jackie shakes her head and removes her boots without comment.

"You see what nonviolence gets you? Killed, that's what. I'm telling you, this country and Mother England are going up in flames if things don't change." Pearl slaps the bed with the magazine. "Medgar Evers?" She goes back to reading the article. After a few minutes, she looks up, frowning. "That face you're pulling is not about this horror, is it?" She dog-ears *Life* to keep her place and puts it on the floor next to the book Jackie's been reading.

"It's horrible," Jackie says. "We need to be careful."

"Little late for careful." Pearl squints. "Did you have a row with Regina? I hate to fight on the telephone. There's no satisfaction in it. Except maybe when you slam the receiver down."

"Her sister answered. Says Regina's out playing bridge." Jackie pours herself a finger of rye.

"The sister's lying," Pearl speculates. "Regina punishing you for calling late? Should I go?"

"Probably." Jackie holds up the bottle of whiskey. "Drink?"

"Why not? We need to change the mood in here." Pearl takes the glass Jackie hands her. "Look, honey. I know the score. You know the score. Florida was supposed to be an opportunity for us to get a leg up." She takes a sip. "We're both lonely and disappointed. You'll be back with Regina soon enough. At least summer is almost over and it's not hotter than hell in here tonight."

"Hot enough." Jackie takes off her pants. "Scoot over. Please."

Pearl loves Jackie's liberal use of the word *please* and slides over. "You can bet when we've finished working here, I'm going to find a well-mannered Black man, a rich bloke, and none of your political types either. An American. A rich American businessman."

189

"I'm starting a pool and putting a ten-spot on nice-enough, Black, and man." Jackie lies on her back.

"Don't you dare!" Pearl barks out a laugh.

In this trailer park there are people willing to bet on anything. Jackie and Pearl are two of the most willing.

"He's got to have good manners, too," Pearl says.

"You know you're not polite, right?" Jackie grins.

"You don't know anything. Opposites attract." Pearl throws a leg around Jackie and rests her head in the crook of Jackie's arm. "Are you saying I couldn't attract a nice polite man?"

Jackie looks up at the ceiling, remembering that Pearl left England because she was about to be prosecuted for a crime she won't name and swears she didn't commit. Before the case went to trial Pearl had insulted her own barrister beyond reconciliation. Jackie chuckles. "Can't say I see you in the happy homemaker role of Mrs. So-and-So."

"People take marriage too seriously. Such an obvious way to get girls to behave. Blokes, too." Pearl is silent for a minute. "Hey." She picks up her head to see if Jackie's eyes are open.

"I'm awake," Jackie says without opening her eyes.

"They should let queers get married. Pair off the degenerates to keep you away from nice girls like me. If you and Regina were married and we got caught, I'd get the blame. Whatever game you're playing, two white lizzies beats one tarty Black girl every time."

"Lizzies." Jackie's never heard the term before. "No argument, stacked deck all around." She kisses the top of Pearl's head. It's not even nine o'clock., but they both have to be up and out before six. Some fucker murdered Medgar Evers. The world is a hell of a place. Jackie can't fathom how Pearl walks through it without losing her mind. Jackie's glad Pearl is yawning now.

"Church and state, cradle to grave," Pearl says. "One thing I guarantee, I'm going to keep a good eye on my husband when I get one."

Pearl continues to murmur her rambling thoughts until they're both asleep. They've changed position and are spooning when knocking on the door shakes Jackie awake.

"Jackie?" Regina knocks softly on the flimsy aluminum door. She listens for an answer. When she gets none, she stands on her tiptoes and peeks through the vent at the top of the door. She sees only dark shadows. Does she have the right address, D5? The narrow dirt rows that pass for roads are marked quite clearly. Since the bus let her off at the park's entrance Regina has been carrying the flashlight Lynn tucked in the carrying case. Regina is tired, and a few minutes ago a man wearing only boxers appeared in an open trailer door and waved a bill at her in exchange for "a little sugar." She shines a beam of light on the trailer. The red D5 is right above the door.

"What is it?" Pearl turns in her sleep without fully waking.

Jackie sits up in bed. "I thought I heard Regina call my name."

"That's guilt talking." Pearl pulls the sheet over her head. "Go back to sleep and dream of all the money you'll bring home to her."

Jackie holds a hand up in the semidark, waiting, listening. The door rattles and then a definite knock. Pearl sits up and silently starts gathering her clothes.

Outside, Regina stands still and listens. For sure she hears rustling, someone moving carefully around inside. When there is no answer to the second knock, Regina leaves her small travel bag on the step and walks around the trailer. Because of the lampposts at the end of each row and the full moon Regina can see well enough outside. She stops at a small open window. There seem to be no lights on inside, and curtains block her view. She puts a finger on the screen and listens. She doesn't hear another sound.

By the time she has circled back to the door she's sure she's being denied entrance to the tin can of a trailer because Jackie is shacked up inside with a platinum-haired tramp who wears her sweaters too tight. Regina makes a noise close to a growl and gives the trailer a dirty look. The thought that really irritates Regina is how most people, when they get to know Jackie, find her to be so damned honest. "The fact that you never tell an outright lie doesn't mean you're not a filthy liar," she yells at the side of the trailer before she kicks it. Regina is enraged, but on top of rage she also feels deep down tired. She hoped it was something else. A gambling slip or the flu. Some glitch with the phone. Jackie, with her sad eyes, always makes it clear enough in her sparsely worded conversations how much she's given up to be with Regina. "Drinking and gambling and girls who love sex but not you, that's what you allegedly gave up." Regina speaks with a little less volume because someone has turned on a light outside the door of the trailer in the next lot. She slams the side of Jackie's trailer with her fist. "It's a beautiful night," she says in a singsong that scares even her. "Come out and enjoy it." That the girl inside the trailer falls asleep, spends the whole night curled up next to Jackie after they're done, makes Regina kick the trailer a second time. "Oh, but I am a fool," she says in her normal voice.

She stands on her tiptoes and shines a beam of light into the vent over the door, then paces in front of the trailer. She remembers what Lynn said to her when she dropped Regina off at the bus station. "I'll kill Jackie myself if she's messing around in Florida while you're watching *Ozzie and Harriet* on TV with Mom and Dad. Mom trying to fix you up with every available bachelor in town while Jackie's gone. Maybe you're all wet? You made Jackie promise before she left, right, Regina? What in the hell is the matter with you? Just because you're both girls you think you don't have to nip this shit in the bud? Give her an ultimatum. Make her believe it. Who wouldn't keep sleeping around if they kept getting away with it?"

After six years of waiting for Jackie to come to the conclusion that Regina's love is worth forgoing the love of all others, on her own, without Regina insisting, Regina bangs on the side of the trailer and repeats what she yelled at her sister after Lynn gave her that lecture, "Shut up, Lynn."

"Shut up is right," a man's voice bellows, and the light a few trailers away flicks on. "Fucking dykes."

The metallic sound of the trailer door across the row banging open is followed by a gravelly voice. "Come on, don't make me put on my pants to walk down to the phone booth and call the cops."

"Hired a girl for a man's job, what'd they expect. If you want to call what lives in that trailer a girl," the first voice yells. "If they don't shut up, we won't need no cop. I'll take care of 'em myself."

The first "shut up" worked on Regina. She stands still, frightened, infuriated.

"That's Joe Simpson. He sleeps with his rifle," Pearl whispers. "Is Regina smart enough to shut up? Who's Lynn?"

"Her sister."

"She brought her bleeding sister?"

"No, it's just Regina." Jackie runs a hand through her hair. "She'll be quiet now, I think."

"Just?" Pearl pulls on her stockings. There's no back door, and the windows are too small to climb out. Pearl is buttoning her blouse, considering the loo as the only place to hide, when Jackie takes the one step necessary to get to the door and opens it.

"Move." Regina looks over her shoulder to see all but one trailer light has been turned off before she steps in, shoving her travel case in ahead, aiming it at Pearl like a weapon.

Pearl takes a step back, still gets poked in the gut, but she doesn't even wince.

"I hate being threatened by a man," Regina hisses. "I hate being humiliated by a woman more."

Jackie gives Pearl a worried, sorry glance, takes the travel case out of Regina's hands, and puts it on the floor. She wants to tell Regina that this trailer park is a dangerous place for a woman to be wandering at night, knows saying nothing is best.

Pearl slips on a high heel without taking her eyes off Regina who sits on the vacated bed.

"I'm going to close my eyes. When I open them, you'll be gone." Regina doesn't close her eyes. Through clenched teeth

193

she says, "Buckle your belt, Jackie."

Jackie buckles her belt and stands stock still with her hands behind her back. The only person she likes less than Regina at this moment is herself. She considers apologizing to Pearl, but knows that will make things worse for everyone, especially Pearl.

Pearl can't find her second shoe. She wobbles on one heel, trying not to take her eyes off Regina as she searches. She almost admires the way Regina sits there directing her anger where she wants it to go, right between Jackie's eyes. A picture of Pearl's pretty mother, who was often enraged at her father and never lost a staring contest, pops into Pearl's head.

Out of the corner of her eye, Regina sees the spike of Pearl's bone-colored high heel peeking out from under the magazine on the floor next to the bed. She picks up the shoe and dangles it by the ankle strap. "I should make you limp back to the rock you crawled out from under." She tosses the shoe at Pearl.

Pearl catches the shoe by the heel. "In her own way," she says as she slips it on, "Jackie is dedicated to you."

"Shut up." Regina laughs bitterly. A book titled *The Group* lies spread-eagled with its spine arching up, right next to a magazine. Regina picks up the book and snaps it closed. "Where's *The Buck in the Snow?*"

Jackie pulls the poetry book from under the mattress and hands it to Regina.

"Under the bed. Jesus." Regina turns toward Pearl. "You think you know Jackie because she reads to you after sex? What do you talk about? Women's liberation, civil rights, the girl back home? Free love?" Regina rattles off the list dispassionately, like questions under consideration in a philosophy course. "Her childhood on the farm if she's feeling particularly chatty?" She watches Pearl struggle to tie the complicated strap of her shoe in the small space. "She hasn't mentioned her stint in the army, has she?" Regina crosses her arms and looks down at her hip next to Jackie's. "Jackie and I on the bed watching you gather your belongings." Regina's voice becomes shaky. It unnerves her. She looks from Pearl to Jackie back to Pearl. "Does she make fun of me and my attempts at poetry?" She waves the book. "She never heard of Edna St. Vincent Millay until she met me." Regina wants to scream something mean and vulgar in Pearl's face. She wants to holler, *Couldn't you just come when she reads you poetry?* She knows she'll start crying if she says another word.

Jackie and Pearl exchange a look. It's uncanny how accurately Regina has summed up their after-sex talk, at least Jackie's half of the conversation. Right down to St. Vincent Millay's "A Buck in the Snow," the title poem taught to Jackie by Regina, a poem they both know by heart.

"I'm sorry." Jackie puts her hands on her thighs and looks straight ahead. "I'm so sorry."

Pearl has the only cabinet, under the hot plate, open.

"Whatever are you looking for now?" Regina regains her steady voice.

Pearl opens a seat that turns into a drawer and pulls out her purse.

Regina lifts herself off the bed to stand in front of the door and block Pearl's exit. She picks up the travel case. "No need to run off. You can have her. A Brit, aren't you? I don't even know your name. Can you say something about what a gas it is to sleep with a big white American buck?" She attempts an English accent.

"You're better than this." Jackie stands and puts a hand on Regina's shoulder. She bends so her head doesn't hit the ceiling.

Regina slaps it off. "*I'm* better than this?"

Jackie looks at her hands. "I begged you to come, Regina."

"You asked, knowing it made no economic sense for me to come down here and blow half your pay on an apartment."

"I wondered when she'd get to skin color." Pearl throws the strap of her pocketbook over her shoulder. "Excuse me." She attempts to shoulder her way past Regina.

Regina ignores Pearl and stares at Jackie who stares back for a long ten seconds.

Ten seconds is all it takes for Pearl to get sick of them acting like she isn't standing a foot away breathing the same air.

"For fuc'sk sake." She rolls her eyes. "Regina, you've done all the talking. Let me ask you a question about one of your special friends." Pearl hesitates. They've made it this far without so much as a slap. She's no stranger to taking an occasional blow but prefers to avoid them, and what she's about to say might hurt Jackie. She quite likes Jackie.

Regina's eyes flash from Jackie to Pearl.

"Pearl, please," Jackie says.

Regina gives Pearl a haughty smirk that inspires Pearl to continue, "She's overplaying the wounded lover. Not what I pictured from the way you talk about her, like she hung the moon."

Jackie puts a hand on Regina's shoulder. This gesture infuriates Pearl. She kicks the door beside Regina's feet, aiming for the bottom of the frame, always the sticking point. The door springs open a full one-eighty degrees and rattles against the side of the trailer.

Regina gives them both a filthy look. Remembering the man in the boxers waving the bill at her, she almost says, "Be careful," but wants Pearl gone, steps aside to let her pass, and says nothing.

Before the door makes a tinny, unsatisfying sound when it slams shut behind her, Pearl says, "Ask her if she's seen Darla since you've been away, Jackie."

Regina puts her case on the bed and sits next to it, leaving no space on the bed for Jackie to sit.

Jackie sits on the covered storage space. The slope of the trailer above the wooden seat makes her lean forward. She spares a thought for Pearl, walking home to her tiny trailer, not even in her own country, fuming no doubt; a slammed door their last communication. She sighs and turns her mind to Regina whose face seems to have crumpled into itself in the last minute.

"Jesus, I'm sorry," Jackie says. Neither of them speaks for a while. Regina sits with her eyes closed. Jackie studies her face. She's never seen Regina look so defeated. Regina defeated is more disturbing to Jackie than Regina infuriated.

After a long time, Jackie says, "Darla?" The color drains from Regina's face when the name is spoken, and Jackie wonders if Regina broke her promise not to see Darla. Regina was lonely as hell, too. Did she sleep with Darla, the woman who has hated Jackie from the moment she found out Jackie and Regina were lovers, Darla who has been trying to worm her way back into Regina's bed for six years? Whenever Jackie's in the doghouse, Darla comes sniffing. Regina has cried on Darla's shoulder, but that's all. As far as Jackie knows.

"You did." Regina opens her eyes slowly. "You told her about Darla." This realization deflates Regina almost as much as finding out Jackie has been fucking Pearl. "Your little friend is right, I've seen Darla, but I haven't fucked Darla. Do you see the difference, Jackie?" Regina sits with her elbows on her thighs, holding her forehead in the palm of her hands, looking down at the dirty, matted carpet and her scuffed brown pumps.

"I'm sorry." Jackie hopes they can both take a couple deep breaths and rest in their own thoughts for a few more minutes. They've had too many conversations on the subject Regina calls "fidelity" for Jackie not to understand that Regina, like most people, has made a religion out of monogamy. "The holy grail of devotion," Jackie says softly, not expecting a response and not getting one. In New York, Jackie had thought she found the silver lining to being a queer—sex without being tied down to the usual notions about how a decent human being behaves, sex without being expected to find a mate and form a couple for life. Jackie doesn't know where she picked up the idea that not everyone has to be in a couple, not every couple has to be only with the other person. Certain books and the way most of the dykes and gay guys who were her friends lived in New York, maybe. Not from her parents who have been together almost forty years. Two people get along, spend time, have sex, and enjoy each other. Why make demands? Except Regina doesn't see it that way. And Jackie doesn't want to give up Regina.

"How did this get turned on me?" Regina asks.

"It didn't."

"Well." Regina stares straight ahead. "I made a promise to you and to myself that I wouldn't have anything more to do with Darla, and I'll be damned if I'll turn into someone who breaks a promise without an explanation."

"Regina," Jackie says.

"Let me explain." Regina holds up a hand. "Can you do this one last thing for me?"

"Yes." Jackie takes Regina's hand, which Regina allows, but her hand stays limp.

"Darla called, miserable, pregnant. Her husband . . ." Regina flips her wrist, dismissing the thought of Darla's horrible second husband. She stares at their entwined hands. Her anger shrinks to a hard nut of loss in the pit of her stomach. She wishes she hadn't come, that she didn't know, but she did, and she does. "It's hard enough, making it work when you love someone."

Jackie nods her agreement. Regina is looking away and doesn't see this.

"I didn't know how it could be until I met you," Regina says. "And then I had you and she had nothing except a series of men she couldn't love." She turns abruptly to face Jackie. "I love you, but I'm not going to let that ruin my life. You want to fuck around, fuck around. I can't do this anymore."

Jackie moves closer. "What we have is worth saving."

Regina puts up both hands to block Jackie's embrace. Her words come in a rush. "When we first got together, you said I wasn't the kind of girl who could live with people hating me. I thought you were wrong, to hell with the ones who stop inviting me to lunch and baby showers. To hell with anyone who is unkind to my Jackie. I found out pretty quickly what you were talking about. On you, who you are—it always shows. Darla and me, we both look so normal, so straight. Lynn didn't even know. But you—even people who don't know you, when they see you . . ."

Regina takes both of Jackie's hands and squeezes them hard before letting them go. "You walk down the street and people know. I've never known how you could stand it." She looks into

Jackie's eyes. "It hurt when Jenny and Mae both stopped returning my calls after they realized we were together. I tried so hard to get them to make a date for the movies, a cup of coffee. They dropped away, one by one. I'm sorry for how hard it's always been for you and for what a bitch I could be when it got hard for me. I've been so alone at my parents'. Only Lynn stood by me. And Darla. Even when I forbade her to call me or come to our place, she persisted."

They sit in silence, Jackie feeling tired and sorry for the truth of what Regina has said. How are they supposed to live their lives with so few people pulling for them? A pang of uninvited sympathy for Darla comes over Jackie. "Does her husband know she's pregnant?"

Regina shakes her head. "Was pregnant." She wants Jackie to know the whole thing. She says the word out loud, "Abortion. No one to drive her, no one to take her home and stay with her to be sure the bleeding stopped."

"Except you." Jackie is sorry for the anger that bubbles up around her compassion. She stops herself from asking if Regina tried to talk Darla out of it. Jackie's friend Lou Ellen had done it and it was horrible. Illegal. Unsafe. Lou Ellen had to borrow money from all her friends to pay for it. Jackie was glad she wasn't asked to help beforehand, only to hold Lou Ellen's hand after. "Abortion," she whispers, the first time she's said that dangerous word out loud. "It was brave of you to help her.

Jackie waits a respectful second. "Don't leave me, Regina."

"I've had enough. You don't have to be the bad guy, but I'm done being the hysterical girlfriend. Maybe sometime, somewhere two people can do this, but not me. It's not just you with other girls, although god knows that's the straw that broke the camel's back." There's pain in Regina's belly. This could be the last heart-to-heart she has with Jackie. "A week after Darla had it done, we met for coffee at Lucky's. Two girls, wives in Darla's social circle walked in. Girls she knew through her husband. They sat in the booth with us. They'd been shopping and pulled what they bought out of their bags to show us, giggling because what they bought was panty hose. We talked about *The Patty Duke Show* and Darla seemed all right for the first time."

Regina shakes her head. "She had to pretend she was all right in front of those girls and laugh over something as silly as panty hose. Then she was really laughing, and she really was all right. For an hour, anyway. I was relieved, not just for her but for myself. I'd been pretending to be all right and sitting in a diner talking about a silly TV show made me feel like I was all right."

Jackie can't think of a thing to say. She nods. She used to think if people would just leave each other alone everything would be okay. She sees she was wrong. Regina needs more. Jackie has her card buddies and her pal Bo to have a drink with and play pool with, but Jackie and Regina both need more friends, a social life. "I thought time apart would give us time to think. But I haven't been thinking. I've been working until all I want is two fingers of rye and sleep," she says.

"And a fuck." Regina lets out an angry laugh. She stares at Jackie, seeing how gaunt her face has become. Even through the sleeves of Jackie's shirt Regina sees that the muscles in her arms are more defined. "You can't live without having sex with other girls and I can't live without having girlfriends to talk to about TV shows, and stockings, and you." Regina stands.

"You talked to those girls about me?"

"Not those girls. Darla."

Jackie groans.

"Hurts, doesn't it?" Regina tries to pull her hand back. Jackie grips tighter. "One lover, that's the way I'm made," Regina says. "I was afraid to lose you, so I just kept coming back to you after you screwed around. Now I'm more afraid I'll lose myself. I really am done. I quit. I'm breaking the Jackie habit." She frowns at their entwined hands. "You plan to hold me against my will?"

"No." Jackie releases Regina and stands, hitting her head on the sloped ceiling. "No, never."

"I'm not strong enough to live in a world that keeps

200

humiliating me, not when the woman I love is humiliating me, too."

The door rattles as it closes behind Regina. Jackie rests her forehead against it and cries.

Regina gets to the terminal nine hours before the next bus leaves for Massachusetts and eight hours before any bus leaves for anywhere. A man in filthy overalls asks her for money. She gives him a quarter. He sits across from her staring, until the man who stands behind the bars at the ticket booth yells over, "Leave the lady be. Get up out of here now, Jimbo." Jimbo leaves. The man answers, "Yes 'um," when Regina asks if he will be there all night. She finally falls asleep sometime after 2 a.m. with her feet propped on the travel case and her chin propped on the purse clutched to her chest. She wakes before dawn to feel someone sitting next to her. Before she has a chance to be frightened or even to turn her head, she knows it's Jackie. The big trunk that left Holyoke with Jackie sits next to Regina's much smaller luggage.

"You know what Lynn said?" Regina asks as if they were in the middle of a conversation.

"What did Lynn say?"

"She said, 'Be a woman. If she's cheating, make her sorry she was born. Make her suffer for a good long time, then fuck her till she's blue.'"

"Great advice." Jackie has a paper sack with bologna and cheese sandwiches and a thermos of hot coffee on her lap. She hands Regina the bag.

"She said I'll never find better than you." Regina takes the bag. She is expressionless with fatigue. "Handkerchief?" She holds out a hand. "I meant what I said. We're done. It's a free country. You can go back to Holyoke or Granby or wherever, but you're not coming home to me."

Jackie reaches into a side pocket and pulls out her last clean bandanna. She hands it to Regina.

201

"Lynn's an idiot." Regina blows her nose. "Will they pay you anything if you leave now?"

"Not if. Foreman's a good guy. Four hundred eighty bucks left, after I bought this." Jackie holds up her ticket.

"You should go to the city. That'll get you started."

"I'll only go to the city if you go with me. There are people like us everywhere. We'll find them. We have to look harder." Jackie thought about this as she packed. There must be men and women in every town who don't care that she and Regina share a bed, people who don't care about the length of Jackie's hair or that she'd prefer not to have breasts. In Holyoke, in New York. "We could start a reading group. Bo is moving to a farm in Hatfield."

"Bo Meeks." Regina laughs. "Oh, she'll keep you on the straight and narrow."

"Yes, she will. She always has people around, parties, gatherings. A social club, maybe." Jackie doesn't mention card games or bars, thinking of the bar in Springfield with a rough reputation that Bo frequents. Jackie knows *rough* is what people who don't know them say about her and Bo.

"More girls for you to fuck around with." Regina uncaps the thermos and pours coffee in the aluminum cup. "Why not bowling or knitting? You've never been close friends with a girl, a girlie girl. I mean only friends, have you?" Regina's been pondering the question for some time and has come up with her own answer. "It's how we're all brought up, boys and girls, isn't it? We're supposed to stop being friends with the opposite sex once we hit puberty. We get interested sexually, and we're expected to couple with one, and stop being friends with the rest. But if you're homosexual? Who are your friends supposed to be?"

"Not supposed to be a dyke. Lesbian." Jackie defers to the word Regina favors. "I won't," she says. "This time is different, I know. I'll do whatever it takes." Jackie's voice quivers. "It's different for me, too. I know I'll really lose you. This time I promise. I can give up . . . I'll wait. For you. As long as it takes."

202

"You can't even finish a sentence to say what it is you promise to give up. What you will or won't do." Regina laughs unhappily. "I don't want a girlfriend I have to argue with about loving only me."

"I won't have sex with anyone but you." Jackie thinks *have sex* not *make love* are the right words. The man in the ticket booth coughs when Jackie says "sex" but he may just be clearing his throat.

Regina shakes her head and gives Jackie a look that says *too little, too late.*

When the bus arrives, Regina walks all the way to the back. The bus is almost empty, but Jackie follows, sitting near Regina, leaving a few feet between them on the long seat that spans the width of the bus. Before the driver pulls out of the lot he walks to the back, cuts his eyes toward Jackie, and asks Regina if *that girl* is bothering her.

"I knew her," Regina says, trying out the past tense. "She used to be a special friend of mine."

Chapter 10

Saturday, February 18, 2017

Regina likes looking out at the snow-covered trash and thinking about their past, but she's had enough of remembering Florida. "Fuck Pearl," she says. "That's a swear, not a request."

"Fuck 'em all big and small," Jackie agrees, thinking Pearl was special, keeping this thought off her face. "You got close to Yvonne after Florida."

"And Bo, eventually. They helped get us back together, then saved us from being too much by ourselves, introduced us to lots of queer people. Lots of people, period."

Jackie nods. "Getting you back was the only good thing to come from the Kennedy assassination."

"I might have ended up a miserable divorcée if we hadn't gotten back together."

"You were a spitfire," Jackie says.

"Second time you've called me a spitfire today." Regina grins.

"You would have kicked your way out of the closet with or without me."

"Would I?" Regina's been questioning if she could have

loved anyone besides Jackie enough. "Would I have defied my mother's iron will? Never mind that we made our peace before she died, she was a homophobe to the bitter end. May she rest in peace."

"Hell of a thing," Jackie says, thinking of her own parents, how steadfast their love was from the very beginning, *unconditional,* Regina would call it. "Hell of a thing," she repeats because the expression reminds her of Bo.

Regina squirms on the seat. "I'm a lot like my mother, aren't I?"

"In some ways. Strong-willed. Pretty," Jackie says. "Smart. Petite."

"We were so scared when Kennedy died. People are scared every time they turn on the news today. But that day," Regina shakes her head, "I thought the world might end. Our world, anyway."

"Those pills you gave me are working." Jackie rubs her hip and flexes her glutes. "Feels better." She can tell by Regina's fidgeting that Regina is about to say it's time to go again.

Jackie pulls Regina close, and to keep her there, sitting on the step of the bulldozer sharing their past as long as possible, she starts to talk about that November day.

November 1963

"Call her." Bo steers their late-model Buick into the dirt driveway with one hand and flicks her Camel out the window with the other hand. "Regina worshipped President Kennedy. She won't refuse a call today. Someone dies, you want a phone call." It's Bo's week to chauffeur them back and forth to their jobs at the paper mill in the sedan they bought and own together, so she gets to keep the car for the upcoming weekend.

The two women barely spoke on the fifteen-minute ride home. A first for Bo. They sit silently with the car idling, looking out the dashboard window at the side of the barn.

"Hell of a thing." Bo puts a hand on Jackie's shoulder. "Hell of a thing, my friend. Me and Regina, we have our differences, but we're all in the life. You love her and I love you. Some good should come out of the misery that happened today. Call your girl."

"Not *my* girl anymore. If she ever was, I blew it." Regina's last word to Jackie was "good-bye" as Regina walked away from the bus toward her parents' house, warning Jackie not to follow. Between missing Regina and the escalating rumors of layoffs at work, Jackie thought she was already carrying all she could handle. Now assassination? Bo's "I love you" touches her so deeply it's all Jackie can do to stare straight ahead without breaking down.

"She's gonna come around," Bo says. "You just gotta keep calling, and when she finally speaks to you, you gotta keep telling her that you're ready to be her one and only."

"Thanks, buddy." Jackie reaches into the backseat for her thermos. "I'll call Regina like I do every Friday night, and she'll refuse to speak to me like she has every week for the last couple months."

"What would make somebody shoot the president?" Bo grimaces. "Too many damned nuts in this country. Had to be planned, though, don't ya think? I better call New York. My folks must know by now. Mama will be a mess, want me to move back home, grow my hair out, put on a skirt. Whatever the trouble, Mama Lucy believes me living at home, calling myself Bonnie Louise, and wearing silk stockings will help the situation."

"Good luck getting your turn on the phone at your place." Jackie refers to the fact that Bo lives with five other girls and shares one phone that's on a party line. She opens the passenger door. "Rain, maybe," she says looking at the horizon, the sun about to set soon in the overcast November sky. "Or snow."

"Don't think we'll be playing cards tonight," Bo says. "Might be something at my church. Wear your overcoat."

"It's 'my' church now?"

"A tragedy happens, people get churchy. Don't be small-minded. Couple of people stood up for me, including the pastor. Long as I don't wear that hat, I'm welcome." Bo offers Jackie a flickering smile. Several parishioners tried to ban Bo from attending when she showed up for services with her fedora in her hand and Yvonne on her arm. "If I was a wiry broad-shouldered girl like you, eight inches taller, less meat on my hips, I'd go ahead and pass."

Jackie returns the smile, but it's not convincing. "In my hometown?"

This is the first time Bo has mentioned that one or both of them should try to pass as male since Bo moved from the big city to western Massachusetts. Bo and Jackie are often mistaken for men. Not that Jackie necessarily tries to pass. Her voice usually gives her away. By passing, Bo means living as a man, day in day out, not just occasionally when the mood suits. Bo has cultivated her naturally low voice. Her breasts are no problem. If Bo wears a T-shirt under a well-cut shirt, her small chest blends right into her belly. Her broad hips are her biggest give-away. In the relative anonymity of Manhattan, Bo held more than one job she never would have gotten if she wasn't passing and held more than one woman she never would have held. She got roughed up more than once for holding the wrong jobs and the wrong women, too.

"You'd have to cut back those lashes," Bo says, still trying to lighten the mood.

In better times, Jackie likes to razz Bo about passing and Bo likes to razz Jackie about her long lashes making her too girlie to pass. Bo should have known better than to think foolish banter would lift anyone's spirits today. This is going to be a hard day, a hard week. A hard year, maybe. They just must help each other through it. Try to stay safe.

Bo keeps talking, leaning halfway across the front seat so her words will reach Jackie who has already slid out of the car. "You think there's gonna be more trouble?" Bo asks. "The killer was against civil rights—that's why he did it?"

Jackie stoops with one hand on the car's hood. "You can bet

he's a racist." She bends her head into the open door. "I hope this doesn't mean more trouble at work."

"Work?" Bo pushes the back of her head against the car seat. "Jesus fucking Christ."

Bo, Jackie, and two other girls in the factory got punch press jobs that some of the guys thought should have been theirs. The other two girls get sneers. Their time cards go missing. Jackie gets the same. Plus, mumbled threats. One of the guys bumped into her, knocked Jackie down last week, feigning an accident. Bo got the worst of it; the safety on Bo's machine was tampered with. The big red button used to stop the punch from taking a bite out of her hand was purposely jammed, and she could have been maimed if she hadn't noticed it.

"We got the union," Jackie says. "Some of the guys will act better not worse." She shudders, hoping this is true.

Bo shakes her head. "Your average racist will be cheered on by this. Happy to see bullets clear out the queers, too. Just when there's less work at the mill. We are so screwed. Call Regina. You want to be someplace safe with people who care about you tonight, more of a crowd than just you and your folks. My guess is the church people will have a service, a food and fellowship thing. Ha," Bo laughs bitterly. "A safe place?" She whistles through her teeth. "Four little girls blown to kingdom come in that Baptist church would have been safer at home."

"Why the hell did I bring up work? Come in. Have a beer." Jackie sticks her head and shoulders farther inside the car.

"They had the balls to murder Kennedy." Bo hits the steering wheel with her fist. "What's that going to mean for the rest of us? That kind of guy would beat on a colored girl because he couldn't figure out if she was a dyke or a fag."

"You do a bad job keeping yourself safe when you're angry," Jackie says with tenderness that catches in her throat.

"Yvonne will be waiting. We'll calm each other down. You go in. *You* have a beer." Bo puts the car in reverse. "Hug your mama."

"You'll pick me up? For the service if there's one tonight?"

"Yvonne probably already invited Regina. Be good for me and Yvonne to be around other Black folks. You'll be welcome, and you won't be the only white girls there. Tell Regina to wear a nice hat. Those church ladies welcome well-behaved white girls, but they will not forgive a raggedy hat." Bo grins. "I'm not going off half-cocked. Get off my car. Lemme go."

"Our car." Jackie straightens up, closes the door, and slaps the top of the Buick, a sign of affection, a gesture unconsciously meant to keep Bo safe. "I love you, too," she says, probably loud enough for her friend to hear. "Hell of a thing." She watches the dust kick up behind the car down the long dirt drive. Bo's reasons for going to church, other than her desire to impress a woman, finally make some sense to Jackie.

"Mom," Jackie calls as she walks into the kitchen. "Dad."

She's not surprised that neither of her parents is in the house. It's milking time. They only have six cows left and do the milking by hand together. She stands by the sink staring at the phone on the wall, thinking about how many bad days her parents made it through together in the last forty years, the death of her soldier brother in a driving accident while he was on leave during World War II when he was still a young man; Selma, the grandchild they thought they would raise after their son's death being taken away from them; almost losing the farm; and the day the letter arrived announcing Jackie's dishonorable discharge from the army. It has taken her these long months alone to understand that having Regina in her life, by her side year after year, would give some shape to the hard days, a reason to persist. She tries to remember easier days, days you could accept as they unfolded, days you didn't have to struggle to understand.

She picks the receiver off the hook, starts to dial. Stops. She should decide what she wants to say in case Regina does take her call this time. She puts the receiver back in the cradle. What if Regina won't take her call, not even today? Never again?

She faces the sink, wraps both hands around the edge of the countertop and bows her head until it almost touches the

209

counter. If Lynn had not gone off to South Dakota with the cattleman she plans to marry as soon as his divorce is final, she could call, ask for Lynn, at least find out how Regina is doing. "Regina," she whispers. It feels like years, not months, since the bus from Florida dropped them off at the station in Massachusetts. The soft bleating from the barn seems to sympathize. The only thing that stops her from weeping is the possibility of her parents walking in. No doubt her mother has already had a good cry over President Kennedy. Probably every mother in Massachusetts has had a good cry. If she's going to call Regina, she should do it while she has some privacy. There is only the one phone in the small farmhouse.

Something stirs in the front room. "Mom?" she calls.

In the front room, Regina rises off the couch and walks slowly toward the kitchen. She stands in the doorway hugging herself.

Jackie and Regina stare at each other, transfixed, not five feet between them.

Regina steps around Jackie into the kitchen. "They're so good, your parents. They gave me big hugs," Regina says. "My parents are so relieved to have me back as a normal unmarried spinster. My dad pretends not to miss you. My mother pretends you never happened."

"You came." Jackie wonders for a moment if she's hallucinating. She's never seen Regina in this stance, drawn into herself, shoulders hunched, arms cradling each other. Always thin, now Regina is downright skinny.

"You heard?" Regina looks away to avoid seeing the tear run down Jackie's cheek. Regina has been living in a state of dogged determination to stay on the track she has chosen for herself. Work and night school. She hates her day job less than the preparatory courses she's taking in hopes of being admitted to nursing school. She even applied for a scholarship. Teaching and nonclinical nursing courses are what the community college offers at night, and she's drawn less to children in grades K-12 than she is to sick people. Neither profession calls her,

210

but if she's doomed to live with her parents for the rest of her life, she'd better prepare herself for something besides selling cosmetics. "Your mom said it would be okay for me to wait in here." She had not known that simply being in Jackie's home would magnify the loss of what happened today and shine such a harsh light on her daily routine of work and school.

"I'm surprised." Jackie moves toward Regina. "Glad you came."

"Yvonne gave me a lift. She's worried all hell will break loose. I am too. There's been so much trouble already. I haven't been able to get in touch with my sister out West." Regina turns, walks back into the front room and puts a hand on top of the television console, rubbing a circle with her finger on the polished blond wood, looking down, talking to the top of the set. "I had to put the TV off before I went crazy." Her voice trembles. "It's disorienting, eerie, because it feels like the nightly news is on but all day long and only one horrible story to tell since it happened, not giving you a second to forget. Not that you could forget. Not that I even want to forget." She glances at Jackie and then back to her own finger still making the same circle on top of the wooden cabinet. "Every radio station, too. It feels like the end of the world. I was trying to sell a customer a tube of lipstick when she told me something bad had happened, but she wasn't sure what. Then the store made the announcement over the intercom, and the whole place went silent. The manager came on and said we were closing, and we should all go home to our loved ones. Yvonne came up from the stockroom to find me. I haven't even seen my parents yet. They must think I'm still at work. Poor Mrs. Kennedy."

She rubs her temple, still not looking at Jackie. "Can you imagine? Hearing a thing like this over the intercom? And Lynn, off with that man. Yvonne says the mill might be getting ready to lay off. Well, I wondered if that's how you'd heard it, too. At the mill? It's one thing to have a lousy job. It's another thing not to have a job. Not to have someone to come home to. Not that your parents. Not that we should get back . . ."

211

Jackie, who had been silently crying, inhales a sob that makes Regina look up mid-sentence.

"Oh, no. Don't cry. Please." Regina hugs herself. "If you cry, I'll start, and I may never stop."

Jackie takes the few steps necessary to embrace her. Regina's arms are wrapped around herself. Jackie pulls her in without being embraced in return. Regina lets herself be held and they both cry until their breath comes out in hitches.

Regina pushes away and goes to the bathroom to fix her face. When she comes back, she finds cups of tea on the coffee table, but walks to the window to look out into the shadows.

Jackie stands behind her, fighting the instinct to put her arms around Regina's waist.

They both stare out at the yard without speaking until Regina says, "It's so dark, so calm while the world falls apart."

"I'm afraid. For all of us. But the *us* I'm talking about now is you and me," Jackie whispers. "If you had asked me outright to be faithful, I would have said yes." She hesitates. "I mean if we had established that rule. If I had given my word. I would have kept it."

Regina turns, feeling a terrible composure. "I doubt you had it in you at first. Sleeping around was a way of life. After we were together for a while, maybe before you left for Florida you might have agreed. I didn't want you to just agree. I wanted you to want what I wanted. Monogamy." There's no judgment. Only resignation in Regina's sigh. "You just don't."

"Are you happier without me?" Jackie asks. Regina doesn't answer. Jackie sits on the couch, leans forward, and rests her elbows on her knees. "Because I'm miserable without you. I should have pretended I wanted what you wanted. From the beginning. To keep the peace. To keep you. In the end that's what people do. Bend." Jackie gestures for Regina to take a seat on the couch next to her.

Regina remains standing. "Yes, we've had this conversation. This fight. Me and my romantic notions. You and your misgivings about 'one and only, till death do us part, true love.' I've had lots of time to think about it. To write a poem about a willow tree." Regina lets out a derisive snip of a laugh and stops talking to give Jackie a moment to smile at the thought of Regina's poetry. Jackie is all sincere attention. "Well, I've come to agree with you," Regina says. "How often does *forever* last? Even for married people? Men and women, couples who have a house and kids and dinner parties with their neighbors to keep them together? How *happy ever after* are most of those couples really? Never mind two girls with no money who get the evil eye from the old biddies in the grocery store?"

"Our parents are happier together than they would be apart. We were too isolated. Bo lives closer now. She and Yvonne have parties. They belong to some women's society in Boston. Boston's not so far. It could be different. You and me, committed to each other."

"We've switched arguments, have we?" Regina says without malice. She moves a family photo to sit on top of the TV console. "I've thought a lot about freedom since we split, who has it, who doesn't. Today I kept thinking that your kind of freedom is a type of bondage too, or no—I don't mean to be melodramatic, not today of all days—a burden maybe. I just mean there's a price no matter which way you jump."

Jackie nods. "Freedom to be alone on this damn day."

Regina hops off the console. "What's happening to me? I'm sitting on the television set." She moves the photo back where it belongs. "I do believe you'd be faithful if I asked. But I don't want to spend my life trying to be better than the hurt and anger that rears up when I think about you and those other girls. I always wanted to be brave. Heroic. The only brave thing I've ever done is loving you." Regina sits on the horsehair chair that was once in their apartment and before that in Jackie's apartment in New York. The comfort of that chair starts her crying again.

Jackie gets up, pulls a chair close to Regina's.

"What are we going to do with our lives?" Regina throws up her hands. "Lesbians? Homosexuals? All of us? We don't even

213

have words to use for ourselves that aren't in psychology books."

"Whatever we do, we should do it together, you and me," Jackie says. "Who we are, that is our lives. I'm sorry I messed our lives up."

"Oh sorry." Regina crosses her arms in defiance of her own regrets as well as Jackie's. "I remember sorry."

To Jackie, Regina seems more herself at this moment than she has since Jackie first saw her in the kitchen doorway.

"I'm sorry, too." Regina frowns at the chair that just gave her comfort. "So what? I'm sick of sorry. I'm sick of sitting around on overstuffed chairs and standing behind cosmetic counters. Some maniac murdered the president who was the best decision this country ever made, and now all hell can break loose or we can get off our asses and do something. What was I doing in August during the March on Washington? I was reading about it in the newspapers and crying over you, that's what."

"We should have been there." Jackie nods. "Bo says the march was something."

"Bo went to Washington?"

"The union sent the steward and two other people."

Regina smirks. "They sent Bo Meeks? They know what she is? Of course, they know."

"Bo pays her dues. She never misses a meeting." Jackie is surprised at how soon irritation slides back into her feelings for Regina.

"She's always had guts. I just can't see Bo in Washington, DC, unless it's at a poker table with a drink."

"Why? She's from a big city," Jackie says flatly. "What if she did have a drink and play cards while she was doing some good there?"

Regina, taken aback by the change in Jackie's tone, hears what she has just said as Jackie heard it. She bites her lip, agreeing. "You see I'm the same old girl, even now in the middle of this mess, quick to judge." She takes Jackie's hand. "I apologize, truly. There. Now you can be sick of sorry, too. Bo did something good. Good for her. It's not fair that I associate Bo with our troubles."

"Not fair," Jackie agrees. "Bo wasn't even here. She was in New York during our worst times. She thinks there'll be a service at her church tonight."

"Mourning, proper respects." Regina walks a small circle in front of the window. "Something to do besides sit numb in front of the TV."

When Jackie's parents walk in, Jackie and Regina are sitting on opposite ends of the couch, watching a loop of horror on the console, waiting for Yvonne to come back for Regina.

Later, alone in the kitchen with Jackie's father, Jackie's mother lowers her voice so Jackie won't hear. "It's not that I object to her having Negro friends. You know I don't." Jackie's mother stands at the stove holding a big wooden spoon, uncharacteristically distracted from her task, letting the food in the pot pop and hiss, spitting a bit of hot gravy on her wrist before she stirs the stew and lowers the heat. "People are nervous. Some may feel tenderhearted, but some will be jittery, looking to cast blame."

She wipes her hands on the dishcloth tucked in the waist of her apron. "Jackie calls enough attention to herself. I like Bo. Jackie and Bo together?" Her mother purses her lips. "Don't look at me like I'm making a mountain out of a molehill, Jack. People pass remarks. You've ignored them. Same as me. We've all lived with this thing since she was a young girl. You know how the good people of this town can be. Four girls going around together. Who knows if they have enough sense not to hang on each other's arms?"

"Our girl lived in New York City. She can handle herself." Jackie's father goes to the cupboard and gets two mugs. "Sit. Have a cup of tea with me before dinner." He places the cups on the table and puts a teabag in each one. "The coward who shot the president would be happy to know he was keeping four girls from attending a church service in Kennedy's honor."

"I can't lose another child." She clicks on the gas burner and fills the kettle with water from the tap. "Talk to her. She listens to you."

215

"They're going to church, not a war zone." Jackie's father pulls out two chairs.

"The president had bodyguards." Jackie's mother makes the sign of the cross, her voice a mix of fear and anger.

Jackie has been standing in the front room, out of sight, eavesdropping, thinking about what Bo said about the four little girls from Alabama getting blown to kingdom come for going to church as she steps into the kitchen. "Mom, I'm not the president. No one's interested in me."

"You girls have dinner here." Her mother stands as tall as her five-foot-eight frame will stretch. "All four of you. I made plenty."

"Thanks. We'll take you up on it. Another night. Tonight, we're going to the Baptist church. There's Bo," Jackie says, responding to the sound of the Buick pulling up in the driveway. She kisses her mother on the cheek. "Good night, Mom."

Her mother holds her by the wrist.

Jackie squats next to her mother. "We can't all stay in our kitchens."

"Why not?" Jackie's mother looks at her father.

He gently removes his wife's hand from Jackie's wrist and gets up to answer the door.

"Good evening." Yvonne steps inside followed by Bo. Yvonne is dressed in black, wearing her best veiled hat and black sheath with matching jacket, looking more like Ruby Dee auditioning for a part as a grieving young widow than a girl who works in the stockroom at a department store. Bo is wearing her best suit. She has stashed her fedora in the trunk of the car.

Back at the car Bo starts for the driver's side, but Yvonne informs Bo she's not driving. "It's going to be Black girl, Black butch in the backseat, white girl, white butch in the front seat. I plan on doing my bit for integration. Not on the way to church and not tonight. It's enough we arrive together."

"Where's the logic? It's a Black church," Bo says. "The parishioners are going to be driving their own cars. White people who see us on the way and give a damn will think

216

I'm the chauffeur."

"Not in a ten-year-old Buick with a dented fender." Yvonne shakes her head. "With a beautiful girl next to you. They'll think you're my pimp."

"Trying to second-guess the minds of bigots? People see me and Jackie in the car every day. Some fool might be angry that a white girl is driving around Black girls." Bo looks to Jackie for support. Jackie just raises an eyebrow. "There's no winning an argument with this one." Bo hands Jackie the keys and asks Yvonne, "So, who do you want to take the backseat until we pick up Regina? Or do we all cozy up front?"

"You're right." Yvonne's shoulders sag. "I'm trying to apply reason. Reason got shot down with Kennedy. I have no godly idea who should sit where."

"It's okay, baby." Bo puts her arms around Yvonne, who is taller and rests her cheek on Bo's forehead.

Yvonne rearranges her hat before she slides in the backseat.

Regina is outside rubbing her arms and fidgeting against the cold when the Buick pulls up.

"Why is Regina waiting at the end of her driveway?" Jackie wonders out loud.

"Mother trouble is my guess," Yvonne offers.

Jackie sticks one foot out of the car, planning to jump out and open the back door for Regina, hoping for a brief word. Regina is inside, seated next to Yvonne before Jackie's second foot hits the ground. Regina slams the car door behind her. Jackie and Bo both turn in their seats to see the look Regina gives her parents' house.

"You all right?" Jackie asks.

"Please, just drive." Regina's lips almost disappear into her smirk.

Yvonne's eyes meet Jackie's in the rearview mirror as Jackie backs out. "Mrs. LaFleche invited me in for tea when I dropped Regina off this afternoon," Yvonne says. "Explained in her pretty little living room why Regina and I must end our friendship."

Bo nods, having just heard the story on the way to Jackie's.

"'For both mine and Yvonne's good'"—Regina wags her head, mimicking her mother—"'for safety's sake,'" sounding much like herself when she's on her own high horse. "Yvonne never flinched. Finished her tea," she says with satisfaction. "Just stood up, said, 'Good-bye, Mrs. LaFleche' and asked if I still wanted a ride tonight."

"Wanna take odds on that three-way battle of wills?" Bo asks Jackie.

At this moment, Jackie is not about to respond to a joke about a wager.

"I wasn't sure you'd make it out of the house tonight," Yvonne says.

"Thank you for coming. I don't think I would have come back if I were you," Regina says. "It got worse. She figured out you and Bo are a couple."

"I assumed," Yvonne says.

"Took an assassination for the woman to figure it out?" Bo points at herself in her vested three-piece suit and whistles through her teeth. "I thought she liked Yvonne, though. Yvonne is a Good Negro. Mothers never do like me."

"My mother tolerates Negroes. She thought she was rid of—"Regina makes a circle above her head to indicate all of them—"us. She flipped out when it was just her and me. We both did."

"You should not be living with your mother," Yvonne says.

"Yvonne," Bo says. "This is no time for an old argument."

"Don't *Yvonne* me. Making your way to a memorial service is no time to fuss over your racist mother." Yvonne arranges her purse on her lap. "*Tolerate.* How I hate that word. Join the NAACP like you keep threatening, Regina. Give Mama something to fuss about." She cuts her eyes at Jackie, who has not stopped glancing at her in the rearview. "Don't look so troubled Jackie. I like Regina. Otherwise I wouldn't be bothered. I'll take her to a meeting. She should lick some envelopes. I guarantee there will be a table in the vestibule after the service tonight where she can sign up."

Regina stares out her window without saying another word until they get to the church.

Weeks later, Regina accompanies Yvonne to a volunteer meeting held in the community room of the Quaker meeting house. She's finding out political work involves lots of sitting on folding hairs, either in halls listening to men talk or, as Yvonne warned, in basements licking envelopes. When it comes to licking envelopes, the volunteers are mainly women. Today most are still in their Sunday clothes and sit at a long table near the front.

Regina and Yvonne sit alone at a small folding table in the back, kitty-corner to each other. They talk quietly as they work. Yvonne is telling Regina about spending last weekend in Boston at her parents' house. "I should never have told Daddy our meetings alternate between the Baptist church and a Quaker meeting house." She lowers her head and her voice. "He's worried about subversives and socialists."

"If begging for money and drumming up audiences for lectures about nonproliferation and Reverend King makes you a socialist." Regina runs a hand over her hair to be sure her bouffant remains smoothly backcombed away from her forehead. Yvonne's hair is in much the same style, although hers is shiny and keeps its round shape without Yvonne fussing with it. At least not in public. Neither of them wears a hat. Quakers don't require hats.

"Doctor King and Jesus calmed Mother down. Daddy's still worried. He thinks Quakers are a white cult." Yvonne secures a pile of envelopes into two neat stacks with rubber bands. "I brought up Sojourner Truth."

Regina tears off a row of stamps from a sheet, licks one, sticks it on an envelope, and says, "One of the Ruths made up the story about Sojourner being a Quaker to make the Baptists feel welcome." There are three Quaker volunteers named Ruth.

"No, it's true." Yvonne looks up from her work. "Oh, you're making a joke." She crosses out the last name. "We conquered this list. Daddy thinks you people are going to be my ruination."

"I'm not a Quaker." Regina sips her tea.

"White people." Yvonne grins.

"That's because you haven't introduced him to Bo." Regina grins back.

"You got me there." Yvonne stops smiling. "I used to think Quakers were the ones who don't drive cars or use electricity."

"That's the Amish." Regina picks up the list of crossed-out names. "What's the matter?"

"Assumptions." Yvonne shakes her head. "You just told me the Amish don't drive or use electricity and within a second, without knowing one such person, notions about the Amish that have nothing to do with the fact that they don't drive or use electricity pop into my head."

"I feel a sermon coming on." Regina waves the list at a man in the front of the room. "Let's get the real pastor over here." She smiles at him as he glides toward them.

"Hello, ladies." The reverend in his white collar and tasseled loafers carries an empty cardboard box. "You've made quick work of this. Can I talk you into another batch?" He places the stacks of addressed envelopes in the box.

"Thank you, Reverend Joe." Yvonne looks at her watch. "My girlfriend," she says in her churchiest voice and sits up a little straighter, "is picking us up in twenty minutes. I'm happy to do as much as I can until that time. Another batch, Regina?"

Both the reverend and Regina skip a beat before they respond.

"Certainly," Regina says, "that's why I'm here."

"Wonderful." The preacher returns seconds later with another list, envelopes, and stamps.

"My *girlfriend?*" Regina says as soon as he's out of hearing distance. "You are a subversive."

"He's part of the club. He likes men more than you do." Yvonne wets a stamp on a sponge, slaps it on an envelope, and shoves it toward Regina who stuffs it in a flyer.

"You don't know that. Because of how he walks? Talk

about bad assumptions."

Yvonne continues to shove envelopes Regina's way, then stops abruptly. "If we can't push the envelope here," her voice rises accusingly, "where can we?"

"Sometimes you're so rude, so ill-tempered," Regina squares her stack of flyers, "it makes me want to behave better myself."

"All right," Yvonne says. "I won't insult your intelligence by pretending I didn't say *girlfriend* in a certain tone. Just once I'd like to scream from the pulpit that I'm a homophile. How dangerous is saying 'my girlfriend'? These ladies," Yvonne gives a nod toward the women seated at tables in front of them, "call each other *girlfriend*."

Regina gestures for Yvonne to lower her voice. "None of them look like Bo," she says. "Saying *girlfriend* is not as dangerous for us."

Yvonne pushes back in her chair, "Which *us* would that be?"

"Women who wear skirts." Regina moves closer to Yvonne. "Girlie queers."

Yvonne flinches at *queers*. "You think I'm a fool who has to be told it's harder for Bo and Jackie because you can tell by looking at them?"

Regina wants to explain that she likes the word homophile even less than queer, but the conversation is going too fast. She crosses her legs and folds her arms over her chest, too. "Why are you being so hard on me?"

"You know what else is hard?"

Regina waits, understanding that Yvonne plans to ask and answer the question.

"Walking around as a colored girl. Try slipping out of that skirt. Ask Jackie who got the worst of it in New York. At the bars? On the street? At the mill, who better say, 'Yes, sir' to the foreman every damn time?"

"Bo." Regina unfolds her arms. "Bo."

Yvonne picks up her coffee and puts the cup down without taking a sip. "Why don't you like Bo?"

"I like Bo just fine." Regina lifts an inch off her chair, runs

221

her hand under her skirt, and resettles.

"And Bo likes you 'just fine' right back." Yvonne turns a few degrees to consider Regina head-on. "Jealous. Both of you."

Regina considers Yvonne's "right back."

"Maybe Bo's too dark, too dangerous for you," Yvonne says.

"That's not true," Regina bristles. "Are you saying I'm prejudiced?"

Yvonne waits a long minute to answer. "I'm saying what Bo says all the time, she is nobody's Good Negro. You said as much a minute ago when you were teasing me about not introducing her to my parents. Anyone with eyes can see Bo is a danger to good people everywhere. Jackie, too. But not like Bo. Bo is the boogie man, come to steal their way of life, their children." Yvonne sucks in a breath and huffs it out. "And their manhood while she's at it."

"None of us is . . ." Regina hesitates, flustered, scared of Yvonne's anger. ". . . good. I know what you're saying to me. Bo is worse than Jackie. I don't mean worse. I mean more dangerous. I mean *in* more danger." She leans in, both hands on the table, disrupting the pile of envelopes, becoming more rattled. "You're right, I'm more afraid for her, for all of us when we're with her. But it's not like I'm at ease when I'm with Jackie in public. It's not like I'm at ease with myself. Afraid. Sorry. Angry. More than once I've wanted to make all of us invisible."

Yvonne moans. "This would be easier if you were just a normal tight-ass white girl."

An elderly Black woman, wearing a hat with a hazardous-looking feather, walks up to their table. Yvonne greets her with a veneer of politeness. "Hello, Mrs. Johnson."

"Hello, Yvonne." Mrs. Johnson smiles and points to her left ear. "My Earle bought me a new hearing aid, catches every little sound. You young ladies might want to keep your voices down."

Yvonne smiles. "Nice of you to mention it, Mrs. Johnson." She gestures to Regina. "You've met my girlfriend, Regina?"

Regina and Mrs. Johnson exchange pleasantries before Mrs. Johnson says, "You girls take care, now," and heads back to her table.

Yvonne continues with her voice lowered. "You've got back-bone, but you need to take criticism. So do I. You hit my last nerve, teasing me about not introducing Bo to my family." She shakes her head. "It's worse than you think. I do love Bo. But I have to choose."

"Why? Your parents live ninety miles away."

"Not between my parents and Bo. Between Bo and Howard. I'm going back to Howard."

"Howard?" Regina stands up and sits back down. "Poor Bo."

"Shhh." Yvonne reaches for Regina's hand. "Not a man. A school. My parents are thrilled. Daddy went to Howard," Yvonne says. "He was furious when I moved away to work here, in western Massachusetts of all places. In a department store. In the stockroom. My mother insists I move back to Boston every time I go home."

"It was too hard." Regina falters, ". . . to be . . ." She fights for a word, "homosexual in your hometown?"

"And now I have to leave Bo if I want to be a doctor."

"A doctor? Medical school?" Regina stares, her mouth half open. She looks down at Yvonne's hand covering hers, places her other hand on top, and says, "A Black female doctor. Jesus, Yvonne. How smart *are* you? How brave *are* you?"

"I'm going to find out." Yvonne places her other hand on top, making a pile of hands.

"Howard? Is that a Black school? A school where they'll give you a fighting chance?"

"It is," Yvonne says.

They sit with their hands piled between them on the table.

"I didn't know your father went to college." It suddenly occurs to Regina that Yvonne is from a wealthy family or maybe just a well-educated family. "Why do you have to leave Bo to go to medical school?" Regina tries to remember if they have ever spoken about what their fathers do for a living. She's never known a Black girl who went to college before. She's never known *any* girl who went to college. She tries to think of any boys she grew up with who went to college. She's never seen Yvonne blush before.

"My parents wouldn't pay for school if they knew about Bo." Yvonne pulls away and slumps a little in the folding chair. "I know, shocking, I'm deceiving them so they'll pay my way. I'm choosing medical school. For now. Bo knows. She agrees with my decision. Or anyway, she understands. So that's my deal with the devil."

Regina holds out an open palm. "Just don't tell them."

"I won't tell them. I won't take Bo to Washington with me either." Yvonne sits tall in her chair. "If I'm ever serious, I mean forever-after serious, about Bo I'll tell them. Right now, I'm more serious about school. Are you stunned or disappointed?"

Regina doesn't answer.

Yvonne stacks the disarray of envelopes, sits back, and says, "You and Bo both love Jackie. You should know that Bo's done nothing but encourage Jackie to get back together with you. You and Bo need each other."

"I am stunned. Proud of you for going to school. Maybe disappointed, too, about Bo. I don't know. It's between you and Bo, of course. I'm going to miss you." Regina wipes a tear. "You said you're going back to Howard. Why didn't I know you went to college?"

"It wasn't yours to know." Yvonne looks around uncomfortably, rubbing her upper arms through her lacy yellow blouse. "There was an incident with a girl. That I loved. We both got sent home. She took getting caught hard. Now I'm going back."

"Oh," Regina says.

"One thing I learned by leaving school and my parents is that I can't stop being what I am. Another thing is that we all need other girls like us." Yvonne sits up, regaining her poise. "Our Bo is having a hard time forgiving you for turning her playmate into a love-struck puppy who wants to settle down and be a full-time husband."

"Husband? Jackie doesn't want to settle down. She'll settle for settling down."

"So? She wants you more than that whole other life she had in New York. Sometimes you give up one thing to have another. Where's the insult?"

"I still don't understand why you have to leave Bo. You just said we all need other girls like us." Regina leans on the table, threatening to topple again the pile of envelopes that Yvonne just restacked.

"Well then, maybe you just won't understand. I need an education more than I need to be with Bo. She's not in love with me the way she'd have to be to stick it out while I slog through premed and medical school. Maybe she will be someday. But not yet."

"Medical school." Regina has so many questions. "I will miss you." She looks at her lap, surprised to be so hurt that Yvonne held this information so long, surprised to find out just how much she's come to care for Yvonne in such a short time, sorry to be losing her friend. The friend who has parties and makes her stuff envelopes with strange religious groups and lends her books she's never heard of. "Congratulations. It's Washington, DC, not the state, right?"

"Yes, DC. I'll miss you, too. I'm not afraid to hop on a bus to Massachusetts for the occasional weekend. Bo and I aren't giving each other up completely. We're just not promising any- thing." Yvonne smiles and sighs.

Regina moans softly. "Bo and Jackie, loose on the town."

"Yes. I thought of that. I do love Bo, but I'm not a believer in quick love." Yvonne purses her lips at Regina who is dabbing at her eyes. "You and Jackie are clearly in it for the long haul. Why don't you move back in with her?" Yvonne's eyes narrow. "Then you won't have to worry about her and Bo on the town. And you won't be living with mama."

"Move in?" Regina says barely above a whisper. "We're not even."

"Don't tell me you haven't gotten back into bed with her since she came back from Florida? Dear god. Anyone paying the least attention—the good reverend, I bet he thinks you

225

and Jackie are a couple," Yvonne smiles wickedly, "of deviants. Going through all the nonsense and not getting a bit of the goodies. Forgive me for saying so, but that is just dumb as a bucket." She stops to take in the fact that Regina is openly crying. "Are you crying for me or for Jackie?"

"You and Jackie. And Bo."

"Well, stop." Yvonne puts up a hand. "If you make me blubber in the Quaker meeting room I'll never forgive you."

"Then you should have told me in the Baptist church where no one would notice."

"You'll take care of them?" Yvonne tears up herself.

Regina pulls tissues from her purse and hands one to Yvonne. "I suppose we'll all take care of each other."

Chapter 11

Saturday, February 18, 2017

"You all right?" Regina asks. Jackie seems winded even though it was Regina who told most of the story.

"Still things to learn about you," Jackie says. "After sixty years."

"Are you crying?" Regina pecks Jackie's cheek. "You old softy."

"Thinking about my dad."

"Your dad? Well, yes," Regina nods, "so many stories remind me of my parents." She understands perfectly how memory meanders, how a story about JFK that ends at a Quaker meeting could get Jackie thinking about her dad. "We'll call Selma. You two can reminisce." She doesn't like the way Jackie looks. "Young people think about the future because they have so much of it. Old people think about the past because we have so much of that."

"His death was good." Jackie leans forward with her hands on her knees, huffing.

"Good?" Regina taps her handbag, waiting for Jackie's breathing to settle down and worrying about the journey back to the car.

"He was calm. It was his time." Jackie looks up. "Christ." Her lower lip quivers. A shadow passes over them. A large, powerful-looking bird, moving with slow, heavy wing beats, flies by them, circling.

"Just a hawk," Regina says. Jackie is not someone who sees omens in wildlife. Still, she looks terrified. "A hawk if you respect it, a buzzard if you don't." Regina tries to get Jackie to smile, but Jackie grabs Regina's arm with a tenuous grip and slides off the bulldozer's seat to the ground in slow motion. Regina attempts to stop her fall but Jackie lands on her butt in the snow.

"It's a bird, just a bird," Regina repeats, trying to convince herself that the strange look in Jackie's eye has been brought on by some sudden belief in angels of death. Jackie is seated with her back against the step. She slumps forward. Regina sits next to her and pulls at the back of Jackie's parka, which got bunched up when she slid off the seat of the dozer. Regina has a little success in getting her to sit up straighter, but Jackie is otherwise too heavy to move. Regina gives up and cradles Jackie's head between her hands to get a good look.

She pushes back Jackie's hood. Her lips are bright red against her too-white skin. Jackie's mouth is not right. Regina takes off her glove so she can feel Jackie's face and the pulse on her neck. She knows there's supposed to be a pulse, but isn't sure how strong it should be, so she settles for present. "You're going to be okay," Regina says.

Jackie gives Regina a patronizing look that infuriates Regina. How dare she? Regina holds Jackie's clammy hand. The right side of Jackie's sagging mouth further infuriates Regina. This is not happening; she refuses to let this be happening. Regina touches a bead of sweat that has formed above Jackie's top lip. "Can you talk? Say something, honey."

Jackie smiles sheepishly. "Don't be mad at me." She slurs her words a bit and her voice is raspy, but otherwise calm.

Regina pulls the cell phone out of her pocket and manages

to flip it open. She's only used the thing once when she mim-
icked the Elder Care demonstration by pretending to press the
correct buttons to alert the EMS team. "Shit." Her fingers are
arthritic. The keyboard is small.

"Button," Jackie says. "On side."

Regina presses every button, elated that Jackie is paying
attention and her voice is clearer than it was a moment before.
Her color is coming back, too.

The phone's screen stays black. "I'll get this thing to work
if it's the last thing I do," Regina says. She pulls Jackie's hood
tight around her face. "Nobody dies. It's not your time. You
understand. Not today. Not here."

"I feel better." Jackie does feel better and would add, please
don't bother the ambulance people. But she's confident Regina's
considerable will won't conquer a phone that probably hasn't
been charged in months. He had a good death, her dad; he had
a good death.

September 2001

It's been twelve days since the planes hit the twin towers.

Jackie sits on the side of the cranked-up hospital bed holding
her ninety-eight-year-old father's hand. He's been dead for
twenty minutes, maybe more. The hospice nurse smiles in at
Jackie as she walks by the room. Her father has taken weeks
to die and Jackie is still not ready to share his death with the
soft-spoken young nurse, so she smiles back. She kisses her
father's hand, still warm in hers, and wonders how long it will
take his hand to become cold. "Beau Pere," she whispers, hoping
her niece Selma and Regina get here soon. Hoping the Mercury
Tracer hasn't died on the way to or from the station. Hoping
Selma made her connection.

Less than an hour ago, making an account of his survivors,
Dad had said in a raspy voice, "Just you and Selma left." Jackie
felt the absence of Regina's name as more weight on a pile of

loss. Her father blinked and added, "and of course, Regina." Then he closed his eyes and Jackie closed her eyes, too. She thinks they were both sleeping when he died.

Her mother has been gone for fourteen years. Jackie does the math to figure out how long her brother's been gone. Could it be over forty years? She stares at the fine wrinkles on her father's face and notices for the first time that even the bridge of his nose and his eyelids are wrinkled. His only grandchild, Selma, is not here yet. They haven't seen her since Jackie's mother died. Jackie has the absurd thought that she'll have to remember details about what Selma says, how she looks, so she can accurately report back to her father. She squeezes his hand. "Sorry, Dad." She has failed to get Selma up from Georgia in time to say good-bye.

She crosses the hand she's not holding over his chest and studies the IV pole. The bag containing the morphine is half full. She's not sure but thinks something bad might happen to his arm if the fluid keeps dripping into his vein after his heart has stopped pumping. She's reaching for the plastic stop on the tubing and squeezing it shut when the click-clacks of high heels on linoleum announces that Regina and Selma are approaching. Jackie's head swivels toward the sound. Regina leads, but steps aside at the door to let Selma enter the room first.

Jackie places her father's other hand across his chest and stands to greet them.

Selma gives Jackie a desperate look. Her hand flies to her mouth.

"He's gone?" Regina asks, knowing the answer. "I'm sorry, Selma. We tried." It had taken them weeks to track Selma down. She was on another religious retreat, this time visualizing the souls of the three thousand victims from 9/11 being uplifted as Selma and the rest of the faithful erected a spiritual safety shield around the United States. When Selma finally heard that her grandfather was dying, she was anxious to come, but didn't have the bus fare. Jackie and Regina scrounged up money for a ticket, but not soon enough.

"Auntie," Selma says. "Oh, Auntie Jackie. I'm so ashamed. Staying away so long. Y'all were so good to me when I was little." She throws her arms around Jackie.

"The distance between Georgia and Massachusetts is the same north to south as is it south to north," Jackie says. "We should have made more of an effort, too. Your name was on his lips just before he passed."

Selma kneels by her grandfather's bed and takes his hand. Her face brightens. "His spirit hasn't left his body yet, Auntie!"

"No?" Jackie can hear the nurse's med cart clanking toward them, stopping a few doors down. "I don't know much about these things."

"We can pray for him. Help his spirit move on. Will you pray with me?" Selma places her shiny black purse on the end of the bed at her grandfather's feet. She wears a powder blue pantssuit in a style that Jackie remembers from the'80s, maybe the '70s. Selma is round, all bump and curve, with a head of well-controlled gray hair. She looks even more like Jackie's mother now than she did fourteen years ago.

"Of course we'll pray with you," Regina says, kneeling. She gestures with her eyes for Jackie to kneel next to them and moves closer to Selma, but Jackie kneels at the foot of the bed, bending her right leg so her right foot is flat on the floor and the bad knee doesn't have to bear her weight.

Jackie has always wondered how Regina, with her radical politics, is always so willing to dip into religion. Religion, traditional, new wave, east or west, God in all His or Her glory has always seemed to Jackie a distraction, a way to avoid the impossible work of shepherding the world directly toward peace and justice. She hopes Selma doesn't get into any of her moaning and writhing. Her father hated that shit but kept his peace about it, at least to Selma, as Jackie will do now if it comes to that.

Selma prays. Catholic prayers that both Regina and Jackie know and join in on, "Hail Mary full of grace. The Lord is with thee . . ." "Through my fault, through my fault, through my most grievous fault," striking their breasts on every *fault*. Selma does a little chanting. She sings "Hallelujah," a Leonard Cohen song, one of Jackie's favorites. A song Regina associates with the dark side of relationships and Jackie associates with the slippery bitch of erotic desire.

Jackie has just thought of that phrase and wants to remember it so she can repeat it to Regina, a slippery bitch of desire if ever there was one. This phrase makes Jackie grin inappropriately. She lowers her head, appreciating Selma's delivery of "Hallelujah" in her solid, sincere voice that has not lost a bit of its high emotion since she announced she was going to be a famous singer when she was six years old.

When Selma finishes the song, Jackie gives Regina a look and mouths, *Hallelujah*. They both look away. The song already has them both crying, but they're amused, too. Too much sorrow has made them ripe for laughter. More eye contact will set them off for reasons they could never explain to Selma. Dad would have loved to hear Selma sing "Hallelujah." He would have been able to appreciate the song and laugh at the fact that she chose to sing it at his death bed without hurting Selma's feelings. Selma recites a couple of psalms and *The Prayer of Saint Francis*. She is telling her grandfather to "Let go and let God," telling him, "Rise, rise, we'll join you by and by," and Jackie is about to tell her to wrap it up when the nurse with her cart stops by the door.

The nurse takes a step into the room. "Oh," she says. "I'll give you a few more minutes."

Selma turns to Jackie. "Can she join us, Auntie?" Jackie nods her assent.

The nurse kneels next to her at the end of the bed and whispers, "Such a lovely man." She touches Jackie's arm. "Now that I'm officially aware, I'll have to start the paperwork soon."

"Of course." Jackie moves her bent leg to make room. It takes less than a minute for her knee to start throbbing.

After the early morning funeral, Jackie and Selma go shopping and spend their inheritance on used cars. The farm Jackie's parents worked most of their adult lives was sold fifteen years ago to pay for medical bills her parents had incurred during her mom's battle with colon cancer. There is to be no probate court, no tax worries, no lawyer's fees, just a manila envelope with Jackie's and Selma's names on it. Inside are two letter-sized white envelopes, each containing $5,500 in cash and the same note in shaky script that reads *Consider buying a used car. Jake Junior at A Plus on Leonard Avenue will give you a good deal. Say Old Man LesPerance is cashing in a favor. He'll know what you mean. Play up the part where I died.* Jackie and Regina get $350 for their Mercury Tracer. Selma hasn't owned a car in ten years so has nothing to trade.

Four days and three trips to the Registry of Motor Vehicles later, Jackie and Regina drive from A Plus Auto to the small ranch house they bought with a down payment from money Regina inherited when her mother died. The car is a low-mileage '96 Buick that Regina immediately dubs "The Bucket" in honor of the seats, and with the foresight that they will own this car for a long time. Selma follows in the Yugo she will drive back to Georgia the next day.

It's a Saturday. Lynn is already at Jackie and Regina's preparing an easy lunch of tomato soup and grilled cheese. They sit at the kitchen table. Regina and Jackie are happy that Lynn is visiting because a week of Selma is a lot of Selma. Lynn and Selma have always gotten on like gangbusters. Regina is uncharacteristically quiet, hoping Lynn will ask Selma the direct questions that Selma would balk at if they came from Regina. Jackie sits back in her seat and closes her eyes. She loves Selma in a wholehearted, parental, totally exhausting way.

Lynn does not disappoint. "What happened with Gerald? I thought the third husband was going to be the charm." Lynn is back at the stove grilling another round of sandwiches. "You two were carrying on like teenagers the last time you were here." Lynn flips a sandwich onto the plate Selma holds out. The smell of bread grilled on butter fills the room.

"Good lord, that was a lifetime ago," Selma says. "Gerald

didn't so much like cuddling after a while, and I didn't so much like his three grown kids coming in and out of our house like it was a motel and I was the maid. Three husbands and no kids of my own. I tried to think of his children as a blessing but lost that struggle. I'm done trying to be a wife." She slashes the air with half a sandwich. "Three strikes, you're out." Her sandwich gives a satisfying crunch when she takes a bite. "My goodness but you look good for an old lady, Lynn."

"Eight years sober. Good for the mind and body." Lynn does a little shimmy, still vain of her figure. They both laugh at this.

"Good for you. What happened to your third husband?" Selma asks. "I'm sorry, I don't remember his name. Beautiful head of hair on that man."

"A woman named Lacy happened to him. But I was never foolish enough to marry him."

"I can't abide a cheater," Selma says.

"Next time, I'd settle for gainfully employed and nicer to me than whoever he's cheating with." Lynn turns off the stove burner. Jackie, Selma, and Regina all raise their eyebrows. "Kidding," Lynn says. "If I ever find another man, he'll have to worship me like the aging goddess I am."

"Now, that's a good plan." Selma laughs.

Regina is dying to find out what Selma's spiritual beliefs are. She tries to will Lynn to ask Selma a question about religion. Lynn has taken a seat and is busy tearing her sandwich into bite-sized pieces and floating them in her soup.

"You travel to religious revivals?" Regina says.

"You know I do," Selma answers.

"Like the main character in *The Apostle*?" Lynn asks.

Selma lights up. "Oh, I did love Robert Duvall in that role. I don't travel far myself and I never preach. Sometimes I testify. If that's part of the tradition. Not always revivals, though I do like them. Holy places of any kind. I'm not fussy. If a faith community claims to love God or mankind or mother earth and doesn't preach hate or burn buildings or books, I'll give it a listen as long as whoever is teaching or preaching or handing out literature doesn't bad-mouth Jesus. I even tried Wicca." Selma leans in and lowers her voice as if someone in the far corners of the small house might be listening. "Witches. Men and women, they all called themselves witches. They were very nice, but too far-out, even for me."

Jackie laughs. "God knows where you'll go with a car."

Regina wonders why she and Selma have never had the easy relationship that Selma shares with Lynn. Rivalry over Jackie, of course, and maybe Selma finds Regina haughty, a character flaw Regina has heard about herself all her life. "Faith community," Regina says. "That's an appealing phrase."

"Remember that *kundalini* group you were in?" Lynn says. "Claimed it was some kind of spiritual thing." She and Jackie share an amused look at Regina's expense.

Regina folds her arms across her chest. "It was a spiritual group. Your Auntie and Lynn are true nonbelievers, Selma." It's all Regina can do not to stick out her tongue at her sister and Jackie.

"Don't let them bother you." Selma winks and smiles at Regina, which surprises Regina. "Ninety percent of religion doesn't pass the smell test. That's why you have to dig so hard to root out the ten percent that smells true."

Regina is impressed. "I believe that, too."

Lynn reaches for the last grilled cheese. "Can I ask you something, Selma?"

"Ask away." Selma picks a cigarette out of the deep pocket of her denim skirt and twirls it between her fingers. She has not smoked in six months, but spends a lot of time doing finger tricks with rolled tobacco.

"How'd you happen to come to the farm to live with Jackie when you were a little girl? And how'd you happen to leave?" Lynn is the only one at the table who doesn't know that Selma leaving the farm is a subject that makes Jackie twitch. The mention of it now makes Jackie wince and push against her chair. Regina takes Jackie's hand.

"Those years on the farm," Selma says. "Best years of my life. Jackie is only seven years older than I am, but she took care of me better than my mama did. Never mind it was a low bar." She smiles at Jackie. "You were so good to me." She coughs. "See why I quit?" She holds up the unsmoked cigarette and takes the last sip of coffee. "I'm not entirely sure why I was brought to live on the farm or why they took me away. Mama never told the same story twice, and none of it made any sense. She and Daddy died so young. I thought I'd have time to ask Grams. Then I thought I'd have time to ask Gramps. Auntie, what can you tell me?"

"Jackie?" Regina puts an arm on the table in front of Jackie as if she might have to stop her from crashing into a windshield. She's heard bits and pieces through the years and would love to hear the entire story, but not if it's going to make Jackie go silent for a week.

"I hit on a touchy subject?" Lynn looks around the table. "Sorry."

"Nobody alive is holding back the story now," Selma says.

Except me, Jackie thinks. "I'll try, but I'm not much of a storyteller." Everyone at the table, excepting Jackie, knows that once she gets going, this statement is not true.

Selma hates to upset her auntie, which is why she knows so little of her own story. "Never mind. You saved me." She frowns, remembering. "I was five years old and mad at the world. You were the skinniest, strangest girl I ever saw. Childhood was hard on you, too. I know the important part. You took me in. You loved me."

"Grew out of skinny." Jackie clears her throat. "Ask me anything you want to, Selma."

Selma takes a deep breath. "Mama never came to see me in the whole five years I was with you. And Daddy mostly stayed away from his own sister and parents just to avoid me, is that right?" She places both hands flat on the table. "Give me a minute." She gets up and picks up the coffee pot. "Gram's old percolator." She takes it to the sink, rinses it out, scoops fresh grounds into the basket, and grins her approval at the click as the gas ignites under the pot. She sits, visibly shaken. "I should have come to see them both more often." Lynn stands and tries to hug her. Selma waves her away. "I won't be like this but a second. If I could just say a little silent prayer." She bows her head. The coffee perks.

When it's brewed, Lynn pours all around. Selma brightens and breathes in the smell.

Jackie says, "He always said, 'As long as we got coffee and each other.'"

"You were so proud of yourself driving that old tractor." Selma cradles her cup in her hands.

"New tractor then." Jackie rubs her hip. "At age eleven I was allowed to drive a tractor all morning without supervision but couldn't listen to *CBS Around the World* on the radio because the news coming in about the war was bad. Don't think there's an eleven- year-old in the country who hasn't seen the Twin Towers fall by now." Jackie wonders where to begin. "You weren't five the first time we met. You were a baby and I was barely seven."

"What?" Selma fiddles with the cigarette in the pocket of her skirt. "Details please, slow as you like." She snaps the cigarette in half on her empty plate. "I got time and I own a car so I get to decide when to step on the gas."

"Harry was so young," Jackie says. "Fourteen."

"Harry?" Lynn says. "Your brother who passed away?"

"Jackie's brother. Selma's father." Regina puts a hand on Jackie's thigh under the table and keeps it there as Jackie speaks.

"Harry farmed himself out at the Belger place in Hatfield, growing cucumbers, making pickles. One morning a car pulled up our driveway. Parked at the edge of Mom's flower garden. We had the tractor, a truck, and a wagon. No one we knew owned a car, except old man Belger. Funny what you remember."

Jackie speaks with her head tilted toward the ceiling. In her imagination, she has told this story to Selma so many times that it comes to her whole cloth. "I ran from the barn yelling for

Mom. Roses and geraniums, her pride and joy. I was afraid the car would hurt the plants and the rose thorns would scratch the car. Old Man Belger himself stood there, holding his hat, looking sheepish for a man who owned the biggest cucumber farm in the state. We all stood in the dirt driveway staring at each other. I knew something had happened for Belger to drive Harry home. Dad said, 'What is it, son?' Old Man Belger coughed and said, 'Speak to your parents, boy.' Before Harry got a word out, a mewling sound came from inside the car. And there you were, in a dresser drawer in the backseat, baby Selma working up to a howl. Harry started crying and Old Man Belger said, 'Your granddaughter.'

"The two men and Harry went for a walk, and I never saw Belger or his car again. Mom fed you cow's milk in a bottle with a rubber tip on it. I wondered how you'd ever grow because you spit up more than you swallowed. She sat me on the couch and placed you in my arms, and I thought it was about the single best thing that had ever happened to me. Later, when I asked Harry how he got you, he turned to face the wall. Mom said, 'Take her in hand, Jack.' So Dad took me for a walk by the stream and promised Mom would tell me the whole story when I came into my womanhood. I was only seven. But I was a farm kid. It was no secret that, at a certain age, females bled and after that they could have babies. I'd seen how the hog got the baby into the sow, but Harry was fourteen and had no wife to get a baby into, so how he came about getting you was a mystery to me. I knew they all wanted me to keep my questions to myself. 'You just need to know she's family,' Daddy said. 'Why, she's your niece, isn't she?' He got excited when he said that. I did, too." Jackie stares into her coffee.

"But Mama wasn't a Belger?" Selma says, confused.

"No," Jackie says. "I'm pretty sure your mother knew Belger's farm was where Harry would be and that's why she left you there."

Selma rolls half of the broken cigarette between her fingers. "So I was dumped off and taken away from you." She stops to

238

make a tiny pyramid of the tobacco that has spilled onto the plate. "Twice." Selma sets her jaw. "Everyone blames Mama. She was just a kid, too and she had no family that I ever met. And she wasn't right." Selma taps her head. "But she wasn't exactly wrong. I mean, she tried. Neglectful." She nods, accepting her own judgment. "Not abusive. How long was I with you that time?"

"A few months that first time. Harry still lived at home, working most of the time. Your mother was a ward of the state, I think. She came for you with a man she introduced as her husband. She looked like a kid playing dress-up, wearing a hat with a veil and high heels. Her husband said he was taking his little family to Georgia. I thought Georgia was a woman, his mother maybe. It was my bedtime and they made me go to my room. When I got up in the morning, you were gone."

"Poor Grams. Poor Jackie and Gramps. I've never been blessed with a child, but to have one taken." Selma sighs.

It's not particularly hot in the kitchen, but Jackie wipes sweat from her brow with a paper napkin.

"Maybe you need to rest for a minute," Regina says.

"I'm fine." Jackie takes a sip of coffee. "The second time we knew you were coming. Daddy and I got the corn planted before Sunday dinner. I figured I'd get out of doing the dishes and get to take care of you until bedtime. The only girl chore that I liked better than boy chores was taking care of babies and little kids." She grins. "Even at that age, it made me sad to know I was probably never going to do what needed to be done to get pregnant."

Selma laughs. "Well, just shows how different people can be. I was all for doing the deed, but the miracle of birth? Babies?" She shakes her head. "That farm taught me enough to know I wasn't interested in all that blood and goop and poop. Look at us, four healthy women and not a child between us." Selma waves her hand to clear the air for the main subject. "I swear I can still see the Fordson tractor rounding the barn with you squinting from the seat, hands gripping the steering wheel,

239

just as Daddy parked the car in the patch of dirt in front of the house that first day he brought me to you—well, the first day I remember. Never knew anyone but Gram to have roses and geraniums featured in the same garden. Daddy had the nerve to complain about the 'battle of fragrances' assaulting his nose from that garden." She pulls her head back. "Could I truly remember such a thing? Does that sound like something my father would say?"

"I remember things from when I was five," Lynn says.

"Sounds exactly like something Harry would say," Jackie says. "I was so excited to see you I was nauseous."

"My mother wasn't mean to me." Selma has wanted to say this to Jackie for years. "My life was hard, but not so bad. Mama was crazy, but she loved me, and she loved Georgia. Bad checks, good times, bad men, God, and Georgia, that was Mama. She loved me, Auntie."

"I'm glad," Jackie says. "I worried."

"She could sing—vaudeville, hymns, it was the same to her—drawing a crowd at the park on Sunday." Jackie can see the fierce little girl in Selma's eyes as Selma speaks. "But she had these times. Black spells she called them. I think she called Daddy and he took me away from her and back to you the second time because she was having one."

"Seems likely," Jackie agrees. "They were still only nineteen, both."

"How did a nineteen-year-old boy come to have a car in those days?" Selma wonders.

Jackie has pondered this, too, and has an unsubstantiated idea that he was involved in the illegal sale of alcohol but does not offer this as a possible explanation. Selma pulls a laminated black and white photo out of her purse and places it on the table. A young woman, smiling, in a simple dress, white gloves, and feathered hat stares out at them. She shares Selma's round face and full lips. "Mama on a good day," Selma says.

Regina studies the picture. "She's lovely. You look like her."

"Thank you." Selma smiles wistfully. "Jealous like her, too.

Bad trait. I pray about it." Her smile vanishes. "When I was a kid, it was a real problem. The cows, the tractor, I was jealous of anything and anyone that took Jackie's attention away from me. But Lucille I flat out hated."

Lynn raises her eyebrows and looks at Regina. "Lucille?" Lynn says. Regina gives her sister a look that makes Lynn sit back and listen.

"Tell about that first day, what a little shit I was," Selma says.

Jackie takes another sip of coffee before she speaks. "Harry took a little girl by the hand as she stepped off the running board, all dressed up in fancy clothes. I knew it was you, but I couldn't fathom the five years that had passed. I jumped off the tractor and was mad when you didn't come running to me. You stomped your foot and yelled."

"No, I will not, Papa. No, I will not, Papa," Selma mimics her five-year-old self.

"Harry snatched you up in his arms. He was cheerful, but Harry's cheerful always made me feel like something was wrong. He had a way of making you feel like you had no right to your own sadness," Jackie says.

"None of us was supposed to peek under Daddy's blanket of fake happiness," Selma says. "What made him so sad? Why did his sorrow always trump everyone else's?"

"The war? He left strange and came back stranger." Jackie suspects that part of her brother's unhappiness was Selma herself, that he couldn't take responsibility for her. Maybe he was born sad and strange. As long as she can remember he strained to be kind, to be happy, to get through a conversation or dinner.

"I just remembered something," Selma says. "He pulled my braid, laughed, and said, 'This is your Auntie. She took good care of you when you were a baby.' I said, 'I ain't a baby.'"

Jackie doesn't remember this and wonders if either of them truly remembers any of it the way it happened.

"He stayed for meatloaf and pie, but didn't spend the night." Selma moves her spoon around in her cold soup but doesn't eat

241

any. "He said it was the best meal he'd had in five years. I hated him for saying that. I hated him for taking me away from Mama and pulling my braid and making me ride in his car. But I was jealous of the meatloaf."

Jackie remembers turkey, a big bird that they ate for days afterward. "You drank two glasses of milk but refused to eat a bite," she says. "Until we were left alone on the porch so the adults could talk in the parlor, Gramps was the only one you'd look at."

"Gramps made those silly faces," Selma says. "Kindest man I ever knew. Can't believe he's gone." They're all silent for a minute in recognition of the kindness of Jackie's father, in recognition of the loss. "I sometimes wonder if I'm hard on other men because I know how good a man can be." She smiles at Jackie. "You are so much like him."

Jackie shakes her head. "I wish that were true."

"Oh, it's true. Kindness," Regina says, "the best inheritance."

"You got that same look he got on his face when someone tried to give him a compliment," Selma says. "Go on. I'll try not to interrupt. We sat side by side on the porch swing. That's a story I know. I love that story."

"You twirled your braid and studied me," Jackie says.

Unconsciously, Selma twirls a strand of lacquered hair now.

"I was still mad at you for being so changed and for not remembering me," Jackie continues. "When you jumped off the swing, twirling your whole body so the skirt of your dress flew around your knees, I couldn't stop myself from loving you. A little ball of anger, but you couldn't stop yourself from letting in some fun."

"You'll never guess the first thing I said to Jackie." Selma looks from Lynn to Regina.

Regina knows the answer but doesn't want to ruin the story so says nothing. Lynn and Jackie also wait silently in Selma's dramatic pause.

Selma grins. "I said, 'You're a girl, right?'"

Lynn laughs. "And what did you answer, Jackie?"

Jackie shrugs. "I said, 'I suppose so.' You scooted as close to me as you could get on the swing. We swung our legs and looked at the field and you said, 'That man, your daddy? He lives in the house with you?'" Jackie is still moved by the strange mix of innocence and worldliness in Selma's questions. "I told you he did. You smiled and curled yourself into a ball, like a cat."

"You sang," Selma says.

"'Over the Rainbow' and 'God Bless America' until you fell asleep." That she sang these songs seems the least likely part of the story to Jackie.

"He left me with the best auntie and grandparents in the world," Selma says. "Without saying good-bye. Five years with only postcards from my father and packages with perfume or a bit of lace from my mother. Then one year Daddy comes to visit for a week in July. He wore a uniform. Two days after Daddy left in his uniform, Mama came and took me away. She brought a cop with her."

"Sheriff," Jackie says.

"Why? After five years?" Lynn asks.

Jackie wipes her face with her napkin. "Harry reenlisted and wanted to see you before he left."

Lynn frowns. "After five years they show up one after the other?"

After a long pause, Jackie says, "Harry found us, me and Lucille, in the barn. We were kissing . . . and more."

Lynn looks around the table. "What's that got to do with Selma's mother showing up?"

Regina has never heard this part of the story but knows the answer.

"Lucille was a grown woman." Selma frowns. "Jackie was barely seventeen."

"She was barely twenty, old enough to pass for twenty-one and buy liquor," Jackie says. "And I was old enough to say no. Anyway, I was the one who . . . I pursued her."

Selma leans toward Jackie. "We heard Daddy yelling that no daughter of his was going to end up on a hay bale with another girl. You'll think I'm a fool, but I swear all these years I thought he was mad because you were drinking. Even after I knew you went with girls, it never occurred to me." She laughs. "He thought if I stayed on the farm, I'd turn out like you and Lucille?" The look on Jackie's face makes Selma grimace. "Oh Auntie, you blame yourself?"

"Your gramps warned me, but I was too . . ." Jackie lets the sentence trail off. "There were acres, cornfields, and woods. It ripped my parents' hearts out to let you go. I wasn't used to alcohol. I knew better than to drink."

"Daddy sent me off with a woman who couldn't provide three meals in a row and who was married to two men at the same time so I wouldn't see girls kissing?" Selma shakes with emotion. "That's how he repaid you for taking care of me? You must have hated him."

"In those days if I hated every person who thought kids should be kept away from me, I would have hated everyone. I made it harder on myself than it had to be. I was shunned because I was stubborn. I'd stay home alone rather than put on a dress."

"Stubborn you were." Selma nods. "Dungarees under your skirts at school. Good lord what we do to each other."

"I did hate Harry for a long time. Until he died. So young. Then I wished I'd stopped hating him sooner. Grams and Gramps fought to keep you. But Harry was your father and Marion was your mother."

"Marion," Regina says, having misheard Selma's mother's name as *Marianne* the one other time she heard Jackie speak it.

Selma gets out of her chair to be nearer to Jackie. Regina takes her hand off Jackie's thigh and angles her chair to make room for Selma.

"Thank you for telling me." Selma kneels and takes both of Jackie's hands in hers. "Even before the business in the barn Daddy hated the way I followed you around." Selma presses her forehead to Jackie's. "We were children," she whispers. "Both of us." Selma stands with a little help from Jackie and directs a comment to Regina and Lynn, "Well, of course I had a little crush on Jackie. It's the way of young girls to have crushes on their aunties." She rolls her eyes in disgust. "They had funny ideas in those days." Selma takes her seat again. "Makes you wonder what funny ideas we hang on to doesn't it, Auntie?" Her face softens. "Please stop blaming yourself. That just makes everything more wrong." Selma dabs her eyes with a tissue. "I wish I could forgive Daddy. I better pray on it."

"Blame the laws that let them take you," Regina says. "Or blame the war."

"Blame the barn door for not having an inside latch," Lynn says.

Jackie laughs halfheartedly and wipes her cheek with the back of her hand. She doesn't say the barn door had an outside latch, and she was locked in when Selma's mother and the sheriff came to take Selma. She doesn't say that she crawled through a broken slat on the back wall and ran after the sheriff's car long after it was out of sight, that her mother followed her and cried on her knees on the dirt road before they walked back to the house.

The doorbell rings. Regina answers it. Two little boys stand on the step. One holds out a bag to Regina.

"Thank you, Ramon. Thank you, TJ." Regina takes the bag. "Now what could this be?" She holds the bag in both hands to feel the heft of it. "Smells like cookies. We still have some of your mama's chicken and rice left, Ramon." Regina stands at the open kitchen door and waves across the yard to Ramon's grandmother, Lotti, who stands by a fence that separates the adjoining backyards. The fence is more decoration than obstruction, only a few feet high with breaches big enough for a four-year-old to wiggle through. Lotti waves back. Lotti holds Ramon's brother, Oscar, a chubby moon-faced boy, by the hand.

Regina stands in the open door with the boys looking up at her expectantly from the step. She turns to look at Jackie, trying to gauge if she wants a visit, knowing Jackie would have to be feeling very low not to welcome the kids.

245

"Lotti made you cookies," Ramon says shyly. Everyone calls his grandmother Lotti. "Cuz Jackie's papi died."

TJ, bolder than Ramon, peeks around Regina and steps inside. He gives Jackie a big grin. "We can only stay and play if Jackie asks us. We can't ask first."

"Well, I guess a formal invitation is necessary," Jackie says. "TJ, Ramon, please come in. Have a seat. And bring that bag. Smells like something we might need help eating."

"It's okay!" Regina yells across to Lotti. "Thanks for the cookies. I'll call before we send the boys home." She smiles down at the boys. "Leave your coats on the chair by the door."

TJ hands his coat to Ramon, runs to Jackie, and climbs on her lap.

Regina gets the pretty plate that was Jackie's mother's out of the cupboard, and Ramon helps arrange the cookies in a neat circle on the dish before he places it proudly in the middle of the table.

"Hello," Lynn says to the boys. "Remember me?"

"Lotti let you borrow her shoes," TJ says.

"Yes, she did. I needed them for a fancy wedding."

"TJ, Ramon," Jackie introduces them solemnly, "this is my niece Selma."

"Well, aren't you the sweetest?" Selma says.

"We ain't sweet." TJ bounces on Jackie's lap. Jackie puts her hand flat on the table and lets him play with her fingers to help him stop fidgeting. "Where you from?" TJ asks Selma. "You talk like you're from somewhere."

Chapter 12

"Didn't know those things came apart," Jackie says.

Regina looks up from the flip phone she's trying to put back together. In her frustration to get the thing working and listen to Jackie's winded story about her father, she inadvertently broke it into two pieces. She and Jackie are still seated hip to hip on the ground in the snow with their backs against the step of the backhoe.

"Honey?" Regina says. "I've been so busy concentrating on the past and the phone." For a moment Regina is frozen in position, holding a piece of phone in each ungloved hand. "Your face. It's gray." Jackie's face has taken on the color of uncooked chicken left in the fridge too long. Regina lifts a hand to touch Jackie's cheek, but the decimated phone stops her. She can't think of a thing to do. Her own face blanches. She stares at Jackie.

"Lucky break," Jackie says. "Must be my heart."

"Lucky break! You make me angry at the worst times." Regina has been holding her breath. She sucks in a lungful, throws both pieces of the phone in the snow, and pulls on her gloves. She leans forward to look down the road. Have they been here an hour? Two? She tries to look at the watch under Jackie's glove, but can't see it without taking the glove off. She doesn't want to expose Jackie to any extra cold air and gives up on the time.

"Sorry." Jackie looks Regina in the eye, all love and tenderness. "You've forgiven me." Her words are jagged, raw, like she's got a sore throat, like the words of their old neighbor when he was on a ventilator, "for a lot worse." She takes Regina's hand.

Regina knows what Jackie wants: to be told that it's all right, but no, it is not all right. No. Jackie is not their old neighbor, nice as he was. She's Regina's Jackie and she's staying right here in this world with Regina. She'll be okay with a little cajoling, a little encouragement. "Thom will have a phone." Regina stands to start the thousand-foot trek to the car.

"Stay," Jackie pleads, the rawest sound Regina has ever heard come out of her mouth. "St . . ." Jackie attempts the word again but fails.

"Okay, honey. I'm here." Regina pats Jackie's cheeks with her gloved hands, frantic to get some color back. "See. You're pinking up a little. We'll get you back home. Relax. Save your energy. I'll stay. We can make you feel better. We can get help. There's help out there. I'm not so tired. I can do all the paperwork. I don't mind waiting in the Senior Housing Office or Elder Care. SSI, we've barely looked into SSI. And those ads on TV." She doesn't know what ads she means but has a vague notion that she's seen ads that claim to help. "And churches, churches help people. And Casa Latino, we're not Spanish, but we're in the neighborhood; they'd point us in the right direction, maybe. Papi and Lotti. The kids. Charlie calls once a month." She's talking a mile a minute, pulling out every social service agency and friend or neighbor they've ever known. "Of course, Yvonne," she says. "Yvonne will do anything for us. And Silver."

Jackie waits patiently, eyes closed. She whispers "I don't crochet" when Regina mentions The Council on Aging. Her body collapses, her head into her shoulders, her shoulders into

248

her chest. She strokes Regina's hand weakly, holding up her head to see Regina, letting it fall again.

"Hang on, baby. Rest. I'll get Thom. You'll go to the hospital. There are things to hang on for. There's you and me, Jackie. You've still got roast chicken. You love to drive."

"Don't leave, Regina." Jackie's words come in a loose string, unraveling. "You'll be sad about it for the rest of your life."

"Our life. Damn it. Hang on. You've got me."

Jackie's arm somehow is around Regina now. She says in a faltering pant, "We could try yoga."

Regina laughs, hysterical. Her cackle cuts the air like an ice pick.

Jackie coughs and sputters.

"Oh, Jackie." Regina stops laughing when Jackie starts coughing. "Sit up," Regina says. She rubs Jackie's arm. "That's better. There, see? That's it, nice easy breaths in and out. I have to get help. Can you speak?" She remembers something from their first aid training about asking a person in trouble if they can speak. "I don't know what to do," she says, barely out loud.

"A story."

"No," Regina says. "You're barely hanging on." She looks down the road and back at Jackie. "And we've been telling stories."

"That's why I'm still here," Jackie whispers. "The time I cleaned out the cellar," she says almost inaudibly but loud enough for Regina to hear. "That's a hang-on story."

"I can just barely hear you, but your speech is better. Say you won't leave me." Regina puts her arm around Jackie's waist. "The cellar thing was a fight, not a story." She pulls Jackie's arm over her shoulder. "A stupid fight about nothing."

Jackie doesn't register Regina's last sentence because she's speaking softly at the same time, "That was before I stopped— gambling? Yes, a couple years before . . . I stopped. I'll start you off. I couldn't get over . . . my father's death." She speaks in short puffs of words. "You saved us. From my depression . . . Homeland Security orange alert foolishness. Until then . . . I thought you-were the one . . . with middle-class values." Jackie coughs out a laugh.

"Save your breath. Say you'll stay with me until help comes and I'll talk about the time you cleaned out the cellar."

"I'll stay with you . . . always," Jackie says. "What year . . . was it, honey?"

March 2003

Jackie pulls into the drive, cuts the engine, and rests her forehead on the steering wheel. If he had lived, today would have been her father's one hundredth birthday. She doesn't mean to keep mourning the death of someone who lived so long and so well, a man who never sat in the driveway with his head on the steering wheel. She doesn't mean to keep fighting with Regina over everything and nothing. She doesn't mean to stay silent for hours at a time.

As far as Regina's concerned, Jackie has been blue for too damn long. Regina has tried to get Jackie to talk about what's bothering her, better yet to cry. Gentle persuasion, tears, stomping out of the house, valerian tea, sex, shoulder massage, scrapbooking pictures and letters from Jackie's mostly dead family, and Michael Moore videos. Nothing has worked.

When she walks into the living room, Jackie finds Regina on the floor with her back against the couch, legs under the coffee table, Green Party materials spread out around her. She inks a mark next to a name on a list. "Did you get the stuff for chili?"

"Ran out of money." Jackie lowers herself into her La-Z-Boy. "I'll make vegetarian. We have beans and rice. Tomatoes too, I think. I spent the twenty bucks."

Regina snaps to attention. She puts a hand to her breast. "Tell me you didn't."

"I didn't." Jackie points with her chin to the Walmart bag next to her recliner.

Regina frowns at the bag. She gathers the flyers and petitions scattered around her and stacks them into folders. "What did you buy?" Her lips thin out the way they do when she's trying not to be pissed off. "Instead of groceries?"

They are both brought back to the last time Jackie came home without the groceries. A couple of months ago, she lost eighty dollars of grocery money on a couple of games of five-card draw that she played in the breakroom of the local grocery store on a Sunday after the store closed for the day. She tried then to explain how gambling excites and calms her before it shames and makes her miserable. Regina had been a comfort for months after her father's death, but Regina's soothing funeral voice faded before Jackie was ready to soothe herself. "You gambled the grocery money," Regina had seethed. "Eighty bucks." Jackie had tried to diminish the loss. "You spent that much on a duvet last week." "Money wasted to escape worry, sorrow and grief." Regina had quoted Gamblers Anonymous literature. "Causing unhappiness in your home life." And Jackie for once had gotten the last word, "Only a sociopath doesn't need to find ways to escape worry, sorrow, and grief."

They'd had the same argument many times, and in the end neither of them wanted a real fight, so, as they had learned to do decades before, they had settled for the abbreviated version.

Now Regina struggles to get her legs out from under the coffee table. Jackie bends to offer a hand.

Regina manages to get off the floor without help. "There better be something good in that sack," she says when she's finally seated on the couch. "I like meat in my chili."

If Jackie felt better, she might get herself to say, "My father is dead, the world has gone crazy, so let's take a nap and hold each other." As it is, she dumps the contents of the plastic bag on the coffee table. Duct tape and sheets of plastic.

Regina groans. "You're taking the advice of those ridiculous men at Homeland Security telling us to prepare for terrorists with duct tape?"

Jackie says nothing.

"Survivalist," Regina says, knowing Jackie hates the word.

251

The next day, Jackie is in the cellar destroying geraniums that have been overwintering in recycled containers on the cold cement floor. Regina has been in the basement for ten minutes, arms crossed, leaning against the cinderblock wall, silently watching Jackie's every move.

Jackie has not spoken a word to Regina since she accused her of being a survivalist. The ban on speaking that Regina inflicted on herself ten minutes ago is already killing Regina.

Jackie grabs a plant. She's always had a special place in her heart for the tough old-fashioned flower that her mom loved. For ten years now the plants have survived from November until April with little water and scant light from a small basement window. Jackie likes the idea of turning a hardy annual into a perennial in this way. The species is called Martha Washington. She even likes the name. By this time of year, even when Jackie isn't yanking them out of their pots by their scrawny necks, the plants look dead. With a little rooting hormone, cuttings produce a border of showy red flowers around the front of the house all summer and well into fall. With only eight weeks left until they can be set in the ground, Jackie wrenches a plant from a container and tosses its remains into a big black garbage bag.

Regina contemplates Jackie's ass, which is back in the air as she bends over a bag. Before they started to get old, Regina did not imagine an old person could move like that, sore hips, bad knees, and all. Regina is seventy-four. She looks frail. She's not. She's just size six. She can carry grocery bags. She can rake the lawn. More exertion doesn't interest her. If Regina didn't feel like strangling Jackie, if Jackie's aching joints weren't so obvious, Regina could happily watch her big ass move by the hour. Watching Jackie's overalls, so out of fashion on anyone who is not a toddler or a teenager, stretch across Jackie's bottom as she bends at the waist almost brings Regina to tears. She's put in mind of other times Jackie has taken this position: making love, moving the coffee table, caring for Regina's mother when she broke her hip. Regina wonders how she can be disgusted and enamored at the same time. She understands that Jackie is still blue about her father's death and the state of the world. But her father died over a year ago and the world has been a mess forever. Why did Jackie pick their old age to be a horse's ass and start listening to reactionary politicians telling her to build shelters in cellars?

Jackie stops tossing plants and looks in the bag. She considers Regina's foray into the basement a good sign. She almost speaks, but reconsiders. They are in the same room at the same time and not openly fighting; speaking might change that. Jackie wants to get back on an even keel, but Regina has been stepping on her last nerve lately. Why does Regina have to lecture her about every damn thing? Jackie considers how she grunted a response that Regina mistook as a "yes," and now Regina believes that Jackie intends to convert the cellar into an actual shelter. She looks at the smirk on Regina's face and decides not to clear up this misunderstanding.

Jackie needs to do something. With her hands. She wishes it were spring. But, no more flowers. She'll plant food this year, potatoes, carrots, beans. Crops her father planted. She yanks the two sides of the trash bag together and ties them in a knot. "Sorry, Martha," she mumbles. At least Regina can't complain that Jackie's moping around. She takes a break, not five feet from Regina, wiping off the husks of several dead wasps before taking a seat on a gutted TV console.

Regina is still watching, arms folded over her chest, head cocked.

When she and Regina are on good terms this posture strikes Jackie as the stance of a woman interested and willing to take on the world. Right now, it seems like the pose of a self-righteous bitch.

Regina, for her part, has correctly read Jackie's mind and is having no problem taking on the role of self-righteous bitch. She tries on the notion of unqualified forgiveness, no expectation in return, but decides no. Fuck Jackie. Regina believes

Jackie has been ready to talk for days but is too proud to spit out what's really bothering her.

Jackie abandons the geraniums even though there are several plants left on the ledge of the window. She strains under the weight of a plastic tub full of Christmas ornaments, which she pushes toward the bulkhead. At seventy-five, Jackie, once lean, mannish, and muscular, has become a round-bodied mannish old woman. If a person pays close attention, which Regina does, she can see that Jackie braces herself every time she lifts a pot or moves a box.

Regina sighs. She does appreciate physical work and how willing Jackie is to do it. Why is Jackie so aggravated with her, Regina wonders. Regina has every right to complain about the old fool's bomb shelter mentality. And this crap Jackie's buying, sheets of plastic, a special wind-up radio, and a space heater that runs on god knows what? This junk all costs money. Regina would almost rather Jackie waste the money on poker. This morning in the grocery store Regina had to leave the ginger tea on the shelf. Tea, they can't afford tea.

She can't hold her tongue a minute longer. "Who ever thought my Jackie would end up a scared old lady? You're delusional if you think duct tape will hold anything together after a nuclear attack." Leaning against the wall becomes uncomfortable. Regina unfolds a lawn chair. "Maybe if you dress up as Barbara Bush again, you'll remember how to speak, and you can talk some sense into Bush Junior."

Jackie mumbles a swear at a tangle of Christmas lights and throws them back into a plastic tub.

"Very close to speech but no cigar." Regina sits and hoists her feet in their pink sneakers up on a broken dehumidifier. "You as Barbara Bush. That was the best Halloween ever."

Jackie frowns at Regina.

Regina laughs. "You're actually glowering at me."

"Not glowering at you." Jackie turns away. She has not felt this kind of bone-deep disgust with herself or her country since she was dishonorably discharged from the Army for *conduct unbecoming* during the witch hunts of the '50s. She needs to move her body. If she can't save Regina and herself from reckles politicians, she can save them from a hoarder's nest in the cellar. Not one, but two, rotary phones on a pile of wooden slats particularly irritate her.

"Glowering at yourself, are you?" Regina watches the curve of Jackie's back bend to the work as Jackie drags the slats to the growing pile of junk near the hatchway.

Jackie says, "Bastards," under her breath, meaning the inquiry board members who sent her parents that damn letter half a century ago. *We are sending your homosexual child home.* It wasn't bad enough they got rid of her. They put it in writing and sent the fucking letter ahead of her. Dishonorably discharged. Almost killed her mother. Damn near killed Jackie. And her father, so proud of her in his quiet way when she signed up. Since she was twelve, her father knew what she was and who she was. He found her and Suzie Norris in the pantry, took them out to the barn, Suzie shaking, expecting a beating, but what they got was a shake of her father's head and the sad truth. "You girls are going to get the shit beat out of you, anyone but me finds you like that." Only time her father ever swore in front of Jackie. And after his homosexual child was sent home, he took her fishing and never spoke of her time in the service again. His only living child and the bastards wouldn't let her make him proud.

Jackie grips a rotary phone in each hand. She glances at Regina, the one person in the world she has told this story. She would smile at Regina now, maybe get out of her own way long enough to make up, to give Regina a chance to wonder out loud how Jackie found so many girls to get in trouble with in rural Massachusetts in that day and age, but Regina is looking at the stack of empty plastic flower pots with that face she puts on when she's right. What did Jackie's father call the old lady down the road when she made that face? On a good day, Jackie could ask Regina to help her remember.

Regina lifts out of her lawn chair and moves it to keep Jackie in view. "Speak up. I swear you just called me priggish. If you mean to insult me, you have to stop grunting."

"Lavender scare, afraid of rough girls and sissy boys. Coward."

"Growling now? Much better. Who's a coward?"

Jackie gives the phones a filthy look. Why did they keep the useless things in the first place? "Eisenhower." Jackie hates all politicians but reserves a special dark place in her soul for her country's beloved Eisenhower, who declared homosexuals a threat to national security. She holds the phones over an empty box. They land with a satisfying crack of thick plastic.

"Oh, we're back on the witch hunts and Ike again? 'Before Eisenhower,'" Regina mocks Jackie, "'it was Truman. At least under Truman they let you alone if you stayed *undercover*.'" Regina had laughed the first time Jackie used undercover to describe the gay women and men who managed to remain completely closeted, so got to remain in the Army, but Jackie hadn't cracked a smile. Regina learned quickly that there was no pun or double entendre in the dishonorable discharge story that could make Jackie smile.

Jackie counts to ten, then twenty. If Regina wants some big reaction, she's not going to get it. She counts to one hundred before picking up a burlap bag. The bottom of the bag rips. Potatoes hit the floor in a rapid succession of thumps and a series of *fucks* from Jackie.

"Insanity," Regina says.

Jackie kicks a potato. It lands near Regina's left foot. "They waited till after the war to get rid of us, didn't they?" Jackie says clearly.

"You think Rosie the Riveter is wasting her anger on dead politicians? Sensible Jackie becoming foolish, folding so late in the game. Sometimes I admire your gruffness. Part of the no-nonsense attitude I fell in love with. It's turning into plain old pigheadedness." Regina looks at the stack of moldy boxes. There must be mismatched plates and mugs in at least one of them. She clicks her tongue, wishing Jackie was the kind of woman who threw dishes. Do her good. It's chilly in the cellar.

Regina zips her hoodie, bringing together the two sides of the pink *Silence=Death* triangle logo on the front. "You're angry. I'm angry. Let's climb the stairs to our warm kitchen and fight it out over a cup of tea so we can spend another decade or two arguing and making up and being thankful for what we have."

Jackie huffs, considering their relative position as old women living on Social Security in a low-income neighborhood. A shadow floats across her face. She hasn't told Regina about the $200 she "borrowed" from Bo and Yvonne to fix the car. They still owe mortgage money Bo and Yvonne "lent" them a year ago. Her father never would have let this kind of debt happen.

Jackie kneels to gather the potatoes scattered around the ripped bag and remembers her father's sorrow when he sold the farm to pay for her mother's medical expenses. How defeated he seemed for the first time. The ache in her knees reminds her of kneeling in front of her father's coffin. She has not prayed in years and she did not pray then, unless whispering to your dead father is a kind of prayer. She never really believed he would die. Death is real. She's going to die. Regina's going to die. It's infuriating that these assholes who control the world might make it sooner and uglier than necessary. Jesus, why is she fighting with Regina? All she wants is to feel useful, to feel like she's protecting them, like Regina wouldn't be better off without her. She looks up, ready to make amends, to speak, but Regina speaks first.

"This shelter is an insult to people who have to hide underground," Regina says.

It's not so much what she says as the self-righteous way Regina says it that gets to Jackie. The desire to apologize drains out of Jackie. Let Regina think what she wants. Jackie is preparing. The house is drafty. The cellar window should have been covered in plastic the first winter they moved in. Nothing insane about what she's doing. Except for the high-end wind-up radio that she got from Radio Shack—that was a nutty purchase. And maybe the heater. That money should have gone back to Bo and Yvonne.

Jackie stands, trips over a sprouting potato, scowls at Regina

257

and says, "Bitch," before she rights herself. As soon as the word is out, she's sorry. In their fights, *fucker* is fair play, but *bitch* is always out of bounds. Jackie considers claiming she was talking to the potato.

Regina will be damned if she'll show Jackie how hurt she is. She leans forward in the lawn chair to pick up the potato near her foot and picks a geranium leaf off the floor while she's at it. She pulls a face at the odor the plant releases when she pinches the leaf. "You stink," she confides to the leaf. "And my girlfriend called me a bitch."

The word *girlfriend*, even said sarcastically, makes Jackie's heart ache. She abandons potato-wrangling to sit on a box in front of a wall of boxes and rub her forehead. Nobody says *girlfriend* anymore. It's *partner*, *significant other*, sometimes *spouse*. And Christ, never *lover*. *Lover* makes people nervous, supposed to slide the tongue quickly over the sex in homosexuality. She longs to stop aiming her anger at Regina and call her *lover* right now. They used to say *lover* on purpose to feel sexy and make other people nervous. Now it's all about assimilation, getting along. "Lover," she whispers.

"What?" Regina considers the dirty potato in her hand and decides it must be organic. "I wonder if you're becoming demented?" Regina sniffs the leaf again. "Amazing, how disgusting these things smell." She taps her head. "Maybe what you have is reactionary dementia." Regina grins, the disingenuous smile that Jackie hates. "How many years has Martha survived down here with just a drop of water every few weeks?" Regina turns to glance out the small window. "And almost no light." She wipes the potato on the leg of her jeans.

Regina's little spiel makes Jackie glad she didn't say "lover" louder. "This a sermon? Little Flower and The Miracle of the Demented Lover? A lot for one story." Jackie grabs the last of the plants off the windowsill. "Even for you."

"And that was a lot of words out of you at one go. Look at you. Hiding in a cellar. You do—" Regina shakes her head, "—you believe the nonsense those unpleasant men in the Bush

White House are spouting."

"Unpleasant?" Jackie has a headache coming on. "Three thousand dead on 9/11. I'm not worried about pleasant. Who's going to take care of us if we don't take care of ourselves?"

"Worry about the mortgage." Regina's head moves like a bobble doll in a slow-moving car. Her head shakes when she's stressed; nothing to worry about the nurse practitioner at the clinic claims. She holds the potato like a grenade she's about to toss. "Speaking of irrational reactions to useless acts of violence," Regina smiles broadly, liking the sound of her words, "tell me again why you are killing the tender perennials?"

"You hate geraniums." Jackie, wielding a plant, walks to Regina. Regina crosses her legs. The naked root dangles a few inches from Regina's nose.

Regina slaps it away and the roots spit little black BBs of soil onto her faded pink sweatshirt. She screws up her face and picks a heart-shaped leaf out of her hair. "They smell like something that used to be pleasant. Like garlic on the breath the morning after a good meal."

"Pleasant again? Nothing's all that pleasant if you get close enough." Jackie tosses the plant on top of its relatives in the big black trash bag and reaches out with both hands to steady Regina's head.

But Regina raises a hand to strike Jackie, stopping at the last possible second. They both stare at Regina's hand. Neither of them has ever hit the other. Regina folds her hands on her lap. "I admit it, I want to slap some sense into you. We should be talking about money and your dead father and how it feels to grow old. What are we arguing over?" She opens her arms. "This."

Jackie bends to touch the plant she just tossed, a descendant from her mother's garden like all the rest in the bag. She has never been fond of what her parents called "God's plan" that in the end we all die. But this fear that she won't be able to take care of Regina, this regret that she didn't do more to prepare for their aging, this is new. She doesn't want to infect Regina with the dread she feels. In her mind, Jackie has braided together her father's death, her own aging, and the feeling that the world is going to hell in a handbasket. She doesn't want to tighten the braid and pull Regina in by putting her anxiety into words.

"I . . ." Jackie sits on a stripped mattress on a metal frame. The mattress sags. "I should leave." She lowers her eyes. "I thought I would plant beans, tomatoes, maybe peas."

"You can have peas *and* flowers." Regina cocks her head. "Leave? You mean leave me? Are you leaving or planting?" She gets off her lawn chair to sit next to Jackie and stare at her tear-streaked face. "Where would you go?" She's incensed. Also, panicked.

"To Bo's," Jackie says softly.

"And Yvonne's? The room over their garage? Yvonne must not know. She would never agree to it. You're not speaking to me, but you've spoken to Bo about leaving me?"

"I called you a bitch," Jackie says. "You almost hit me. We need . . ."

"Don't you dare say 'some space.' We're too old for this. Is there someone else?"

"Christ, no. Just. For a while."

"For fuck's sake." Regina's tears disgust her. What if neither of them can bend enough to get through this? This has gone far enough.

Jackie's head falls. She looks at the floor. "Just for a while until I'm not so . . ." She covers her face with her hands.

"You drop this bombshell in your bomb shelter?" Regina moves six inches away so their legs aren't touching. She remembers with repulsion that sexy women used to be called bombshells and tightens her jaw, causing a tremor to travel down her left shoulder to her arm. She gives the arm a dirty look and tries to calm her growing fury so she can think straight. "Good, go somewhere else to be a sullen prick. Don't talk about your fear or anger or whatever is depressing you with the person who loves you most in the world." Regina turns away, throws the potato she's holding in the air, and catches it. "You need a washing," she

260

tells the potato. "Not a speck of green on you." She squeezes it. "Nice and hard." She pets her cheek with the potato, leaving a smudge. She glances at Jackie. "You still here?"

Jackie winces, not wanting to see a potato get the affection she craves but has been pushing away. She had whispered, 'I don't know how to be old and scared,' to her father as he lay in his coffin, almost wept then for herself, and because she was so moved by what she thought of as her ninety-eight-year-old father's last gift, dying just when she and Regina were contemplating moving him into their house. She weeps silently now, head bowed, glad Regina is turned away.

Out of the corner of her eye Regina watches the slight movement of Jackie's shoulders that lets her know Jackie is crying. Crying, Regina thinks, is a start, but she wants words, conversation.

Jackie wipes her tears on her sleeve and turns to see the stony look on Regina's face.

"Still edible." Regina throws the potato in the air and catches it. "Why wait for famine?" She takes a bite.

"Jesus." Jackie grimaces. "There's dirt on those things. They're old and raw."

"Old and raw." Regina chews and nods her approval, putting on a show. "Gritty. Remind you of anyone?" She concentrates and tries to swallow. She tries to cough. The lump of potato sits in her throat. Bad move, talking and eating.

"Okay. Enough shock and awe," Jackie says. "You win. Spit it out before you choke to death." She waits while Regina stares at her. "Please."

Regina spits a bit of potato into the trash bag that holds the geraniums. She attempts an exhale but only a wheeze escapes.

"Thank you." Unaware of Regina's distress, Jackie spreads her hands on her thighs, looks at her sneakers, and begins simply, "You're right. You usually are. I should have been talking to you right along. My father dying right when 9/11 happened. This damn war. Bo gave me the money to fix the car. It started with that. I don't know why I didn't tell you."

Regina attempts to exhale again but manages only another faint wheeze.

Jackie continues her slow stride of words, "I meant to take care of you, I mean, all along. Now we're old and . . ." Jackie shakes her head, looking at her feet, jiggling one foot, forcing herself to continue, ". . . I'm. Ashamed. Afraid. It doesn't seem fair to ask you to take care of me emotionally. When I couldn't even provide a decent place for us to live all those years."

Regina wonders if her head tremor is complicating the potato's passage down her throat. Her eyes widen. She points to her neck and tries to speak but is only able to produce a squeak that Jackie, still head-down, her bad ear toward Regina, painstakingly pulling words from herself, doesn't hear.

Regina kicks Jackie's jiggling foot.

For a moment, Jackie thinks the kick is delivered out of annoyance, but Regina staggers over to the bulkhead. Jackie jumps off the mattress. Regina tries unsuccessfully to slide the rusty bolt and push open the hatchway. Jackie yanks the bolt and shoves a shoulder against the slanted metal door.

Regina stumbles up the steps and tumbles into the backyard where she hops around in the snow coughing and spitting.

"Baby, are you all right?" Jackie asks, even though she's sure neither of them is all right. She tries to remember what she learned in CPR. "Can you speak?"

Regina's eyes water. She exhales, points to her throat, and bends over, gagging, with her hands on her knees. Jackie thumps her on the back with the flat of her hand. A piece of potato flies out of Regina's mouth. She holds on to Jackie's arm, bends further toward the ground, sucks in a lung full of air, coughs, and spits out pink saliva and more chewed potato. When she's done with the heaviest hacking, Regina stands, and Jackie takes her in her arms. Regina coughs on Jackie's shoulder.

Jackie kisses Regina's forehead. "Jesus, I could have lost you."

"What do you care?" Regina asks hoarsely. "You're leaving me."

"Damn fool." Jackie steadies the back of Regina's head.

"You?"

"Yes, me."

Regina cries. It feels good, so she keeps crying.

Holding Regina is the first time Jackie hasn't felt like crying in weeks.

Regina's cough becomes intermittent throat clearing. "You called me a bitch." She steps away.

"Sorry." Jackie tries to pull Regina back into a hug but gets a *not so fast* look.

"What were you talking about, *take care of* me? We take care of each other. We always have." Regina folds her arms across her chest. "Take care of me in a bomb shelter?"

"Never was building a shelter. Just cleaning the cellar, getting rid of the drafts, trying to keep us warm, keep down the heating bills. I thought the plastic and duct tape would look better than it does. Why were you so mad about plastic sheeting? I'm sorry for all of it. I don't want to suck the life out of you because I'm so . . ." Jackie runs out of patience with words.

Regina tries to wait her out. She holds on for ten seconds, then twenty. "You're so what? Depressed? Old? You think I don't know you're scared? I'm scared, too. Scared of being old and broke. Scared of the greedy fools running this world. Now I have to be scared you're going to leave me?"

Regina lets Jackie pull her into a hug.

"We'd be richer apart?" Regina rests her head on Jackie's shoulder. Her breath is on Jackie's neck. "If you weren't holding me down, I'd be an executive for Exxon?" She steps out of the embrace, shivering.

"Let's go inside," Jackie says.

Regina sticks her hands in the pockets of her hoodie and ignores the comment.

Jackie is wearing only a long-sleeved T-shirt under her overalls. She puts her hands in her armpits. "I don't understand sometimes the point."

"The point? Of us? Of life? You expect me to have answers?"

Regina coughs up a last scrap of potato and spits it out on the snow.

Jackie searches in her back pocket for a handkerchief to offer Regina. Her pocket is empty. She puts a hand on Regina's arm.

Regina brushes the hand off, saying, "We're supposed to care about each other enough to want to stay together. If one of us is a mess, we go to the clinic. Figure it out. Together. Get some drugs. Talk to each other. Our friends. We take care of each other."

Jackie sighs. "If your Mom hadn't left you and Lynn her house to sell when she died, we'd still be living in a fourth-floor walk-up."

"So? What are you saying? It was your job to provide a house? Living in an apartment is shameful? What?" Regina assumes her fighting stance, hands on hips, elbows back. "We live in a neighborhood of hard-working people. Lots of them have a hard time making ends meet. Are they bad people? Lazy? Lotti has a second mortgage. Are you ashamed of us? Our neighbors? Of the choices we made? Because I'm not."

"I'm saying I should have done better."

"Better than what? We took jobs women could get in those days. I lost my shot at working myself up to middle class more than once because of my big mouth. We both could have used more common sense." She flaps a hand. "You never had a chance at decent-paying work because no man wanted to find out you could do his job." Regina's face is red with cold and exertion. She likes a good argument. Particularly when she thinks she's winning. Talk fighting is so much better than silent fighting. "Especially a girl who had the balls to look like you."

"Balls," Jackie snorts, her laugh taking her by surprise. "Do we want to claim that term? If anyone had balls it was you. You would have been promoted at the Big Y if you hadn't called the manager a bigot."

Regina ignores what she takes as a sideways compliment. "You didn't think any less of your father when he lost the farm. Life isn't fair. I refuse to go into old age being ashamed about money. By the way, we own this house," Regina says.

"The bank owns this house," Jackie says, but nods her general agreement with the sentiment that they are fortunate to be in the house.

"And I'm proud that my homophobic mother saw the light in her last days and left us half of what she had for a down payment," Regina says. "I worked hard to push my mother that far. We've had a good life and we're not done. I'm not stupid. I know I can't talk you out of depression, but damn it, Jackie, if you think you're going to make decisions about leaving me, even overnight, to stay at Bo and Yvonne's without talking to me first . . ." Regina takes her hands off her hips and stares Jackie down.

"I thought you'd be better off without me moping around for a while." Jackie meets Regina's eyes. "I'm not going anywhere."

"Miss Regina! Miss Regina!" They both turn to see their neighbors, six-year-old Ramon and his constant companion, TJ, walk through the widening gap in the fence that separates the yards. Ramon is carrying a jar of honey, holding it away from the one-piece snow suit with matching boots he's wearing that his grandmother, Lotti, and Regina picked up at the Goodwill. TJ is carrying a spoon and wearing a leather jacket that reaches his calves, the arms rolled to his elbows, the shiny lining exposed.

Ramon hands the jar to Jackie. "Lotti says Regina should swallow a spoon of honey."

"Thanks, pal." Jackie takes the honey.

TJ hands her a spoon.

"Thanks, Buddy." Jackie takes the spoon.

TJ is wearing a Batman cape over the leather jacket. He spreads his arms and for some reason, growls.

Ramon watches, his little forehead tight with concern as Jackie spoons some honey into Regina's mouth. As Regina swallows, she looks up at Lotti's kitchen window, which overlooks both yards. Even though she can't see her because of the way the winter sun is striking Lotti's window, Regina holds up a hand to say thanks and let Lotti know she's all right.

"I'm glad we landed here, in this neighborhood," Jackie says.

"You ladies having a fight?" TJ asks. "You making up now?"

"Now why would you think that, honey?" Regina's body is stiff with cold. Her sneakered feet are numb.

"When my cousins fight, Lotti throws them out till they say sorry," Ramon says.

"Lotti says it looks like you're fightin'. You ladies need a go inside." TJ has a stern look on his face.

"I'm sorry." Jackie bows to Regina. "You're right, TJ; we need to go inside."

"I'm sorry, too," Regina says.

Jackie promises to help the boys build a snowman that weekend. She asks them to thank Lotti for the honey and sends them back across the yard to her.

At the kitchen table, Regina blows her nose and clears her throat; otherwise, she and Jackie sip their tea in silence until a jet announces that it is flying overhead with a loud crack of the sound barrier. Jackie startles and grimaces. As if they could spot a plane from their seated angle, they both look out the window.

"Air Force is sending up more planes, switching up flight patterns. Not a good sign." Jackie gets up and stands by the window to see if the boys are outside, but the only sign of them is their tracks in the snow. "The noise terrifies TJ," she says.

"Lots of things terrify TJ. That's why he's such a little shit." Regina gets up and stands beside Jackie.

"He's got reasons to be afraid," Jackie says.

"You turn me into an old lady who dotes on other people's kids and then you make plans to leave us all?" Regina rubs Jackie's arm. She kisses the scruff of her neck but she's not kidding about what she just said.

"I'm sorry. I'm a jackass." Jackie drapes an arm across Regina's shoulder. "Don't leave me."

"I'm sorry you're a jackass, too. You're going to the clinic on Monday. It's you who threatened to leave me this time, remember?" Regina feels sorry for the times she's left or thrown Jackie out, and leans into Jackie's side.

"Proof of insanity," Jackie says.

Another plane booms overhead. Regina wraps an arm around Jackie's waist. They watch TJ tear around the side of Lotti's house. Ramon and Pock are right behind him. The boys run to the back door which swings open to accept them before they reach it. The little girl stops to stare up and wave at the plane before she runs in the house.

"Can't be good for their ears." Regina puts her hand in Jackie's back pocket. This is her favorite way to look at the world, leaned into Jackie with Jackie's arm around her. "You should tell TJ how much the planes scare you, while he still idolizes you."

"Good idea." Jackie leans her cheek against Regina's head. "It might help him understand we're all scared sometimes."

Chapter 13

Regina stops speaking only to take in air, desperate to keep the tide of words moving, to believe that the stream of their story has the power to keep the air flowing in and out of Jackie. She slips her hand inside Jackie's parka to feel the rise and fall of her chest.

Jackie smiles. One side of her mouth stays put. "TJ?" she says out of the side that moves.

"TJ is fine. All the kids are fine, sweetheart." The bulldozer's step, which they have been leaning against for quite some time now, is causing a dull pain where it presses against Regina's back. Regina thinks it must be causing the same pain for Jackie. She takes off her scarf and stuffs it behind Jackie's back. "Is that more comfortable?" She kisses Jackie's face all over. "Your skin feels cool against my lips already, my love."

Regina recoils, her body stiffening at her own use of the word *already*. "No. No," she tries to take the word back. She kneels in front of Jackie and tries to embrace her, but Jackie is too slumped, and Regina settles for sitting next to Jackie again.

"Good kids," Jackie whispers. She wonders if her words are

coming out so Regina can understand them. She feels sleepy and closes her eyes. She means to say, "The kids will help, like they did a few years ago when I had my hip replaced." She means to say, "Don't be frightened; it's not so bad; the worst part is that I seem to be scaring you." But she can't rouse herself enough to concentrate on speech.

Regina is not afraid of Jackie's garbled words. She's afraid Jackie will stop talking altogether, afraid Jackie will go to sleep and not wake up again. Regina has a vague notion about keeping people awake when they've had a stroke, but maybe this isn't a stroke or maybe that advice is for when a person has a concussion.

"Jackie." Regina gently shakes her shoulder. "Stay with me." She looks desperately at their car parked 1,000 feet away across the snow on the side of the rutted road. "I should have gone for help."

"You stay with me," Jackie says. "The kids . . ." She fades out with a sigh and comes back with, "when my hip."

"Does your hip hurt?" Regina asks loudly. "Stay awake, honey. Here, lean on me. That's right." They are angled so Regina can see the back of The Bucket. She stares at their car, which is far enough away to look like a toy. It seems so alone on the side of the road. "Someone will come soon. Someone will see our car and the tracks we made in the snow." Regina takes a deep breath of cold air. "Yes," she says. "Thom will come and see us sitting on the ground in the snow, leaning against his bulldozer." She has her arm around Jackie now. "Wake up, honey." She grasps Jackie's shoulder tightly as if to bolster them both. "Don't be startled. I'm going to yell as loud as I can."

Regina turns her face away from Jackie, so she's not screaming in her ear, throws her head back, and howls, "Hello." She listens for an answer. It's only a matter of seconds before the *Oh-Oh-Oh*, bounces back and Regina realizes she is being answered by an echo. She tries a second time, adding, "Help," after "Hello." Again, she's answered by the echo of her own voice.

Jackie is beyond being startled. Her world is out of focus,

but she knows Regina is here with her and she's grateful. Glad that Regina is here and sorry that Regina is frightened. Because Jackie is feeling less and less frightened for herself, but more frightened for Regina. "The kids," Jackie says, getting frustrated with the struggle to stay awake, "help you," and the amount of effort it takes to get a simple thought into words. "I'll try . . ."

"You're worried about the kids?" Regina sits up straighter, pulling her head back, trying to get a good look at Jackie, trying to figure out what in the world she can do to make her more comfortable. To keep her alive. "Does something hurt you?"

Jackie rallies, trying and failing to pull herself up a little taller, grabbing for Regina's hand and finding it, suddenly frantic to get Regina to understand. Jackie starts talking fast, jumbling words.

"What?" Regina says. "Slow down," she says, more relieved by Jackie's burst of energy than concerned by her agitation. "One or two words." Regina takes off a glove and puts a hand on Jackie's cheek.

"The kids," Jackie says slowly, stopping for a long moment between words, looking into Regina's eyes. "Helped." Her speech is clearer. "With my hip."

"Yes," Regina says, holding Jackie's hand. Jackie is slumping against the step of the dozer again. Regina lets her head and spine curve forward, to match Jackie's, a more comfortable position than sitting up straight. "It's okay, you can close your eyes if you want to. If I'm calm, you'll be calm, too," she whispers. "If you're calm, I'll be calm. The kids helped. We couldn't have done it without them. Sit back now, relax. Lean against me. The kids, they'll help us. Rest. Maybe sleep is best. I'll tell you about the kids, you fall asleep, and I'll get help."

"Stay," Jackie says.

November 2014

Jackie lies on her back on a rented hospital bed in the middle of the living room. Pain in her hip and the clink of a cup in the kitchen wake her. She thinks it must be morning. "Shit." She throws an elbow over her eyes, regretting having spoken out loud, possibly alerting TJ that she's awake. How she hates spending her days and nights trapped in full view of whoever happens into their living room, every well-wisher, neighbor, and Girl Scout selling cookies having full access to the spectacle of eighty-six-year-old Jackie's decidedly slow recovery from her hip replacement. Regina was aggressive enough to get Medicare to agree to pay for the rental of the bed, but no amount of will-power could get the bed down their small hall and through their bedroom door.

Jackie peeks through the crook of her arm. TJ stands in the doorway of the kitchen, the dawn light streaming in behind him. How soft he looks in that light. TJ has been spending his nights in their den, sleeping on her La-Z-Boy, helping Jackie with her daily exercises and walks, until Regina thinks it's safe enough for her and Jackie to go it alone again. Jackie squints at him, unmoving, not wanting to break the spell of TJ hunched in the door, patiently waiting with a cup of tea in one hand and a bottle of pills in the other. Her tea, her pills. She sees him like this, barefoot in his T-shirt and tight jeans, his hair mussed up, all sleepy concern and she thinks no wonder Ramon is in love with him. Even though she has always loved TJ herself, before he started taking care of her postsurgery, Jackie never fully understood why Ramon would love him in the romantic way boys sometimes love each other.

TJ watches Jackie's chest rise and fall. Regina has told him these operations are routine. But a fat old lady like Jackie, out of shape, huffin' when she walks? TJ frowns. He's read all the little booklets that came home with her, all the instruction sheets. TJ thinks Jackie should be doing better by now.

Jackie lowers her arm and says his name softly so as not to wake Regina.

He says, "Good morning," and places the tea and pill bottle on the coffee table next to the hospital bed.

Jackie watches. What a pain in the ass she has become. "You

let Regina sleep. Thanks."

"That's Tylenol." TJ nods at the bottle on the coffee table. "I can get you ibuprofen. If you want something stronger, I have to wake up Regina. She doesn't trust me with those pills," he says calmly, in a way that makes Jackie think the program really did help.

In fact, oxycodone is of no interest to TJ. Never was. But if it makes *The Ladies* feel like they're keeping him safe by hiding the drug, fine by TJ. His drug is alcohol. Watching Charlie get carried away on a stretcher and almost die was enough oxy for TJ. TJ knows where his trouble comes from—Smirnoff and his temper. And having an asshole for a father. "It's time to taper off the painkillers," he tells Jackie, not for the first time.

Jackie starts to push herself up in bed. "Tylenol's fine for now."

TJ points to the control panel on the side of the bed. "You know what to do." He shakes his head. "You gonna go through all that then mess up because you don't want to press a button?"

"You sound like Regina." Jackie pushes the icon and the bed raises her knees. She presses another icon and the top of her body rises to a forty-five-degree angle.

"Regina's right." TJ watches Jackie push with her hands flat on the mattress to maneuver to the position she prefers. "You gotta do that breathing thing, too." He picks up a plastic box with a tube that Jackie is supposed to exhale into to lift the little red ball inside. "And you're getting up for breakfast. Eggs." TJ has become a bodybuilder, one of the few addictions they approve of in the program. He knows protein.

"Nurse Ratched." Jackie smiles. "If you manage to hold your temper for six months, you can get your high school equivalency and apply to nursing school."

"Now you sound like Pock." TJ sets the plastic box back on the coffee table. "We walk outside today. This room is too crowded. Who's Nurse Ratched?"

After school Ramon carries a platter of food straight from his house to Jackie and Regina's. He looks over his shoulder before he knocks on the door. Better the neighborhood punks don't see Ramon with his chicken and potatoes and come slouching over pretending they mean to take the aluminum foil-wrapped plate from him; better he doesn't have to tell them to fuck off. Better he doesn't have to mess with some kid who disrespects one of The Ladies. Above all, he doesn't want any of them to hear Regina say, "Ramon, you dear boy," when she opens the door.

Ramon knocks and waits. When TJ stopped coming to school, the other boys thought Ramon would take any kind of shit from them. They found out he won't. It's just, Ramon doesn't want to be TJ. Ramon's going away to college next year. If he gets in. He will get in. He'll get a scholarship or take out a loan. Why shouldn't he get in? It's just the damn essay. He'll get in if he doesn't smash one of these punks in the face first. Papi says, "Smashing a damn fool's face would look bad on an application." Since he's been eight years old Ramon has wondered how it felt for TJ to be wound so tight that any punk with a big mouth might make him snap. Lately, Ramon doesn't have to wonder.

Regina comes to the door in her slippers. Ramon doesn't like the slippers. It's only four o'clock. She should be wearing her pink sneakers or her ugly black shoes with bows. How he hates being a guy who has an opinion about what kind of shoes the neighbor lady wears.

Regina puts a finger to her lips and points to Jackie sleeping. Ramon slips in the door as Regina whispers, "Ramon, you dear boy."

TJ is right behind her mouthing the words with Regina as she takes the plate. Ramon grins at TJ. This is as close to a normal exchange as the boys have had for six months, since before TJ got driven home by an Adjustment Counselor, kicked out of school, and enrolled in a special program for kids too fucked up to stay in public school.

Jackie washes a hand across her face. "I'm up. You don't have to whisper. I smell Mary Soto's chicken, worth waking up for. Thanks, Ramon."

Regina kisses the top of Jackie's head and carries the plate of food to the kitchen.

"How you doin?'" Ramon sits on the end of the coffee table near Jackie. He puts an iPad and spiral notebook on the already cluttered table.

"Okay." Jackie wonders who will make her get out of bed this time.

"She's taking too many painkillers," TJ says. "They're addictive."

Ramon keeps his face neutral, not sure if TJ is making a joke. TJ's specialty, why he got kicked out of school, is alcohol. Ramon's not ready for TJ to be making an addiction joke. And an old lady becoming a drug addict? Ramon adds that to the list of fucked-up shit that can happen. "You want to go for a walk, Jackie?" Ramon says. "It's not too cold out."

"No thanks."

"Yes, thanks." Regina is back with Jackie's jacket over her arm. "At least fifteen minutes," she says to Ramon.

When Jackie and Ramon get back from the walk, TJ is in the bedroom teasing Pock who's helping Regina fold clothes. Ramon gets Jackie an oxycodone from Regina's hiding place, which is a box of prunes in the cabinet above the stove.

Why, Jackie wonders, does Regina think the new improved TJ wouldn't consider eating a dried plum? Regina must be overwhelmed. Losing Lynn last year took its toll. Then a few months later, TJ got thrown out of school for being drunk and getting caught with alcohol in his locker a third time. Now Jackie's hip. Eighty-six seems to Jackie too old to start life with a titanium hip. And poor Regina at eighty-five has to manage both Jackie, the patient, and TJ, the addict, taking care of the patient. Jackie may be the only person, besides TJ, who believes TJ doesn't have a problem with narcotics. Temper, mental health, big problems. Alcohol, big problem. But Jackie is sure that TJ's not going after oxy. TJ's got a healthy fear of narcotics.

Jackie is sitting on the side of the bed about to lie down when Regina, TJ, and Pock come out of the bedroom. Before Regina can put words to her disapproving glance, Jackie says, "It's the most comfortable seat in the house."

"Hips higher than knees," Regina says. "Did you notice Pock changed the sheets for you?"

Pock curtsies. She's wearing a short skirt and tight-fitting top. Her birthmark is covered up by her hair and makeup. Jackie supposes Pock looks good, just older. Jackie would stop them all from aging if she could.

"How did we get such good kids?" Jackie doubts she's ever again going to be able to get her leg up on the bed without bending forward and using both of her arms to do it.

"By being good grown-ups," Pock says. "Before TJ took over the den, you let us pile in there to watch TV." She makes a face, first at TJ who's sitting on one end of the couch, then at Ramon, sitting on the other end. "This is stupid. How long are you guys going to be mad at each other?"

Both boys smirk at her. "Not mad," Ramon says.

"Yes, you are. Since before TJ got busted. TJ hides in the den when you bring food over for The Ladies after school."

TJ says, "Am I hiding, Pock?"

"Not today," she admits.

"So how about you put a sock in it and let me and Ramon figure out our own business?" This statement comes out of TJ so reasonably that everyone in the room, even Pock, nods in agreement.

She picks an apple out of a basket on the coffee table. "So much food since Jackie's new hip." Pock takes a bite, making a note to herself to tidy up the table.

"I thought you kids visit because we're lovable. Grab me

275

a banana, please." How, Regina wonders, can she be so tired when she's getting so much help? How much longer can she take having TJ and the other kids in the house so much of the time, and how would she and Jackie have gotten through this without them? "You boys want something? There's cookies and I don't know what else in the kitchen."

"We love you, love you, love you." Pock waves the banana in a separate arc for each *love*. "One from me, one from TJ, one from Ramon." She hands Regina the banana and sits on the arm of the couch. "Boys are too emotionally immature to tell people they love them."

"We love you, too." Regina wishes she and Jackie knew, when the kids were toddlers, that this couch was going to have to last the rest of their lives so they could have made some rules about not sitting on the arms, but supposes if the couch held up this long it's likely to get hauled out with whoever dies last. Pock pops up to throw her apple core and Regina's peel in a basket near the bed. "Ramon or TJ, you need to empty this," she says.

Both boys respond to this command by pulling out their phones and engaging with the tiny screens.

"See, if you were being normal," Pock wags her head, "you'd be telling me I'm not your mommy or you'd be in the den telling boy secrets." She sits on the end of Jackie's bed. Jackie's shoes are already off. Without asking, Pock plucks a bottle of body lotion off the coffee table and removes Jackie's socks.

The first time Pock offered to give Jackie a foot rub Jackie was mortified. Excepting Regina and a podiatrist, no one but Jackie had touched her feet in fifty years. Now she's lying here having her toes massaged by a teenaged girl while teenaged boys play with their phones. Jackie's pretty sure the painkillers are dulling some of the indignity of her exposed body.

While trying to parse out exactly what is going on between Ramon, TJ, and Pock, Regina falls asleep. She wakes up when Pock clinks the bottle of lotion on the coffee table. "You'd think I was getting the massage." Regina feels the corners of her mouth, which are, thank god, dry.

Pock pulls Jackie's socks back on.

"Thanks, Bo." Jackie's startled awake by speaking her dead friend's name. "Pock." She corrects herself. "Thank you, Pock."

"You can call me Bo." Pock hops off the bed. "Bo was cool. I can't get anyone to call me Patricia anyway."

Regina can't stand seeing the boys so uneasy with each other, so she puts them to work. A living room shade has been stuck rolled halfway up for weeks. The mechanism that makes it move needs fixing. The boys take the shade off the window and roll it tightly by hand.

Jackie watches the boys put aside whatever pride or anger separates them as they bend toward each other. So much awkward relief in their movement. They must miss each other. They'd been constant companions. TJ holds on to one end with both fists, keeping the shade wound, while Ramon twists the spring and locks it in place on the other end. Jackie wishes she could tell them how quickly life passes, how in the end your friends pass one by one. What wouldn't she give to see Bo? She misses Regina's warm body in bed at night. It seems like weeks since they've been alone for more than a few minutes at a time. She longs to hear what meaning and bad poetry Regina could make out of the boys fixing a broken window shade.

Regina and Pock offer advice that the boys disregard.

TJ twists the metal end of the shade, trying to get it to stay tightened in place for the third time, but the overwound mechanism is spent. The spring pops. The shade unfurls in Ramon's fist.

"This thing's shot," TJ says. "You're gonna have to buy a new one or keep pulling the curtains closed like you been doing."

Jackie closes her eyes. She wonders what Ramon thinks about this new alliance between Pock and TJ. Is it too much medication or too much company making her second-guess what everyone else is thinking? Funny how a person can crave company and privacy at the same time. She doesn't exactly want Regina and the kids to leave the room, but she doesn't exactly want them to stay. What Jackie really wants is to be able to walk in and out of a room on her own, clearheaded and pain free. What she wants is to have been alone and to know she's going to be alone again soon. She wants to have some control over the flow of her own life. Regina and Pock start talking about the Common App Essay Ramon's been working on to try to get into college.

The last thing Jackie hears as she dozes off is TJ saying, "Ramon, you been working on the essay for like, a month. You writing the Gettysburg Address?"

Jackie wakes a few minutes later to Ramon saying, "Not if I don't finish this essay and I can't write for shit." She takes a few sips from the water bottle that's always near her bed, more to help herself wake up than because she's thirsty.

"True. I've read it," Pock says. "You got the technical part down. Grammar, punctuation, you can build a sentence. But—" she grimaces.

"The boy cannot tell a story, never could. Now you and me, we can bullshit all day long." TJ raises his hand to fist-bump Pock.

"Unless you're in a crappy mood." Pock grins and raises her fist to meet TJ's. "Then you get all taciturn."

TJ shakes his head. "Girl loves to say *taciturn.*"

Regina sits on the couch with a boy on each side and Pock hopping from one arm to another. Regina can't help but notice how the kids are filling out, what nice-looking adults they're becoming. Ramon as handsome as ever: thin, tall, with a shock of jet-black hair. TJ more relaxed in his short, well-built body since his father disappeared, almost two years ago now, after not appearing in court for a domestic abuse charge filed by his "real" wife. Pock becoming more graceful, more poised every day.

Pock stands now and reads the hard copy of the first page of Ramon's essay titled *Pride and Heritage.*

"Sorry." She taps the paper when she's done reading. "But this is boring. I like Papi. I always wanted to be Puerto Rican, or part of some ethnic group, not watered down, a little of this, a little of that. I used to have an epic crush on you, Ramon, and

I'm still bored."

"So it's boring," Ramon says. "I don't care." He's sick of caring. Sick of trying to fit in. "I want to be an engineer. I'll never be cool. Nobody raps about being an engineer." He wants to be a father. Nobody raps about their queer daddy, either. Ramon looks at his hands. He looks up, sick of looking at his hands.

"Those birdhouses you wrote about were boring when you and Papi were making them. What's the story? We sawed wood together?" TJ says. "Relax. I'm trying to help. For real. Even in rehab, in group therapy, there's got to be a story. You gotta give up something here—" TJ slaps his hand over his heart, "—or make up something if you want to keep their attention. You want them to talk to you outside when you're passing around a cigarette and drinking shitty coffee, you gotta give them a good story. You write about your father, he gotta have some juice, a hook. Work it. Make him a hero. Papi's a class act daddy, working two jobs, making sure his boy goes to college, making sure his retarded kid . . ." TJ, into the rhythm of his own voice, skips a beat, corrects himself. ". . . excuse me, making sure his developmentally challenged son gets the best care, respects his wife and the old lesbians next door. And still takes care of the birdies. Throw in some shit about him serving dinner at Casa Latina at Thanksgiving. His fucked-up childhood."

"Lotti took care of Oscar. Papi went to Catholic school." Ramon sinks into the couch.

"Where the nuns beat him," TJ punches the air.

"Fool." Pock grins at TJ. "I begged my parents to send me to Catholic school."

"He never goes near Casa Latina. Jesus," Ramon says, "I'm not making up shit about my father."

"Nah," TJ says with grudging respect. "You wouldn't."

"We're going to brainstorm." Regina turns the essay over so she holds blank pages. "Throw out ideas. Nothing is too ridiculous."

Regina writes *Addiction, Bullying,* and *Life with Differently Abled Brother* on the page.

Jackie clears her throat. "Privacy," she says. "These days, people say every damn thing out loud. God forbid we think or do something without telling the world about it, take a picture of it, email it, tweet it, put it on Facebook. YouTube." She's aware that she sounds like the old crank in sweatpants at the clinic who comes in early and sits by the reception desk so he can be in the best position to find fault with everyone who walks in. She knows she's talking louder than she normally does, too. She lowers her voice. "It's getting so privacy is suspect. Write about that."

They all wait to see if Jackie's done.

She isn't. "Write about how everyone isn't a writer, and writing isn't the only reason people should get into school." Jackie falls back on her pillows winded and huffing. Why does she talk so much since surgery?

"You all right, honey?" Regina stands to get a better view of Jackie.

"Write about the neighborhood," Jackie says.

"Good idea," Pock agrees. "Diversity sells."

"Yeah." TJ leans into the idea. "Regina listens to NPR all day long. Poor people with problems is their big story. This street got an old white lesbian who's learning to walk, people of all colors addicted to all kinds of shit, a white girl with no baby daddies but two sets of twins." He holds up four fingers. "A developmentally challenged brown boy with a hot retarded white girlfriend. We got good daddies, bad daddies, good mommies, bad mommies, no daddy, no mommy, every kind of parental influence known to man, man." TJ is smiling the way he used to before he got busted—only this smile is easier, less edgy. Regina and Pock laugh.

Ramon remembers how good it was with TJ when it was good. He smiles, remembering cuddling with TJ under TJ's bed when they were little boys, how they pressed against each other there and giggled, how they pressed each other against the big oak tree in the woods miles away when they got older. TJ's laugh was always easier and his smile less edgy after he'd been held, after he'd been loved. After sex.

"You're an idiot, TJ," Ramon says, still smiling. "Oscar will punch your lights out if he hears you call his girlfriend retarded."

"Must be love if he's willing to fight me." TJ flexes his biceps and flashes all his teeth at Ramon. "Don't get all righteous on me. You and Oscar used to call me retarded."

"You did," Pock says.

"I miss that boy." TJ grins his crooked grin at Ramon.

Ramon closes his eyes, lets his head fall back, and grins. TJ seems better. Better since he's been off Smirnoff's and off Ramon. Ramon should be glad for TJ. It was good with TJ. Bad, too. But they had each other's backs, mostly tried to anyway. Ramon spent the first day of first grade explaining to their teacher that no, TJ did not think he was smarter than she was, and no, TJ did not know he wasn't supposed to stuff Marie and Karly Roux's matching lunch boxes in the sleeves of his sweater and stash them in the coat closet. Why is TJ getting better without Ramon now?

Pock runs her hand over her skirt. "I wrote about Tommy. My guidance counselor loved my essay."

"You gave up your own father?" TJ says. "That's cold."

"You just told me to give up my father." Ramon pushes himself forward and looks around Regina so TJ can catch the shade coming his way.

"Your father's a fucking saint. What's Pock gonna say about Tommy?"

"I showed it to Tommy," Pock says. "He was proud. Mr. Merrick said it was the perfect blend of ethos, pathos and logos."

"You sucked up to the English teacher." TJ flashes his quick, crooked smile again. "What's that mean? Ethos, pathos, logos?"

"Bleed on the page and sound smart and sincere about it." Pock gives him a face full of attitude.

TJ would smack her with the pillow that's sitting on his lap, but then someone might notice the hard-on under it. Pock and TJ stare at each other a beat too long, and the fact that they have been holding back on serious flirting becomes obvious.

They both cut their eyes at Ramon who has already looked away.

Jackie studies Ramon from her slightly higher position on the bed. It's odd to be in the room, so close to them all, but alone in this bed, the odd person out, the four of them sitting in a row so close together on the couch, with her opposite them. Jackie is the only one in the room who is situated in the right position to see the sneer flash across Ramon's face. She looks at her watch. Way too soon for another pill. Poor Ramon. She wonders again what he's thinking.

Ramon is wondering if Pock is a virgin. He's positive she's a straight girl who spent a lot of their childhood making eyes at him. Now she wants to get in TJ's pants, maybe already has. Fuck TJ. Maybe Pock is. Literally. Fucking TJ.

"Write about gay neighbors, old guys, so it doesn't have to be Jackie and Regina," Pock says. "Maybe one of them got arrested, in the past, went to jail for being gay. Do an intergenerational thing. I have a book about it. You could have footnotes. A then and now, how the world has changed, thing."

"I'm not writing about old gay guys who went to jail," Ramon snaps at her.

"She's trying to help. You're being kind of a bitch, Ramon," TJ says.

Ramon puts a hand on his thigh to stop it jiggling. He gets off the couch and walks into the kitchen.

Regina wiggles her feet back into the slippers she kicked under the couch. "Give him a minute." Within thirty seconds she's on her feet following him.

Ramon squats in front of the cabinet to the left of the sink, the one with the missing door. He looks up at her. "Is it in the cellar?"

"What?" She puts a hand on his shoulder. "Ramon," she says softly.

"The cabinet door. It's just the hinge." He runs his hand along the inside of the frame.

"Another day. After the essay gets written."

"I don't need MIT." Ramon stands. "I can get into a

community college without an essay. Maybe I won't go at all."

"You're going to college." Regina considers writing the essay herself. She used to be good at it, probably too scattered to pull it off now. Maybe with enough coffee. "You're going to have a good life." She looks over at TJ and Pock who are standing in the kitchen doorway. "All you kids are."

Ramon looks down at the exposed Quaker Oats, Salada Tea, and graham crackers in the open cabinet. "This needs help." He gestures with an open hand to take in the kitchen.

They all look at the busted stove with only two working burners and below it the thin gray line of water dripping from the refrigerator that drains on the uneven floor into a crack in the linoleum.

Ramon feels tired, old-man tired. He's felt tired since TJ left school. He knows they think he's making some point about The Ladies' run-down kitchen. He's not afraid of ending up in the neighborhood. That would be okay. "I didn't mean . . ." He isn't afraid of going to college either. He's afraid of coming out of college without learning anything that makes sense or maybe becoming somebody that doesn't make sense. "I meant, maybe I don't go to school. I could stay here and fix things, build things."

Jackie's walker scrapes against the living room's hardwood floor. She's halfway to the kitchen and proud of herself for having made it this far this fast. Her hip hurts like hell.

Regina hears the scraping and yells, "You okay, honey?" even though a speaking voice would suffice.

Pock goes to help Jackie. She puts a hand under Jackie's elbow and starts to speak, but Jackie gestures for Pock to take her hand away and be quiet so they can keep walking and hear the conversation, twenty feet away, in the kitchen. The throbbing ache in her hip radiates down her leg. It occurs to Jackie that there's no way through this without a lot more pain.

After Ramon rudely declines TJ's offer to go down to the cellar to look for the cabinet door, TJ sticks his face in Ramon's and says, "What's your problem?"

"I got a problem?" Ramon stares him down. "Why don't you

tell me what my problem is?" He takes a step back. "Be a man."

TJ steps back, too. "We were going to tell you."

Pock and Jackie make it to the kitchen.

"Never mind." Ramon glares at TJ. "I don't wanna hear it."

"I wanna tell it," TJ says.

"It had to be Pock?" Ramon stands very straight. "Pockie?"

Regina pulls out a kitchen chair and sits. "Sit, all of you."

Pock and Jackie sit at opposite ends of the table.

"She said sit." Ramon yanks out a chair for himself and sits next to Regina.

TJ sits across from them. "Pock helped me." He opens both hands. It's not like he's not amazed himself. He wanted to go running to Ramon to tell him all about it the first time Pock picked him up from the program in Jackie and Regina's car. Some guy said, "Who's the hot chick?" It was like seeing her for the first time. "Because of her father . . ." TJ trips over his words. "She knows a guy can, you know, be trouble, but be okay, be worth something anyway." How can he tell Ramon it's not just that she's hot and smart? "She's solid," he says, looking at the table, "like you." How can he tell Ramon he'd never have made it to ten years old without him? That he will always love Ramon, but that doesn't stop him from loving Pock. How can he tell Ramon any of that stuff if he tells him that sex with Pock feels right?

"You're a coward." Ramon's chair grates against the floor as he stands abruptly.

"I'm sorry. I was a coward, too." Pock has her back against the counter. "TJ," she says, "Ramon thinks you're afraid to be . . ."

Ramon's head whips towards her. "Shut up, Pock."

"He thinks I'm too pussy to be queer," TJ says. "But I'm not the one afraid to tell my daddy."

Ramon slams a fist on the table.

From the silence that follows Ramon says coldly, "That's not what this is about," and walks out the door.

"Okay, Ramon. You're right, man," TJ yells out the door behind him. He turns to ask the women, "What am I supposed to do? I love the guy, but I never said I don't like girls."

"Go tell him that," Jackie says.

Pock folds her arms across her chest. "Or maybe you're not pussy enough?"

The door slams behind TJ.

Chapter 14

Saturday, February 18, 2017

Regina has been holding Jackie in a sideways hug and quietly talking about the hip replacement and the kids. At first Jackie was clearly listening, offering an occasional sigh of agreement, or grunt of argument, a spoken "yes" or "no." Even a full sentence of "TJ never said that." Now Regina realizes Jackie hasn't moved or made a sound in several minutes and she panics. She's run out of calm.

Regina's hand is back inside Jackie's parka on Jackie's chest. Jackie is breathing a little louder than usual. Regina tries to think of more to say, something about the kids. They always interest Jackie. "Are you cold?" She doesn't feel cold herself, but worries their warm bodies sitting against the bulldozer will melt the snow beneath them and by the time someone finds them the temperature will have dropped enough to freeze them to the ground. "Can you talk, honey?" Regina's own voice has become unsteady. "Just say 'yes' if you can."

Jackie makes a quivering sound. Then a definite, "Yes."

"Why isn't anyone else coming to this dump?" Regina's voice shakes. Then not wanting Jackie to feel her panic, adds,

"Thom will show up to see what happened to us."

"Don't be scared." Jackie is not panicked. She is short of breath. Her voice is soft, but Regina can understand it. "We're all right," Jackie says.

Jackie cries softly, sad at the thought she is really leaving Regina, tears leaking out of only one eye. Regina cries harder. Jackie stops breathing. Regina doesn't breathe either, until Jackie takes a sharp inhale, coughs and sputters like an engine trying to start up, and says, "Tell me a dirty story," in a wheeze that is almost as scary as no breath at all.

Regina becomes disoriented, like she's the one who's had the stroke or heart attack or whatever has happened to Jackie. Is Jackie teasing her? After gasping for breath? Jackie hasn't asked for a dirty story since they were in their thirties and Jackie was away working in Florida. Regina disregards the cheating aspect of Florida and concentrates on the desperate need Jackie had to hear her voice, even then. Regina almost laughs remembering how they had squandered a good part of Jackie's paycheck on phone sex, but cries again, remembering how Jackie craved the audio version of sex they'd already had. That was so sweet.

Regina realizes she must be saying these things out loud because Jackie coughs out, "Sweet? No. It was good." Jackie's chest heaves. "Our sex."

"Don't talk, my love," Regina shushes her and tries to concentrate. She must find her wits. There must be some way to get them out of this predicament. Old women don't die in dumps. Homeless men die in dumps.

Jackie lifts her head an inch off Regina's shoulder and says, "I didn't untie . . ." Her head falls. She sucks in air noisily and says, "the tree."

Jackie's concern helps Regina gather herself. "Please don't worry about the tree." Regina pulls Jackie in and tries to rock her, but Jackie is much bigger than Regina and they are sitting against the hard metal of the bulldozer, so it's a gentle sideways sway. Their puffy jackets stop Regina from holding Jackie as close as she wants to hold her.

287

"I'll laugh for you, baby," Regina says stupidly, tears running down her face. Jackie says something Regina almost catches. Jackie's head goes slack on Regina's shoulder. Regina slips her hand inside the neck of Jackie's bulky sweater. Jackie keeps whispering, but her words are too mumbled and soft to understand. Jackie's neck is warm. Her heart is beating. Regina puts her mouth close to Jackie's ear. "You're all right. We're all right."

"We're all right, you're all right," Jackie whispers and keeps whispering.

Words Regina understands and words she doesn't. She wipes drool off the side of Jackie's mouth. "We'll play your birthday in the lottery and win a lot of money. We'll tell the kids the stories. We'll meet Ramon's boyfriend," Regina says.

Jackie's eyes are closed. Her mouth twitches and sounds spill out, none of them actual words.

And then the only sounds are the gulls and the words coming from Regina. "Shh, my love, yes, yes, you're all right. There, see, you're all right; your hip doesn't hurt, does it?" Yes, her Jackie is all right. Regina holds on tight and keeps talking. "We're all right."

Sunday, February 19, 2017

TJ dribbles a basketball in front of the hoop at the end of the driveway Ramon's family shares with Jackie and Regina. He slips on a patch of ice and rights himself. Ramon comes out his front door grinning at TJ as though not falling while he's dribbling is an accomplishment that might get TJ a spot on the varsity team. If guys studying for their high school equivalency exams had teams.

"Skipping work this morning?" Ramon says. "Ruining your perfect attendance?" He notices the look on TJ's face. "What?"

TJ starts dribbling the ball again without answering.

Ramon throws up his hands. "Last night you and Pock were all over me and Gene like we're all best friends." He turns to walk back in his front door.

"I gotta tell you something." TJ looks down at his Nikes, wet from walking in the snow. He looks at Ramon's Reeboks, still dry. "We should wear boots."

"Boots? You gotta tell me we should wear boots? Pock's been bragging about how great you're doing." Ramon holds up a hand. So something bothering you? Say it."

"I will." TJ stops dribbling. He stands there shaking his head at the ground. "It's just . . ."

"What? Somebody die?"

"Shoot a few hoops with me. Come on." TJ passes him the ball.

"Jesus." Ramon shoots halfheartedly. He's been home from UMass at least ten times, and every time TJ seems better. Last night was as close to a normal double date as Pock, TJ, Gene, and Ramon could expect. If Gene wasn't such a flaming queer, Ramon might be jealous of all the attention Pock gave him. So what kind of shit is TJ pulling this morning?

Ramon takes another shot. TJ blocks the shot and easily takes the ball back. TJ makes a basket, retrieves the ball, shoots again. TJ is wearing two hoodies. Neither of TJ's hoods are pulled up and Ramon gets a good look at the head of the serpent that inks its way from TJ's shoulder to the back of his thick neck right up into the shaved edge of his hairline. The tattoo is new. Last night Ramon could tell that Pock loves the tat by the way she kept resting her hand on TJ's neck. Ramon hates it.

"Why aren't you at work, anyway?" Ramon stands in one spot, not even trying to block TJ's shots. "Come on, Little Man, let's hear it."

"Don't call me that." TJ stares at Ramon who just keeps shaking his head until TJ wales the ball at him.

Ramon turns just as TJ throws and the ball catches him way too near his crotch. Both boys flinch. "What's your fucking problem?" Ramon slams the ball at TJ's chest. TJ catches it. Ramon turns, giving TJ the double finger as he walks away.

When Ramon is all the way to his front door, TJ says, "She's dead," like a threat or an insult, like it's Ramon's fault he doesn't know what TJ is talking about.

Ramon freezes and asks without turning around, "Who?" Not TJ's mother. TJ wouldn't be playing basketball if it was his mother. His grandmother, the one he likes, in New Jersey?

"Jackie," TJ says.

Ramon spins on the heels of his Reeboks. He nods at the house next door. "We saw Jackie yesterday."

TJ wraps his arms around himself. "They think she had a heart attack and a stroke." He squeezes the ball between red chapped hands. He looks like he might go for Ramon's junk on purpose this time, but puts the ball down on the driveway and sits on it.

Ramon walks back to TJ and crouches next to him. "We helped them tie that dead tree to the roof of their car." He hooks his thumb toward The Ladies' car at the edge of the driveway. "She looked fine. Well, like her usual self. I would have heard an ambulance. I can see them going in and out of their front door from my bedroom window."

"She died after we saw her," TJ says. "At the dump."

"Don't be stupid." Ramon frowns. "You can't have a heart attack and a stroke. Jackie's flat on her back on her La-Z-Boy, with the TV on, snoring." Ramon looks at the side of the house. "Right there in that window."

"No." TJ shakes his head. "My mom stopped me when I was leaving for work, says there was nothing they could do." He shakes his head some more. "Jackie was gone before the ambulance even got there." TJ's mother works at All Saints, where Jackie arrived, DOA.

Ramon stands up and zips his parka. "No offense. Your mom's a laundry worker." *And she was probably eavesdropping,* Ramon thinks. "She got the name wrong."

TJ stands up too and looks at the ground slowly shaking his head while Ramon wonders aloud how so many people can get so many things wrong.

"Jackie is dead." TJ puts an arm over Ramon's shoulder and

starts blubbering like a two-year-old. Ramon stops breathing. His eyes dart around. He pulls away from TJ.

"You want to run?" TJ wipes his nose on the sleeve of his hoodie, watches Ramon's face, and steadies himself for whatever happens next. He feels almost grateful to have something to concentrate on besides Jackie being dead. "You look like you wanna run. This how it felt watching me all those years I was going crazy?" TJ can't help but think it would be better for both of them if Ramon was crying too.

Jackie dead. The thought is so ridiculous Ramon laughs, one of those horror movie laughs. TJ doesn't even flinch when Ramon laughs. They just squat in the driveway together.

"We should have gone with The Ladies yesterday," Ramon says.

"Yeah," TJ agrees. "I better sleep on their couch for a while."

Ramon wonders how often TJ sleeps at The Ladies' house these days. The whole neighborhood knows who sleeps where. They know that TJ's father hasn't been around in a few years, and his mother has a new boyfriend who calls TJ "son" in a formal, respectful way. They know that Lotti's boyfriend stays over on Friday and Saturday nights and eats her *maizena* in the morning. Everybody knows where TJ sleeps now. Except Ramon.

"You ever wonder if she minded that we called her a lady?" TJ says. He sounds like somebody else to Ramon. Someone who cries in broad daylight. TJ's voice is soft, like when they used to walk in the woods behind the strip mall and it was Ramon, not Pock, touching the back of TJ's head.

"What do you mean?" Ramon says this even though he knows what TJ means. The boys and Pock have always called Jackie and Regina "The Ladies." All the kids in the neighborhood call them The Ladies. But Jackie is Jackie: buzz cut, men's pants, work boots. Calling her and Regina The Ladies never changed that.

"Doesn't matter." TJ's shoulder twitches like it used to when he was trying not to hit someone or trying not to cry.

Now, it's twitching because he's trying to hold things together for Ramon. TJ watches Ramon who looks like he might spit on TJ. Not that he would. Probably not. TJ remembers that he spit on Ramon's sneaker one time. Poor Ramon, apologizing every time he comes home: for not being here when Pock's favorite cousin got mangled by a hit-and-run, for not being here when Oscar got mugged his first time alone on a public bus, for not being here when TJ punched a hole in the bathroom wall instead of that asshole at work.

Ramon sees TJ's shoulder moving. "Your arm is spazzin'." He jumps up. "Let's go see."

"See what?"

"If she's in there, sitting in her chair. People on this street . . ." Ramon's voice lifts with disdain for the bullshit that gets passed around. "You see an ambulance? You hear sirens?" Ramon's heart races. Maybe he has hit on the essential point that's going to save Jackie from being dead. Maybe TJ's quiet mother, this one time, carried a rumor without checking it out, without making sure it was true before it came out her mouth.

"I told you she died at the dump," TJ says. "The ambulance went there."

Ramon sprints to the side of the house, stops dead in his tracks to stand with his back against the faded clapboard a few feet from the window. TJ follows, leans against the house, and stands shoulder to shoulder with Ramon.

"Look inside." Ramon crouches and hugs his knees, his butt against the house.

"Jesus." TJ slides down next to Ramon, half convinced that Ramon is right. It's possible Jackie is sleeping in her chair a few feet away. His mom got it wrong? Why isn't Yvonne here? Her car isn't in the driveway. Wouldn't his mom have told Ramon's mom by now? The neighbor ladies should be here with casseroles and chicken and cake. Some people talk shit about The Ladies because they're queer, but Jackie and Regina have lived here since before the boys were born. The neighbor ladies will turn out for them. The men will cut Regina's grass and take out her trash for a few weeks. "TV's not on," TJ says. It's still early, not nine o'clock yet.

Ramon stands. "The window is closed. How do you know the TV isn't on?"

TJ stands slowly. "Come on, Ramon. You know she likes the TV loud." They used to catch the score of a Patriots game by listening right where they stand now, didn't matter if the window was closed or not.

Ramon stops breathing and listens hard. There is noise coming through the window. Not snoring, not the TV. Whimpering. Moaning. Ramon leans forward on the tips of his sneakers toward the window to catch the sound. "Jackie," he whispers.

TJ stands smack in front and squints through the window. His hand shades his eyes from the glare that bounces from the snow to the glass. "Regina," he says.

Ramon stands behind TJ. They stare in at Regina who sits on Jackie's chair. They see a side view of her. There's no light on in the room. The boys can't see her very well. They can tell it's her, though. She's on the edge of the seat, staring straight ahead, making a sound that's getting louder, or maybe sounds louder because the boys are listening so hard. She's so close that if the window were open, they could lean in and touch her.

Ramon puts a hand flat against the window. Regina cocks her head to the sound of the loose pane rattling. Ramon pulls his hand away. The boys watch Regina's slow movements as her head swivels in their direction. They watch her fight with the sash to unlock and raise the swollen window. They watch her close her eyes and bite her lip as she manages to move the stuck frame.

Something is happening in Ramon's chest, like somebody shoved a fist in and is squeezing his lungs, maybe his heart. It hurts bad.

When the window is up Regina says, "Oh, TJ. Oh, Ramon," and Ramon understands it was Regina, seeing her alone, that he dreaded as much as he feared Jackie being dead. Ramon knows how it is to lose the person you love.

TJ and Regina stare at each other. TJ's mouth is open.

Ramon thinks TJ's open mouth makes him look stupid, like Oscar before the occupational therapist taught him to lose his slack jaw. Ramon feels like he's doing something bad looking at them. It's the same feeling he gets when he thinks too hard about how it should have been him and not Pock who took care of Oscar after school when they were younger. It feels dirty watching Regina's sad face and TJ's open mouth, too private. It hurts too much. Regina looks older by the second. TJ's hoodie is wet in the front.

TJ turns to Ramon, sees the expression on Ramon's face, and thinks maybe Ramon is about to lose his shit. The thought of Ramon losing his shit scares TJ, who wants to run himself, but he won't leave Regina. He won't leave Ramon. Not this time.

"Remember when Jackie caught you peeing on the rhododendron in the backyard?" Regina says. "That bouquet of her own sunflowers you picked her. She still has those, all dried up on our dresser." It's like she's looking at the boys and through them at the same time. "Ten, fifteen years of dust. She pulled them out of the trash when I tried to toss them."

Ramon wants to scream that TJ doesn't know the difference between a rhododendron and an oak tree.

"You were all of six years old," Regina says. "I never meant to fall in love with children. Such handfuls, you kids. Jackie." Regina stops talking to look into space. "She showed me," she says abruptly. "You boys and Pock." She smiles sadly and sighs. "You know what I mean?"

TJ nods. Ramon wonders if Regina remembers it was him, Ramon, not TJ who got caught pissing on the rhododendron. He watches TJ's fists clench and thinks TJ's mind might not be in fighting mode, but his hands want to put themselves through something.

Regina puts her fingertips on the screen, and TJ places his finger against hers. She offers Ramon a fingertip. Her touch is another stab to Ramon's chest. Her hair is uncombed, her wrinkles deep.

"She loved you boys," Regina says. "She didn't want to embarrass you or herself by saying it too often." She usually has pink lips and cheeks. Her face is all the same gray today. Her voice sounds younger than usual, a girl's voice.

Ramon pulls his hand away and tries to breathe the fist out of his chest, tries to calm himself while TJ and Regina stare and touch fingertips. Ramon thinks of all the people he knows who died and all the times he didn't panic. He held a baby, a little girl who lived right down the street, held her while her mother picked up the shit that fell out of her purse. A few weeks later that baby died. Ramon liked holding the baby. She smelled good. He felt bad, but he didn't panic when she died. His uncle died. And Pock's cousin. Old people, that's what they do; they die. But Jackie—he thought Jackie would wait until TJ got better. All the way better. He thought Jackie would be living next door every time he came home from school, until he graduated, at least. What if Ramon is gone and TJ does something stupid and dies? Jackie is dead. TJ is too calm.

Lotti steps into view behind Regina. "I thought I heard you boys. Why are you talking through the screen? Come in." She wipes away a tear and kisses Regina on the forehead. "Maybe you can get her to take a few bites of scrambled eggs. Lucky you're home from school, baby." She smiles at Ramon. "We're going to need help."

Regina has one spotty hand over her heart. Lotti takes the hand. "We have to get you dressed." She puts an arm around Regina to shepherd her to the bedroom.

Ramon grips the windowsill and watches them go.

"Come on," TJ says. "You my ironman, remember?"

"She forgot to tie the neck of her nightgown," Ramon says.

"You're freakin'. They left the window open. We gotta go inside and close it."

"Her chest it was . . . like pepperoni. Her skin."

"Yeah, she's an old lady." TJ throws an arm over Ramon's shoulder. Ramon allows it this time and TJ holds him in a sideways hug.

"Jackie's skin," Ramon shivers, "must be cold by now."

TJ speaks softly in Ramon's ear, "Remember what you and Papi used to tell me, 'breathe.'" TJ takes a long breath. "Do it for me." He exhales and takes another deep breath. "I did it for you. Like, a thousand times."

Ramon ignores the instructions. "I think they take the blood out of the body," he says. "She should have a coffin. A really good one, so the insects. She'll freeze and thaw."

"Shut up." TJ shoves Ramon. "Why you saying this? Of course her skin's cold. Course they're gonna put her in the ground. She's going to disintegrate. Ashes to ashes." He starts crying, letting his tears run angry now. "My arm's spazzin' again. That what you want?" TJ slaps his bicep. "What's the matter? Jackie fuck up your perfect life by dying?" TJ can feel the need for a drink and the need to put his fist through something solid coming on strong. His new mantra *walk away* kicks in. He walks away. Fast.

Ramon tackles him on the front lawn. They roll over each other, almost acrobatically at first. Neither of them is any good at gymnastics, so they let their bodies slam together, needing above all else just this: to be near each other, rolling over the lawn, hanging on like they'll drown if either one of them lets go.

"Get off me," TJ moans, half cry, half growl, hanging on tighter. The boys tumble over each other, collecting snow on the tangle of themselves, like a snowball. They stop rolling, eventually land on their knees facing each other.

"Good Ramon thinks he gets to be the crazy boy now?" TJ has snow on his lashes and sees Ramon as a blur.

Their breath comes out in cold bursts that mingle and disappear.

"Call me Good Ramon again, Crazy Boy, and maybe I'll go crazy for real on you." Ramon gets up on one knee intending to stand, intending to be the one to walk away now.

TJ locks his arms around Ramon's chest.

Ramon struggles, but he's nowhere near as strong and he's

fighting against too much, including a lifetime of loving TJ. Ramon collapses, borrowing an old tactic of TJ's, trying to make TJ put down his guard for a second so Ramon can rally then bust out of the hold. But TJ invented this trick. Before Ramon can make it happen, TJ wedges his head between Ramon's neck and shoulder and makes sure both knees are firmly planted in the snow. He holds Ramon in a bear hug that Ramon struggles futilely to break.

"Come on, man, quit. I could kill you right now if I wanted to," TJ says into Ramon's neck.

"Why don't you, then?" Ramon huffs, realizing TJ is barely out of breath.

"How many times you save me?" TJ's voice is too tender for either boy to bear. Then there's the moment that both boys long for and dread, when TJ pulls his head back and looks Ramon in the eye, and their shared grief hangs in the air for a few long seconds. TJ loosens his grip but does not let go. "Ramon, I don't want to fight you. Don't make me." He kisses Ramon's neck softly, lingers a moment feeling the beat of Ramon's heart on his lips.

"What the fuck is wrong with you?" Ramon whispers, his voice a tangle of new and old heartache.

TJ leans his forehead on Ramon's shoulder. He knows kissing Ramon's neck was wrong, the wrong thing to do in The Ladies' yard with Jackie dead and Regina heartbroken. Wrong for Ramon. Wrong for TJ. The boys kneel in their wrong embrace, TJ holding Ramon until Ramon's body goes limp again. This time TJ pulls away slowly. The boys sit next to each other in the snow, their knees pulled toward their chests, their backs to Jackie and Regina's house. They stare at the road.

Ramon says, "Shit. Poor Jackie. Poor Regina." Tears roll down his cheeks until he gets too self-conscious to keep crying and laughs low in his throat. "Right here on the frozen lawn next door to my house?" He shakes his head. "Asshole. You kiss me here. Not even out in the woods by the strip mall?" The fringe of woods where no one ever found them, or only the one close call when TJ waved around a comb that the other boys thought was a blade, making the punks scatter and TJ laugh like a maniac.

Ramon laughs harder. "Now that I got a boyfriend?"

"Yeah, I tried to tell you, I'm the fucked-up one." TJ laughs, too. "You don't get to be the crazy boy. You come home with beautiful unfucked-up Gene. Jackie dies. I got Pock, but we all know she's better than me. She's leaving, too. She'll be living at school, not even commuting next semester. Girl loves me this much." TJ throws open his arms to demonstrate how much Pock says she loves him. Ramon pulls his head back so he won't get whacked by TJ's elbow. TJ's arms fall back in his lap. "But she 'has to be honest.'" TJ's voice pitches high like Pock's. "She's not *in love* with me." He goes back to his own voice. "I love you both anyway."

TJ's crying again.

"You expect me to feel bad?" Ramon is trying with all his heart not to feel bad for TJ. Or Pock. "Kissing my neck. Messed up. Even for you." He doesn't want to wipe his snot on his sleeve, but he has no choice. "Don't touch me like that again." The boys are still sitting in snow. Ramon grabs TJ's arm. "Ever."

TJ winces. The injury has long healed. But even through the double sleeves of the hoodies, Ramon's grip still hurts the arm that TJ's father broke.

"Shit." Ramon lets go and winces, too. "I forget. How'd you live through all that?"

"My mom. You. Jackie." TJ stands and starts slapping snow off himself. "Regina. Pock. Pock's gonna kill me for kissing on you."

"You are crazy." Ramon unzips his parka and shakes the snow off. "Don't tell Pock."

"No?" TJ shrugs. "Okay. Fuck therapy." His hair is white with snow. "I'll just tell the therapist I told Pock." He starts shaking his shoulders and head like a wet dog and laughs when Ramon scrambles to get his parka back on before his dry shirt gets snow on it. TJ grimaces when he moves his sore arm to zip his hoodie. "Might tell the therapist *you* kissed *my* neck."

"Punk." Ramon puts two fingers gently on TJ's forearm and shakes his head. "Still hurts."

TJ shrugs and points his chin at a car driving toward the house. "Bo and Yvonne's car."

"Just Yvonne's car now," Ramon says.

"Yeah. Good ol' dead Bo. Why we so stupid to love so many old ladies?" TJ grins at Ramon. "Buried in a tuxedo. Like, a man's tuxedo." They watch Yvonne parallel park in the street.

Ramon grins back. "Wasn't so stupid when they were letting us hang at their house and feeding us ice cream. Who bought you those Reeboks?"

"Every year." TJ grins. "You gonna be CEO somewhere and Yvonne's gonna be buying you sneakers." Once a year Bo and Yvonne took the kids to the mall to buy sneakers. The last few years it's been gift certificates to the shoe store at Christmas.

"Remember that big wooden box full of toys?" Ramon starts walking to the car.

"It's still next to the TV, full of my weights now." TJ follows Ramon.

Ramon extends his hand to help Yvonne out of the car. She cocks her head. "Have you boys been told?"

They answer, "Yes, ma'am," in unison.

"Please get my cane out of the backseat, TJ." Yvonne takes Ramon's arm and stands as straight as her bad back will allow. TJ hands her the cane. She clears her throat and looks deliberately ahead as if she were reading from a teleprompter. "One of the finest people any of us are likely to meet has died, a woman who helped raise you. A woman who helped me keep my faith in humanity." Teary, she looks directly at the boys. "You aren't some random young men. You have an invaluable inheritance." She is wearing a cape that she wraps around herself. "Let's gather ourselves and make Regina proud."

The only people left in the living room where a hundred came to respect Jackie over the last two days are Yvonne, Lotti and

Regina. And Jackie herself in her coffin up against the wall opposite the couch where the three old women sit. Folding chairs, some leaned against the wall, some open, are scattered around the small room. The women are waiting for the funeral director to come and take Jackie away until the burial in the morning.

"So much better to lay out a body at home." Lotti pulls three chairs towards them and hoists her feet up on the seat of one. "Take a load off." Both Regina and Yvonne accept this advice. "Still don't know how you pulled it off, Regina," Lotti says.

"Entirely Yvonne's idea." Regina takes Yvonne's hand. "Paid for most of it, too."

"It's what we did for Bo. Once you know the ropes, who to contact, just as easy as any other kind of wake. Cheaper. More dignified. What kind of trouble do you suppose those two are getting into without us?" Yvonne squeezes Regina's hand.

All three women stare at Jackie. Regina has been seriously considering the question of an afterlife, something she never believed in before Jackie's death. After a good long look, she answers Yvonne's question. "Depends what's offered."

Yvonne nods. "Imagination fails. I keep thinking, hang on Bo, I'm coming." She puts an arm around Regina, and Regina rests her head on Yvonne's shoulder.

"She looks a little amused," Lotti says. "I always thought Jackie was in on a joke I never got."

The other women smile at Lotti's comment. From the kitchen comes the sound of a cabinet door banging shut, followed by Pock's loud, "Shush," followed by the clatter of dishes and the rattle of knives and forks being tucked in drawers.

"Those kids." Yvonne presses her lips together before she corrects herself. "Young men and young woman. Ramon. TJ. Pock," she says their names slowly. "So much help. Jackie would be proud."

"She would." Regina keeps telling herself it's not Jackie in the coffin, so she'll be able to bear it when the men come to take her body away. "I think that was my favorite part. How the kids came through." Regina laughs and looks at the coffin. "You hear that, Jackie? If Lynn were here, she'd have something to say about my having a favorite part of our funeral."

"Our?" Lotti raises her eyebrows at Yvonne.

"What?" Regina says.

"You said *our*, honey," Yvonne says. "I know what you mean. I felt that way when Bo died. Lynn would remind you that you're still alive. But if we're talking favorite parts, I vote for Selma's 'Amazing Grace.'" Yvonne sighs. "Never mind Selma's voice is shot. The woman's soul is intact."

The three women exchange looks and nods. It's true. Selma sang a sad, embarrassing rendition of Nina Simone's "Feeling Good" first. She had the good sense to stop after one verse of "Ave Maria," Jackie's mother's favorite hymn. But "Amazing Grace" somehow lent itself to Selma's heartfelt off-pitch notes. What could have sounded plain pitiful sounded like an assertion of pity, an admission of human weakness and failing. "I offer music," Selma said when she was finished singing, "as a forgiveness prayer to our beloved Jackie, so maybe she'll forgive us for all we failed to do to make her journey easier while she was with us. And maybe we'll forgive her for her failings. Find only praise in our hearts now, because there is so much in our beautiful Jackie to praise."

Selma is with the funeral director now, arranging for a brief no-nonsense grave site ceremony that her auntie would approve.

Silver, who at ninety teaches a Fit at Any Age class at the Y, pushes Lynn's wheelchair through the door. "Wish we had done this for Lynn." He bows to Jackie in her coffin. "Anyone need a ride to their car?" He points to the empty chair he always keeps with him in the wheelchair van he drives everywhere, three years after her death, "to keep Lynn close," and in case somewwone needs his service. "Or a ride in the van?" he asks. When the women thank him, and decline, he takes his offer into the kitchen where Ramon, TJ, and Pock are cleaning up.

Charlie had stayed for a while to help clean up, too. He's studying world religions at the community college, working at the brake shop where Jackie recommended him. He lives in a "sober household" with three other men. He gave a beautiful testimonial about how Jackie had helped him before and after he got clean "for good." He wore a brown "monk" robe that no one asked about.

The moment Regina has been dreading arrives. The hearse drives up to take Jackie away. Her hearing is not acute, but she hears the car. Everyone and everything in the room vanishes for Regina except Jackie in her coffin. She does not hear the doorbell ring, does not hear Yvonne ask if she would like a few minutes alone.

The men in their black suits agree to wait ten minutes while Lotti and Yvonne join the kids in the kitchen.

Regina kneels in front of the coffin, drapes her upper body over Jackie, and cries.

"You're so cold, honey," she says as she straightens up. "You're already gone. Still, I don't know if I can let your body go." She kisses Jackie's cold lips. "Yes, I'm crying for myself." She goes to the door and waves to the men in the hearse.

Regina stands with an arm through Lotti's on one side and Yvonne's on the other. The kids huddle next to them to watch Jackie leave the house for the last time. Silver watches from the kitchen door. Regina closes her eyes as the lid of the coffin closes, but opens them to watch the slow arc of the coffin turning as the somber men maneuver the casket in the small room and wheel Jackie out their front door.

"You did the right thing," Yvonne whispers from Regina's left side. "She would have died alone."

"Yes," Lotti agrees from her right side. "She died in your arms. Your voice in her ear."

Later, after Silver has left and the hearse has taken Jackie away, Regina sends Lotti and Yvonne home, too. Selma is back and asleep on the La-Z-Boy in the den. The kids have folded up all the chairs for the van from the funeral home to take away. Now they place the living-room chairs back in the usual spots and sit opposite Regina who is still on the couch.

TJ says, "I'll sleep here in case you or Selma need something."

"I'll stay, too," Pock says.

Ramon leans forward as if he's about to speak but says nothing.

Even through her exhaustion, or maybe because of it, Regina senses tension between the kids despite their effort to subdue it. She smiles at them. She knows how much they mean to each other. How much they want to stay friends. Yvonne has given Regina a valium. It's the first time Regina has taken a sleeping aid of any kind in all of her eighty-nine years. She closes her eyes.

"Maybe just one of us should stay?" Pock says.

"You think?" Ramon lets a sarcastic sniff slip out. "I'll stay."

Regina's head falls forward. She can hear them. It's so pleasant to just sit on the couch, dozing, and listen. "She okay?" one of the kids whispers. "Just sleeping," another one answers. "Should we wake her up, put her in her bed?" It's the girl, Pock, such a good girl, such a very good girl, such good kids.

Sleeping? Regina wonders. Is that what we're doing now, Jackie? The kids will be all right, don't you think? "Tell them there seems like so much time." Jackie's voice is so comforting. "But we waste so much."

"She's dreaming," a boy says. Ramon.

Sweet Ramon, mad about something. Shhh, Ramon. Let Jackie talk. Even sleeping, Regina knows Jackie's voice may not come again. "Tell them to take a shortcut and just forgive each other, forgive everything now," Jackie says. Oh, no one would ever behave if everything was forgiven in the now. Regina laughs. You never would have settled down. "Forgive, not give in." Jackie laughs, too.

"Is she giggling?" Pock says.

TJ kneels close to the couch. "Not really," he whispers. "Smiling."

"Leave her where she is," Pock says. "Get the afghan, Ramon. Help me pick up her feet, TJ."

"Sleep. It's just the kids tucking you in," Jackie says. Stay. Oh, please stay, Jackie.

"We will," TJ whispers. Pock puts a finger to her lips.

"There seems like so much time to get things right, but there's no future really," Jackie says. Well, not for you, honey. Regina almost wakes herself answering, but settles into the afghan Ramon tucks around her.

About the Author

Sally Bellerose is the award-winning author of *The Girls Club*, which was awarded a Creative Writing Fellowship from the NEA. Excerpts from the novel have been published in *Sinister Wisdom, The Sun, The Best of Writers at Work, Cutthroat, Quarterly West* and have won the Rick De Marinis Award, the Writers at Work Award, and a Barbara Deming Award. The manuscript was shortlisted for the James Jones Fellowship, the Thomas Wolfe Fiction Prize, The Backspace Scholarship, a Lambda Literary Award, an Independent Publishers Award, and a Golden Crown Literary Society Award. As an author, she loves to work with rhythm, rhyme, and awkward emotion. She is also drawn to humor and transcendence, and writes about class, sex, sexuality, gender, illness, absurdity, and lately, growing old.

Acknowledgements

What follows is an incomplete list of the many people who have helped this manuscript become a book.

Thanks to Janet Aalfs for years of friendship and generous exchange of work and ideas. And for giving *Fishwives* a final critique during a pandemic.

Thanks to Susan Stinson for decades of collaboration and affection.

Thanks to Mary Beth Caschetta and Meryl Cohn for sharing their talents and work and for opening their home to the Croissants Writing Group. I also thank SuEllen Hamkins, Norma Akamatsu, Mary Beth Brooker, Ellen Carter, Karen Randall and all the Croissants.

Thanks to Carol Edelstein, Renee Schultz, Alison Smith, Cynthia Kennison, Lida Lewis, Brett Averett, Sarah Coates, and the Friday Writing Group for friendship, inspiration, and keeping my butt in the chair.

Gratitude to Jane Christensen and Sarah Halper for Tuesday writing, critiquing, and culinary delight.

Thanks to The Clams, bivalves extraordinaire, Ellen LaFleche, Oonagh Doherty, EJ Seibert, and Lori Desrosiers.

Thanks to Nancy Rose, Rita Bleiman, and Joan Cenedella, for

criticism, support, and community.

Thanks to Jane Fleishman for becoming fast friends while wrestling with our manuscripts.

Thanks to Diane Lederman, Bonnie Atkins, and Rosie McMahan for writing support and friendship.

Thanks to Leslea Newman for encouragement, practical advice, friendship, and sparkle.

Thanks to my friend Gail Thomas for years of work exchange, personal support, and for poetry/prose groups that allowed me to be inspired by her, Michael Goldman, Mary Clare Powell, Becky Jones, Terry Johnson, and Ellen LaFleche.

Thanks to Aaron Hamburger, Maureen Brady, and Rob Williams for invaluable critiques.

Forever grateful to Forbes Library for unwavering commitment to the reading and writing community.

Thanks to my agent Laura Blake Peterson for believing in the manuscript.

Special thanks to Bywater Books, Salem West, Elizabeth Andersen and all the people at the press who work so hard to keep our literature in print.

At Bywater Books we love good books about lesbians
just like you do, and we're committed to bringing
the best of contemporary lesbian writing
to our avid readers. Our editorial team is dedicated
to finding and developing outstanding writers
who create books you won't want to put down.

For more information about Bywater Books,
our authors, and our titles, please visit our website.

www.bywaterbooks.com